MANIFEST DESTINY

CHRIS DINGESS — WRITER

MATTHEW ROBERTS — PENCILER & INKER #13-15

STEFANO GAUDIANO & TONY AKINS — INKERS #16-18

OWEN GIENI — COLORIST

PAT BROSSEAU — LETTERER

ARIELLE BASICH — ASSISTANT EDITOR

SEAN MACKIEWICZ — EDITOR

MATTHEW ROBERTS & OWEN GIENI
COVER ART

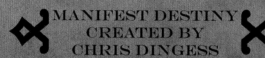

MANIFEST DESTINY
CREATED BY
CHRIS DINGESS

IMAGE COMICS, INC.
Robert Kirkman – Chief Operating Officer
Erik Larsen – Chief Financial Officer
Todd McFarlane – President
Marc Silvestri – Chief Executive Officer
Jim Valentino – Vice-President

Eric Stephenson – Publisher
Corey Murphy – Director of Sales
Jeff Boison – Director of Publishing Planning & Book Trade Sales
Jeremy Sullivan – Director of Digital Sales
Kat Salazar – Director of PR & Marketing
Emily Miller – Director of Operations
Branwyn Bigglestone – Senior Accounts Manager
Sarah Mello – Accounts Manager
Drew Gill – Art Director
Jonathan Chan – Production Manager
Meredith Wallace – Print Manager
Briah Skelly – Publicity Assistant
Randy Okamura – Marketing Production Designer
David Brothers – Branding Manager
Ally Power – Content Manager
Addison Duke – Production Artist
Vincent Kukua – Production Artist
Sasha Head – Production Artist
Tricia Ramos – Production Artist
Jeff Stang – Direct Market Sales Representative
Emilio Bautista – Digital Sales Associate
Chloe Ramos-Peterson – Administrative Assistant
IMAGECOMICS.COM

For SKYBOUND ENTERTAINMENT
Robert Kirkman – CEO
David Alpert – President
Sean Mackiewicz – Editorial Director
Shawn Kirkham – Director of Business Development
Brian Huntington – Online Editorial Director
June Alian – Publicity Director
Rachel Skidmore – Director of Media Development
Jon Moisan – Editor
Arielle Basich – Assistant Editor
Dan Petersen – Operations Manager
Sarah Effinger – Office Manager
Nick Palmer – Operations Coordinator
Genevieve Jones – Production Coordinator
Andres Juarez – Graphic Designer
Stephan Murillo – Administrative Assistant

International inquiries: foreign@skybound.com
Licensing inquiries: contact@skybound.com

www.skybound.com

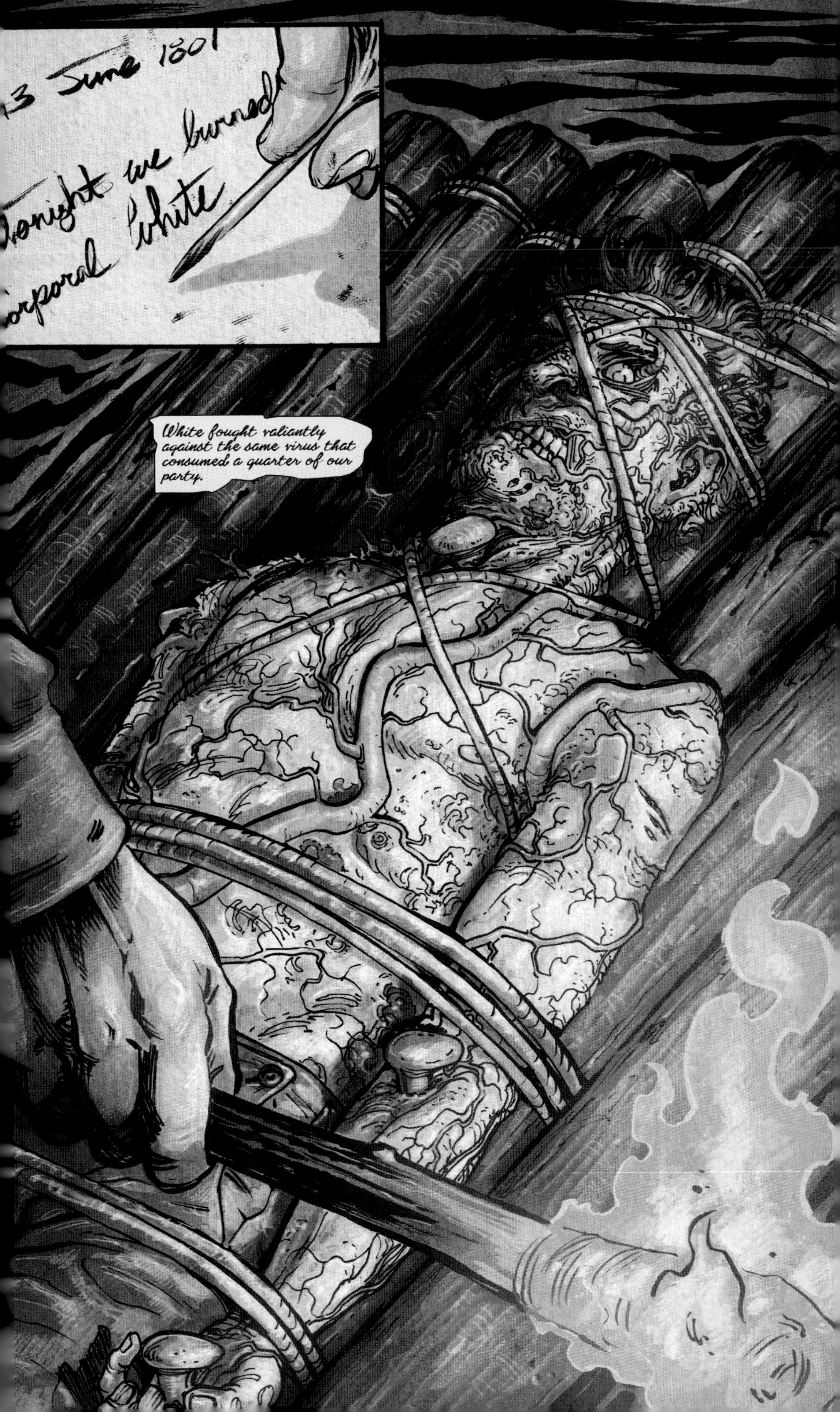
3 June 1801
Tonight we burned
Corporal White
White fought valiantly against the same virus that consumed a quarter of our party.

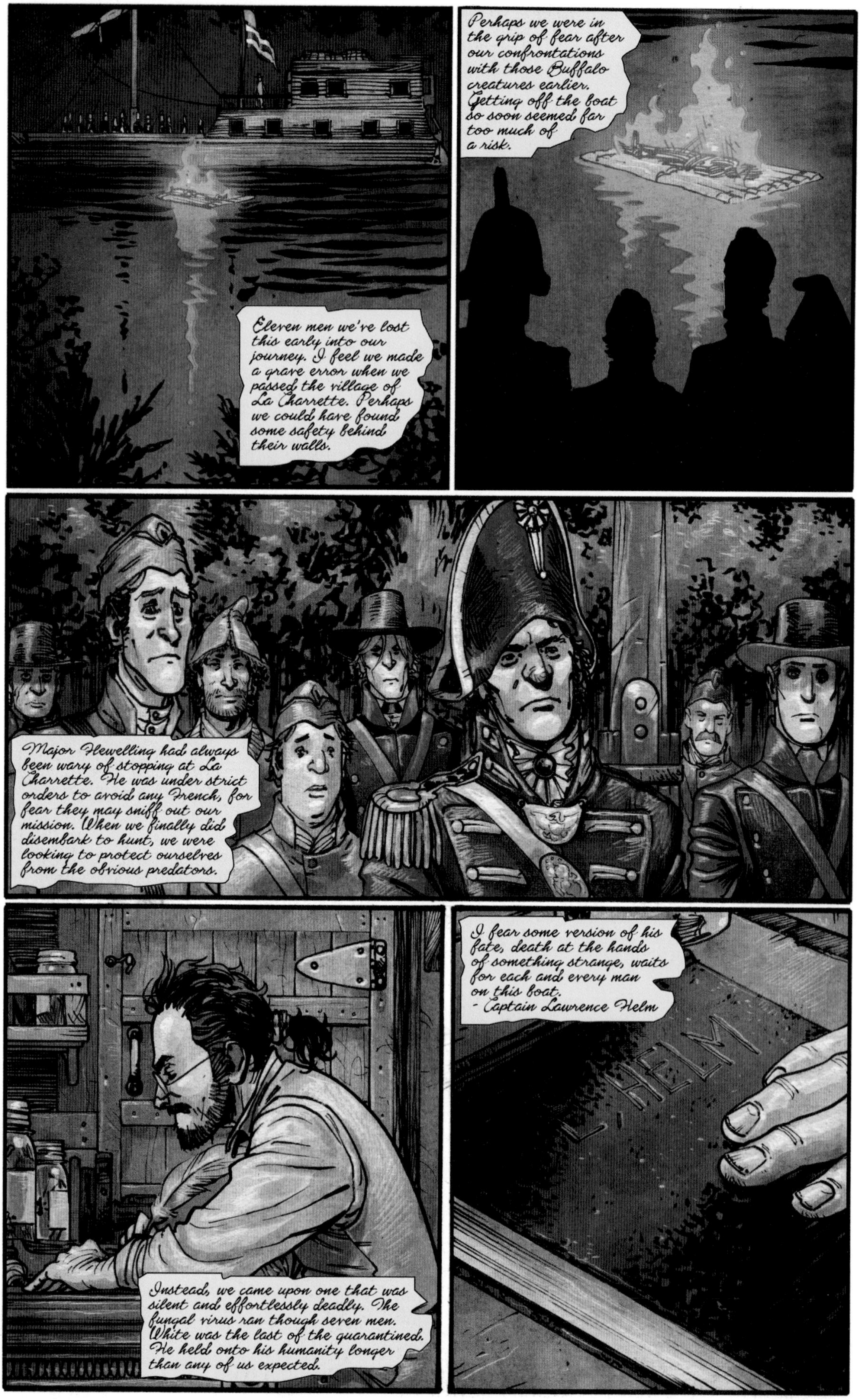
Eleven men we've lost this early into our journey. I feel we made a grave error when we passed the village of La Charrette. Perhaps we could have found some safety behind their walls.
Perhaps we were in the grip of fear after our confrontations with those Buffalo creatures earlier. Getting off the boat so soon seemed far too much of a risk.
Major Flewelling had always been wary of stopping at La Charrette. He was under strict orders to avoid any French, for fear they may sniff out our mission. When we finally did disembark to hunt, we were looking to protect ourselves from the obvious predators.
Instead, we came upon one that was silent and effortlessly deadly. The fungal virus ran though seven men. White was the last of the quarantined. He held onto his humanity longer than any of us expected.
I fear some version of his fate, death at the hands of something strange, waits for each and every man on this boat.
- Captain Lawrence Helm
L. HELM

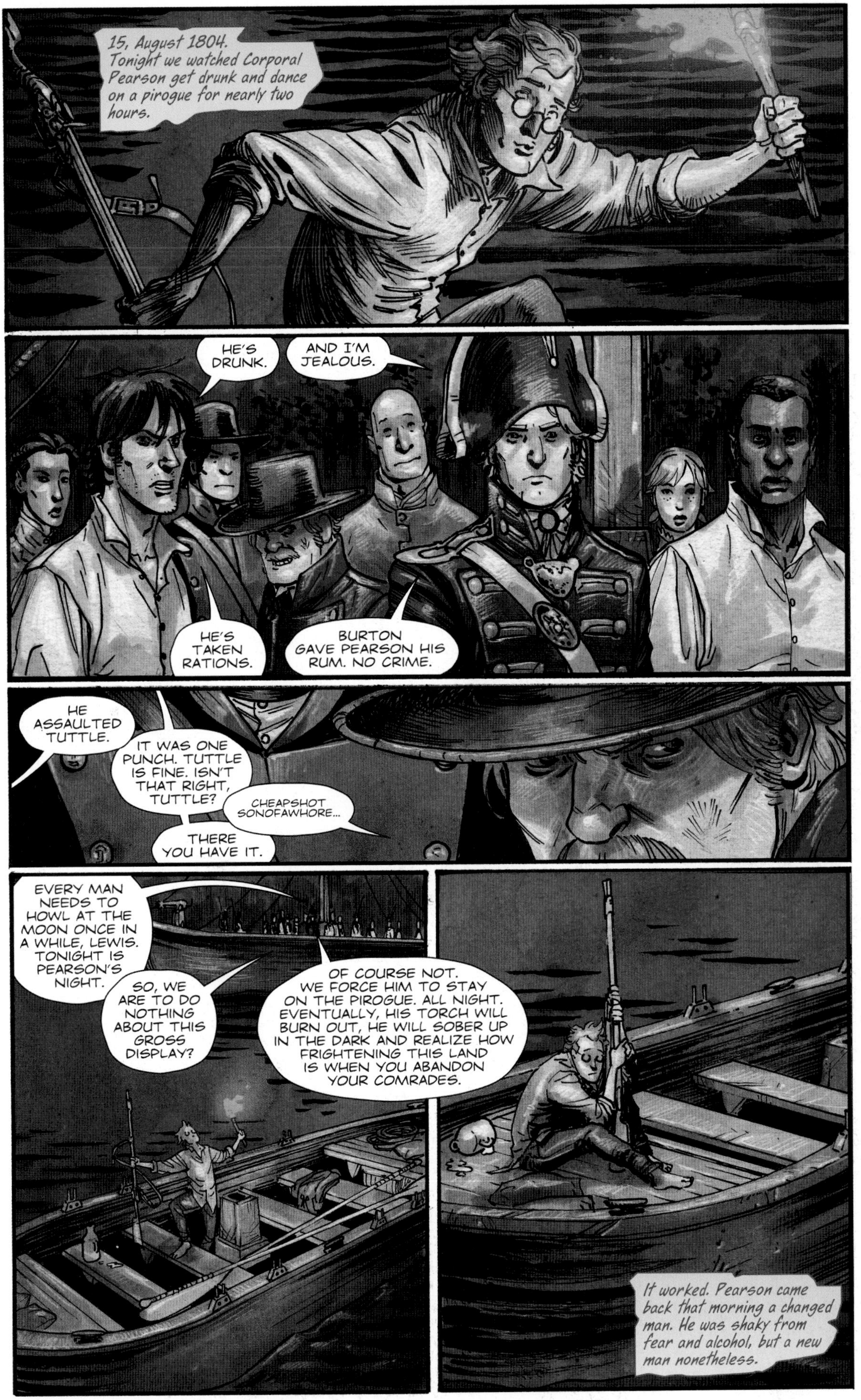
15, August 1804.
Tonight we watched Corporal Pearson get drunk and dance on a pirogue for nearly two hours.
HE'S DRUNK.
AND I'M JEALOUS.
HE'S TAKEN RATIONS.
BURTON GAVE PEARSON HIS RUM. NO CRIME.
HE ASSAULTED TUTTLE.
IT WAS ONE PUNCH. TUTTLE IS FINE. ISN'T THAT RIGHT, TUTTLE?
CHEAPSHOT SONOFAWHORE...
THERE YOU HAVE IT.
EVERY MAN NEEDS TO HOWL AT THE MOON ONCE IN A WHILE, LEWIS. TONIGHT IS PEARSON'S NIGHT.
SO, WE ARE TO DO NOTHING ABOUT THIS GROSS DISPLAY?
OF COURSE NOT. WE FORCE HIM TO STAY ON THE PIROGUE. ALL NIGHT. EVENTUALLY, HIS TORCH WILL BURN OUT, HE WILL SOBER UP IN THE DARK AND REALIZE HOW FRIGHTENING THIS LAND IS WHEN YOU ABANDON YOUR COMRADES.
It worked. Pearson came back that morning a changed man. He was shaky from fear and alcohol, but a new man nonetheless.

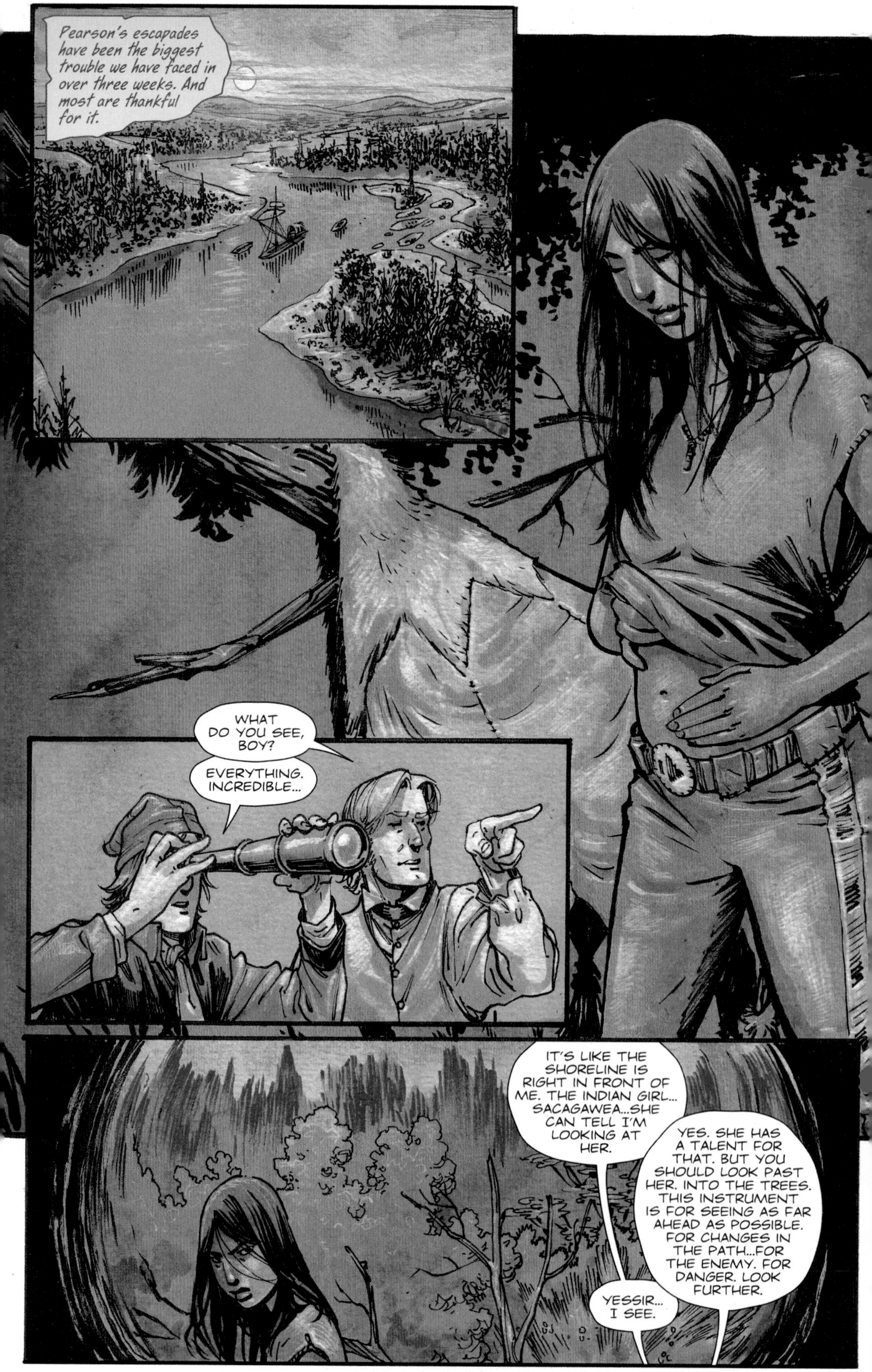
Pearson's escapades have been the biggest trouble we have faced in over three weeks. And most are thankful for it.
WHAT DO YOU SEE, BOY?
EVERYTHING. INCREDIBLE...
IT'S LIKE THE SHORELINE IS RIGHT IN FRONT OF ME. THE INDIAN GIRL... SACAGAWEA...SHE CAN TELL I'M LOOKING AT HER.
YES. SHE HAS A TALENT FOR THAT. BUT YOU SHOULD LOOK PAST HER. INTO THE TREES. THIS INSTRUMENT IS FOR SEEING AS FAR AHEAD AS POSSIBLE. FOR CHANGES IN THE PATH...FOR THE ENEMY. FOR DANGER. LOOK FURTHER.
YESSIR... I SEE.

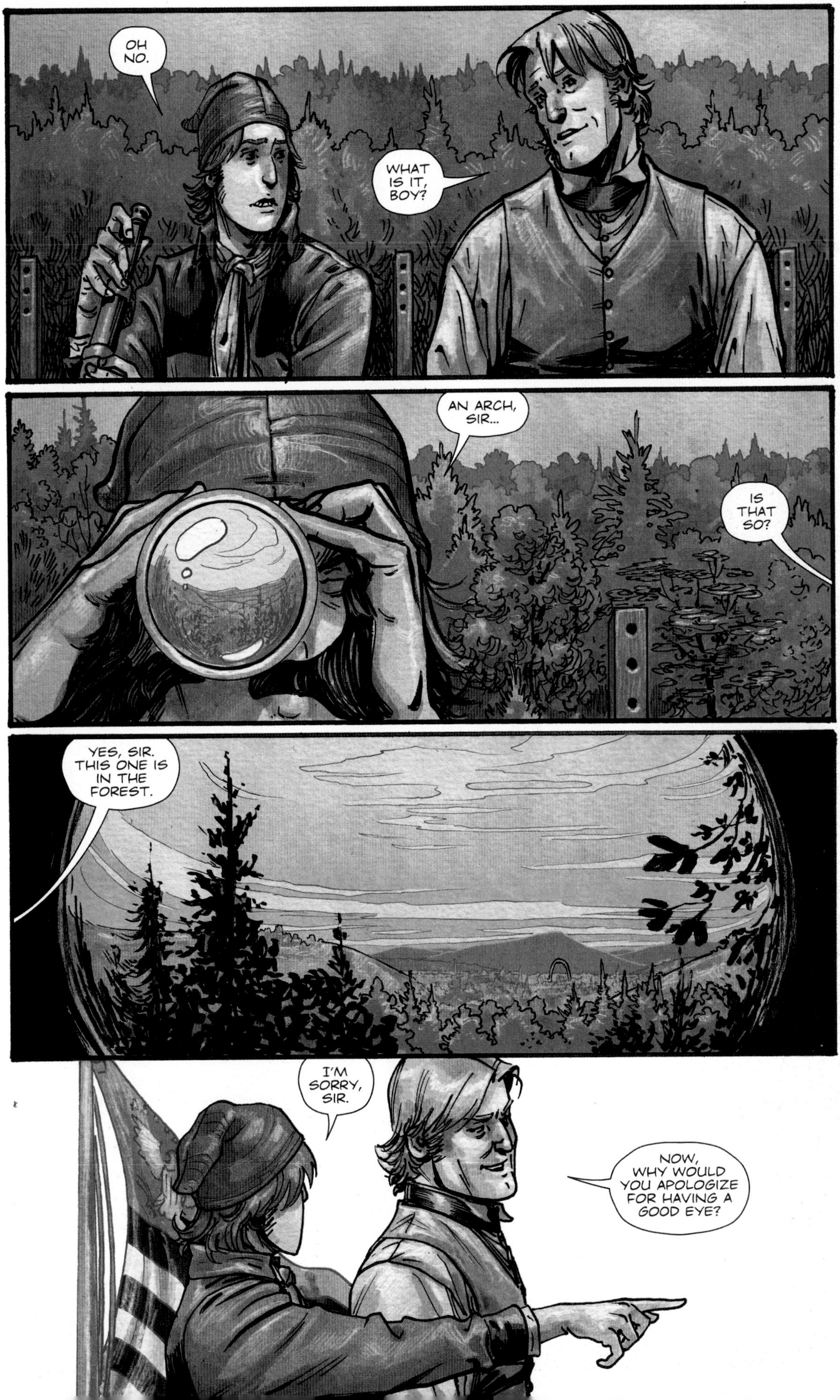
OH NO.
WHAT IS IT, BOY?
AN ARCH, SIR...
IS THAT SO?
YES, SIR. THIS ONE IS IN THE FOREST.
I'M SORRY, SIR.
NOW, WHY WOULD YOU APOLOGIZE FOR HAVING A GOOD EYE?

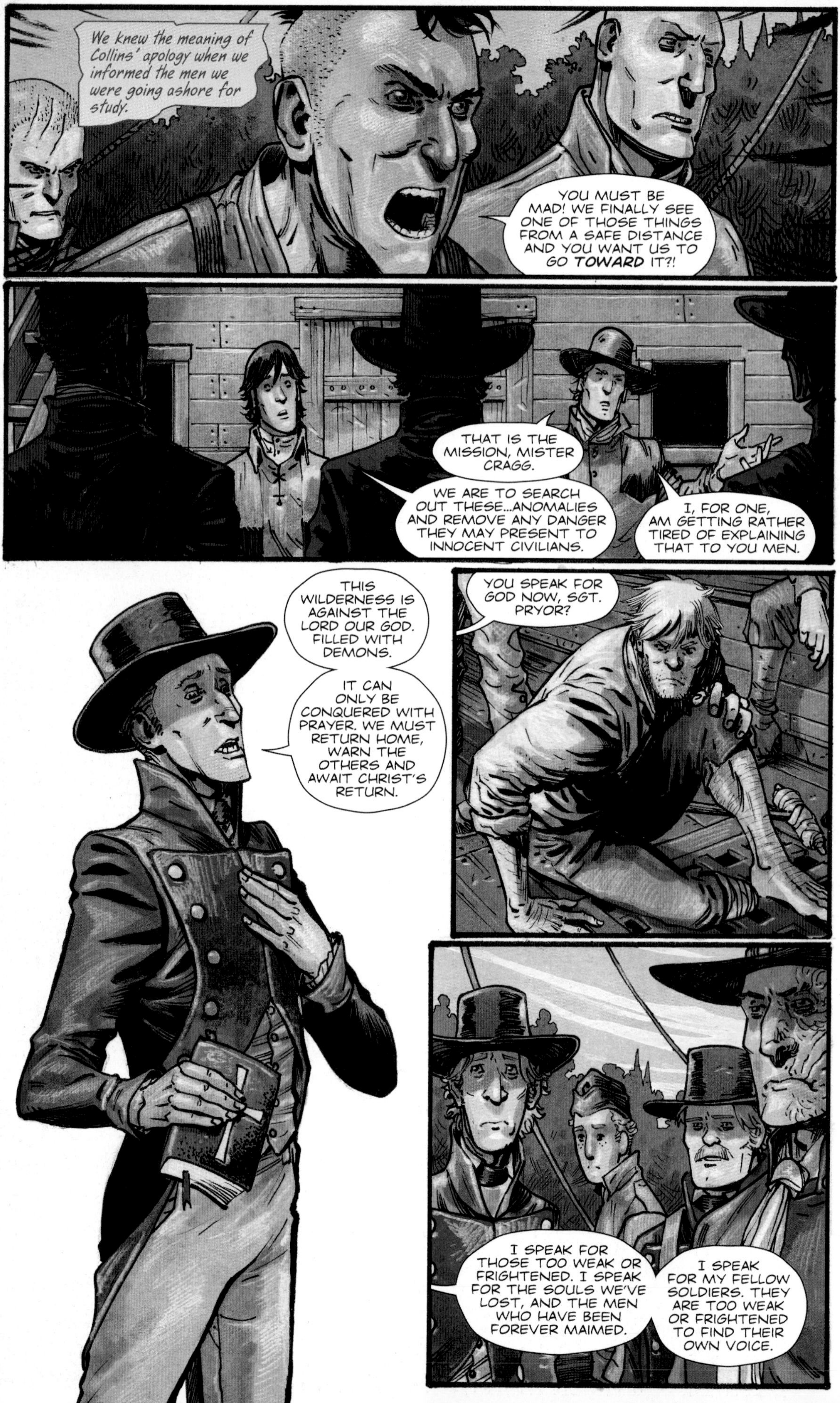
We knew the meaning of Collins' apology when we informed the men we were going ashore for study.
YOU MUST BE MAD! WE FINALLY SEE ONE OF THOSE THINGS FROM A SAFE DISTANCE AND YOU WANT US TO GO **TOWARD** IT?!
THAT IS THE MISSION, MISTER CRAGG.
WE ARE TO SEARCH OUT THESE...ANOMALIES AND REMOVE ANY DANGER THEY MAY PRESENT TO INNOCENT CIVILIANS.
I, FOR ONE, AM GETTING RATHER TIRED OF EXPLAINING THAT TO YOU MEN.
THIS WILDERNESS IS AGAINST THE LORD OUR GOD. FILLED WITH DEMONS.
IT CAN ONLY BE CONQUERED WITH PRAYER. WE MUST RETURN HOME, WARN THE OTHERS AND AWAIT CHRIST'S RETURN.
YOU SPEAK FOR GOD NOW, SGT. PRYOR?
I SPEAK FOR THOSE TOO WEAK OR FRIGHTENED. I SPEAK FOR THE SOULS WE'VE LOST, AND THE MEN WHO HAVE BEEN FOREVER MAIMED.
I SPEAK FOR MY FELLOW SOLDIERS. THEY ARE TOO WEAK OR FRIGHTENED TO FIND THEIR OWN VOICE.

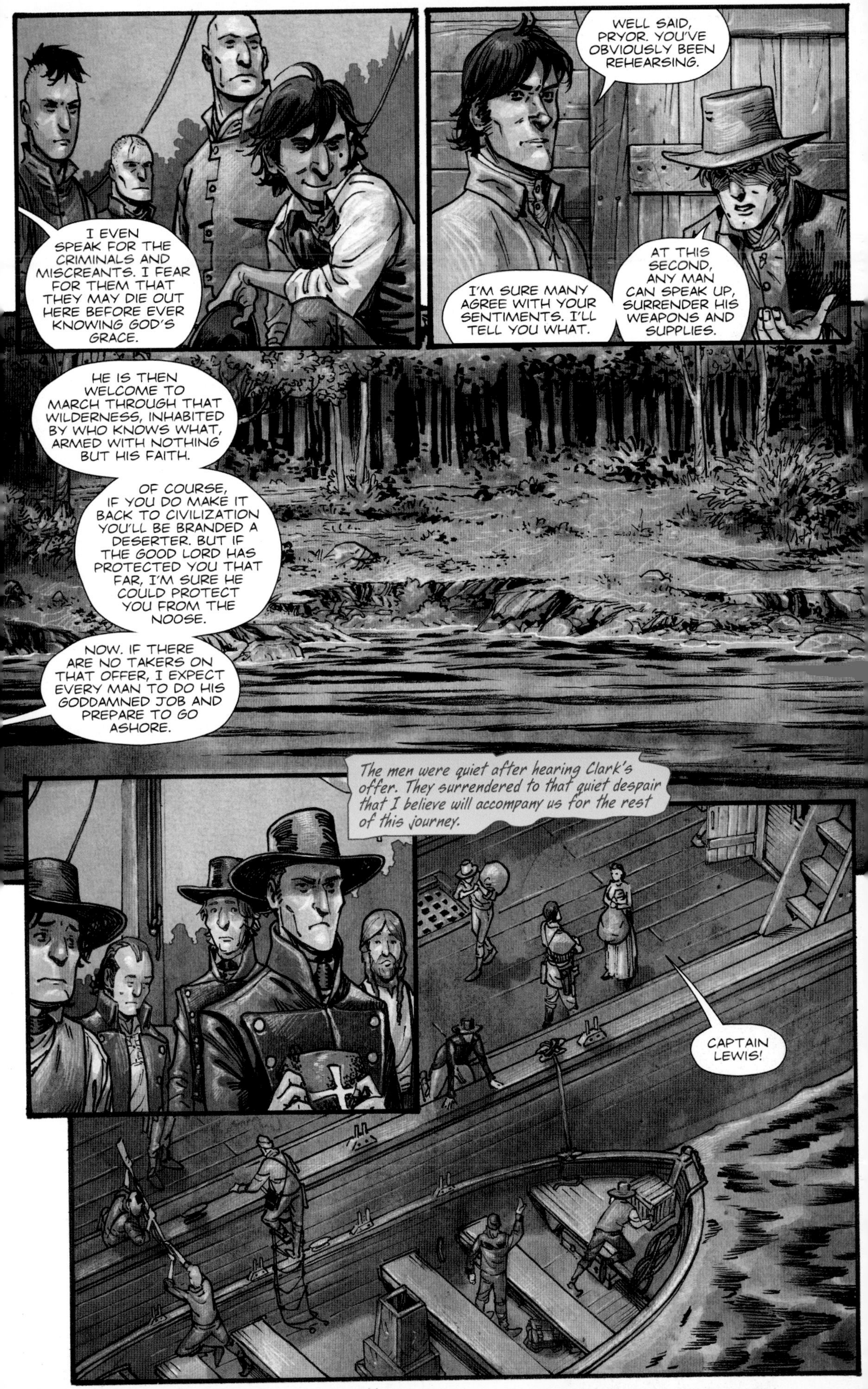
I EVEN SPEAK FOR THE CRIMINALS AND MISCREANTS. I FEAR FOR THEM THAT THEY MAY DIE OUT HERE BEFORE EVER KNOWING GOD'S GRACE.
WELL SAID, PRYOR. YOU'VE OBVIOUSLY BEEN REHEARSING.
I'M SURE MANY AGREE WITH YOUR SENTIMENTS. I'LL TELL YOU WHAT.
AT THIS SECOND, ANY MAN CAN SPEAK UP, SURRENDER HIS WEAPONS AND SUPPLIES.
HE IS THEN WELCOME TO MARCH THROUGH THAT WILDERNESS, INHABITED BY WHO KNOWS WHAT, ARMED WITH NOTHING BUT HIS FAITH.
OF COURSE, IF YOU DO MAKE IT BACK TO CIVILIZATION YOU'LL BE BRANDED A DESERTER. BUT IF THE GOOD LORD HAS PROTECTED YOU THAT FAR, I'M SURE HE COULD PROTECT YOU FROM THE NOOSE.
NOW. IF THERE ARE NO TAKERS ON THAT OFFER, I EXPECT EVERY MAN TO DO HIS GODDAMNED JOB AND PREPARE TO GO ASHORE.
The men were quiet after hearing Clark's offer. They surrendered to that quiet despair that I believe will accompany us for the rest of this journey.
CAPTAIN LEWIS!

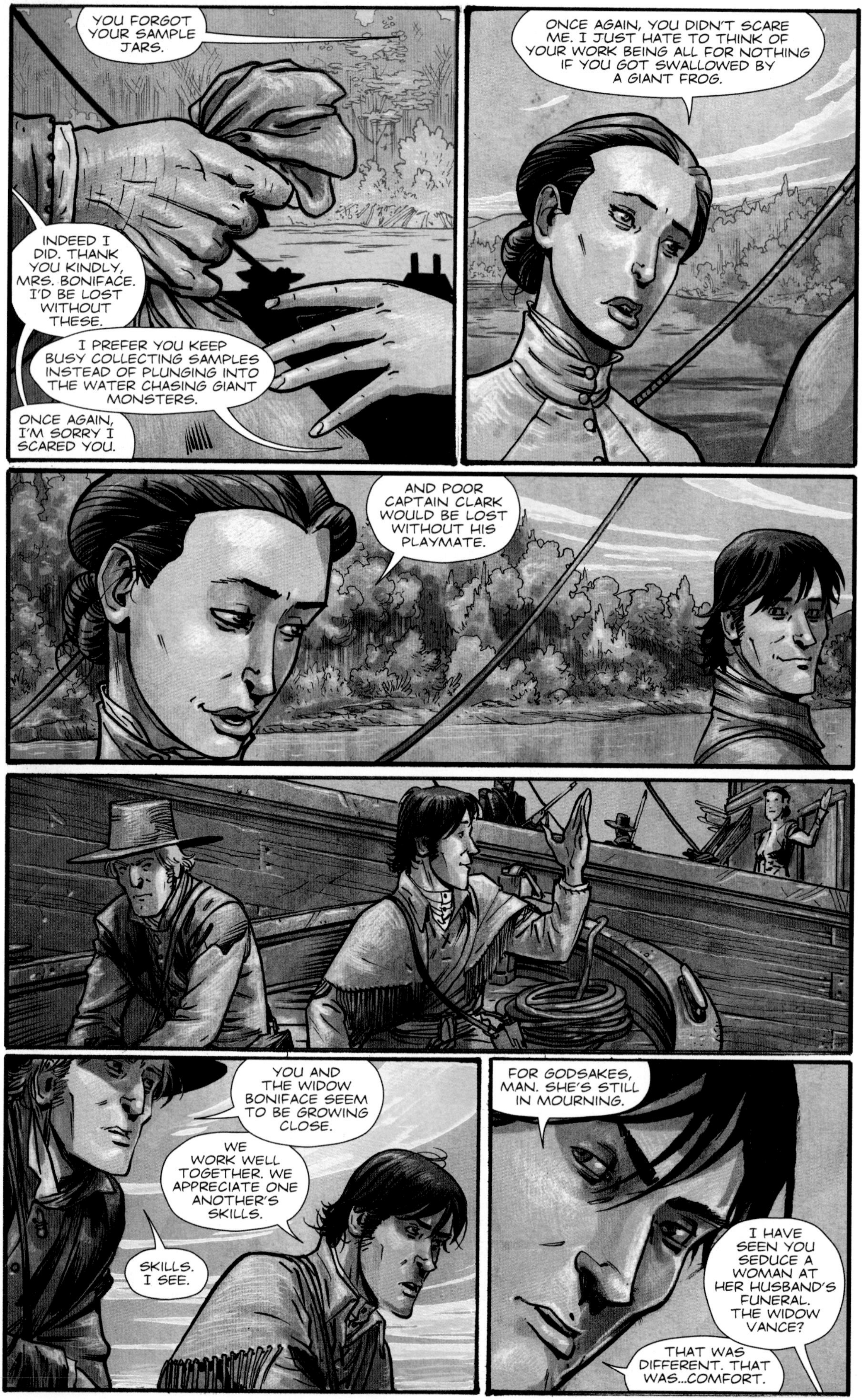

YOU FORGOT YOUR SAMPLE JARS.
INDEED I DID. THANK YOU KINDLY, MRS. BONIFACE. I'D BE LOST WITHOUT THESE.
I PREFER YOU KEEP BUSY COLLECTING SAMPLES INSTEAD OF PLUNGING INTO THE WATER CHASING GIANT MONSTERS.
ONCE AGAIN, I'M SORRY I SCARED YOU.
ONCE AGAIN, YOU DIDN'T SCARE ME. I JUST HATE TO THINK OF YOUR WORK BEING ALL FOR NOTHING IF YOU GOT SWALLOWED BY A GIANT FROG.
AND POOR CAPTAIN CLARK WOULD BE LOST WITHOUT HIS PLAYMATE.
YOU AND THE WIDOW BONIFACE SEEM TO BE GROWING CLOSE.
WE WORK WELL TOGETHER. WE APPRECIATE ONE ANOTHER'S SKILLS.
SKILLS. I SEE.
FOR GODSAKES, MAN. SHE'S STILL IN MOURNING.
I HAVE SEEN YOU SEDUCE A WOMAN AT HER HUSBAND'S FUNERAL. THE WIDOW VANCE?
THAT WAS DIFFERENT. THAT WAS...COMFORT.

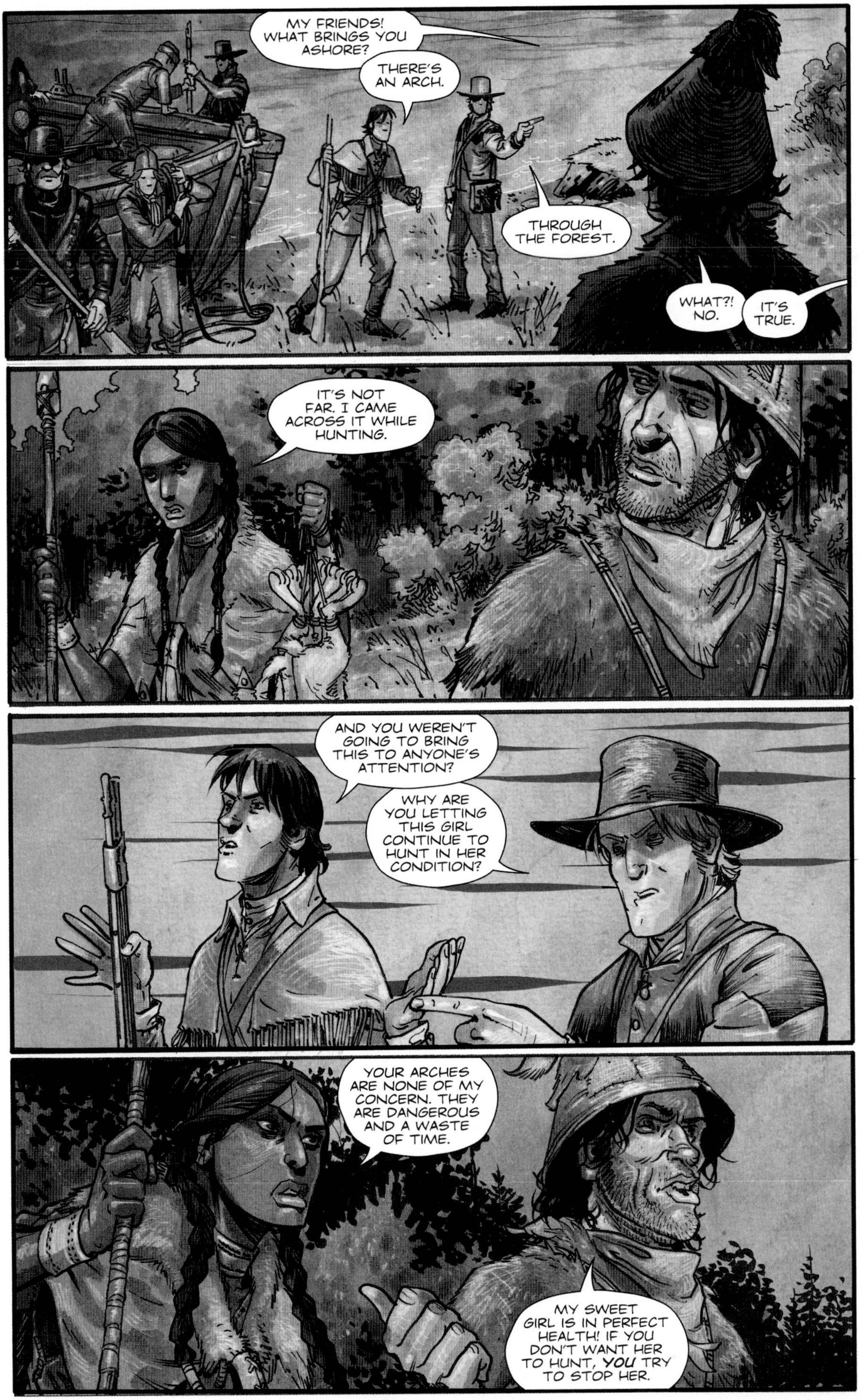
MY FRIENDS! WHAT BRINGS YOU ASHORE?
THERE'S AN ARCH.
THROUGH THE FOREST.
WHAT?! NO.
IT'S TRUE.
IT'S NOT FAR. I CAME ACROSS IT WHILE HUNTING.
AND YOU WEREN'T GOING TO BRING THIS TO ANYONE'S ATTENTION?
WHY ARE YOU LETTING THIS GIRL CONTINUE TO HUNT IN HER CONDITION?
YOUR ARCHES ARE NONE OF MY CONCERN. THEY ARE DANGEROUS AND A WASTE OF TIME.
MY SWEET GIRL IS IN PERFECT HEALTH! IF YOU DON'T WANT HER TO HUNT, *YOU* TRY TO STOP HER.

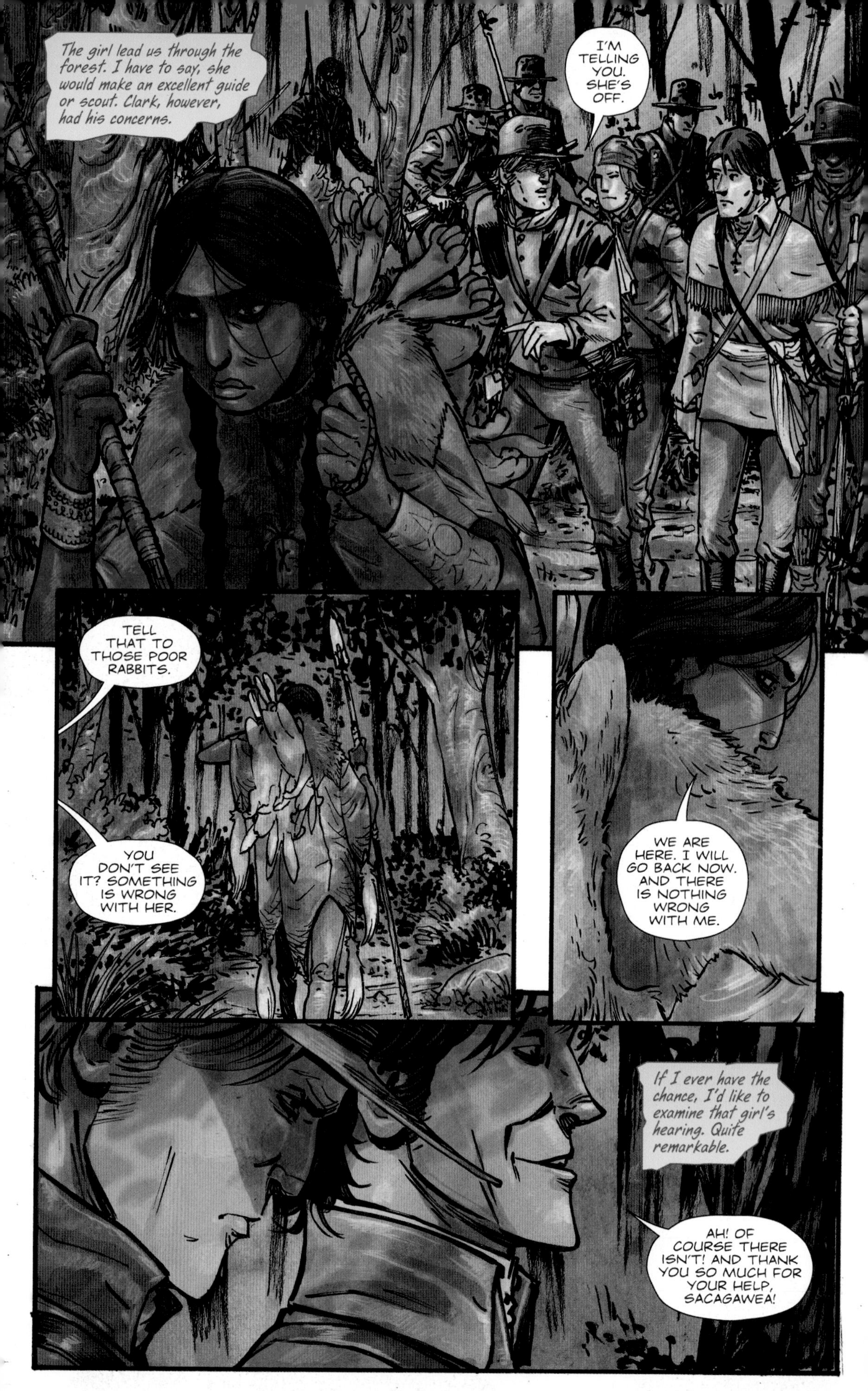
The girl lead us through the forest. I have to say, she would make an excellent guide or scout. Clark, however, had his concerns.
I'M TELLING YOU. SHE'S OFF.
TELL THAT TO THOSE POOR RABBITS.
YOU DON'T SEE IT? SOMETHING IS WRONG WITH HER.
WE ARE HERE. I WILL GO BACK NOW. AND THERE IS NOTHING WRONG WITH ME.
If I ever have the chance, I'd like to examine that girl's hearing. Quite remarkable.
AH! OF COURSE THERE ISN'T! AND THANK YOU SO MUCH FOR YOUR HELP, SACAGAWEA!

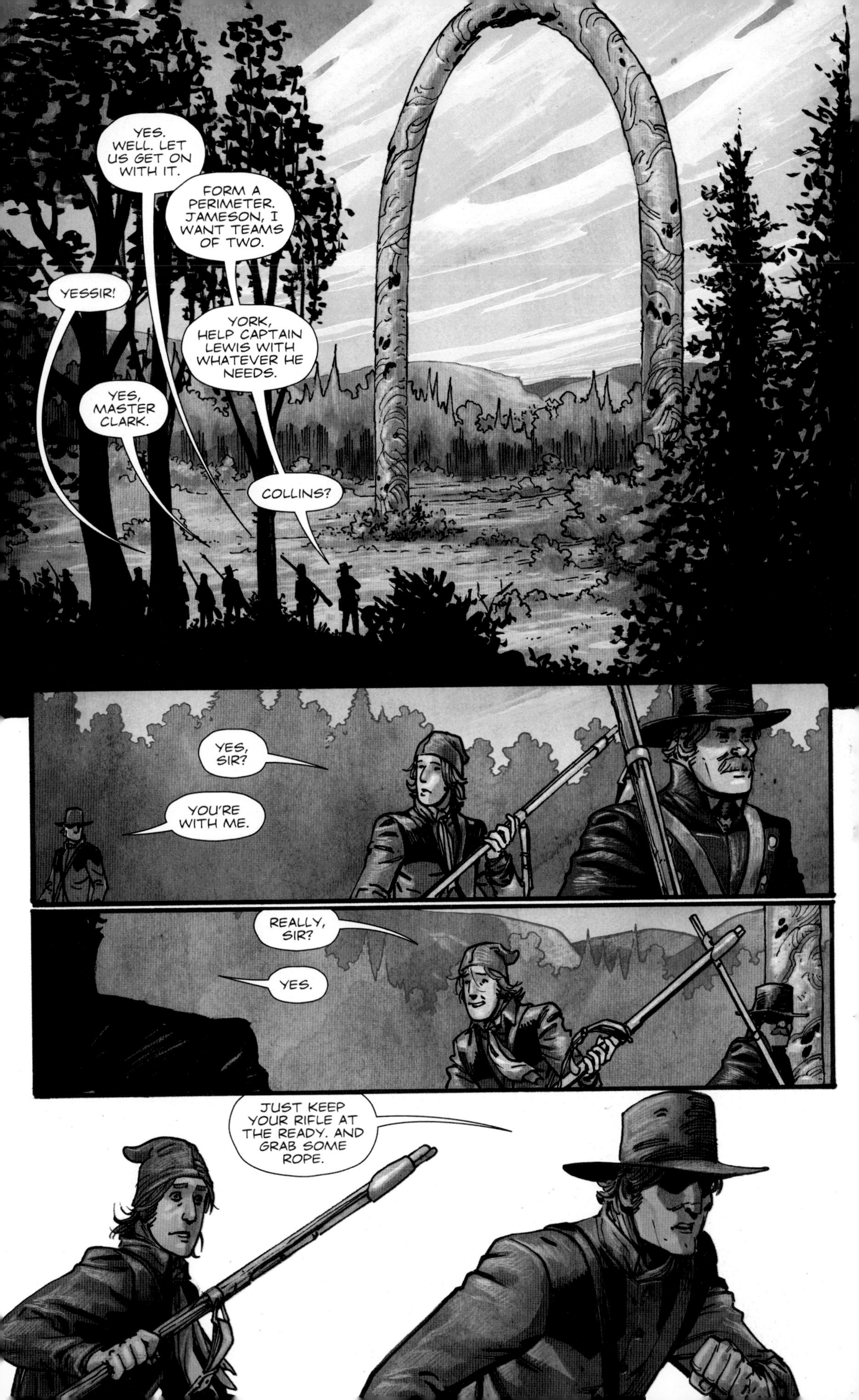
YES. WELL. LET US GET ON WITH IT.
FORM A PERIMETER. JAMESON, I WANT TEAMS OF TWO.
YESSIR!
YORK, HELP CAPTAIN LEWIS WITH WHATEVER HE NEEDS.
YES, MASTER CLARK.
COLLINS?
YES, SIR?
YOU'RE WITH ME.
REALLY, SIR?
YES.
JUST KEEP YOUR RIFLE AT THE READY. AND GRAB SOME ROPE.

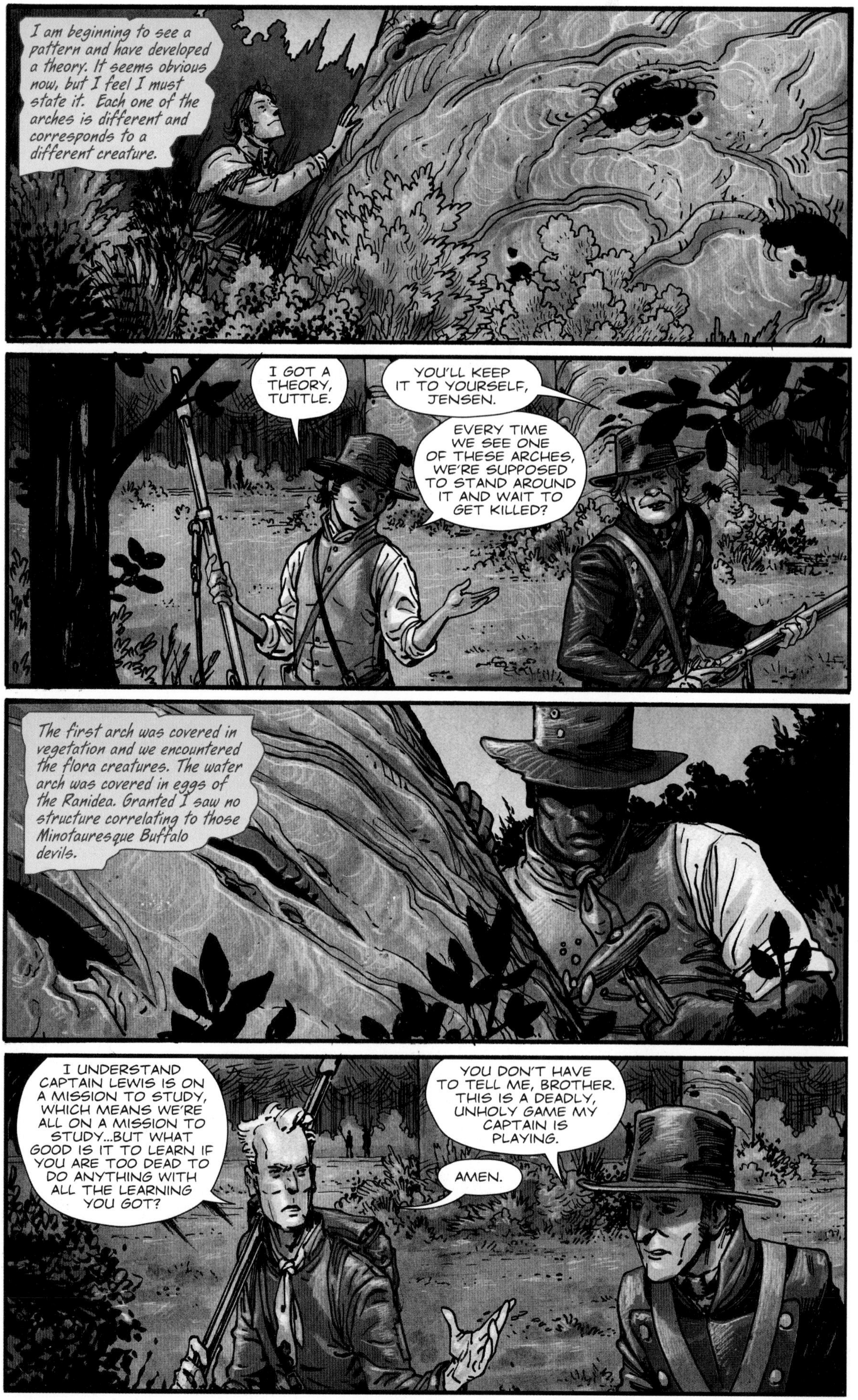
I am beginning to see a pattern and have developed a theory. It seems obvious now, but I feel I must state it. Each one of the arches is different and corresponds to a different creature.
I GOT A THEORY, TUTTLE.
YOU'LL KEEP IT TO YOURSELF, JENSEN.
EVERY TIME WE SEE ONE OF THESE ARCHES, WE'RE SUPPOSED TO STAND AROUND IT AND WAIT TO GET KILLED?
The first arch was covered in vegetation and we encountered the flora creatures. The water arch was covered in eggs of the Ranidea. Granted I saw no structure correlating to those Minotauresque Buffalo devils.
I UNDERSTAND CAPTAIN LEWIS IS ON A MISSION TO STUDY, WHICH MEANS WE'RE ALL ON A MISSION TO STUDY...BUT WHAT GOOD IS IT TO LEARN IF YOU ARE TOO DEAD TO DO ANYTHING WITH ALL THE LEARNING YOU GOT?
YOU DON'T HAVE TO TELL ME, BROTHER. THIS IS A DEADLY, UNHOLY GAME MY CAPTAIN IS PLAYING.
AMEN.

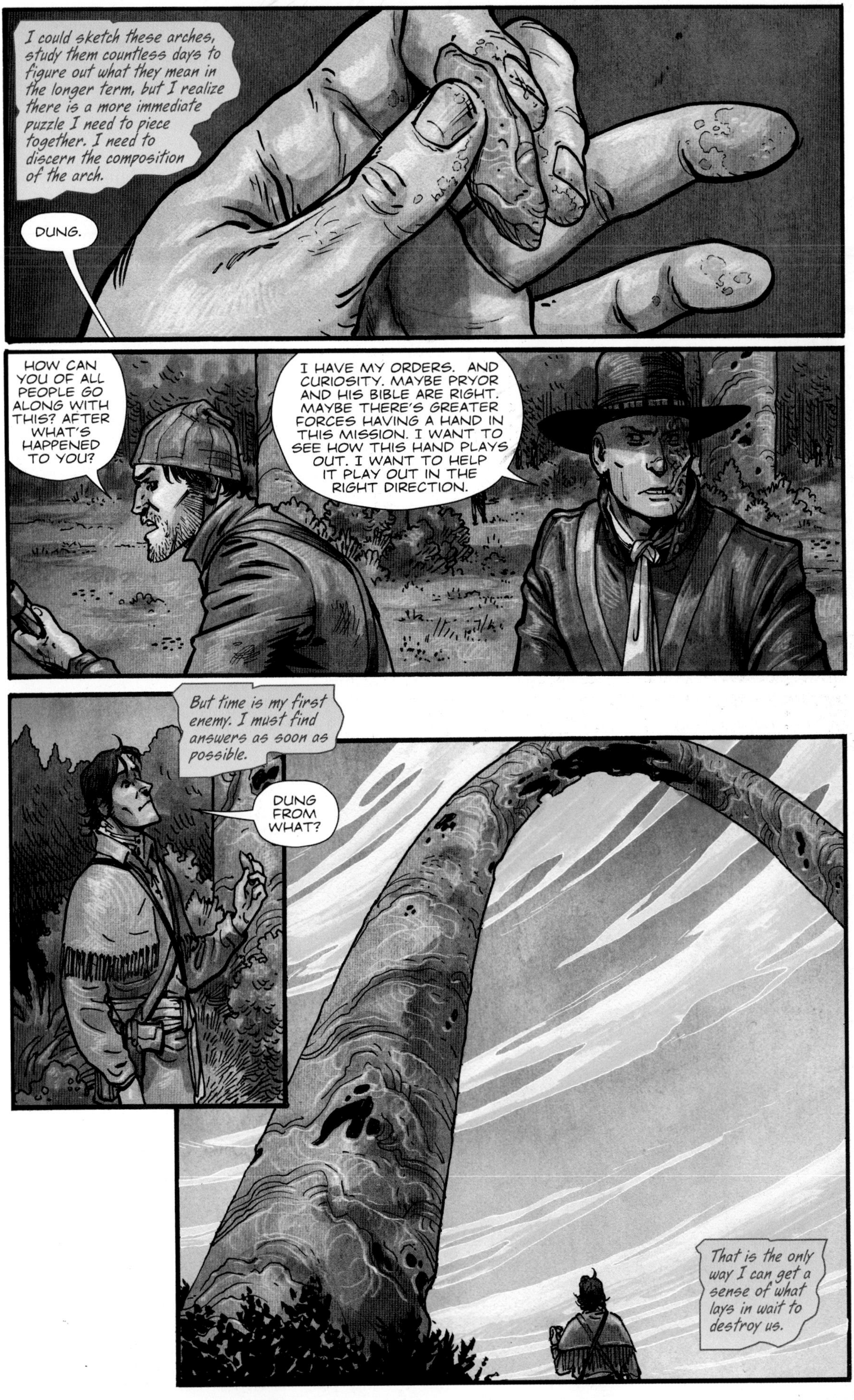
I could sketch these arches, study them countless days to figure out what they mean in the longer term, but I realize there is a more immediate puzzle I need to piece together. I need to discern the composition of the arch.
DUNG.
HOW CAN YOU OF ALL PEOPLE GO ALONG WITH THIS? AFTER WHAT'S HAPPENED TO YOU?
I HAVE MY ORDERS. AND CURIOSITY. MAYBE PRYOR AND HIS BIBLE ARE RIGHT. MAYBE THERE'S GREATER FORCES HAVING A HAND IN THIS MISSION. I WANT TO SEE HOW THIS HAND PLAYS OUT. I WANT TO HELP IT PLAY OUT IN THE RIGHT DIRECTION.
But time is my first enemy. I must find answers as soon as possible.
DUNG FROM WHAT?
That is the only way I can get a sense of what lays in wait to destroy us.

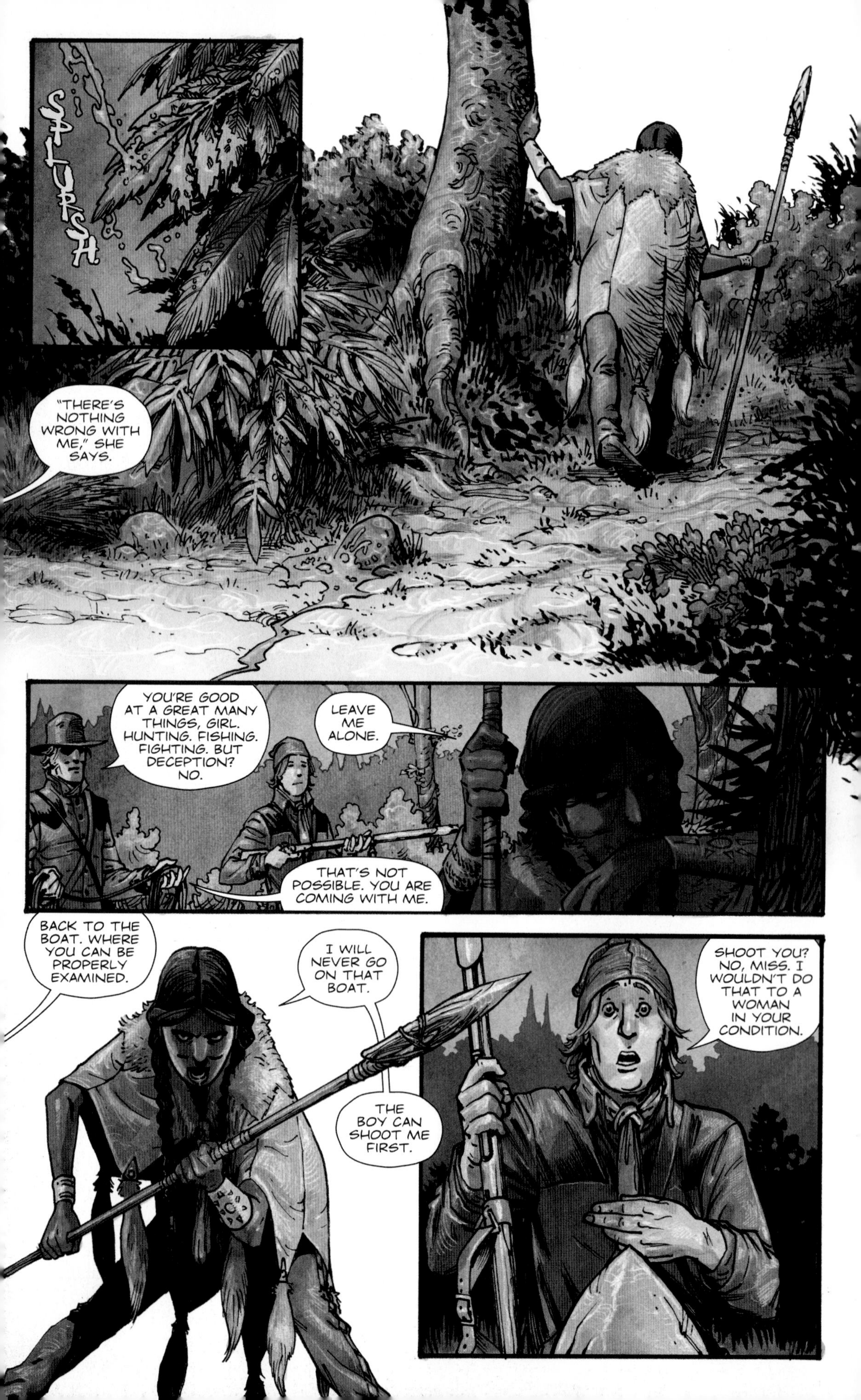
SPLURSH
"THERE'S NOTHING WRONG WITH ME," SHE SAYS.
YOU'RE GOOD AT A GREAT MANY THINGS, GIRL. HUNTING. FISHING. FIGHTING. BUT DECEPTION? NO.
LEAVE ME ALONE.
THAT'S NOT POSSIBLE. YOU ARE COMING WITH ME.
BACK TO THE BOAT. WHERE YOU CAN BE PROPERLY EXAMINED.
I WILL NEVER GO ON THAT BOAT.
THE BOY CAN SHOOT ME FIRST.
SHOOT YOU? NO, MISS. I WOULDN'T DO THAT TO A WOMAN IN YOUR CONDITION.

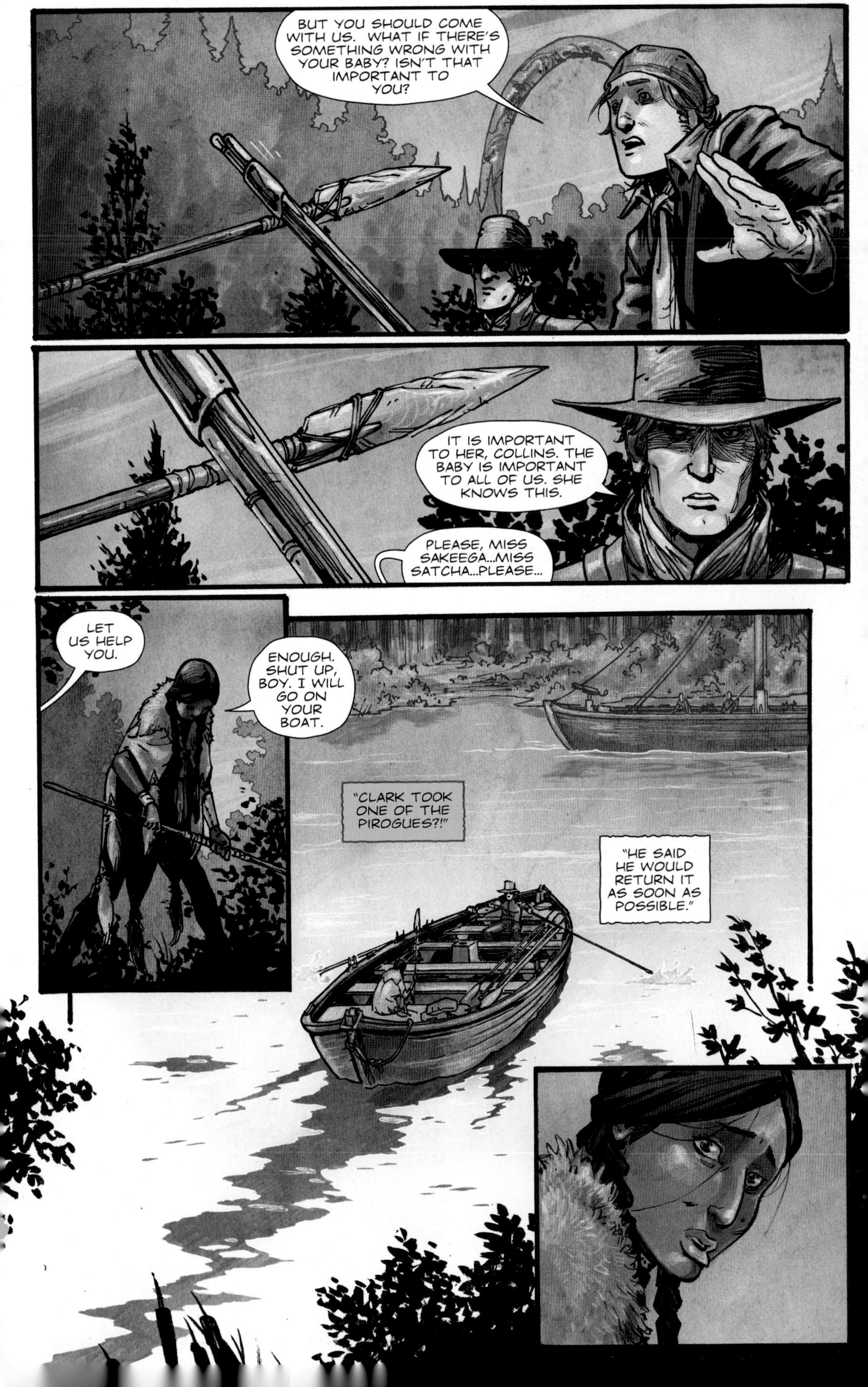
BUT YOU SHOULD COME WITH US. WHAT IF THERE'S SOMETHING WRONG WITH YOUR BABY? ISN'T THAT IMPORTANT TO YOU?
IT IS IMPORTANT TO HER, COLLINS. THE BABY IS IMPORTANT TO ALL OF US. SHE KNOWS THIS.
PLEASE, MISS SAKEEGA...MISS SATCHA...PLEASE...
LET US HELP YOU.
ENOUGH. SHUT UP, BOY. I WILL GO ON YOUR BOAT.
"CLARK TOOK ONE OF THE PIROGUES?!"
"HE SAID HE WOULD RETURN IT AS SOON AS POSSIBLE."

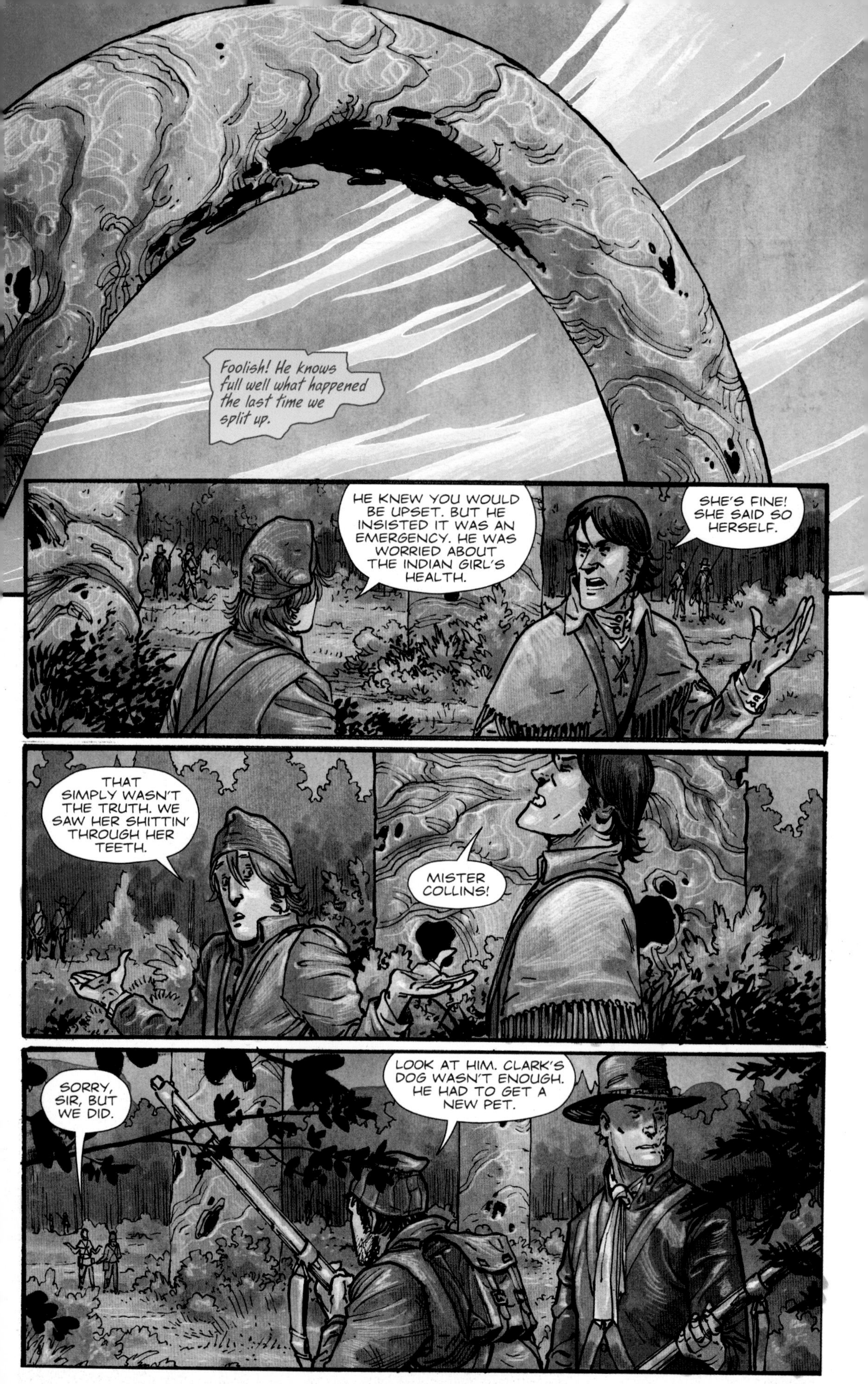
Foolish! He knows full well what happened the last time we split up.
HE KNEW YOU WOULD BE UPSET. BUT HE INSISTED IT WAS AN EMERGENCY. HE WAS WORRIED ABOUT THE INDIAN GIRL'S HEALTH.
SHE'S FINE! SHE SAID SO HERSELF.
THAT SIMPLY WASN'T THE TRUTH. WE SAW HER SHITTIN' THROUGH HER TEETH.
MISTER COLLINS!
SORRY, SIR, BUT WE DID.
LOOK AT HIM. CLARK'S DOG WASN'T ENOUGH. HE HAD TO GET A NEW PET.

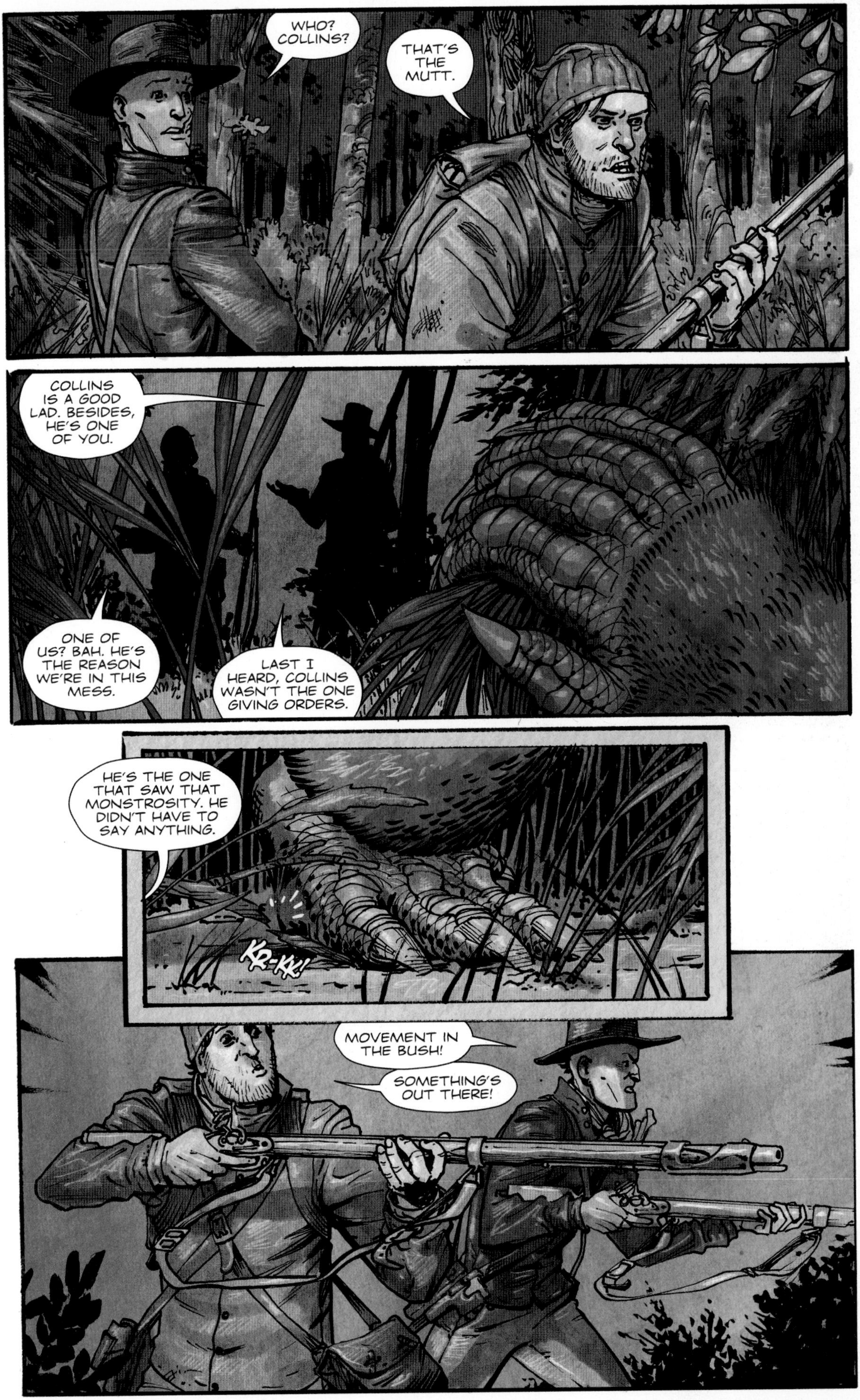
WHO? COLLINS?
THAT'S THE MUTT.
COLLINS IS A GOOD LAD. BESIDES, HE'S ONE OF YOU.
ONE OF US? BAH. HE'S THE REASON WE'RE IN THIS MESS.
LAST I HEARD, COLLINS WASN'T THE ONE GIVING ORDERS.
HE'S THE ONE THAT SAW THAT MONSTROSITY. HE DIDN'T HAVE TO SAY ANYTHING.
KR-KK!
MOVEMENT IN THE BUSH!
SOMETHING'S OUT THERE!

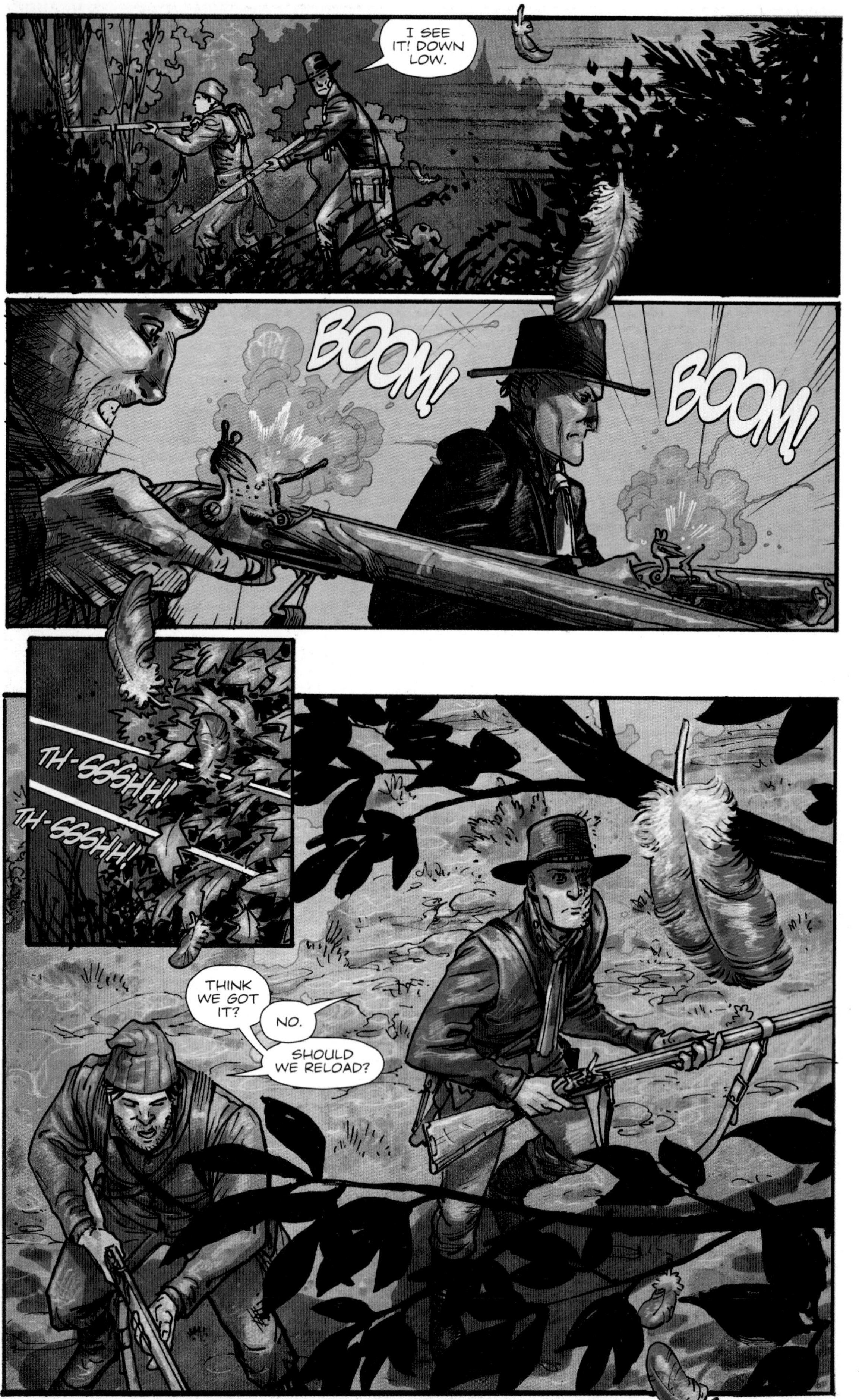
I SEE IT! DOWN LOW.
BOOM!
BOOM!
TH-SSSHH!
TH-SSSHH!
THINK WE GOT IT?
NO.
SHOULD WE RELOAD?

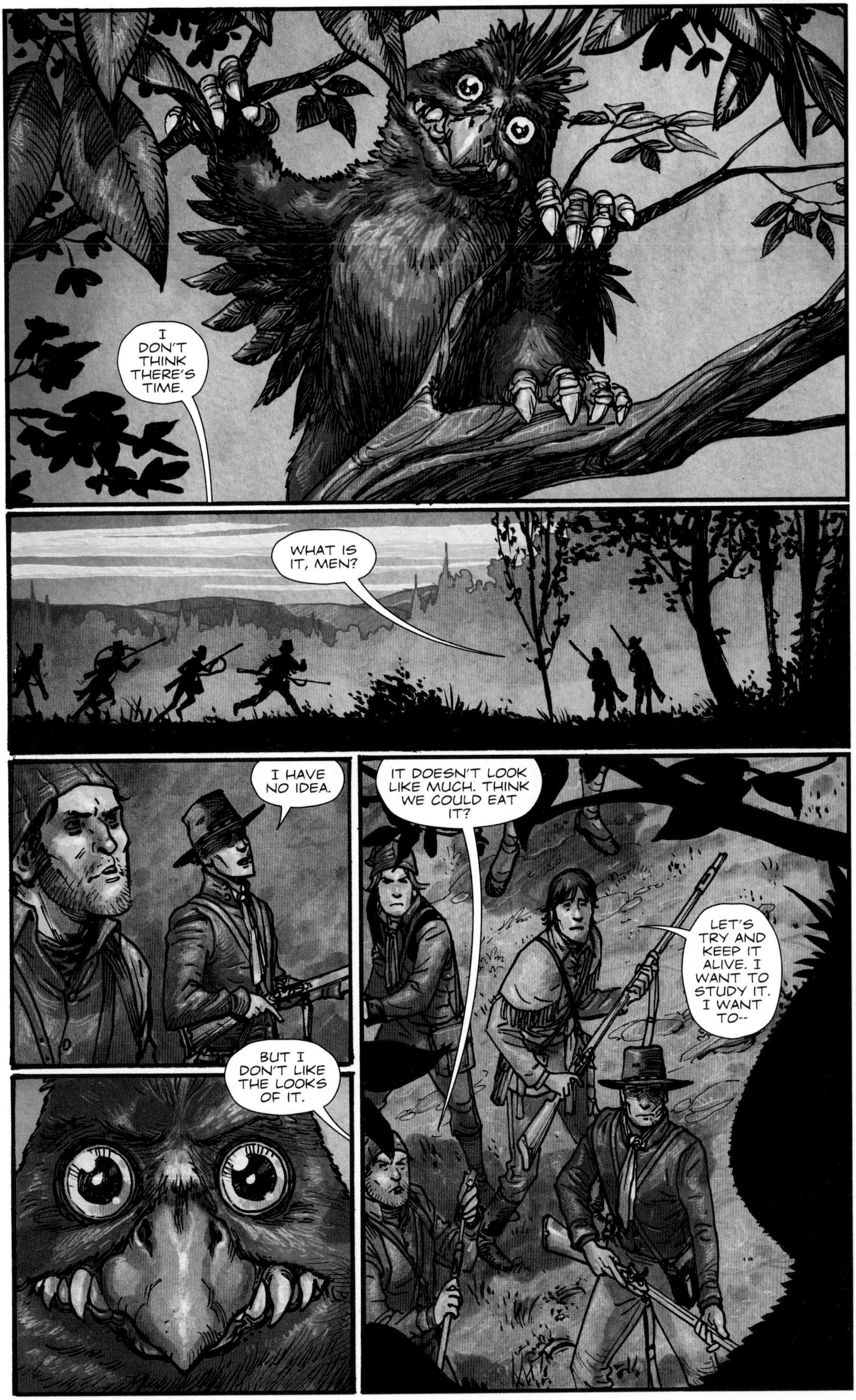
I DON'T THINK THERE'S TIME.
WHAT IS IT, MEN?
I HAVE NO IDEA.
BUT I DON'T LIKE THE LOOKS OF IT.
IT DOESN'T LOOK LIKE MUCH. THINK WE COULD EAT IT?
LET'S TRY AND KEEP IT ALIVE. I WANT TO STUDY IT. I WANT TO--

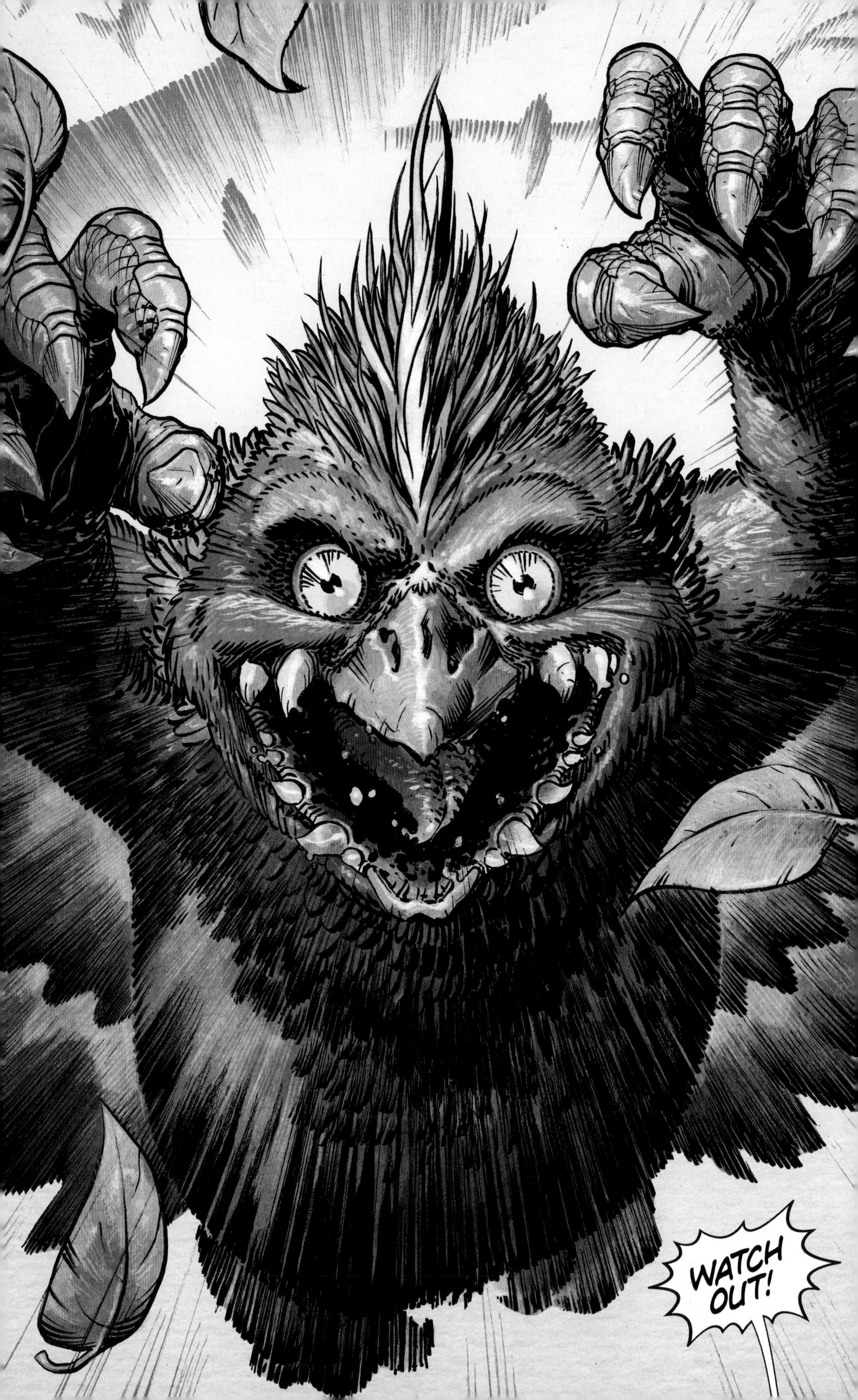
WATCH OUT!

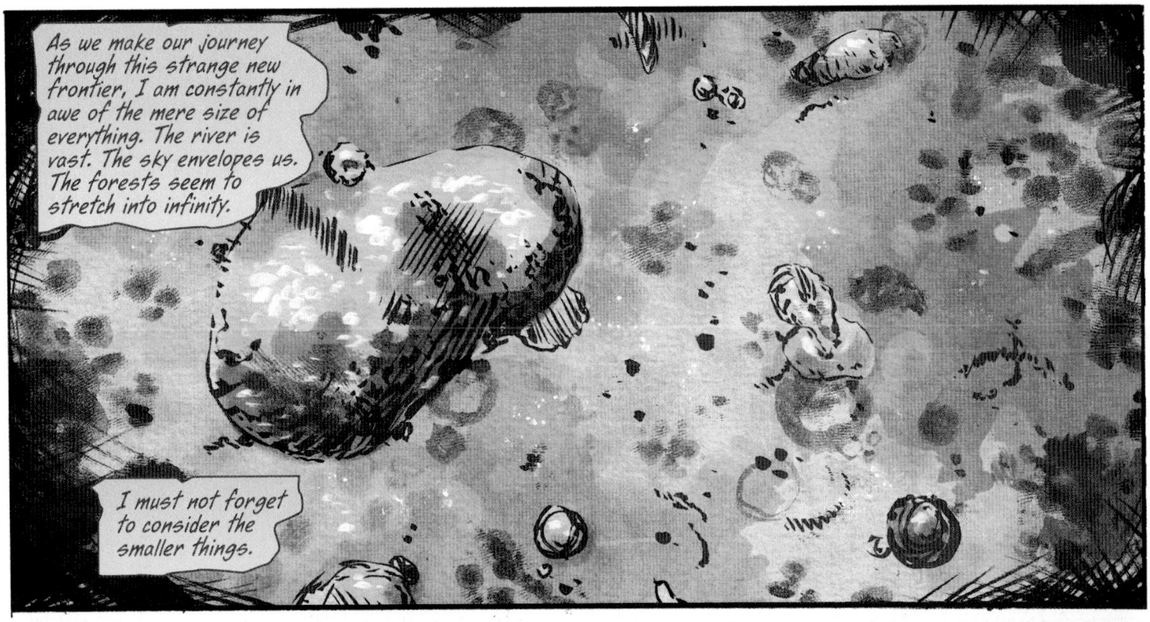
As we make our journey through this strange new frontier, I am constantly in awe of the mere size of everything. The river is vast. The sky envelopes us. The forests seem to stretch into infinity.
I must not forget to consider the smaller things.

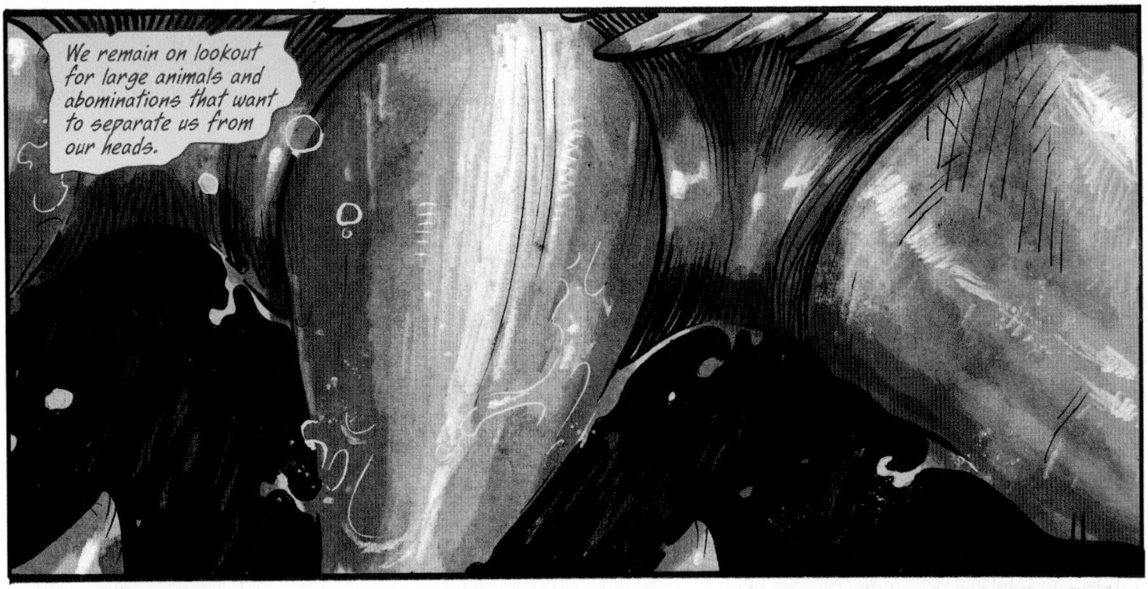
We remain on lookout for large animals and abominations that want to separate us from our heads.

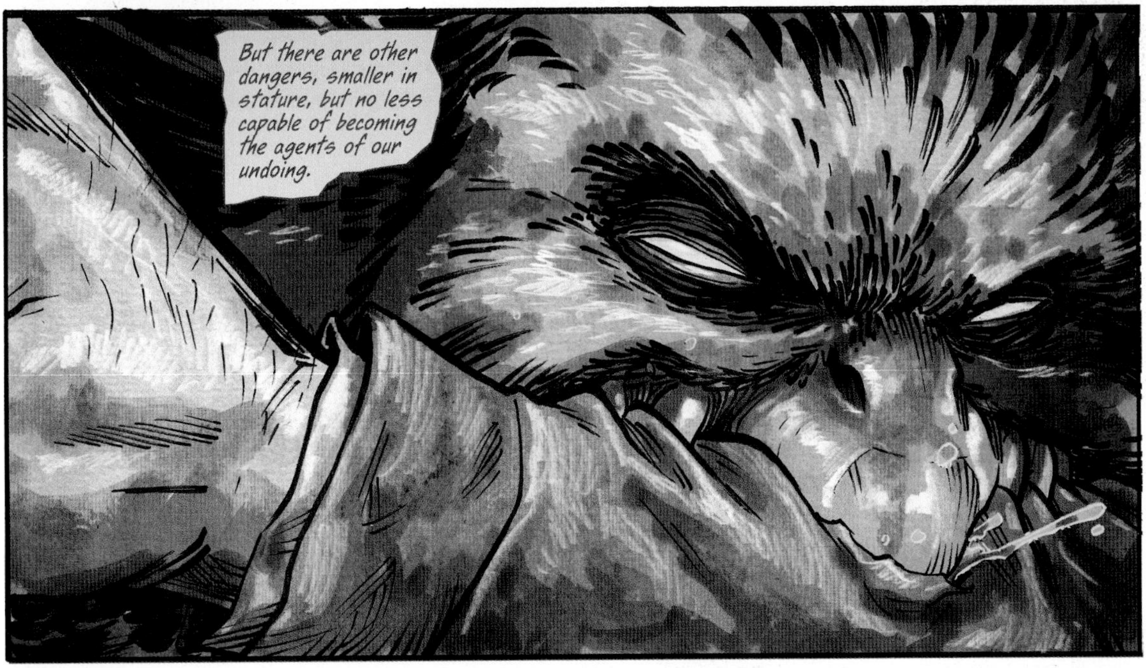
But there are other dangers, smaller in stature, but no less capable of becoming the agents of our undoing.

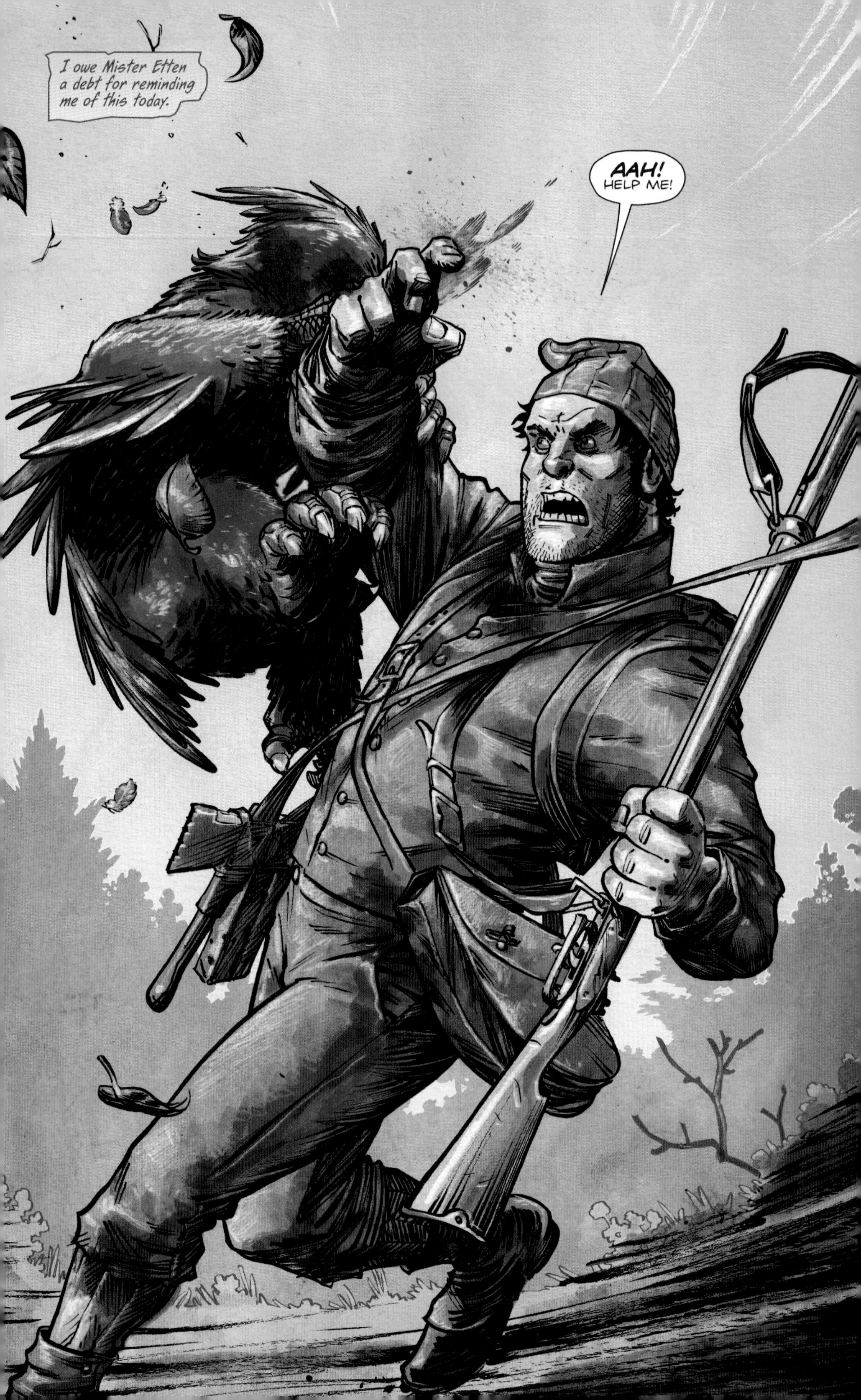
I owe Mister Etten a debt for reminding me of this today.
AAH! HELP ME!

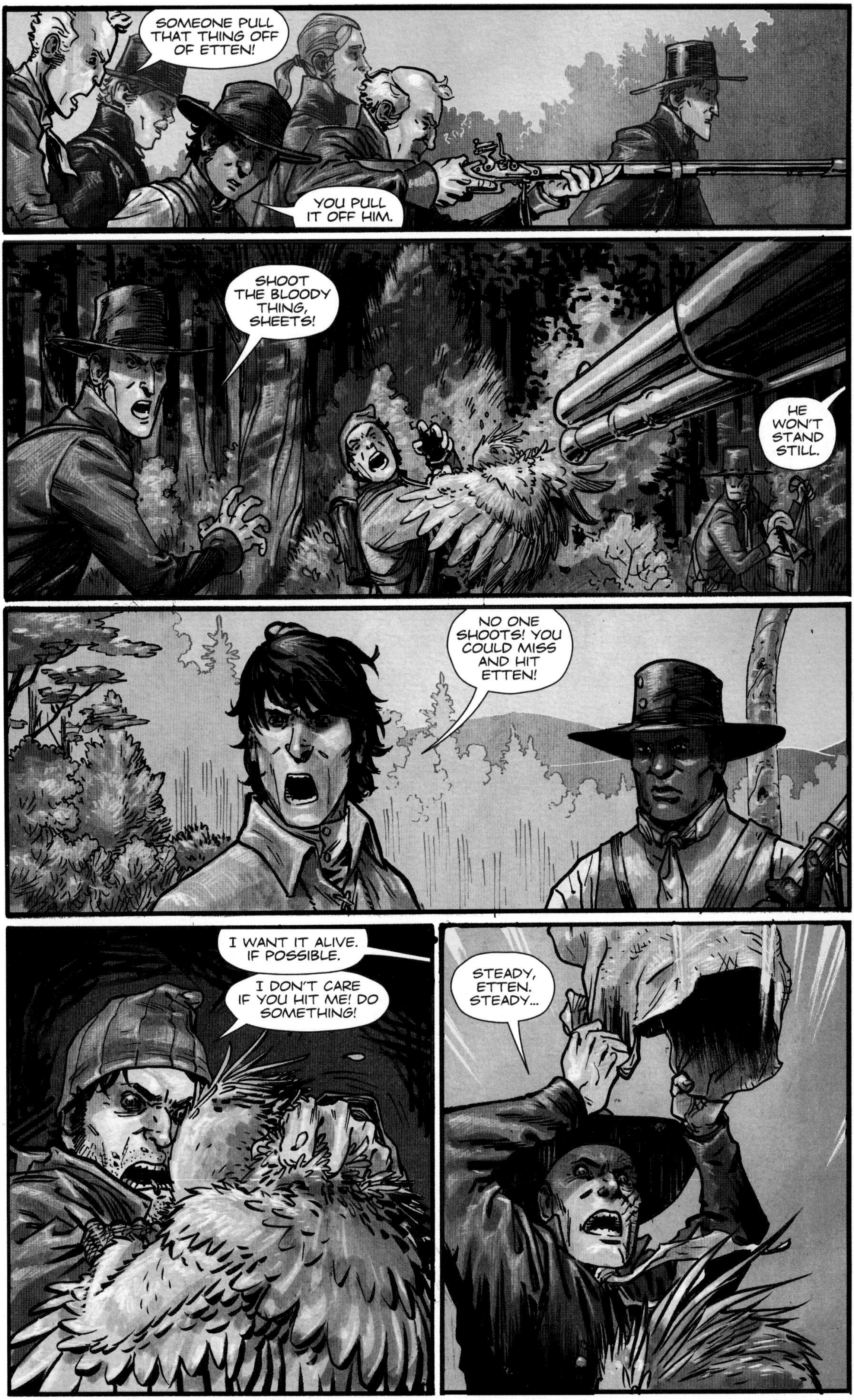
SOMEONE PULL THAT THING OFF OF ETTEN!
YOU PULL IT OFF HIM.
SHOOT THE BLOODY THING, SHEETS!
HE WON'T STAND STILL.
NO ONE SHOOTS! YOU COULD MISS AND HIT ETTEN!
I WANT IT ALIVE. IF POSSIBLE.
I DON'T CARE IF YOU HIT ME! DO SOMETHING!
STEADY, ETTEN. STEADY...

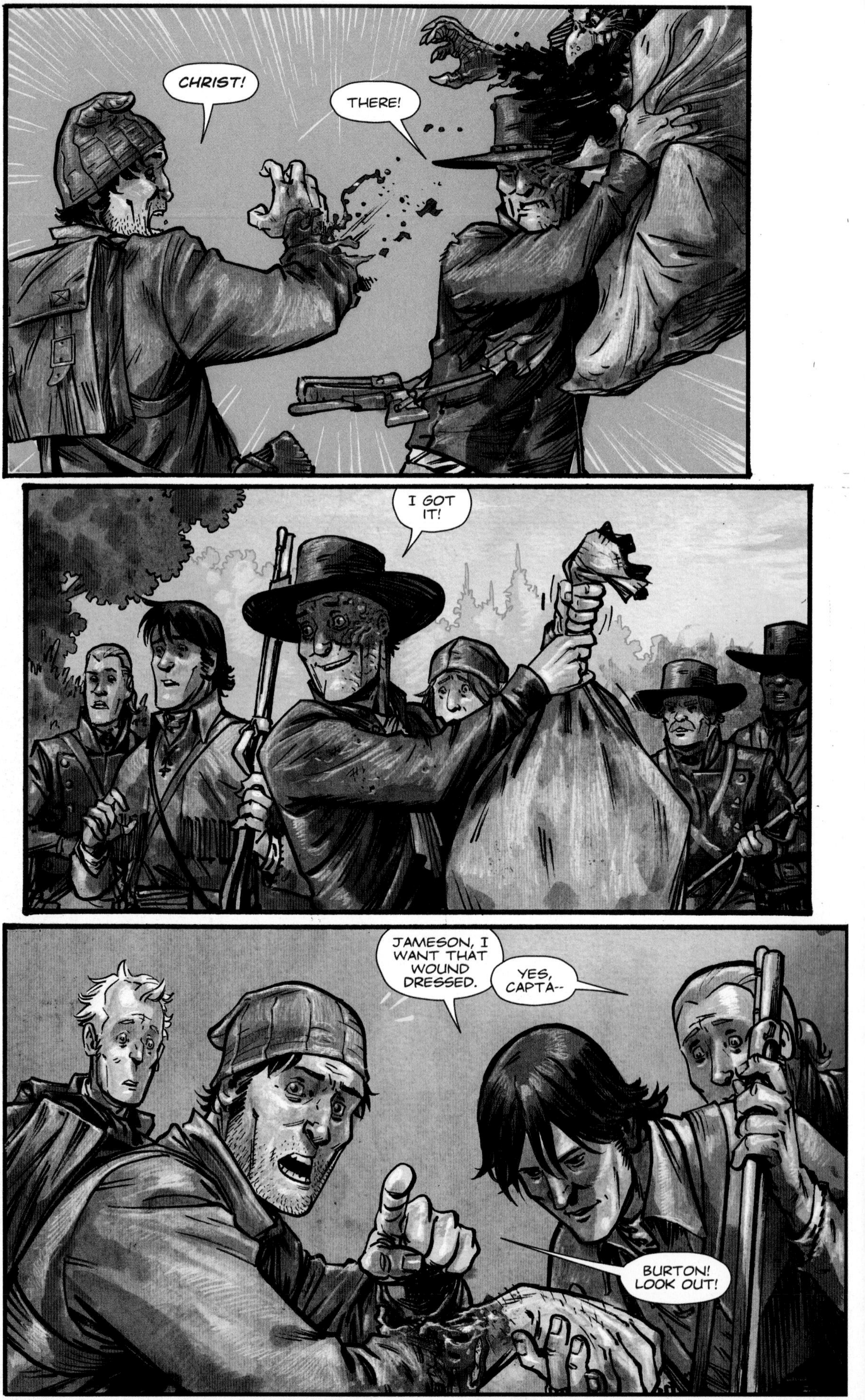
CHRIST!
THERE!
I GOT IT!
JAMESON, I WANT THAT WOUND DRESSED.
YES, CAPTA--
BURTON! LOOK OUT!

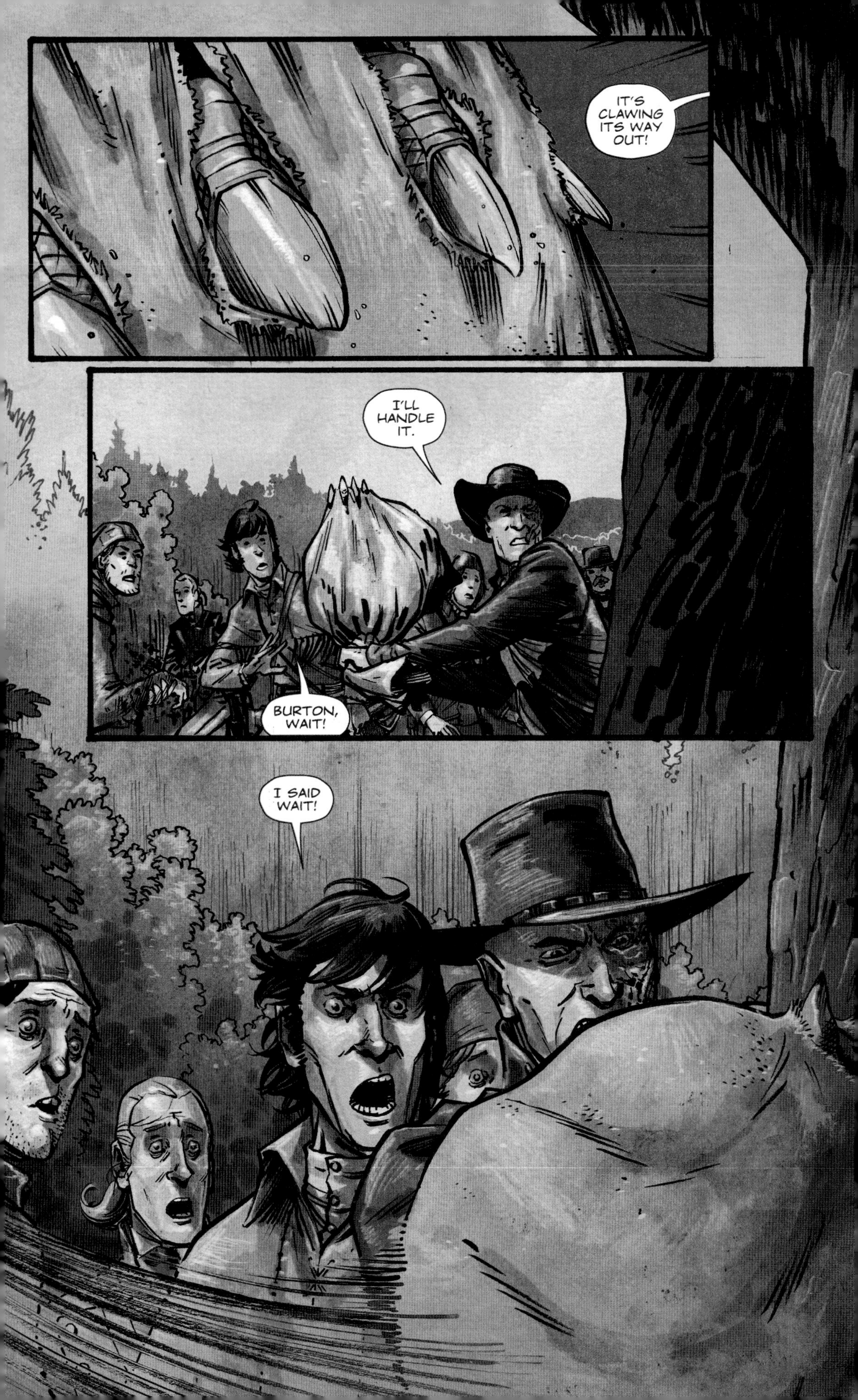
IT'S CLAWING ITS WAY OUT!
I'LL HANDLE IT.
BURTON, WAIT!
I SAID WAIT!

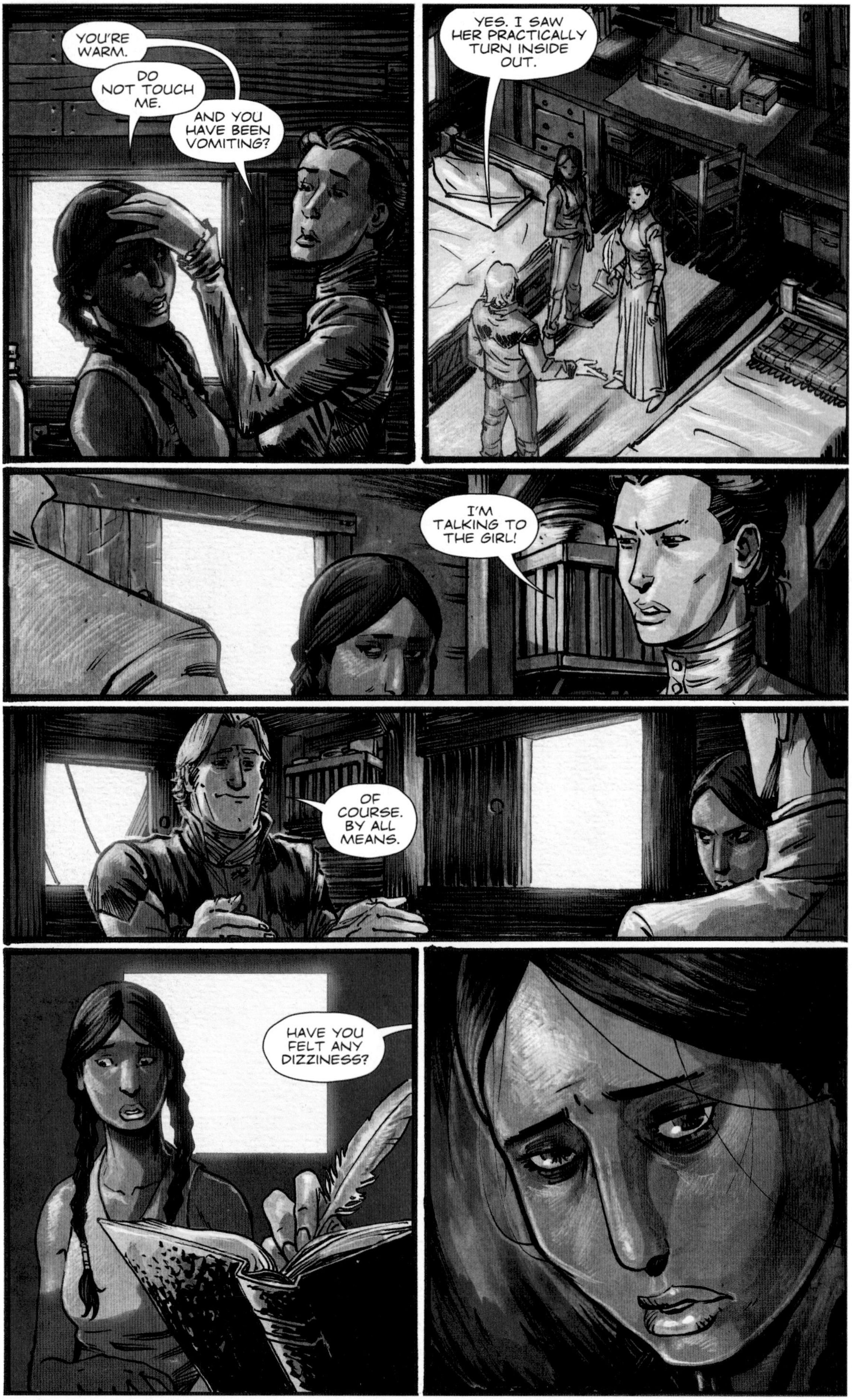
YOU'RE WARM.
DO NOT TOUCH ME.
AND YOU HAVE BEEN VOMITING?
YES. I SAW HER PRACTICALLY TURN INSIDE OUT.
I'M TALKING TO THE GIRL!
OF COURSE. BY ALL MEANS.
HAVE YOU FELT ANY DIZZINESS?

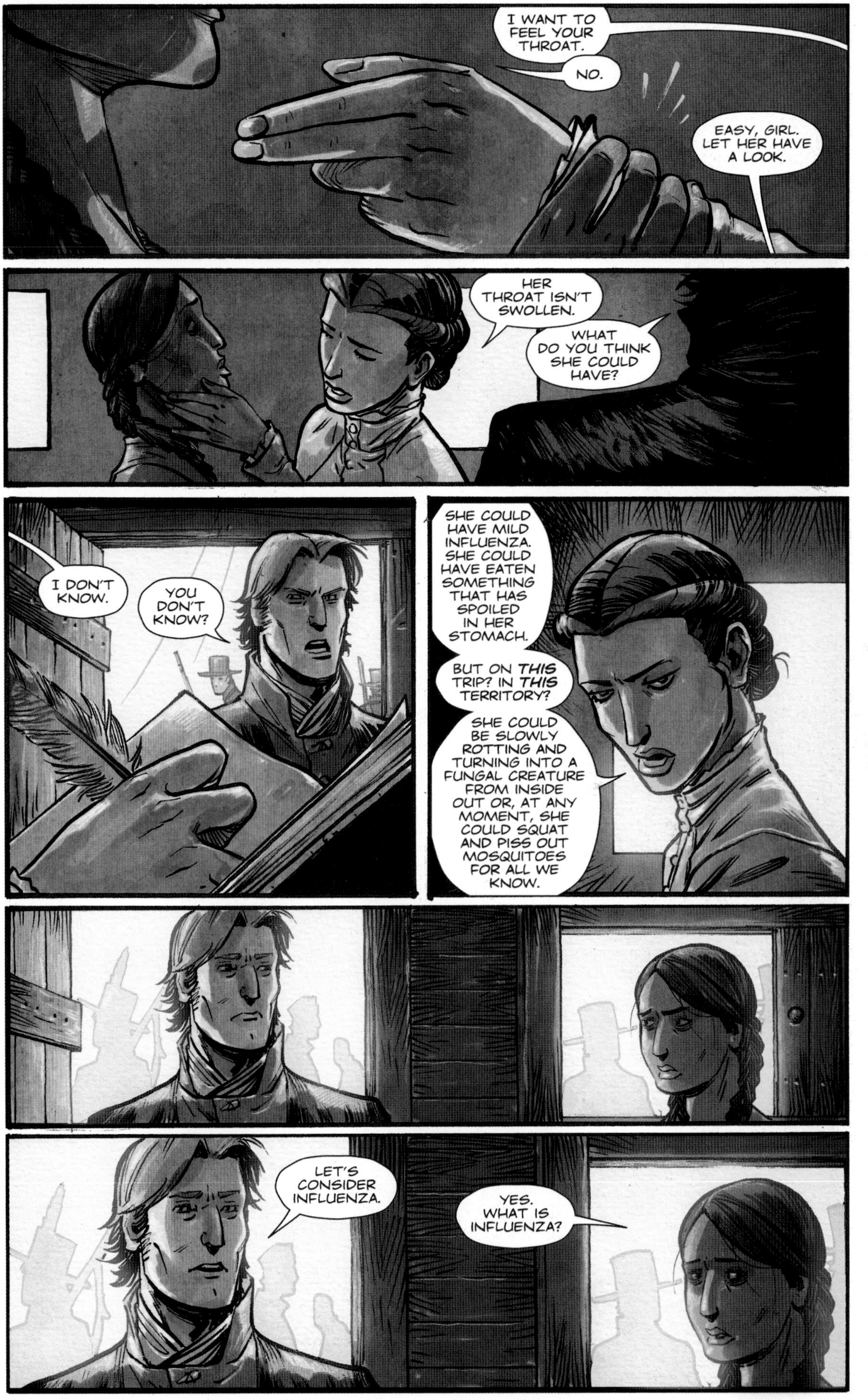
I WANT TO FEEL YOUR THROAT.
NO.
EASY, GIRL. LET HER HAVE A LOOK.
HER THROAT ISN'T SWOLLEN.
WHAT DO YOU THINK SHE COULD HAVE?
I DON'T KNOW.
YOU DON'T KNOW?
SHE COULD HAVE MILD INFLUENZA. SHE COULD HAVE EATEN SOMETHING THAT HAS SPOILED IN HER STOMACH.
BUT ON THIS TRIP? IN THIS TERRITORY?
SHE COULD BE SLOWLY ROTTING AND TURNING INTO A FUNGAL CREATURE FROM INSIDE OUT OR, AT ANY MOMENT, SHE COULD SQUAT AND PISS OUT MOSQUITOES FOR ALL WE KNOW.
LET'S CONSIDER INFLUENZA.
YES. WHAT IS INFLUENZA?

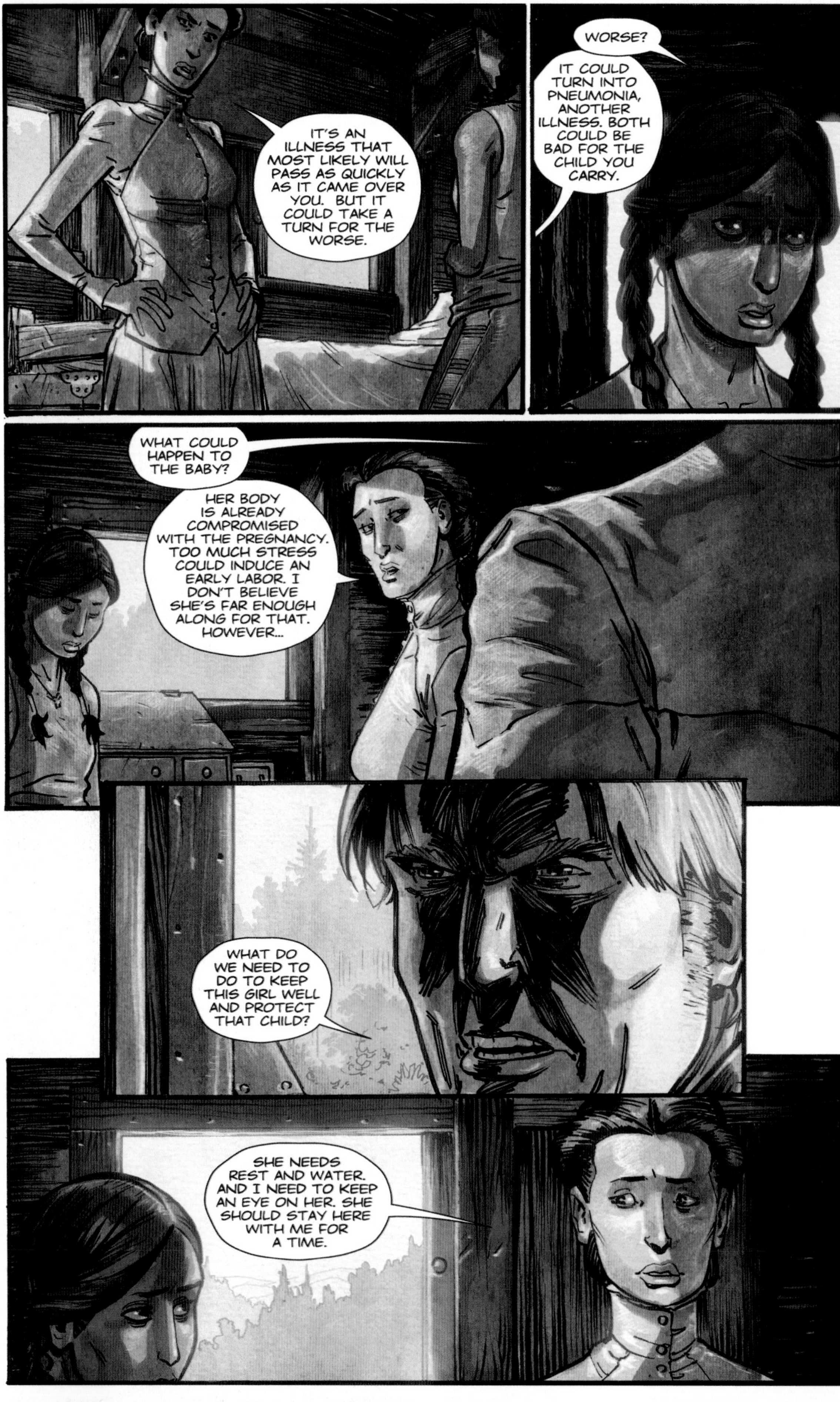
IT'S AN ILLNESS THAT MOST LIKELY WILL PASS AS QUICKLY AS IT CAME OVER YOU. BUT IT COULD TAKE A TURN FOR THE WORSE.
WORSE?
IT COULD TURN INTO PNEUMONIA, ANOTHER ILLNESS. BOTH COULD BE BAD FOR THE CHILD YOU CARRY.
WHAT COULD HAPPEN TO THE BABY?
HER BODY IS ALREADY COMPROMISED WITH THE PREGNANCY. TOO MUCH STRESS COULD INDUCE AN EARLY LABOR. I DON'T BELIEVE SHE'S FAR ENOUGH ALONG FOR THAT. HOWEVER...
WHAT DO WE NEED TO DO TO KEEP THIS GIRL WELL AND PROTECT THAT CHILD?
SHE NEEDS REST AND WATER. AND I NEED TO KEEP AN EYE ON HER. SHE SHOULD STAY HERE WITH ME FOR A TIME.

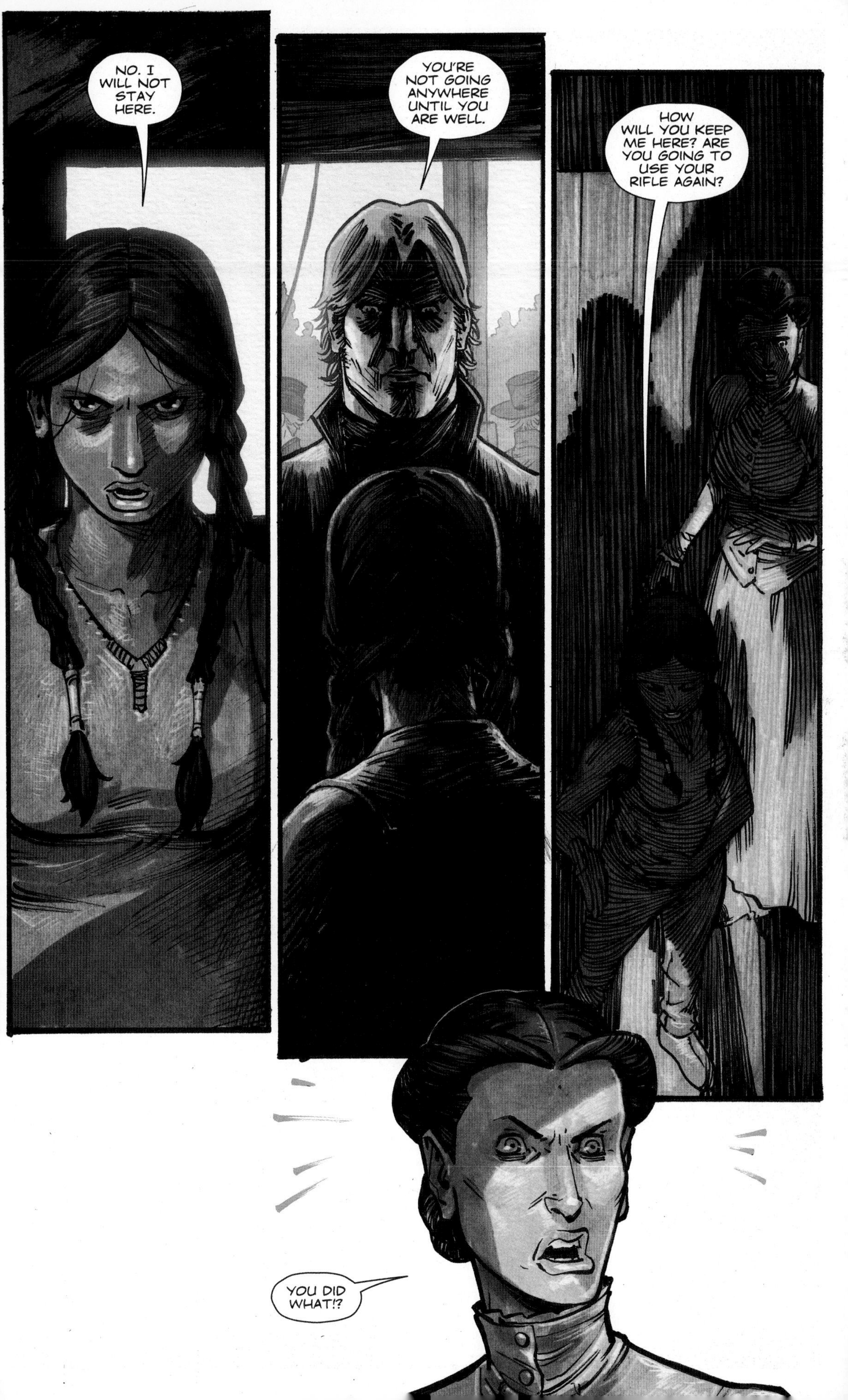
NO. I WILL NOT STAY HERE.
YOU'RE NOT GOING ANYWHERE UNTIL YOU ARE WELL.
HOW WILL YOU KEEP ME HERE? ARE YOU GOING TO USE YOUR RIFLE AGAIN?
YOU DID WHAT!?

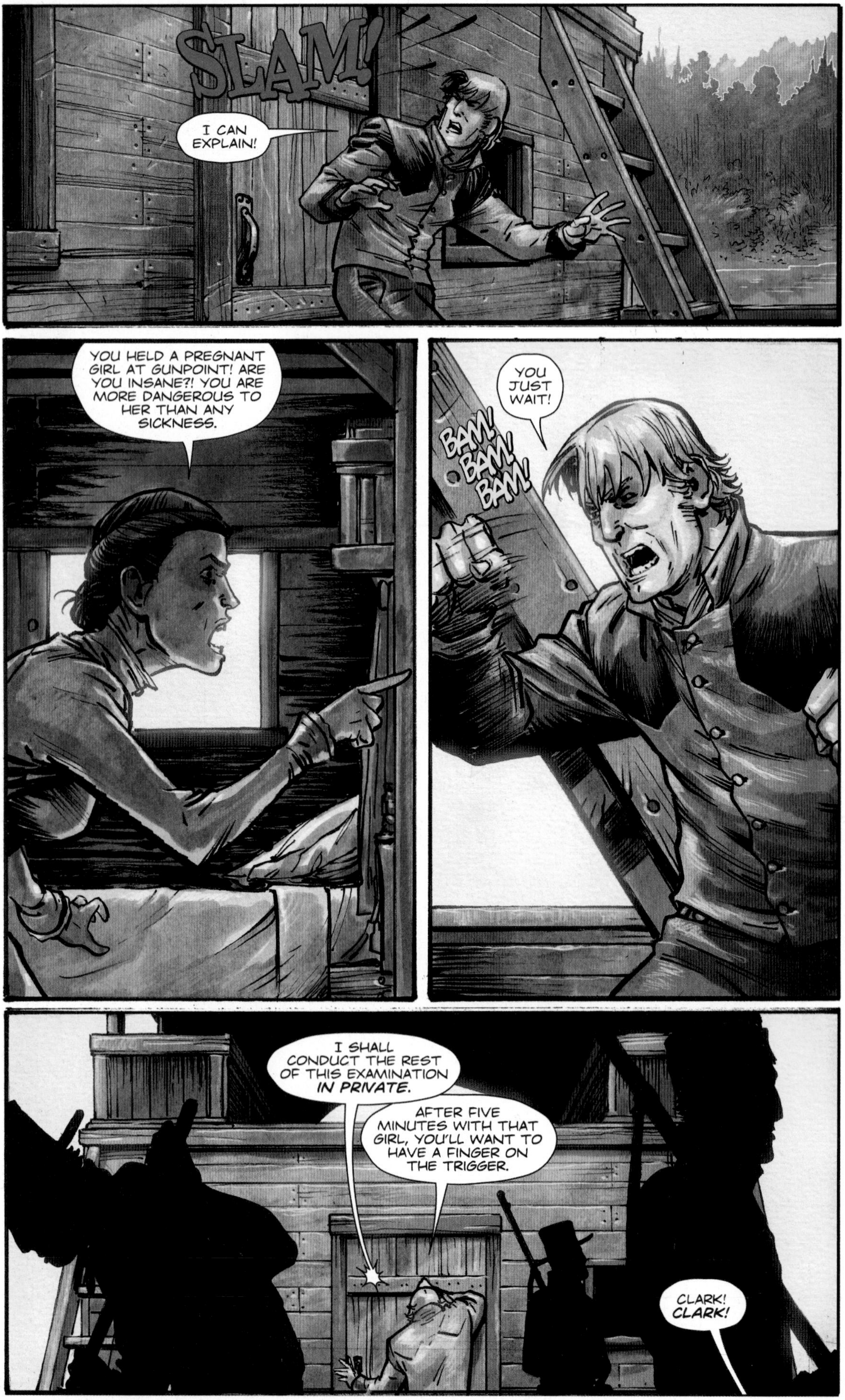
SLAM!
I CAN EXPLAIN!
YOU HELD A PREGNANT GIRL AT GUNPOINT! ARE YOU INSANE?! YOU ARE MORE DANGEROUS TO HER THAN ANY SICKNESS.
YOU JUST WAIT!
BAM! BAM! BAM!
I SHALL CONDUCT THE REST OF THIS EXAMINATION IN PRIVATE.
AFTER FIVE MINUTES WITH THAT GIRL, YOU'LL WANT TO HAVE A FINGER ON THE TRIGGER.
CLARK! CLARK!

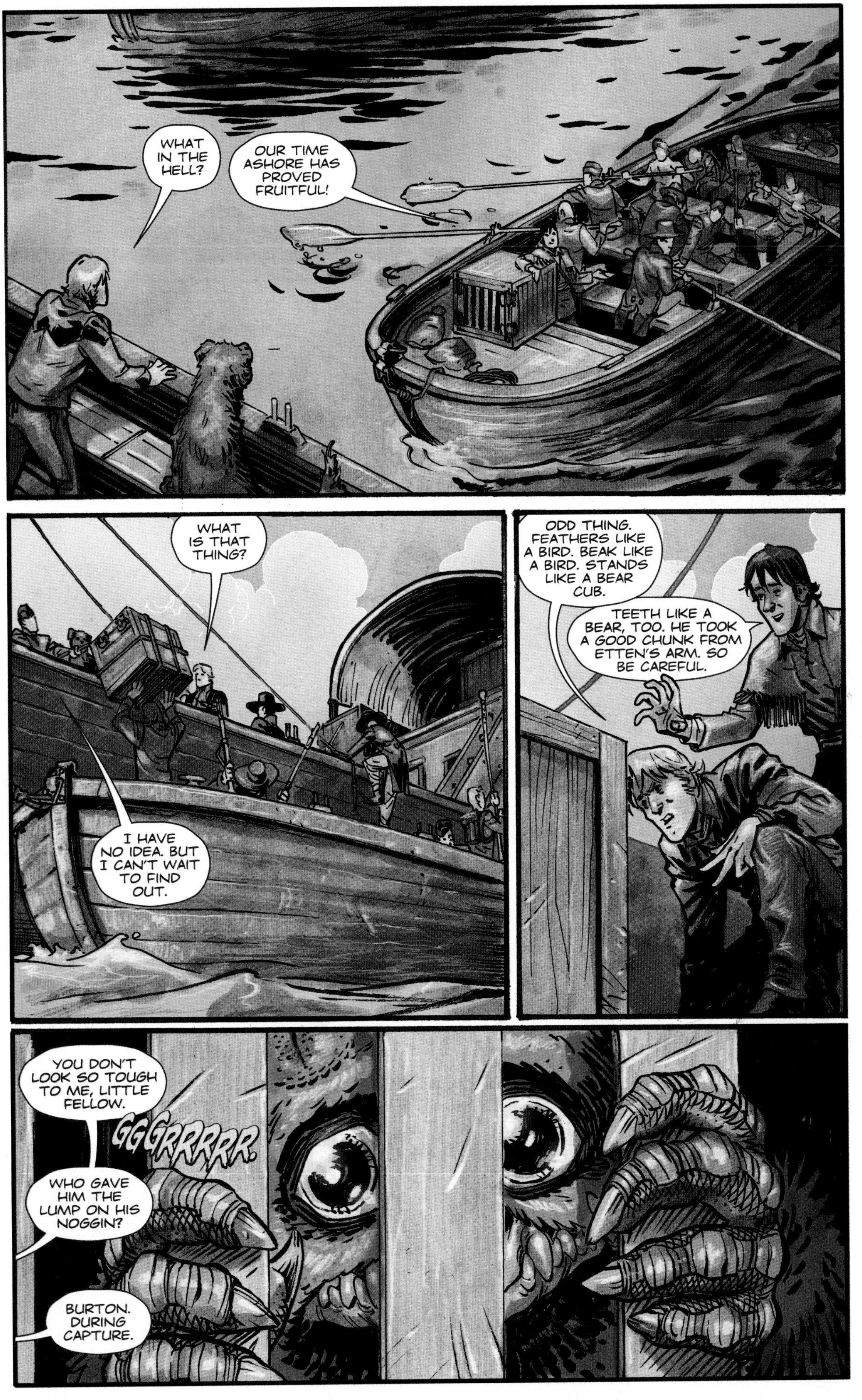
WHAT IN THE HELL?
OUR TIME ASHORE HAS PROVED FRUITFUL!
WHAT IS THAT THING?
I HAVE NO IDEA. BUT I CAN'T WAIT TO FIND OUT.
ODD THING. FEATHERS LIKE A BIRD. BEAK LIKE A BIRD. STANDS LIKE A BEAR CUB.
TEETH LIKE A BEAR, TOO. HE TOOK A GOOD CHUNK FROM ETTEN'S ARM. SO BE CAREFUL.
YOU DON'T LOOK SO TOUGH TO ME, LITTLE FELLOW.
GGGRRRRRR.
WHO GAVE HIM THE LUMP ON HIS NOGGIN?
BURTON. DURING CAPTURE.

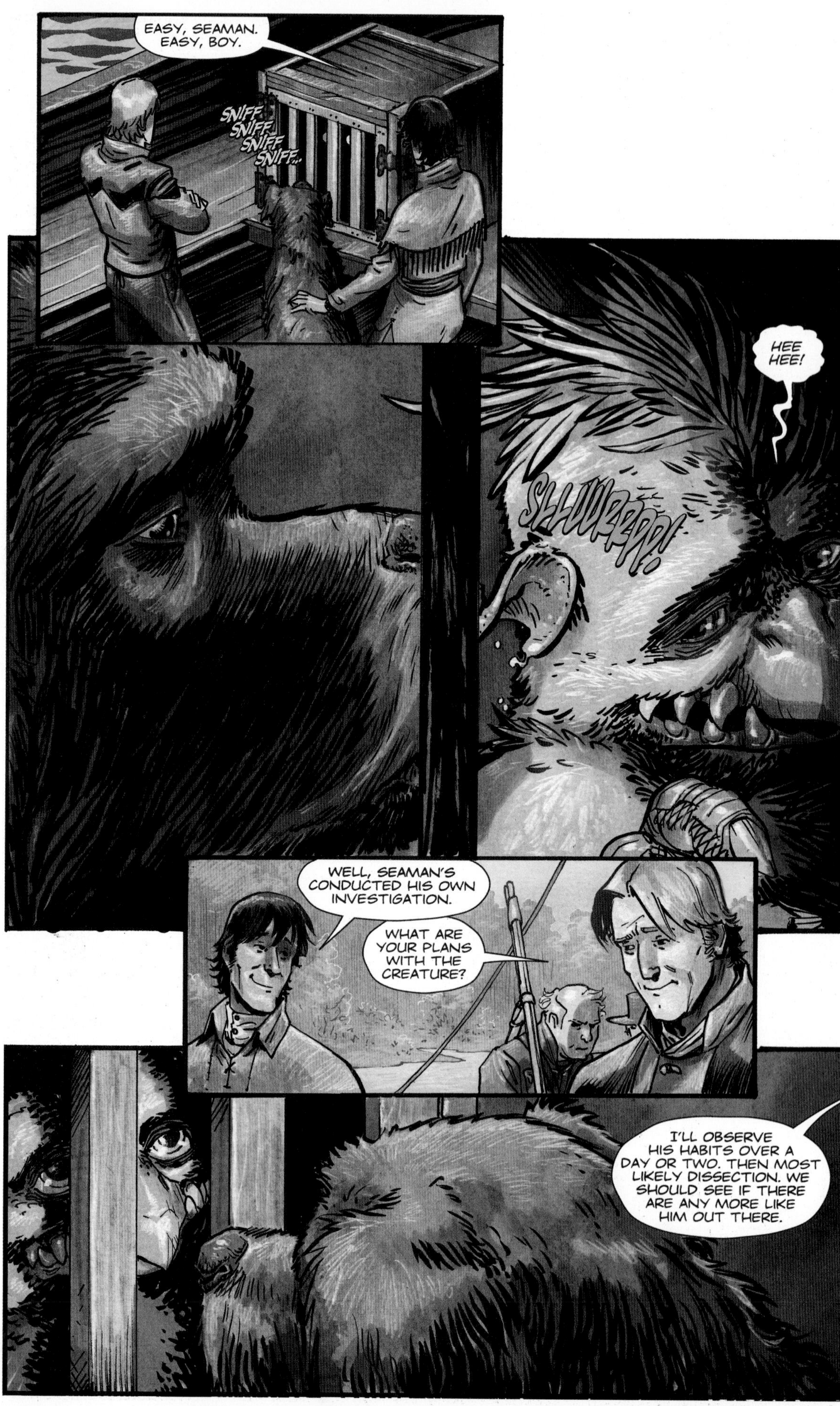
EASY, SEAMAN. EASY, BOY.
SNIFF SNIFF SNIFF SNIFF...
HEE HEE!
SLLURRPP!
WELL, SEAMAN'S CONDUCTED HIS OWN INVESTIGATION.
WHAT ARE YOUR PLANS WITH THE CREATURE?
I'LL OBSERVE HIS HABITS OVER A DAY OR TWO. THEN MOST LIKELY DISSECTION. WE SHOULD SEE IF THERE ARE ANY MORE LIKE HIM OUT THERE.

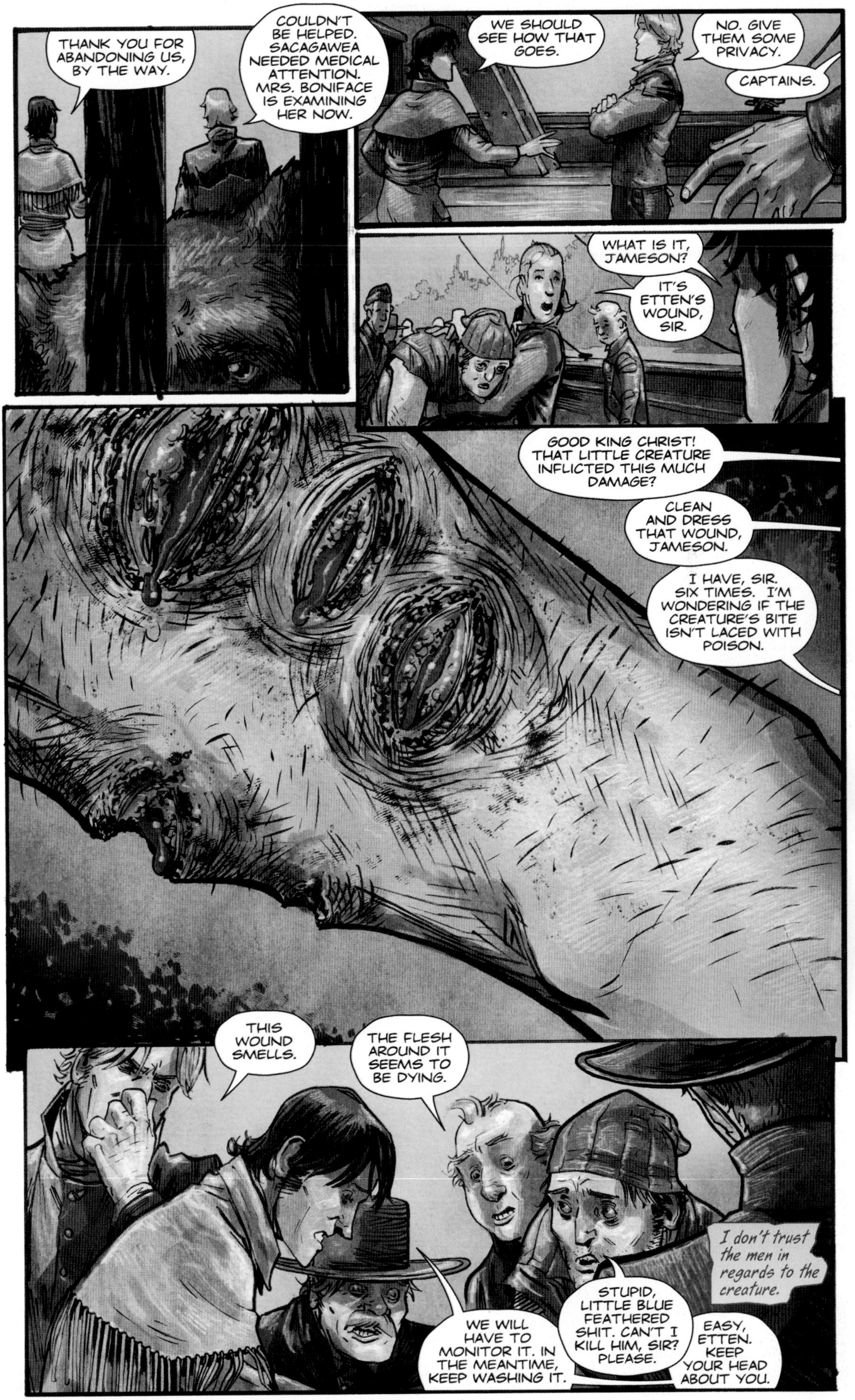
THANK YOU FOR ABANDONING US, BY THE WAY.
COULDN'T BE HELPED. SACAGAWEA NEEDED MEDICAL ATTENTION. MRS. BONIFACE IS EXAMINING HER NOW.
WE SHOULD SEE HOW THAT GOES.
NO. GIVE THEM SOME PRIVACY.
CAPTAINS.
WHAT IS IT, JAMESON?
IT'S ETTEN'S WOUND, SIR.
GOOD KING CHRIST! THAT LITTLE CREATURE INFLICTED THIS MUCH DAMAGE?
CLEAN AND DRESS THAT WOUND, JAMESON.
I HAVE, SIR. SIX TIMES. I'M WONDERING IF THE CREATURE'S BITE ISN'T LACED WITH POISON.
THIS WOUND SMELLS.
THE FLESH AROUND IT SEEMS TO BE DYING.
I don't trust the men in regards to the creature.
WE WILL HAVE TO MONITOR IT. IN THE MEANTIME, KEEP WASHING IT.
STUPID, LITTLE BLUE FEATHERED SHIT. CAN'T I KILL HIM, SIR? PLEASE.
EASY, ETTEN. KEEP YOUR HEAD ABOUT YOU.

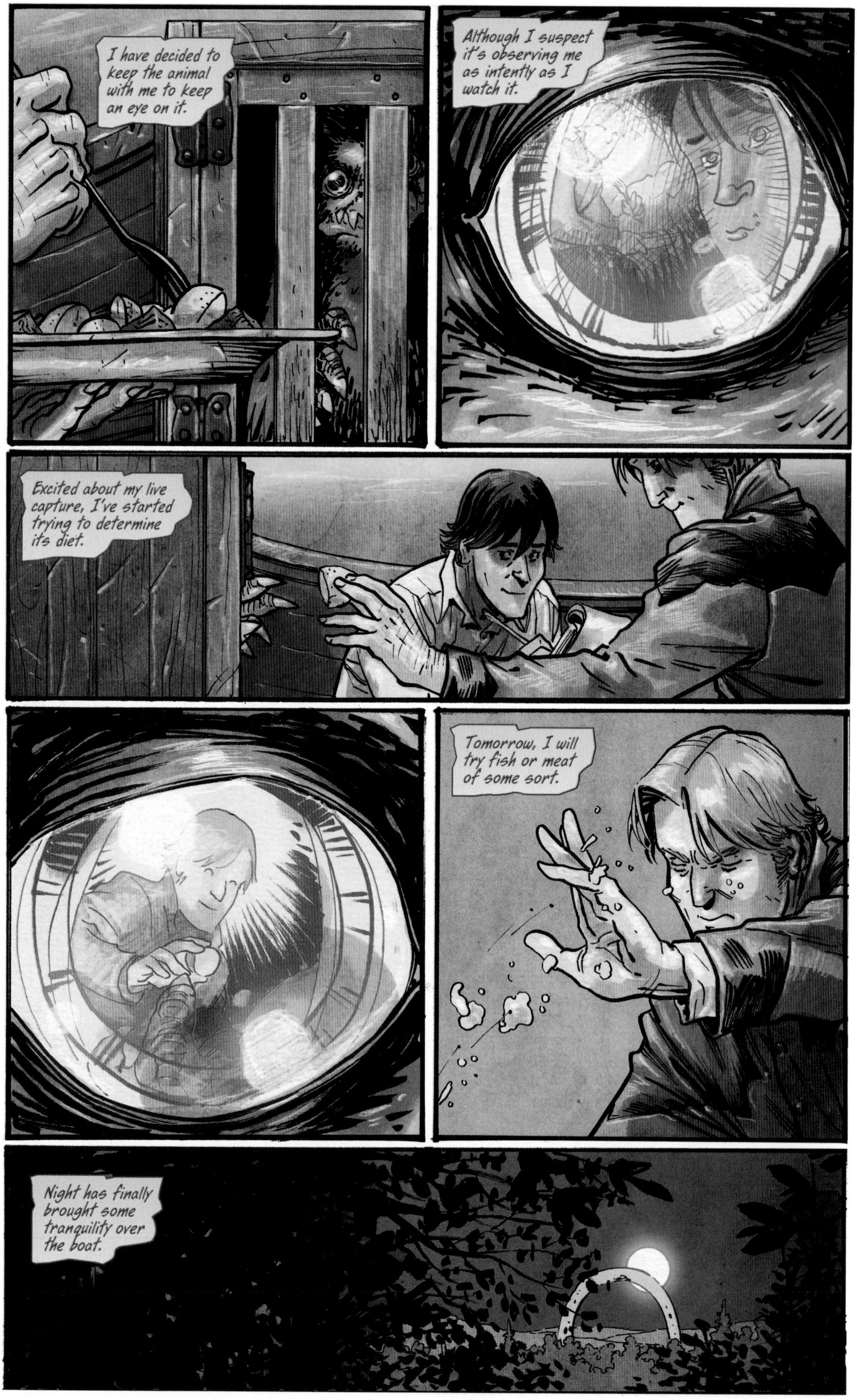
I have decided to keep the animal with me to keep an eye on it.
Although I suspect it's observing me as intently as I watch it.
Excited about my live capture, I've started trying to determine its diet.
Tomorrow, I will try fish or meat of some sort.
Night has finally brought some tranquility over the boat.

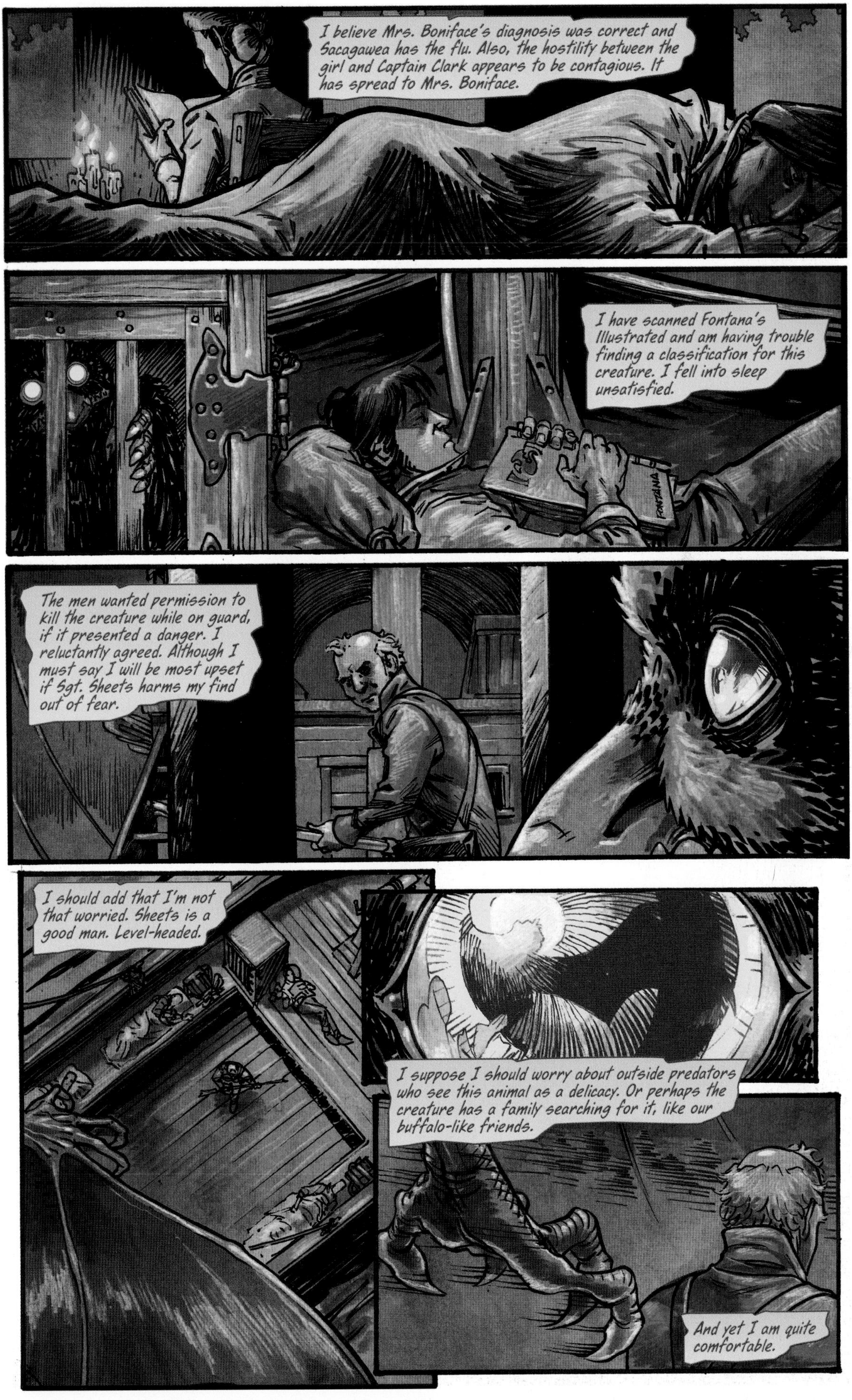
I believe Mrs. Boniface's diagnosis was correct and Sacagawea has the flu. Also, the hostility between the girl and Captain Clark appears to be contagious. It has spread to Mrs. Boniface.
I have scanned Fontana's Illustrated and am having trouble finding a classification for this creature. I fell into sleep unsatisfied.
FONTANA
The men wanted permission to kill the creature while on guard, if it presented a danger. I reluctantly agreed. Although I must say I will be most upset if Sgt. Sheets harms my find out of fear.
I should add that I'm not that worried. Sheets is a good man. Level-headed.
I suppose I should worry about outside predators who see this animal as a delicacy. Or perhaps the creature has a family searching for it, like our buffalo-like friends.
And yet I am quite comfortable.

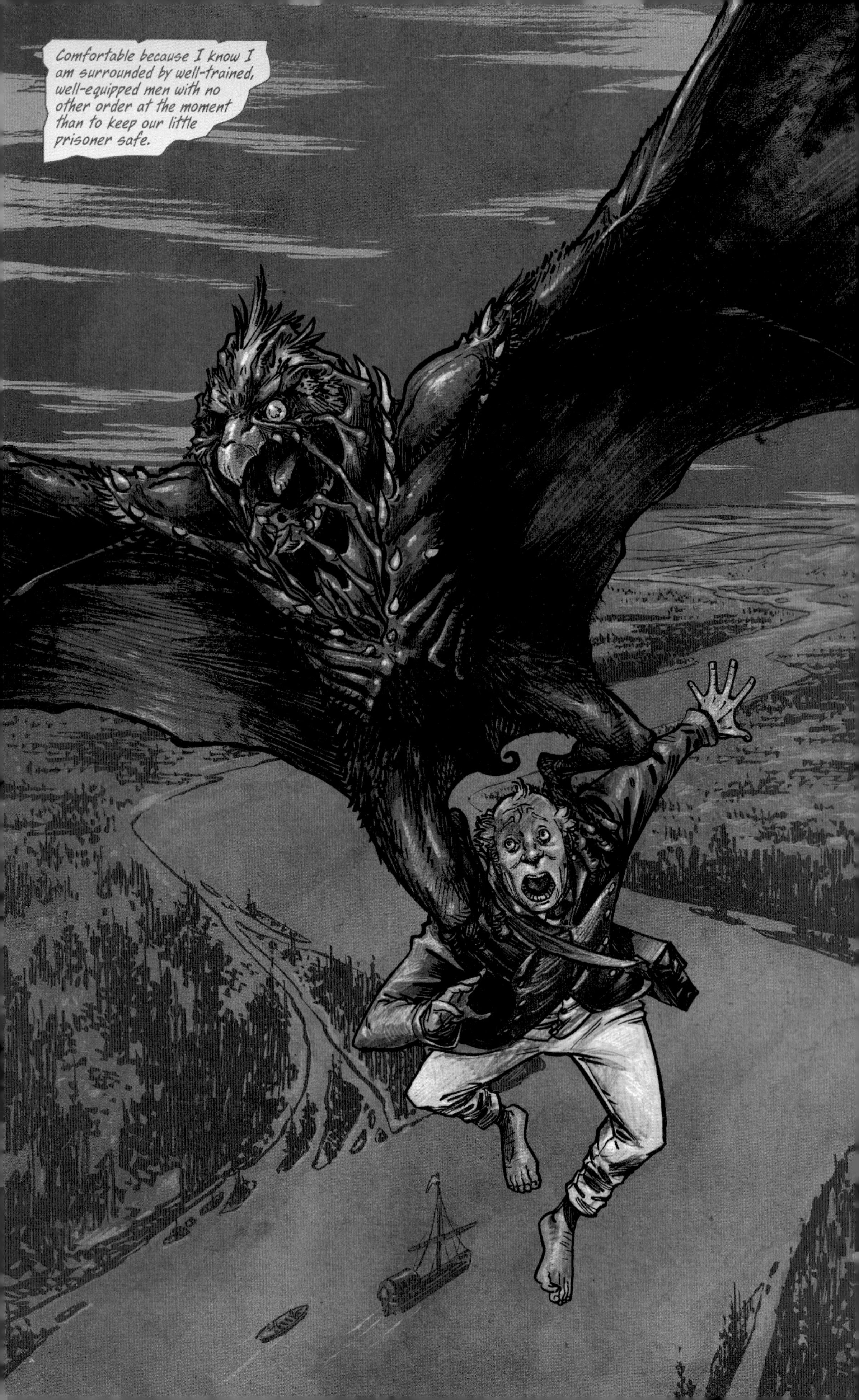
Comfortable because I know I am surrounded by well-trained, well-equipped men with no other order at the moment than to keep our little prisoner safe.

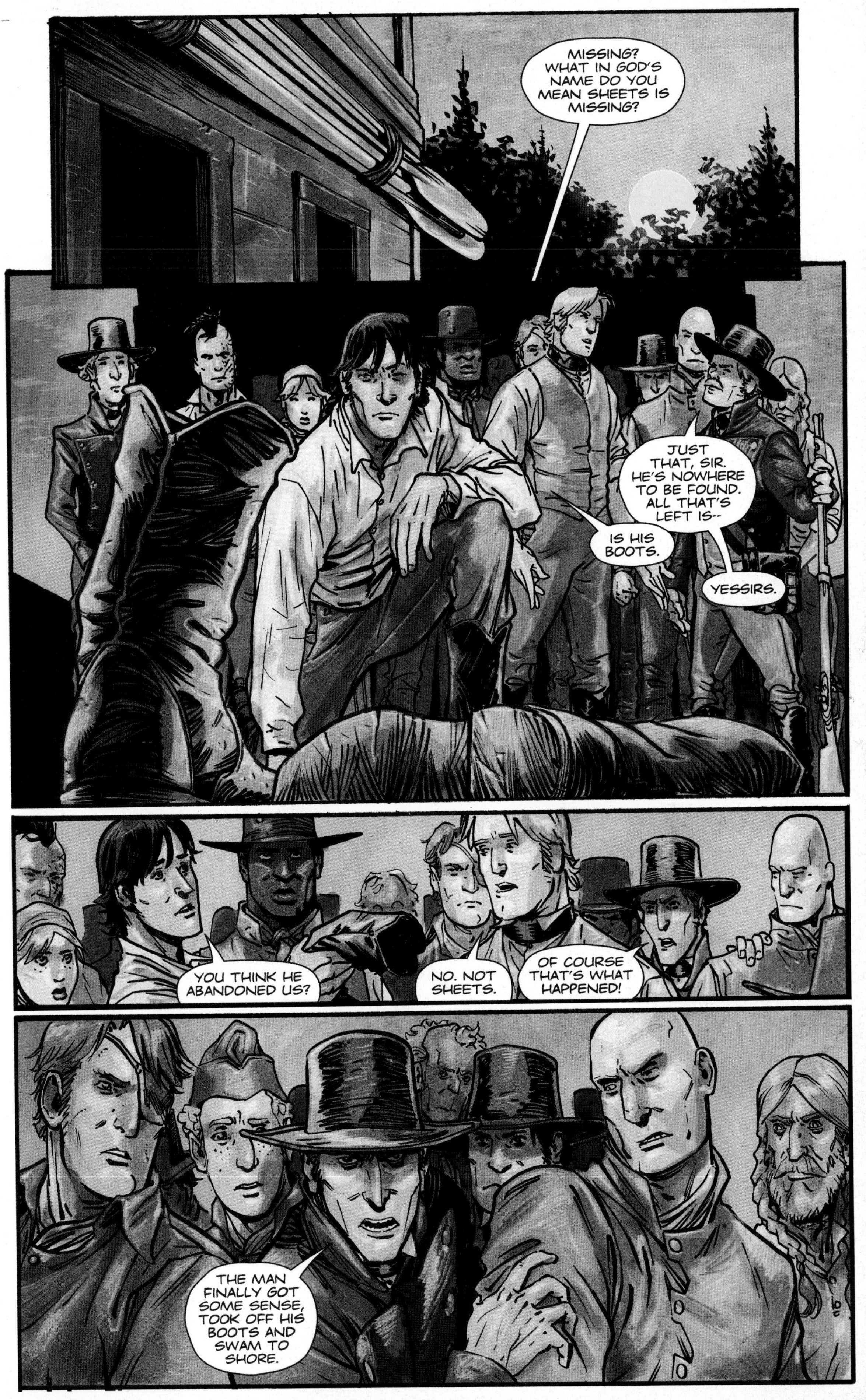
MISSING? WHAT IN GOD'S NAME DO YOU MEAN SHEETS IS MISSING?
JUST THAT, SIR. HE'S NOWHERE TO BE FOUND. ALL THAT'S LEFT IS--
IS HIS BOOTS.
YESSIRS.
YOU THINK HE ABANDONED US?
NO. NOT SHEETS.
OF COURSE THAT'S WHAT HAPPENED!
THE MAN FINALLY GOT SOME SENSE, TOOK OFF HIS BOOTS AND SWAM TO SHORE.

HE WON'T GET FAR WITHOUT HIS BOOTS.

OR A BOAT.

AND THEN THERE'S THE FACT THAT SHEETS ISN'T A COWARD.

CAPTAIN'S RIGHT. SHEETS WAS COURAGEOUS, IF NOTHING ELSE.

WHAT COULD IT BE THEN? MAYBE SOMETHING GOT HIM.

IF YOU ARE HUNTING DEMONS...I MUST GO... YOU ARE ALL TOO STUPID AND WEAK TO KILL IT...

BUT I MUST SLEEP FIRST.

YES, DEAR. LET'S LAY BACK DOWN.

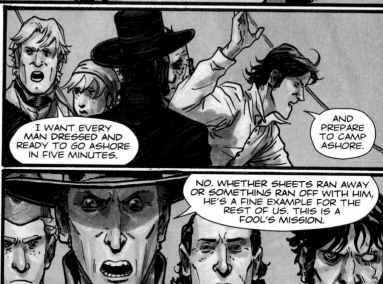

I WANT EVERY MAN DRESSED AND READY TO GO ASHORE IN FIVE MINUTES.

AND PREPARE TO CAMP ASHORE.

NO. WHETHER SHEETS RAN AWAY OR SOMETHING RAN OFF WITH HIM, HE'S A FINE EXAMPLE FOR THE REST OF US. THIS IS A FOOL'S MISSION.

PRYOR, NOW IS NOT--

ENOUGH! I'VE HAD IT WITH YOUR FLIRTATIONS WITH MUTINY, PRYOR. THAT GOES FOR THE REST OF YOU. IT ENDS *NOW*.

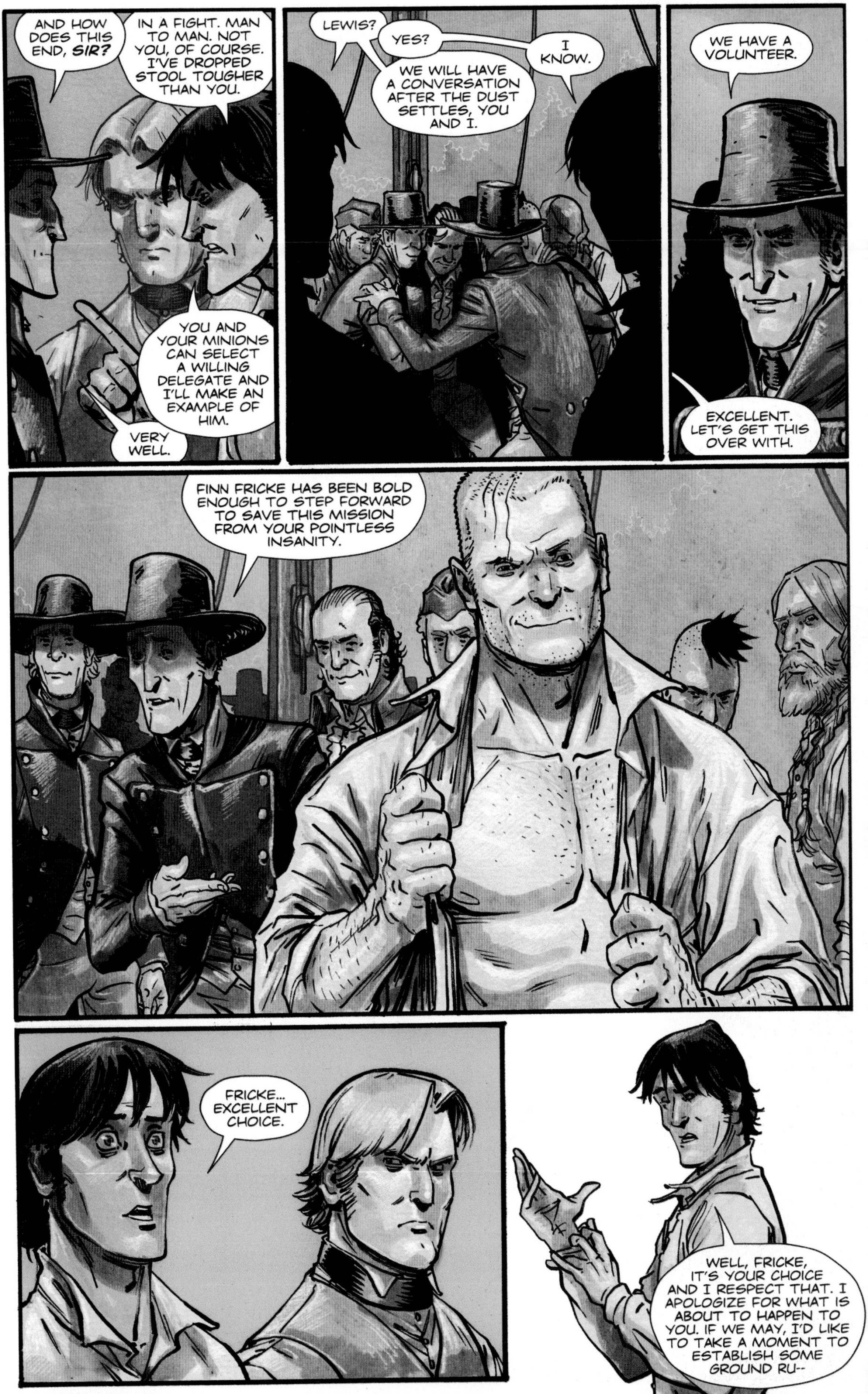

AND HOW DOES THIS END, SIR?
IN A FIGHT. MAN TO MAN. NOT YOU, OF COURSE. I'VE DROPPED STOOL TOUGHER THAN YOU.
YOU AND YOUR MINIONS CAN SELECT A WILLING DELEGATE AND I'LL MAKE AN EXAMPLE OF HIM.
VERY WELL.
LEWIS?
YES?
WE WILL HAVE A CONVERSATION AFTER THE DUST SETTLES, YOU AND I.
I KNOW.
WE HAVE A VOLUNTEER.
EXCELLENT. LET'S GET THIS OVER WITH.
FINN FRICKE HAS BEEN BOLD ENOUGH TO STEP FORWARD TO SAVE THIS MISSION FROM YOUR POINTLESS INSANITY.
FRICKE... EXCELLENT CHOICE.
WELL, FRICKE, IT'S YOUR CHOICE AND I RESPECT THAT. I APOLOGIZE FOR WHAT IS ABOUT TO HAPPEN TO YOU. IF WE MAY, I'D LIKE TO TAKE A MOMENT TO ESTABLISH SOME GROUND RU--

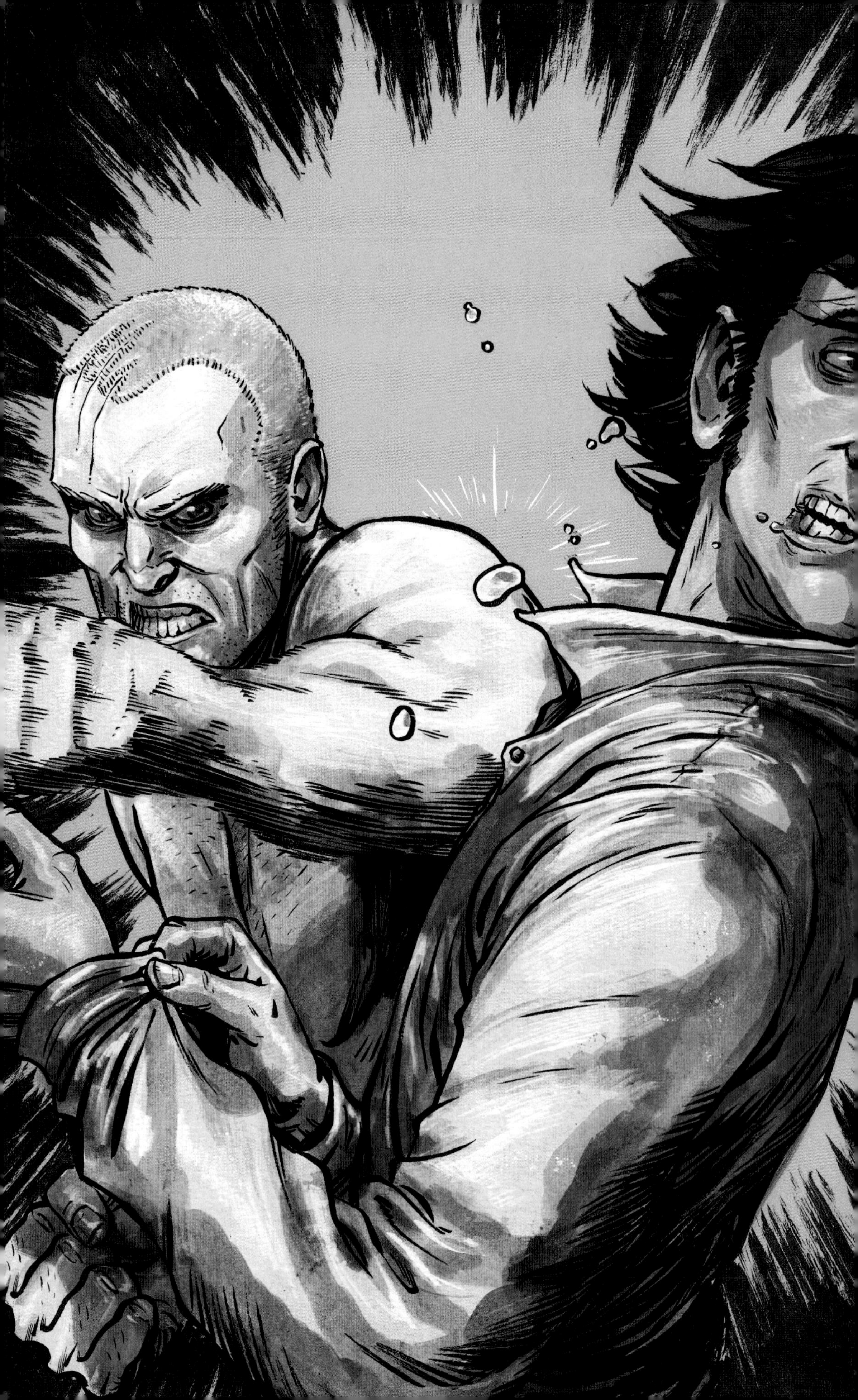

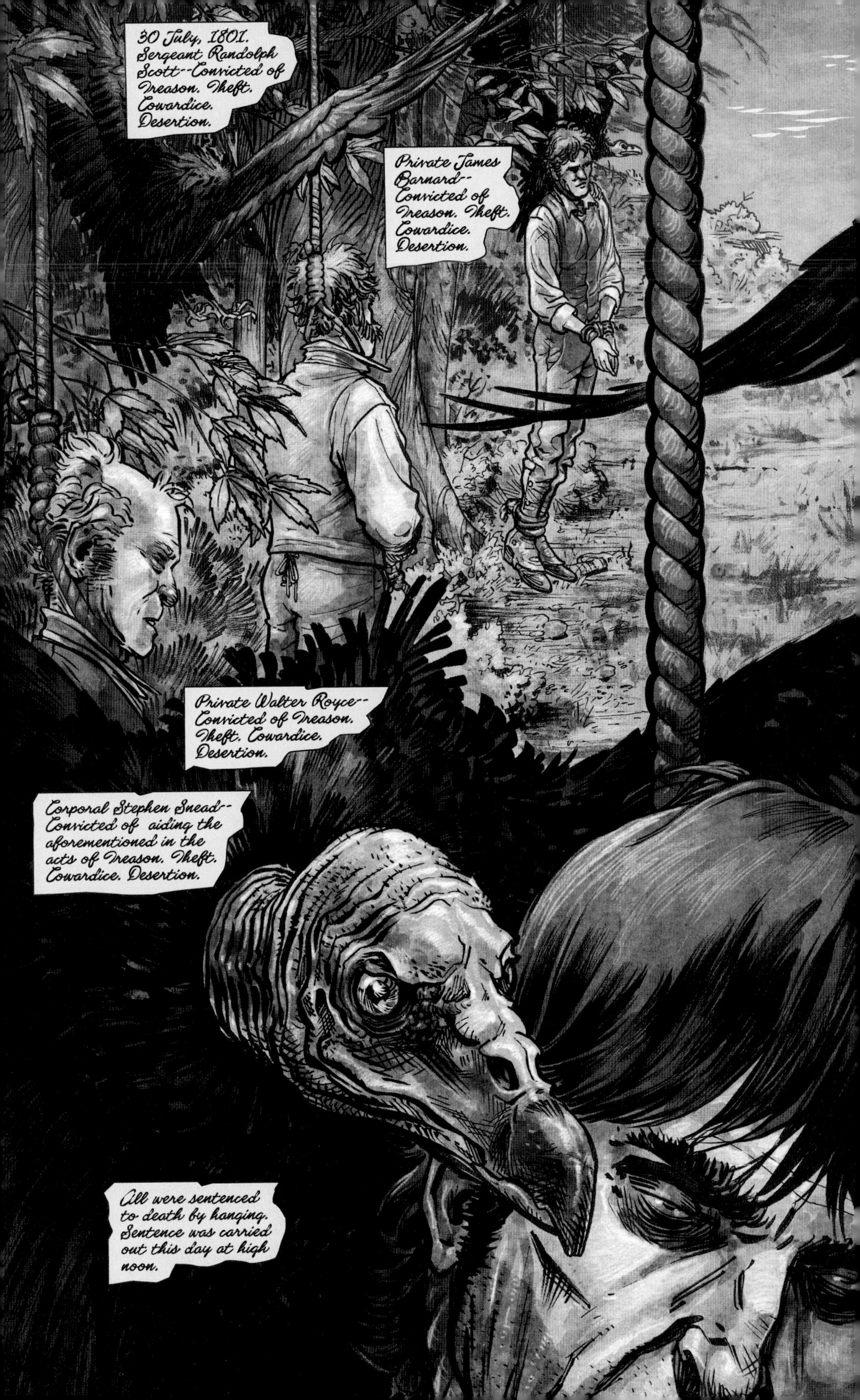
30 July, 1801. Sergeant Randolph Scott--Convicted of Treason. Theft. Cowardice. Desertion.
Private James Barnard--Convicted of Treason. Theft. Cowardice. Desertion.
Private Walter Royce--Convicted of Treason. Theft. Cowardice. Desertion.
Corporal Stephen Snead--Convicted of aiding the aforementioned in the acts of Treason. Theft. Cowardice. Desertion.
All were sentenced to death by hanging. Sentence was carried out this day at high noon.

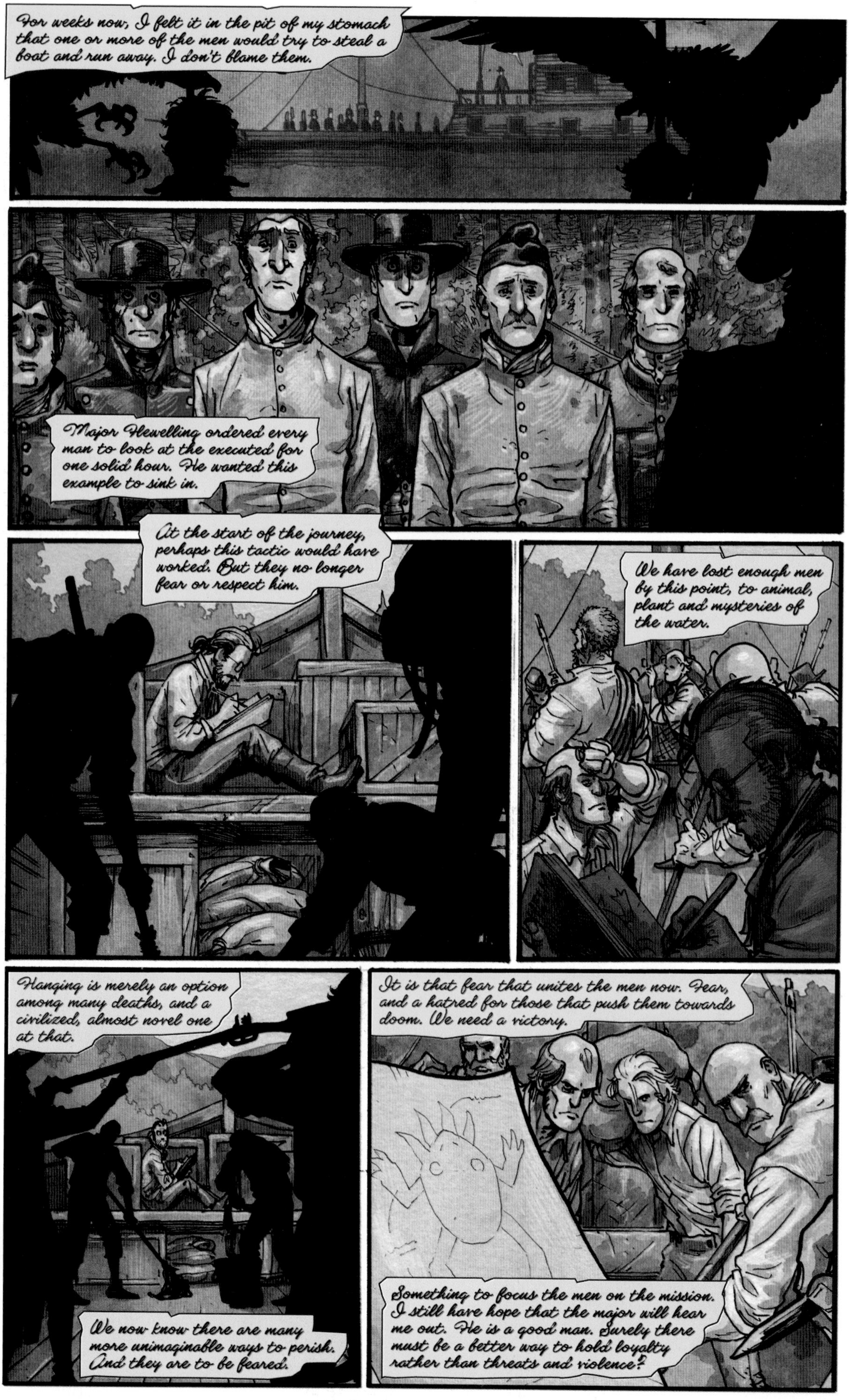
For weeks now, I felt it in the pit of my stomach that one or more of the men would try to steal a boat and run away. I don't blame them.
Major Flewelling ordered every man to look at the executed for one solid hour. He wanted this example to sink in.
At the start of the journey, perhaps this tactic would have worked. But they no longer fear or respect him.
We have lost enough men by this point, to animal, plant and mysteries of the water.
Hanging is merely an option among many deaths, and a civilized, almost novel one at that.
We now know there are many more unimaginable ways to perish. And they are to be feared.
It is that fear that unites the men now. Fear, and a hatred for those that push them towards doom. We need a victory.
Something to focus the men on the mission. I still have hope that the major will hear me out. He is a good man. Surely there must be a better way to hold loyalty rather than threats and violence?

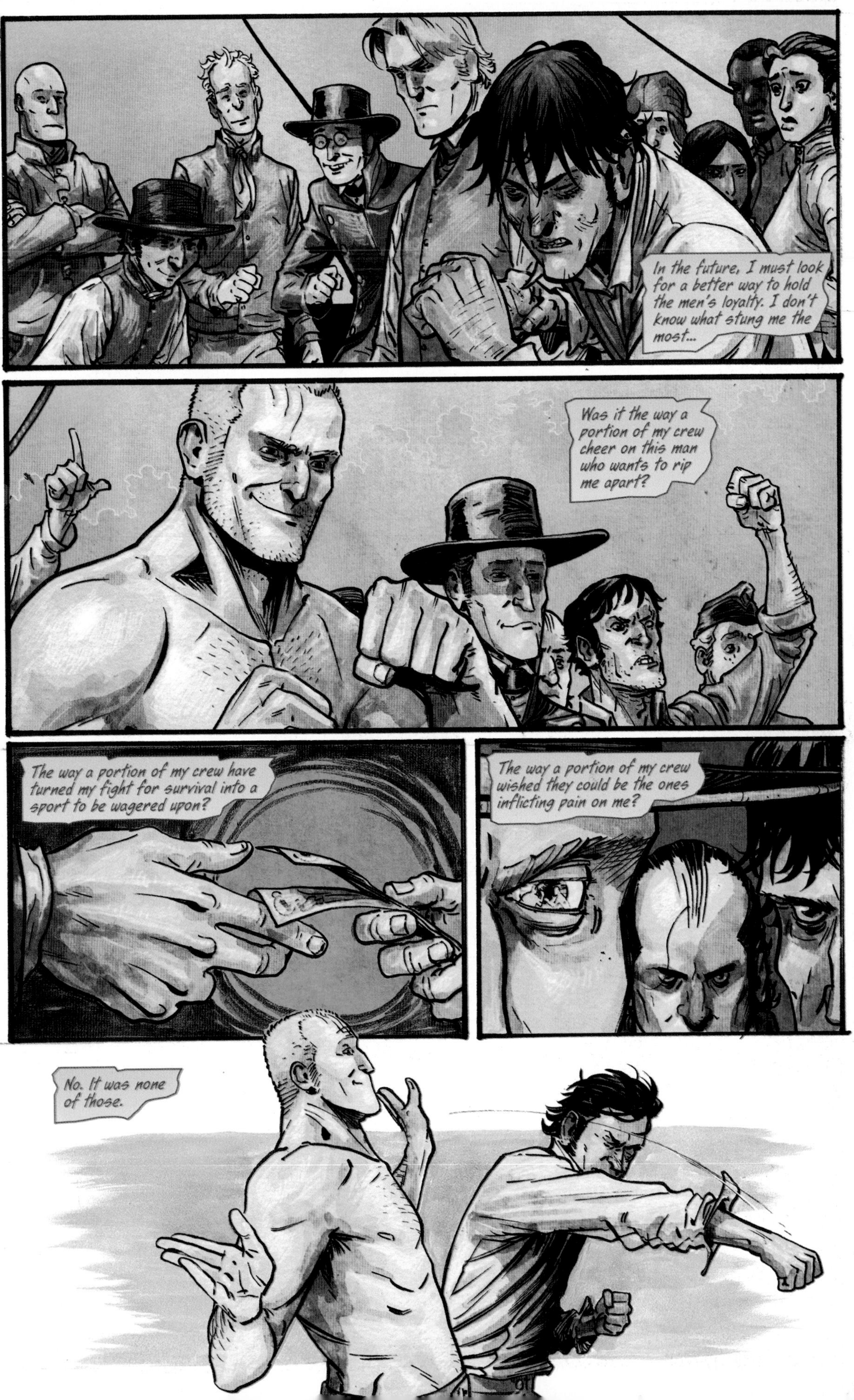
In the future, I must look for a better way to hold the men's loyalty. I don't know what stung me the most...
Was it the way a portion of my crew cheer on this man who wants to rip me apart?
The way a portion of my crew have turned my fight for survival into a sport to be wagered upon?
The way a portion of my crew wished they could be the ones inflicting pain on me?
No. It was none of those.

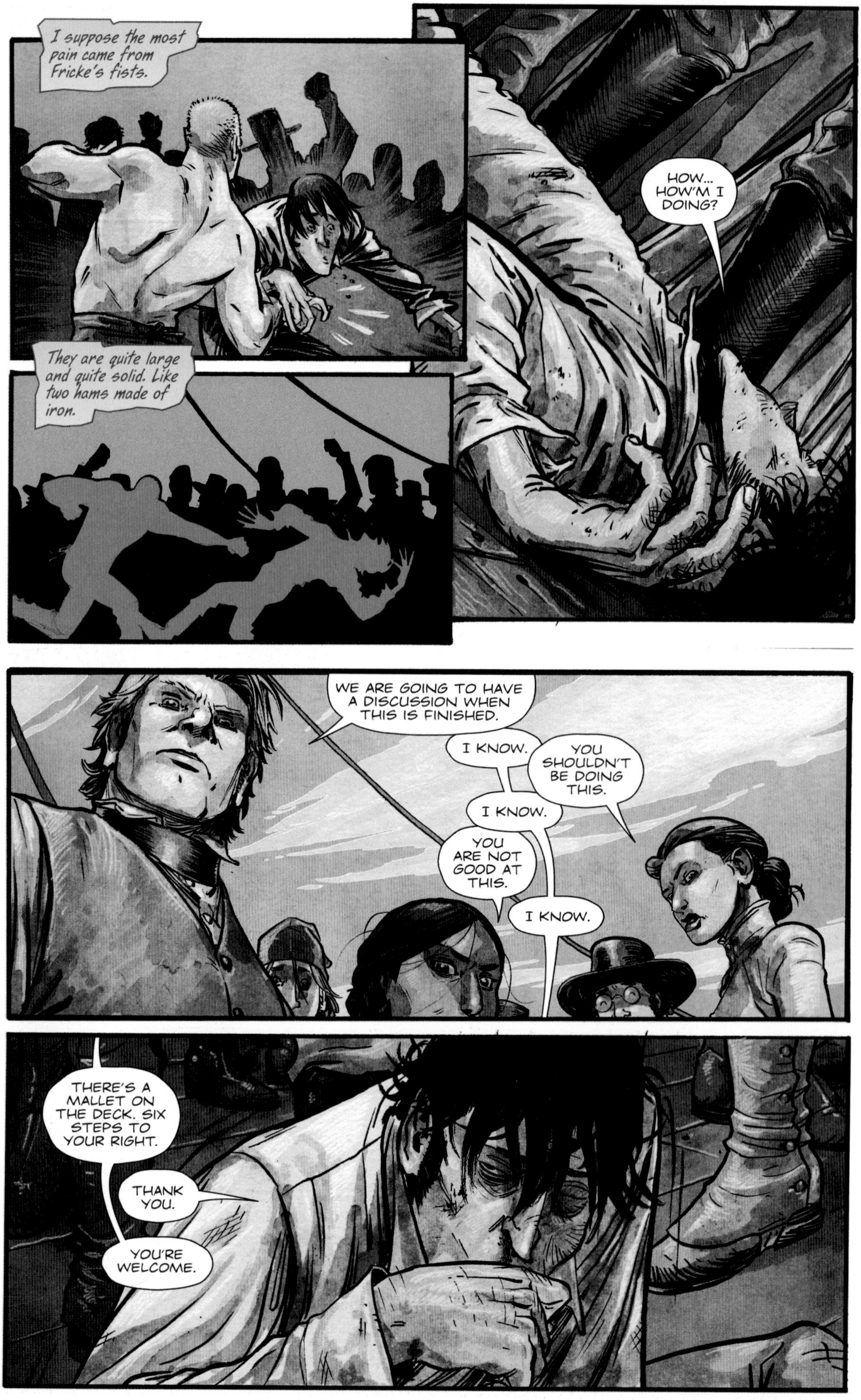
I suppose the most pain came from Fricke's fists.
They are quite large and quite solid. Like two hams made of iron.
HOW... HOW'M I DOING?
WE ARE GOING TO HAVE A DISCUSSION WHEN THIS IS FINISHED.
I KNOW.
YOU SHOULDN'T BE DOING THIS.
I KNOW.
YOU ARE NOT GOOD AT THIS.
I KNOW.
THERE'S A MALLET ON THE DECK. SIX STEPS TO YOUR RIGHT.
THANK YOU.
YOU'RE WELCOME.

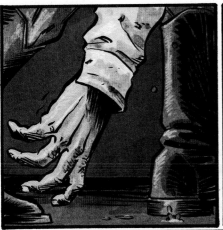

YOU NEED TO STOP THIS. AT ONCE.

LEWIS KNOWS WHAT HE'S DOING.

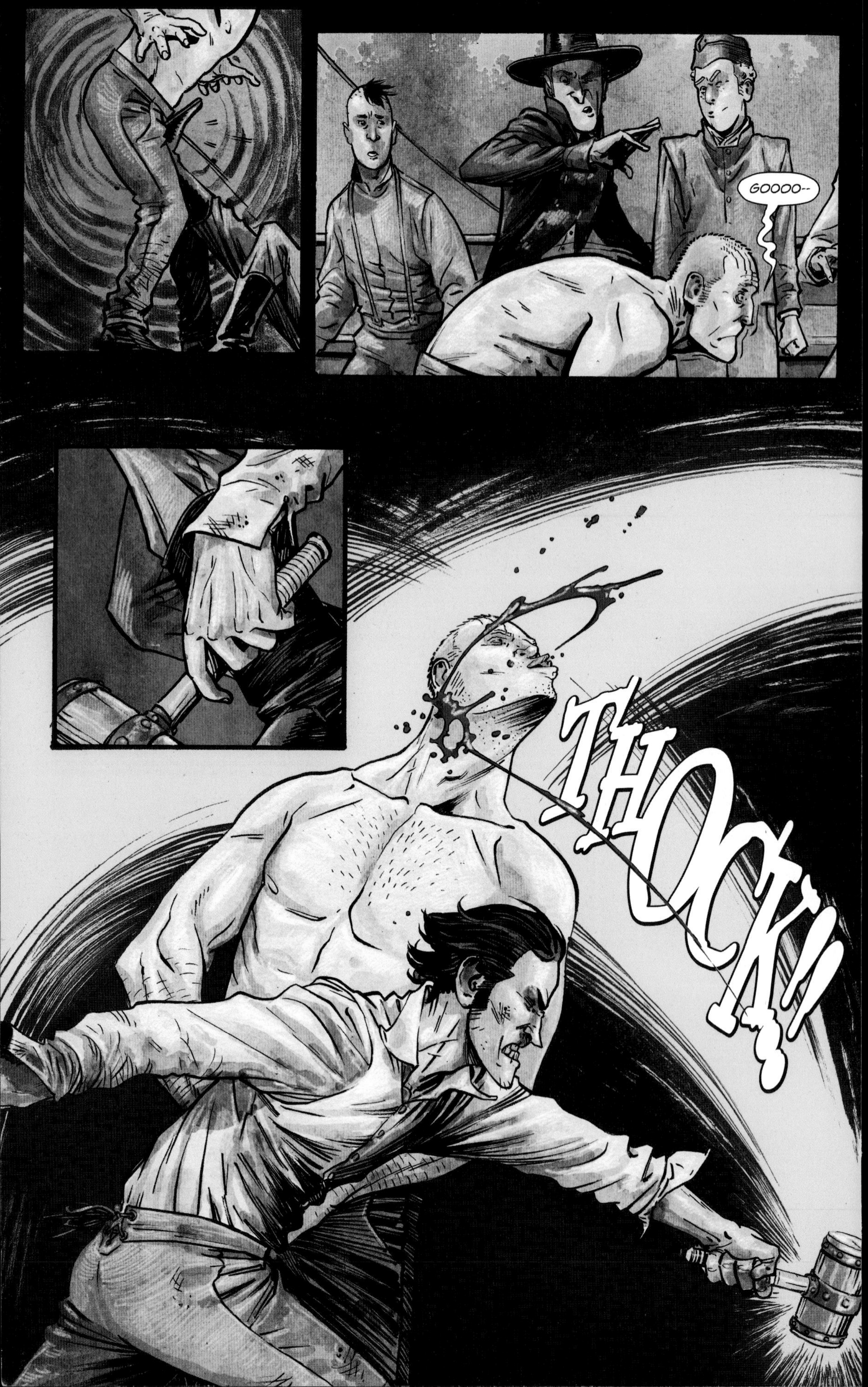
GOOOO--
THOCK!!

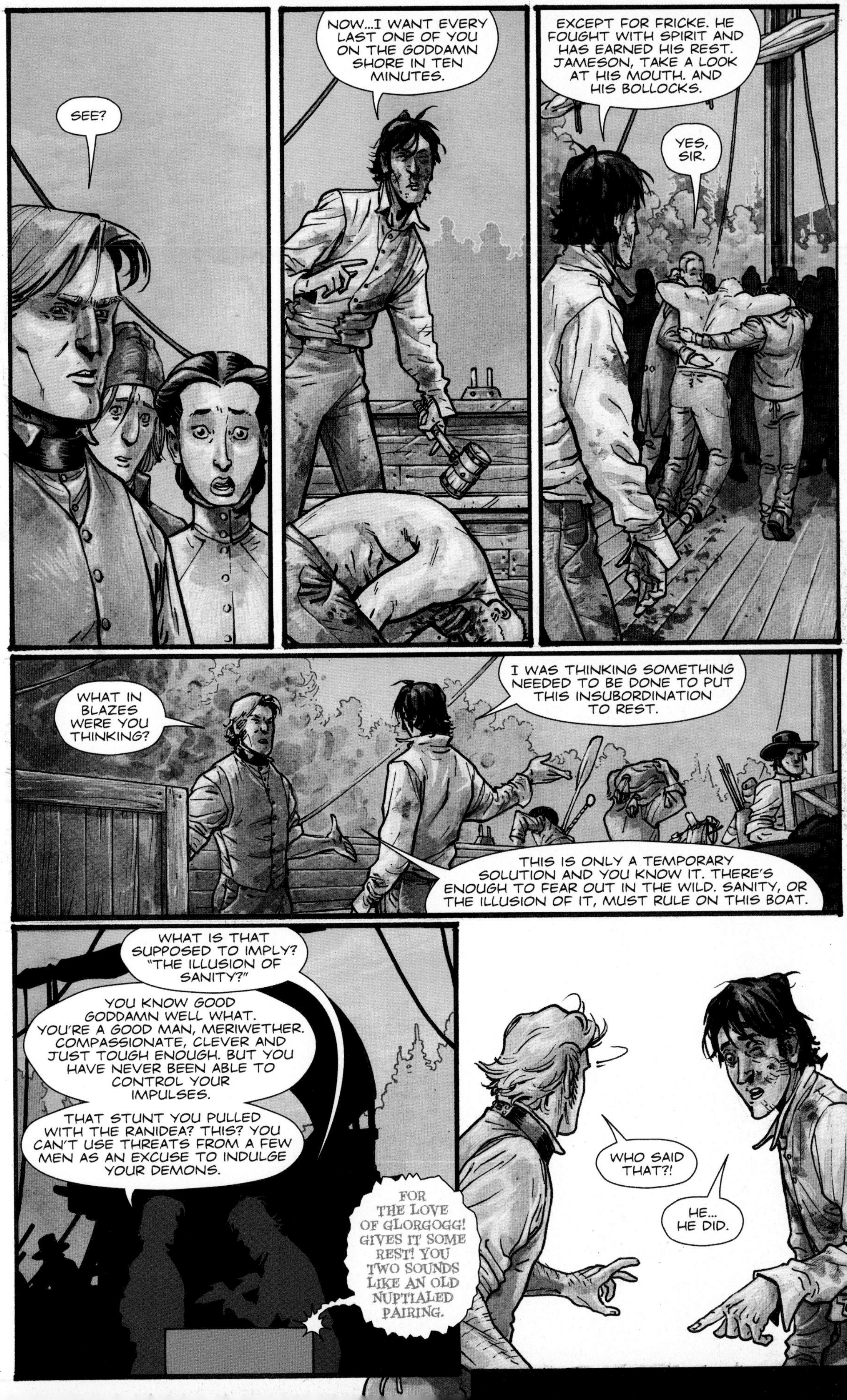
SEE?
NOW...I WANT EVERY LAST ONE OF YOU ON THE GODDAMN SHORE IN TEN MINUTES.
EXCEPT FOR FRICKE. HE FOUGHT WITH SPIRIT AND HAS EARNED HIS REST. JAMESON, TAKE A LOOK AT HIS MOUTH. AND HIS BOLLOCKS.
YES, SIR.
WHAT IN BLAZES WERE YOU THINKING?
I WAS THINKING SOMETHING NEEDED TO BE DONE TO PUT THIS INSUBORDINATION TO REST.
THIS IS ONLY A TEMPORARY SOLUTION AND YOU KNOW IT. THERE'S ENOUGH TO FEAR OUT IN THE WILD. SANITY, OR THE ILLUSION OF IT, MUST RULE ON THIS BOAT.
WHAT IS THAT SUPPOSED TO IMPLY? "THE ILLUSION OF SANITY?"
YOU KNOW GOOD GODDAMN WELL WHAT. YOU'RE A GOOD MAN, MERIWETHER. COMPASSIONATE, CLEVER AND JUST TOUGH ENOUGH. BUT YOU HAVE NEVER BEEN ABLE TO CONTROL YOUR IMPULSES.
THAT STUNT YOU PULLED WITH THE RANIDEA? THIS? YOU CAN'T USE THREATS FROM A FEW MEN AS AN EXCUSE TO INDULGE YOUR DEMONS.
FOR THE LOVE OF GLORGOGG! GIVES IT SOME REST! YOU TWO SOUNDS LIKE AN OLD NUPTIALED PAIRING.
WHO SAID THAT?!
HE... HE DID.

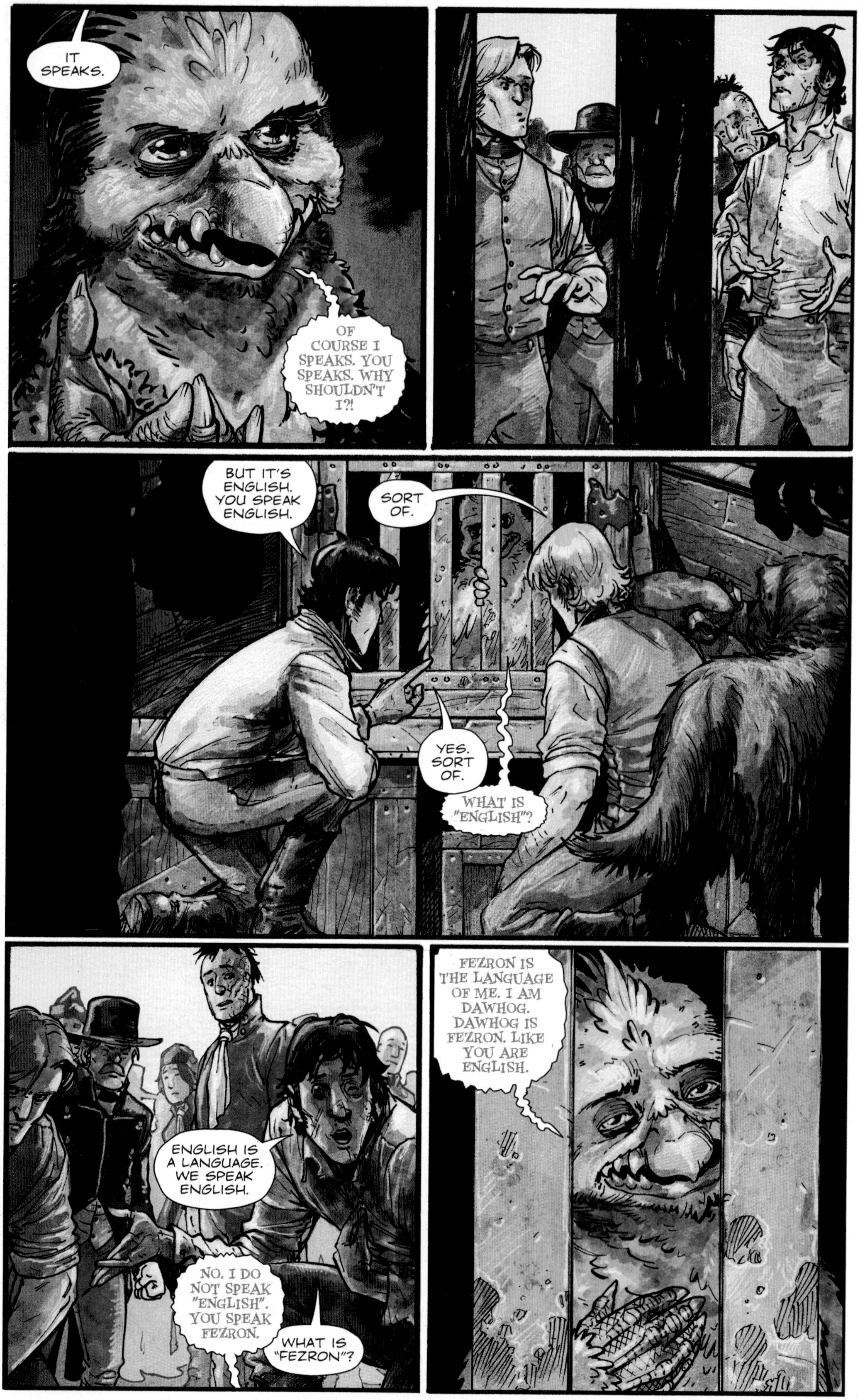
IT SPEAKS.
OF COURSE I SPEAKS. YOU SPEAKS. WHY SHOULDN'T I?!
BUT IT'S ENGLISH. YOU SPEAK ENGLISH.
SORT OF.
YES. SORT OF.
WHAT IS "ENGLISH"?
ENGLISH IS A LANGUAGE. WE SPEAK ENGLISH.
NO. I DO NOT SPEAK "ENGLISH". YOU SPEAK FEZRON.
WHAT IS "FEZRON"?
FEZRON IS THE LANGUAGE OF ME. I AM DAWHOG. DAWHOG IS FEZRON. LIKE YOU ARE ENGLISH.

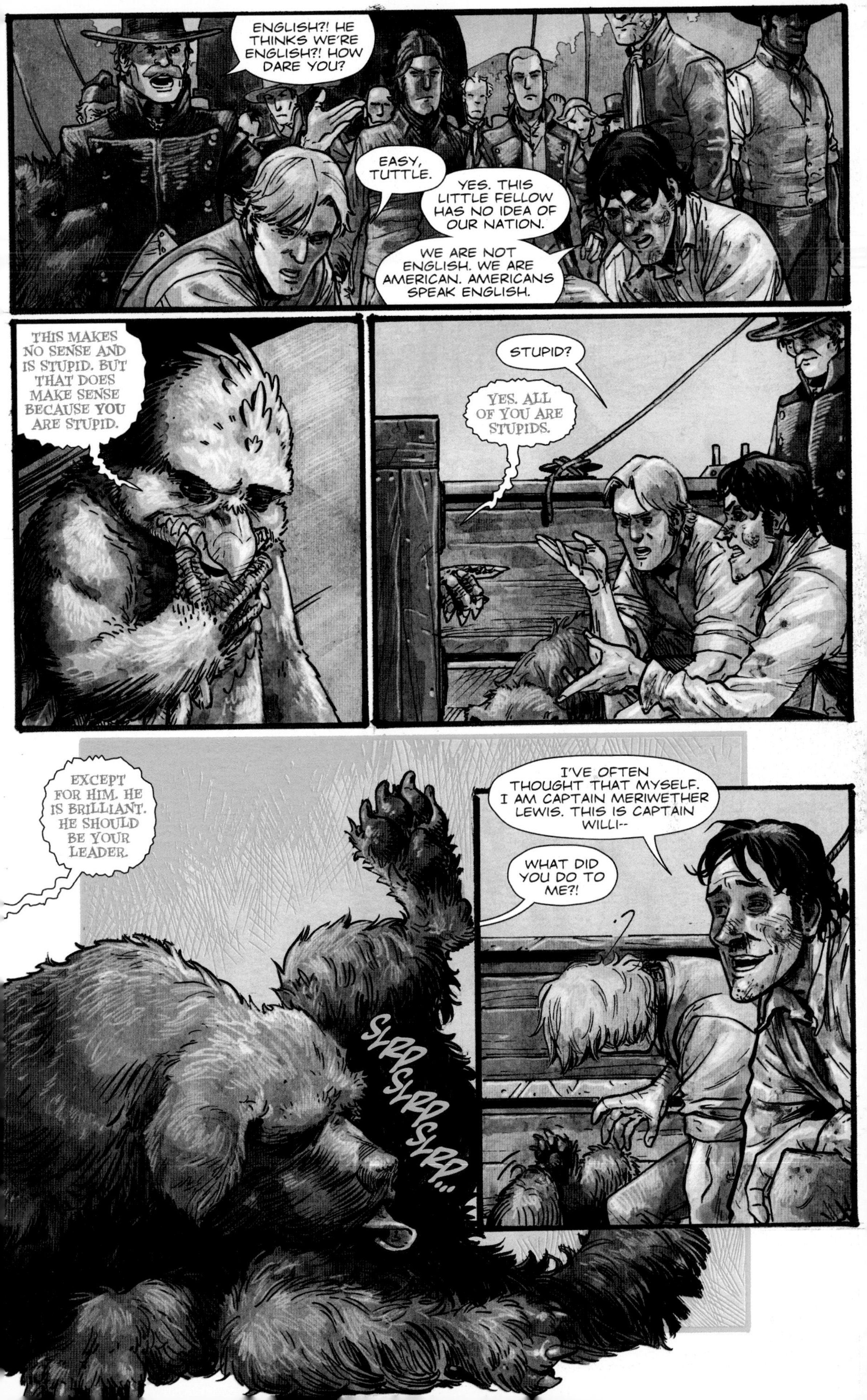
ENGLISH?! HE THINKS WE'RE ENGLISH?! HOW DARE YOU?
EASY, TUTTLE.
YES. THIS LITTLE FELLOW HAS NO IDEA OF OUR NATION.
WE ARE NOT ENGLISH. WE ARE AMERICAN. AMERICANS SPEAK ENGLISH.
THIS MAKES NO SENSE AND IS STUPID. BUT THAT DOES MAKE SENSE BECAUSE YOU ARE STUPID.
STUPID?
YES. ALL OF YOU ARE STUPIDS.
EXCEPT FOR HIM. HE IS BRILLIANT. HE SHOULD BE YOUR LEADER.
I'VE OFTEN THOUGHT THAT MYSELF. I AM CAPTAIN MERIWETHER LEWIS. THIS IS CAPTAIN WILLI--
WHAT DID YOU DO TO ME?!
SYRRSYRRSYRR...

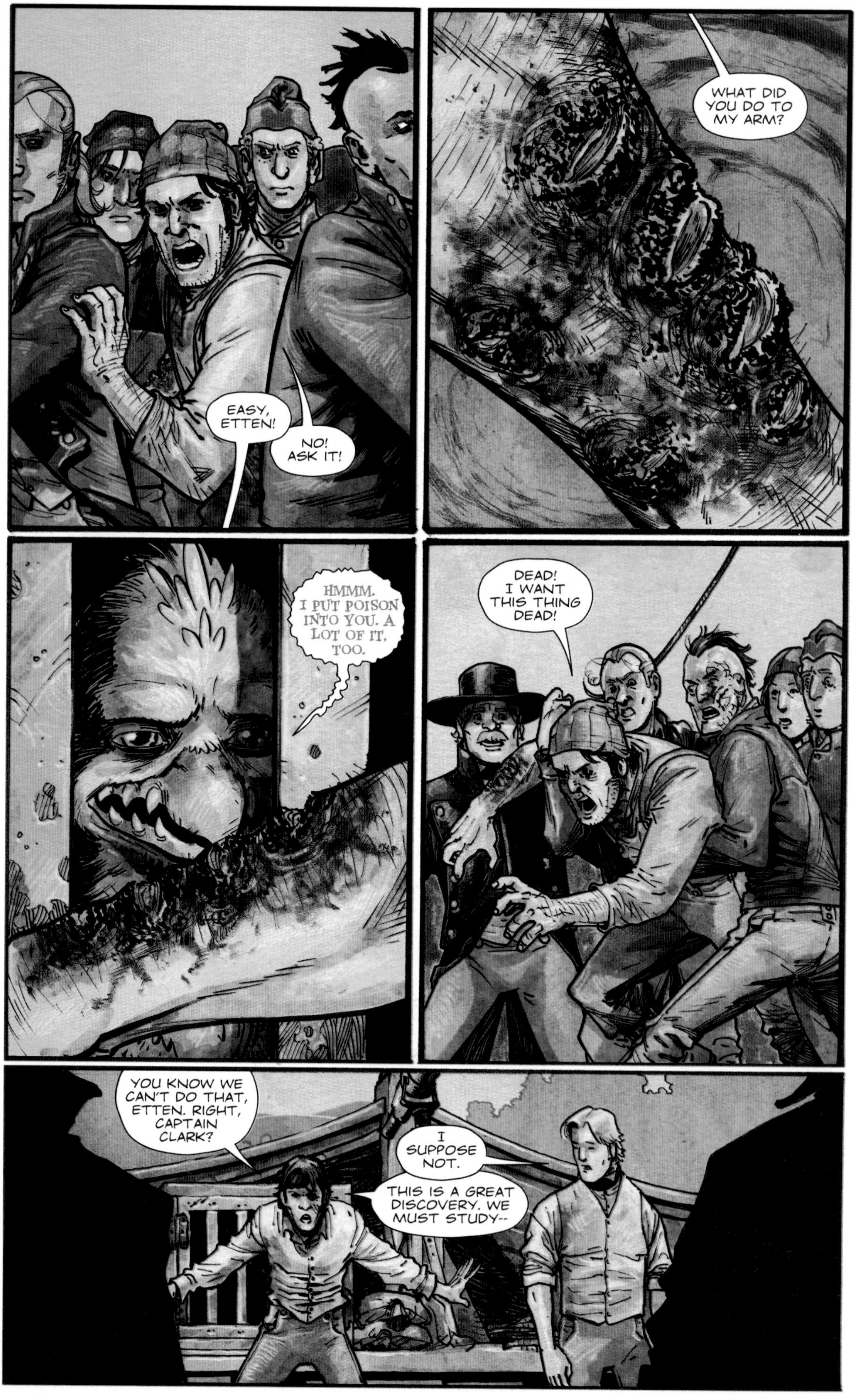
EASY, ETTEN!
NO! ASK IT!
WHAT DID YOU DO TO MY ARM?
HMMM. I PUT POISON INTO YOU. A LOT OF IT, TOO.
DEAD! I WANT THIS THING DEAD!
YOU KNOW WE CAN'T DO THAT, ETTEN. RIGHT, CAPTAIN CLARK?
I SUPPOSE NOT.
THIS IS A GREAT DISCOVERY. WE MUST STUDY--

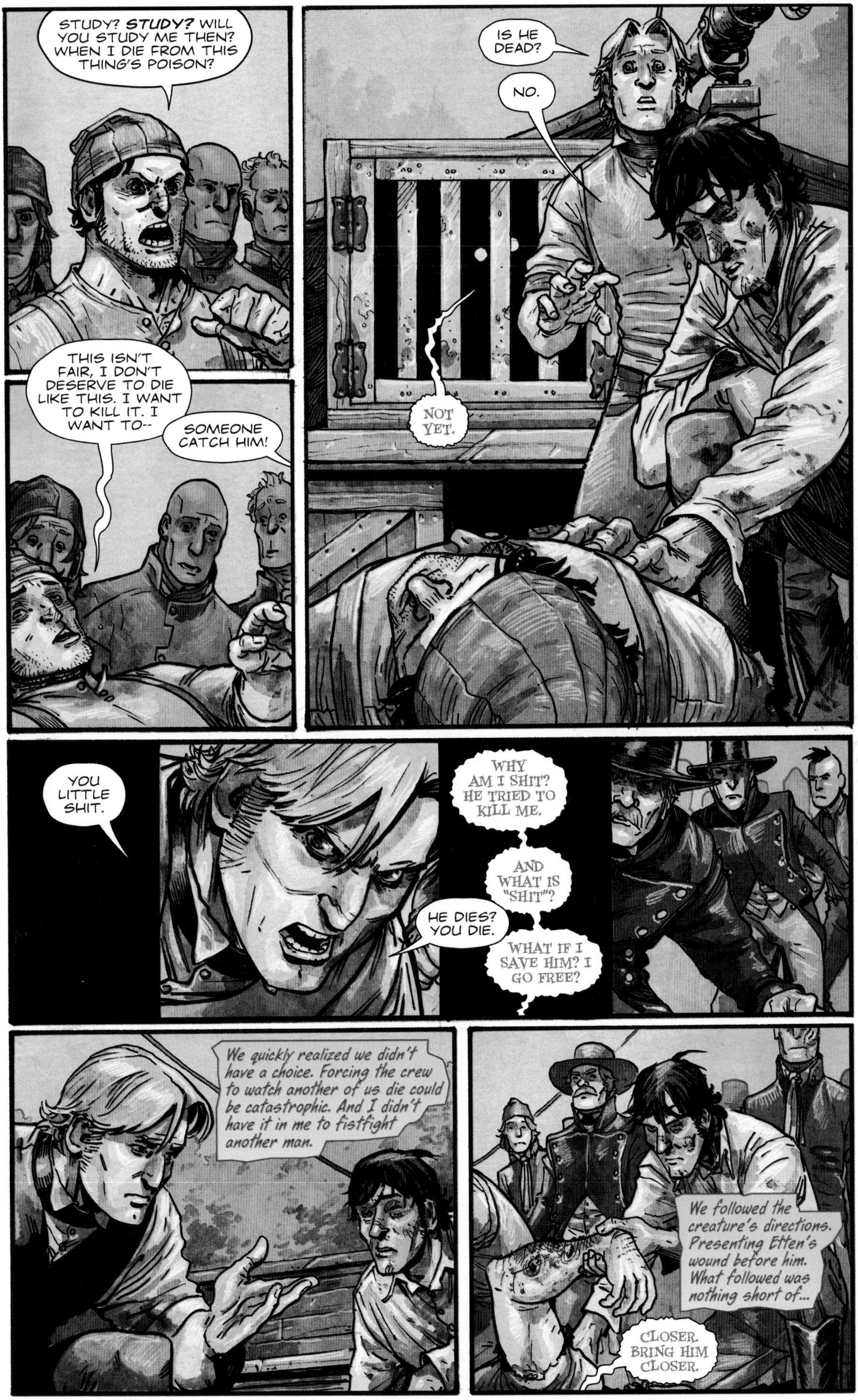
STUDY? **STUDY?** WILL YOU STUDY ME THEN? WHEN I DIE FROM THIS THING'S POISON?
THIS ISN'T FAIR, I DON'T DESERVE TO DIE LIKE THIS. I WANT TO KILL IT. I WANT TO--
SOMEONE CATCH HIM!
IS HE DEAD?
NO.
NOT YET.
YOU LITTLE SHIT.
WHY AM I SHIT? HE TRIED TO KILL ME.
AND WHAT IS "SHIT"?
HE DIES? YOU DIE.
WHAT IF I SAVE HIM? I GO FREE?
We quickly realized we didn't have a choice. Forcing the crew to watch another of us die could be catastrophic. And I didn't have it in me to fistfight another man.
We followed the creature's directions. Presenting Etten's wound before him. What followed was nothing short of...
CLOSER. BRING HIM CLOSER.

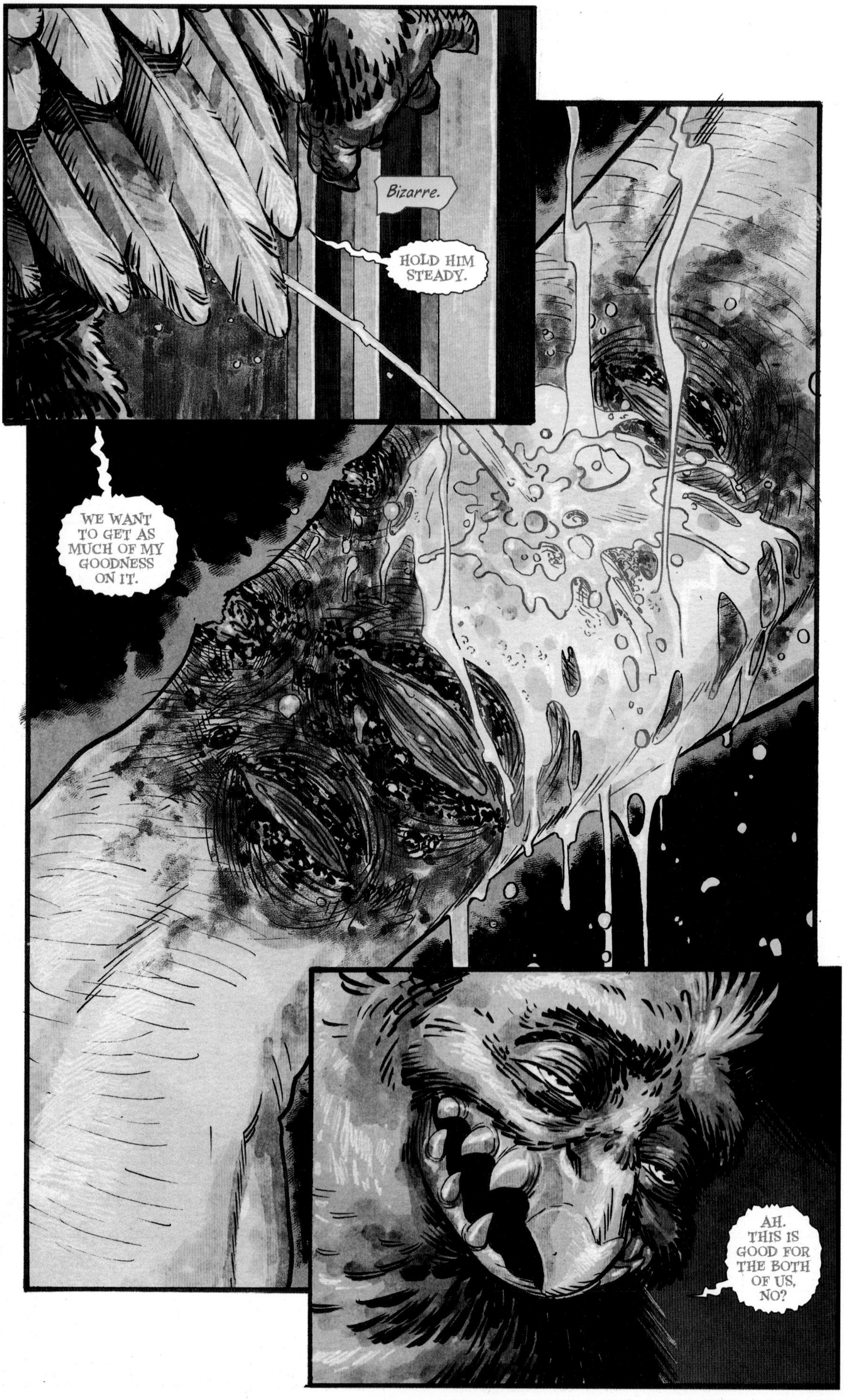
Bizarre.
HOLD HIM STEADY.
WE WANT TO GET AS MUCH OF MY GOODNESS ON IT.
AH. THIS IS GOOD FOR THE BOTH OF US, NO?

IF THIS IS SOME SORT OF JOKE, I PLUCK AND GUT YOU MYSELF.

WAIT! SOMETHING'S HAPPENING!

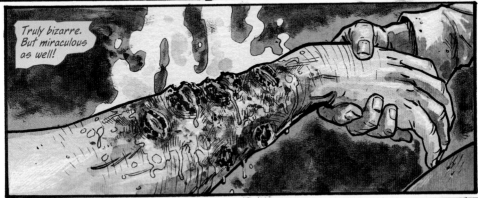

Truly bizarre. But miraculous as well!

Had I not witnessed the power of this little monster's urine myself, I would never believe it.

IT'S WORKING. BY GOD, IT'S WORKING!

As excited as I was over Etten's improved condition, I made a note to collect a sample for study should the opportunity arise.

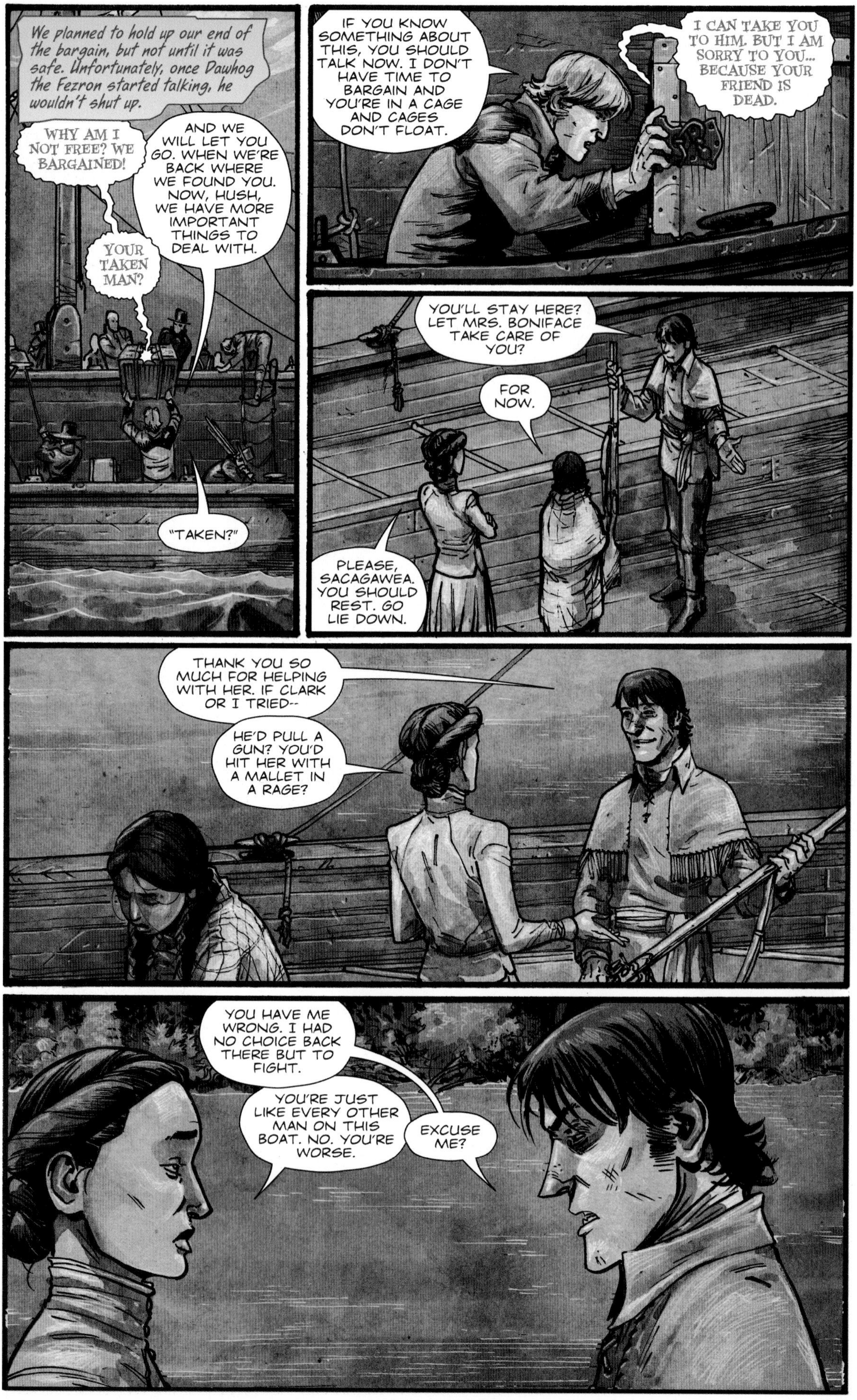
We planned to hold up our end of the bargain, but not until it was safe. Unfortunately, once Dawhog the Fezron started talking, he wouldn't shut up.
WHY AM I NOT FREE? WE BARGAINED!
AND WE WILL LET YOU GO. WHEN WE'RE BACK WHERE WE FOUND YOU. NOW, HUSH, WE HAVE MORE IMPORTANT THINGS TO DEAL WITH.
YOUR TAKEN MAN?
"TAKEN?"
IF YOU KNOW SOMETHING ABOUT THIS, YOU SHOULD TALK NOW. I DON'T HAVE TIME TO BARGAIN AND YOU'RE IN A CAGE AND CAGES DON'T FLOAT.
I CAN TAKE YOU TO HIM. BUT I AM SORRY TO YOU... BECAUSE YOUR FRIEND IS DEAD.
YOU'LL STAY HERE? LET MRS. BONIFACE TAKE CARE OF YOU?
FOR NOW.
PLEASE, SACAGAWEA. YOU SHOULD REST. GO LIE DOWN.
THANK YOU SO MUCH FOR HELPING WITH HER. IF CLARK OR I TRIED--
HE'D PULL A GUN? YOU'D HIT HER WITH A MALLET IN A RAGE?
YOU HAVE ME WRONG. I HAD NO CHOICE BACK THERE BUT TO FIGHT.
YOU'RE JUST LIKE EVERY OTHER MAN ON THIS BOAT. NO. YOU'RE WORSE.
EXCUSE ME?

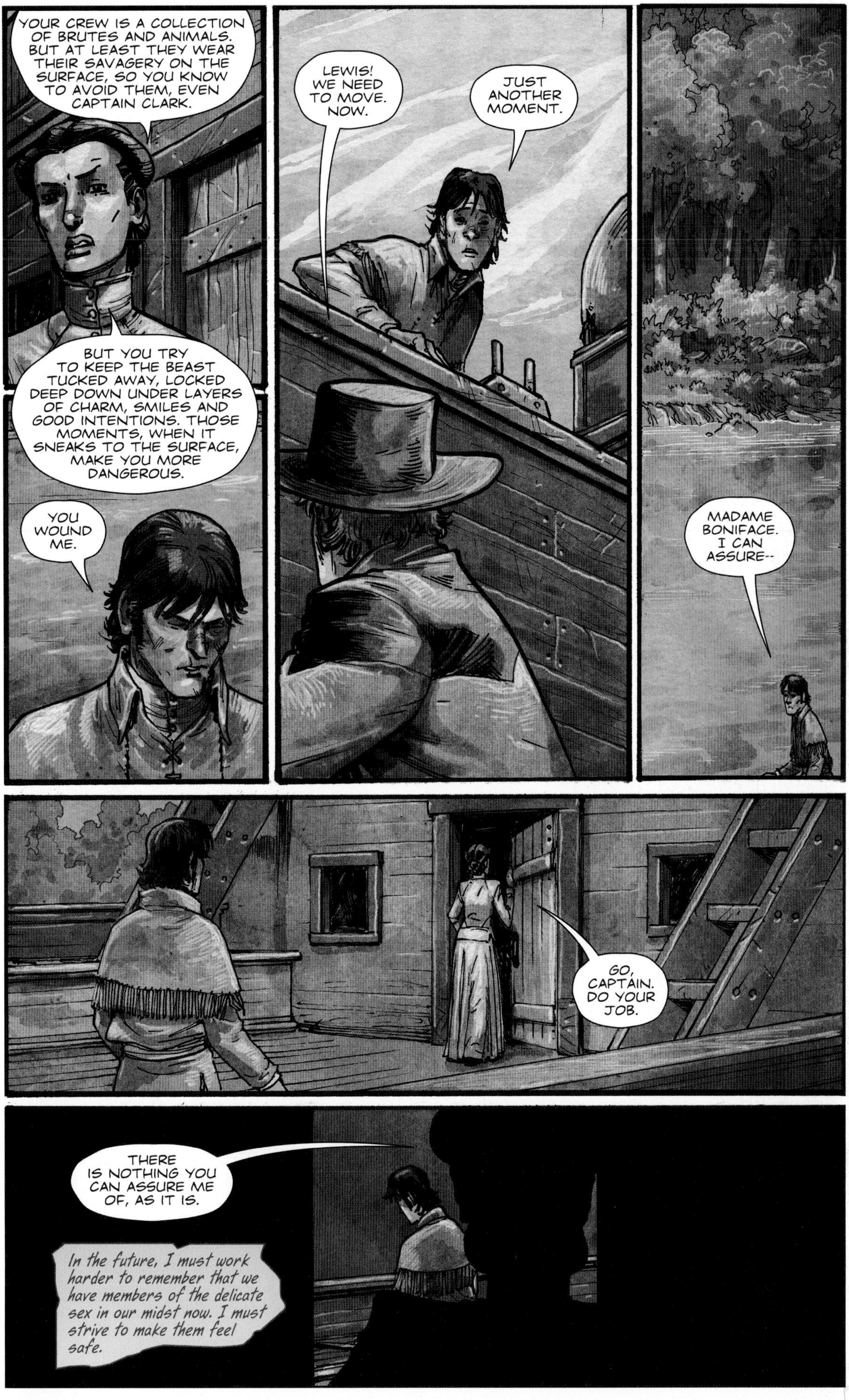
YOUR CREW IS A COLLECTION OF BRUTES AND ANIMALS. BUT AT LEAST THEY WEAR THEIR SAVAGERY ON THE SURFACE, SO YOU KNOW TO AVOID THEM, EVEN CAPTAIN CLARK.
BUT YOU TRY TO KEEP THE BEAST TUCKED AWAY, LOCKED DEEP DOWN UNDER LAYERS OF CHARM, SMILES AND GOOD INTENTIONS. THOSE MOMENTS, WHEN IT SNEAKS TO THE SURFACE, MAKE YOU MORE DANGEROUS.
YOU WOUND ME.
LEWIS! WE NEED TO MOVE. NOW.
JUST ANOTHER MOMENT.
MADAME BONIFACE. I CAN ASSURE--
GO, CAPTAIN. DO YOUR JOB.
THERE IS NOTHING YOU CAN ASSURE ME OF, AS IT IS.
In the future, I must work harder to remember that we have members of the delicate sex in our midst now. I must strive to make them feel safe.

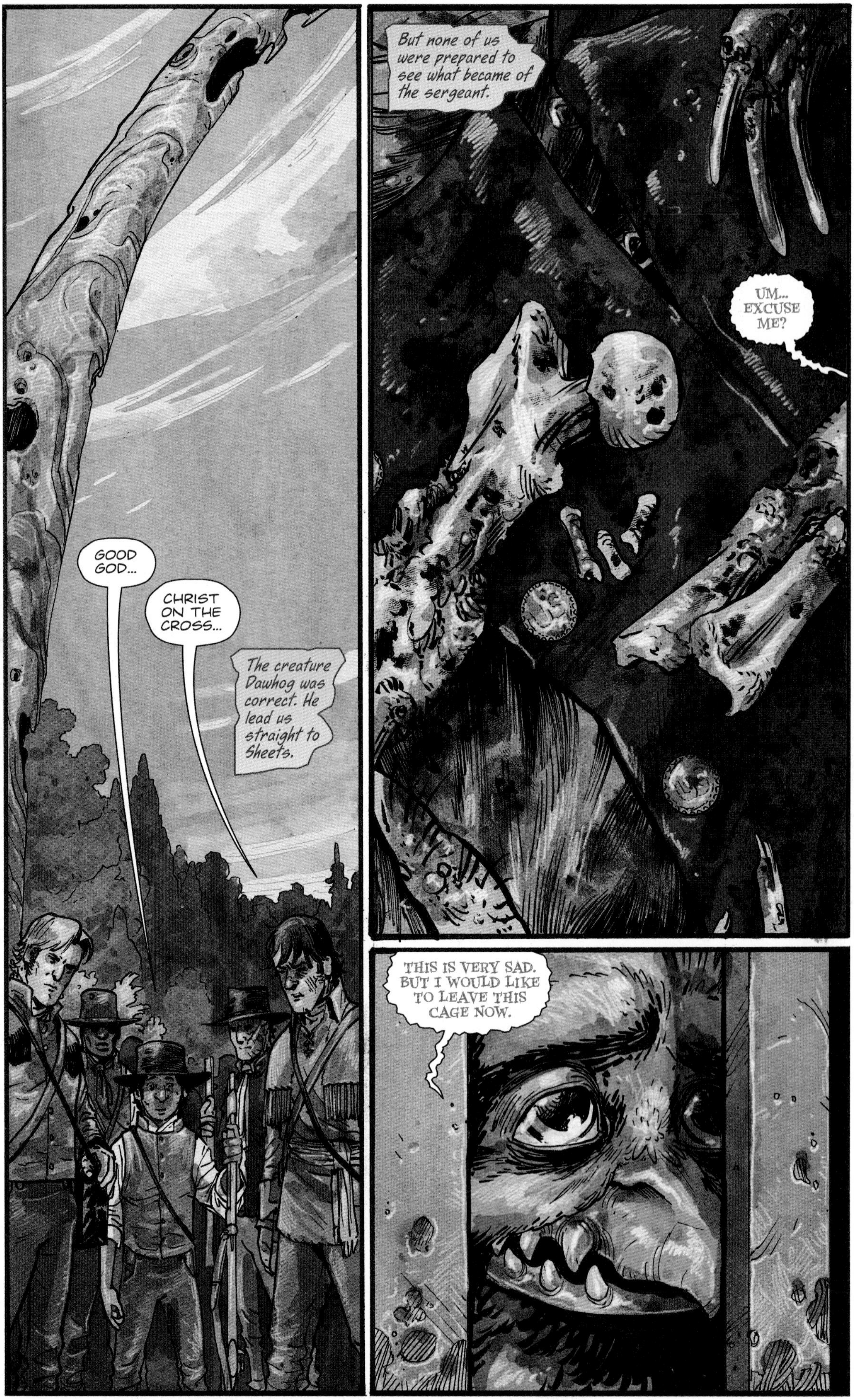
GOOD GOD...
CHRIST ON THE CROSS...
The creature Dawhog was correct. He lead us straight to Sheets.
But none of us were prepared to see what became of the sergeant.
UM... EXCUSE ME?
THIS IS VERY SAD. BUT I WOULD LIKE TO LEAVE THIS CAGE NOW.

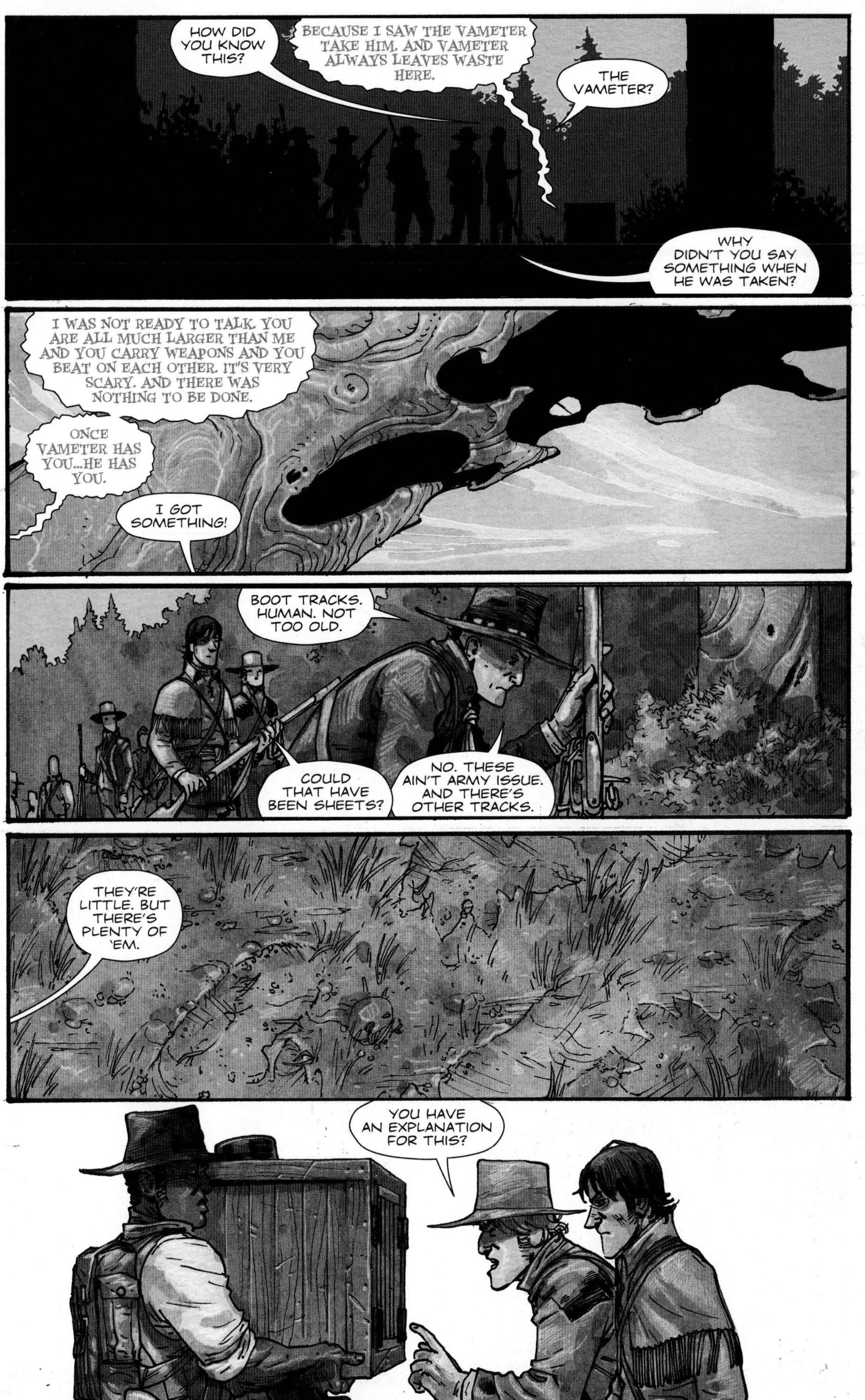
HOW DID YOU KNOW THIS?
BECAUSE I SAW THE VAMETER TAKE HIM. AND VAMETER ALWAYS LEAVES WASTE HERE.
THE VAMETER?
WHY DIDN'T YOU SAY SOMETHING WHEN HE WAS TAKEN?
I WAS NOT READY TO TALK. YOU ARE ALL MUCH LARGER THAN ME AND YOU CARRY WEAPONS AND YOU BEAT ON EACH OTHER. IT'S VERY SCARY. AND THERE WAS NOTHING TO BE DONE.
ONCE VAMETER HAS YOU...HE HAS YOU.
I GOT SOMETHING!
BOOT TRACKS. HUMAN. NOT TOO OLD.
COULD THAT HAVE BEEN SHEETS?
NO. THESE AIN'T ARMY ISSUE. AND THERE'S OTHER TRACKS.
THEY'RE LITTLE. BUT THERE'S PLENTY OF 'EM.
YOU HAVE AN EXPLANATION FOR THIS?

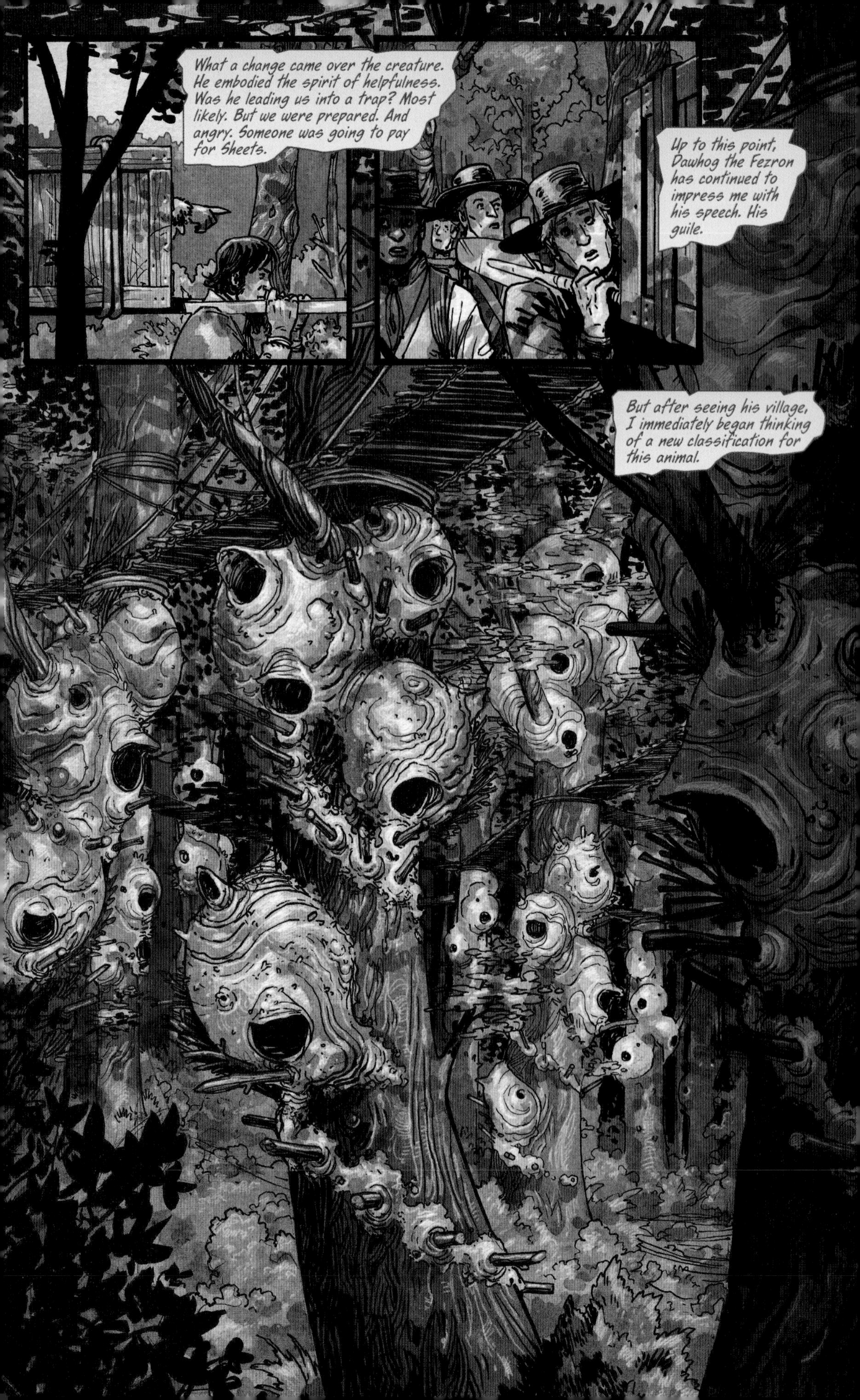
What a change came over the creature. He embodied the spirit of helpfulness. Was he leading us into a trap? Most likely. But we were prepared. And angry. Someone was going to pay for Sheets.
Up to this point, Dawhog the Fezron has continued to impress me with his speech. His guile.
But after seeing his village, I immediately began thinking of a new classification for this animal.

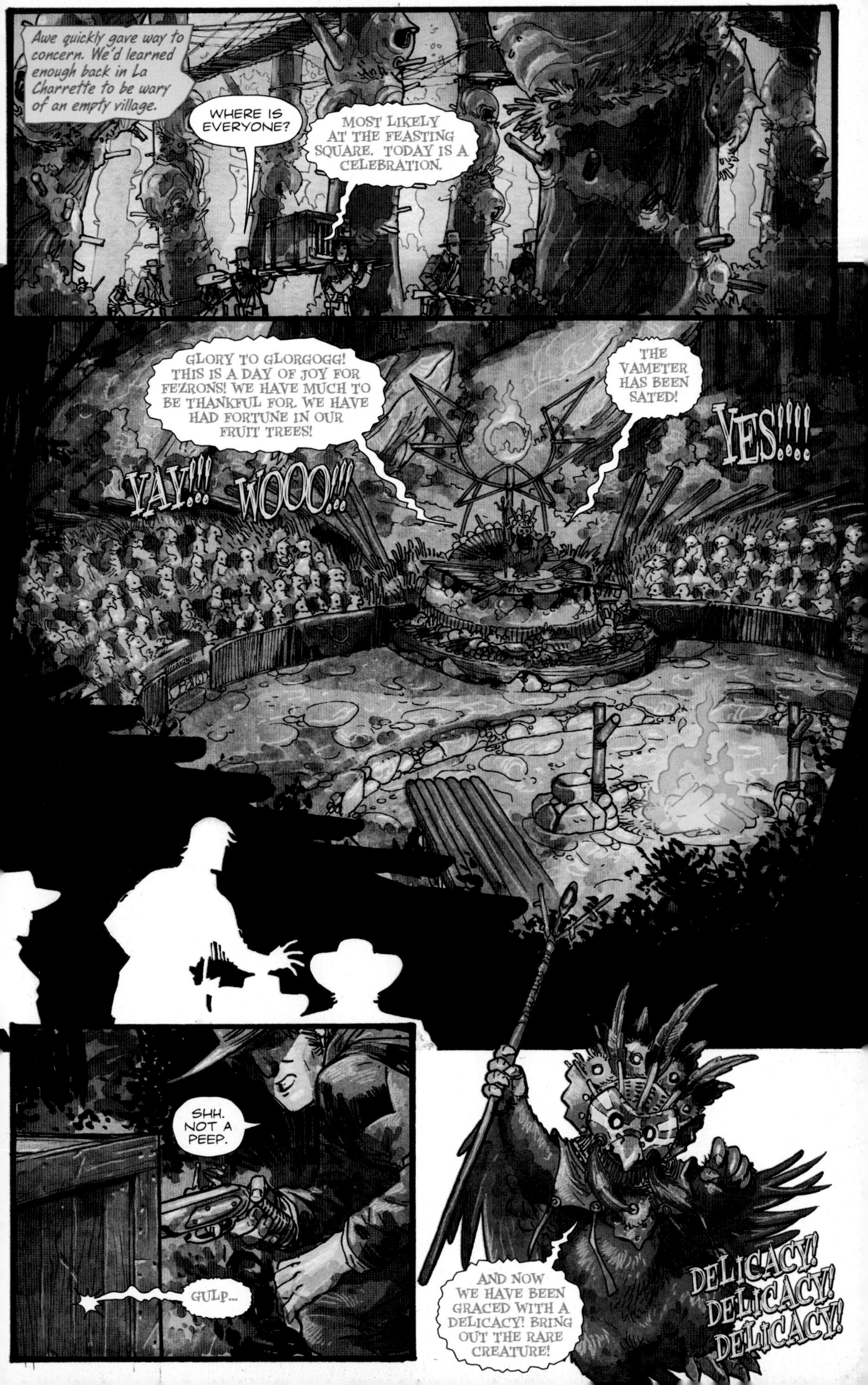

Awe quickly gave way to concern. We'd learned enough back in La Charrette to be wary of an empty village.
WHERE IS EVERYONE?
MOST LIKELY AT THE FEASTING SQUARE. TODAY IS A CELEBRATION.
GLORY TO GLORGOGG! THIS IS A DAY OF JOY FOR FEZRONS! WE HAVE MUCH TO BE THANKFUL FOR. WE HAVE HAD FORTUNE IN OUR FRUIT TREES!
THE VAMETER HAS BEEN SATED!
YAY!!! WOOO!!!
YES!!!!
SHH. NOT A PEEP.
GULP...
AND NOW WE HAVE BEEN GRACED WITH A DELICACY! BRING OUT THE RARE CREATURE!
DELICACY! DELICACY! DELICACY!

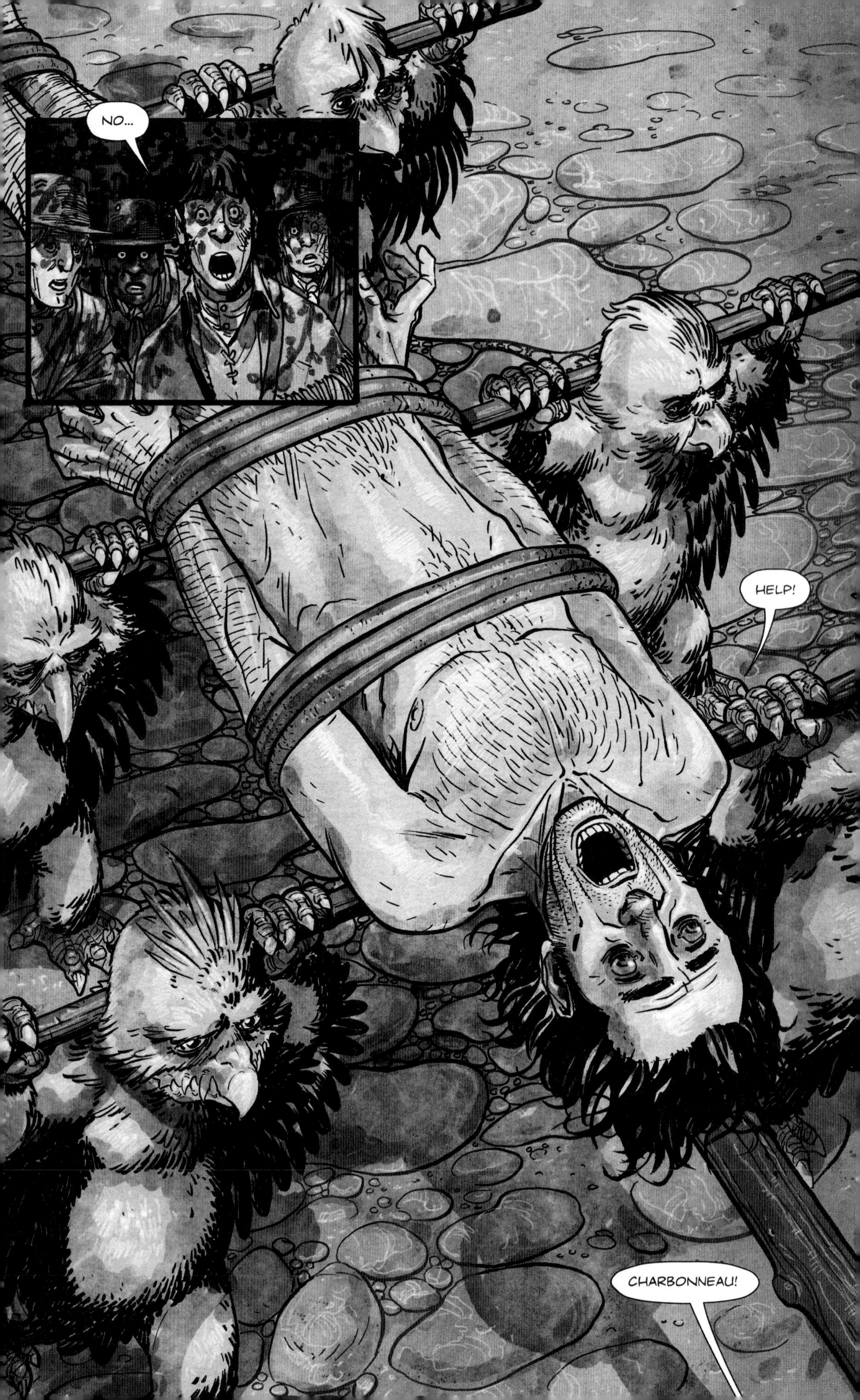
NO...
HELP!
CHARBONNEAU!

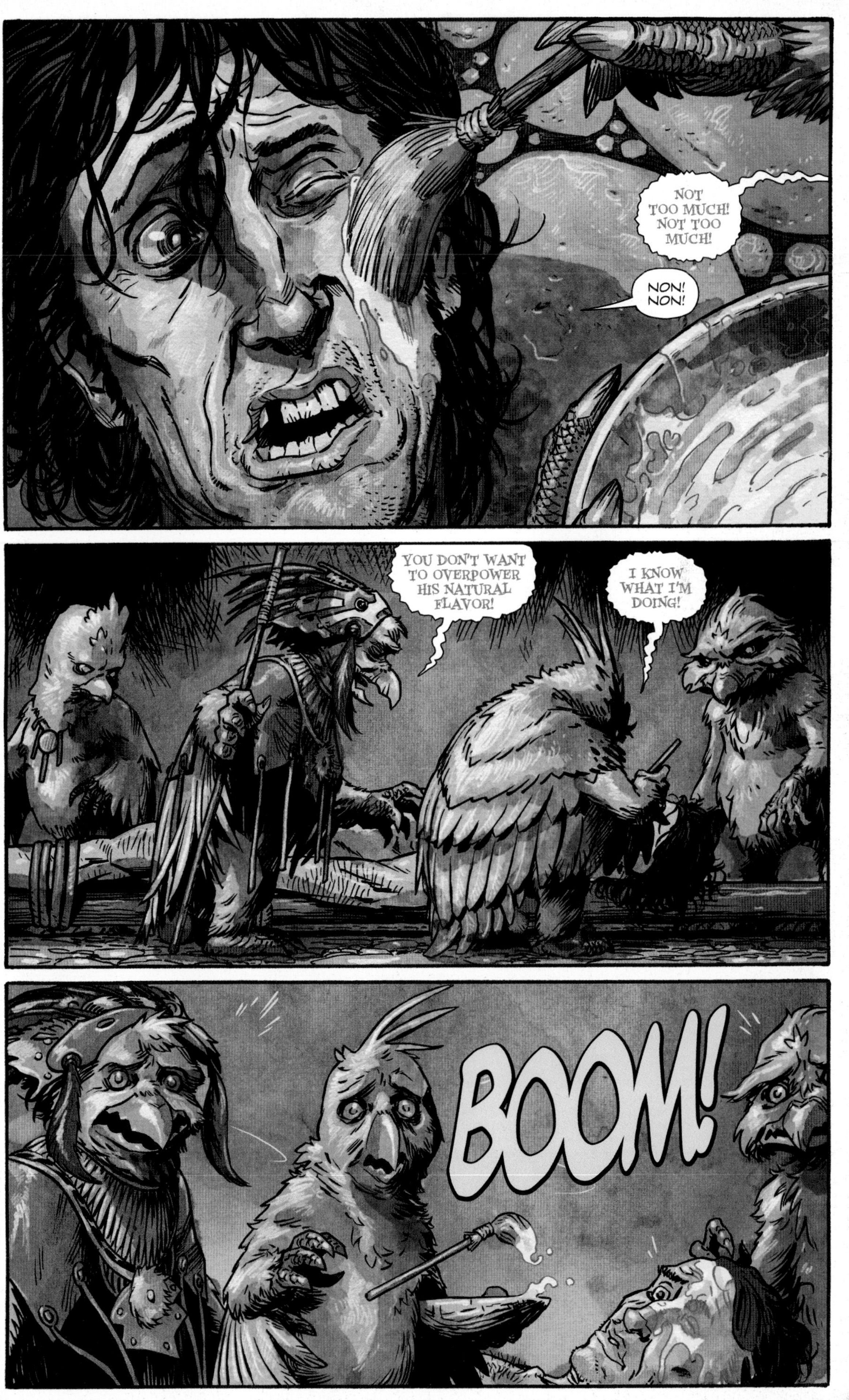
NOT TOO MUCH! NOT TOO MUCH!
NON! NON!
YOU DON'T WANT TO OVERPOWER HIS NATURAL FLAVOR!
I KNOW WHAT I'M DOING!
BOOM!

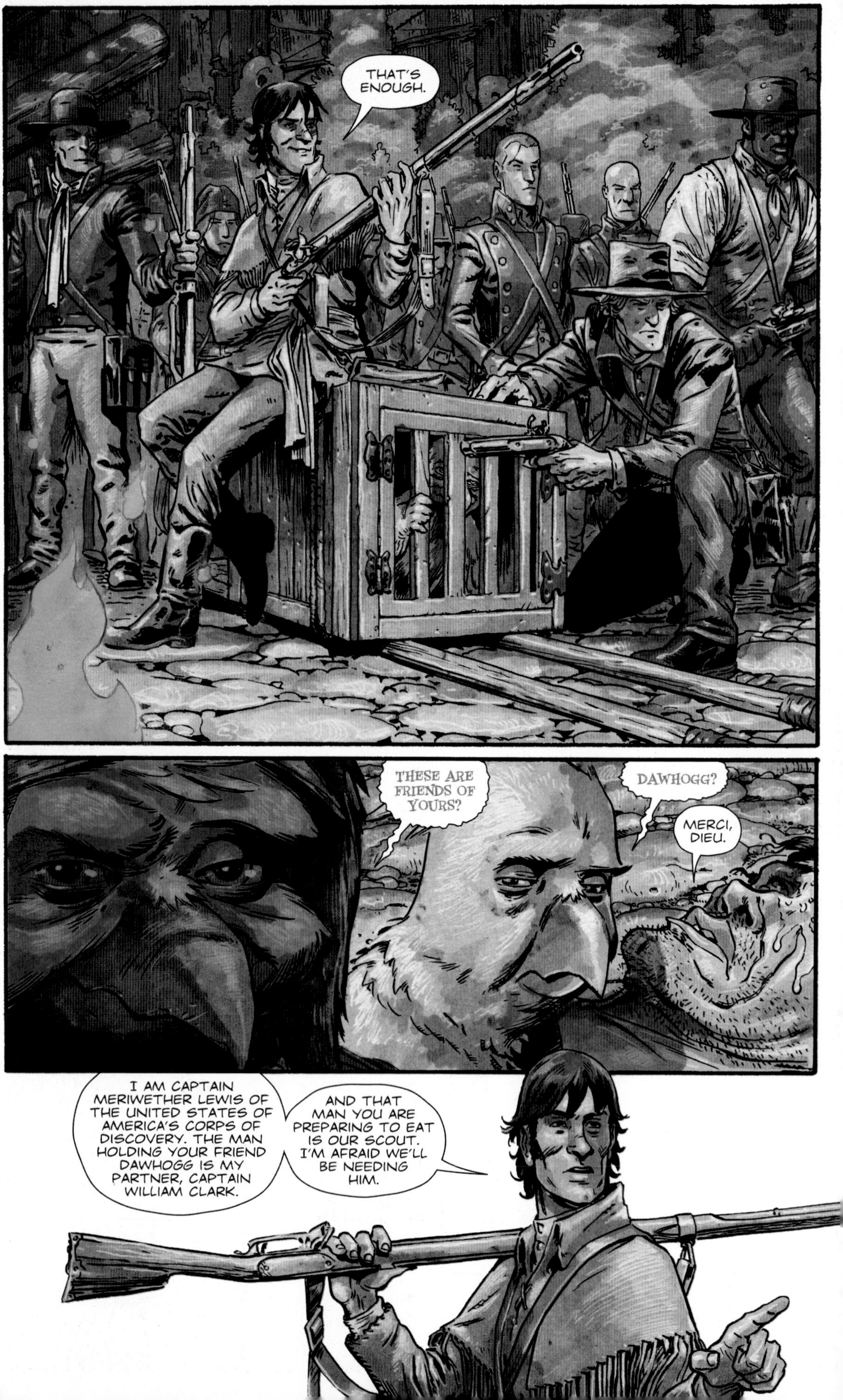
THAT'S ENOUGH.
THESE ARE FRIENDS OF YOURS?
DAWHOGG?
MERCI, DIEU.
I AM CAPTAIN MERIWETHER LEWIS OF THE UNITED STATES OF AMERICA'S CORPS OF DISCOVERY. THE MAN HOLDING YOUR FRIEND DAWHOGG IS MY PARTNER, CAPTAIN WILLIAM CLARK.
AND THAT MAN YOU ARE PREPARING TO EAT IS OUR SCOUT. I'M AFRAID WE'LL BE NEEDING HIM.

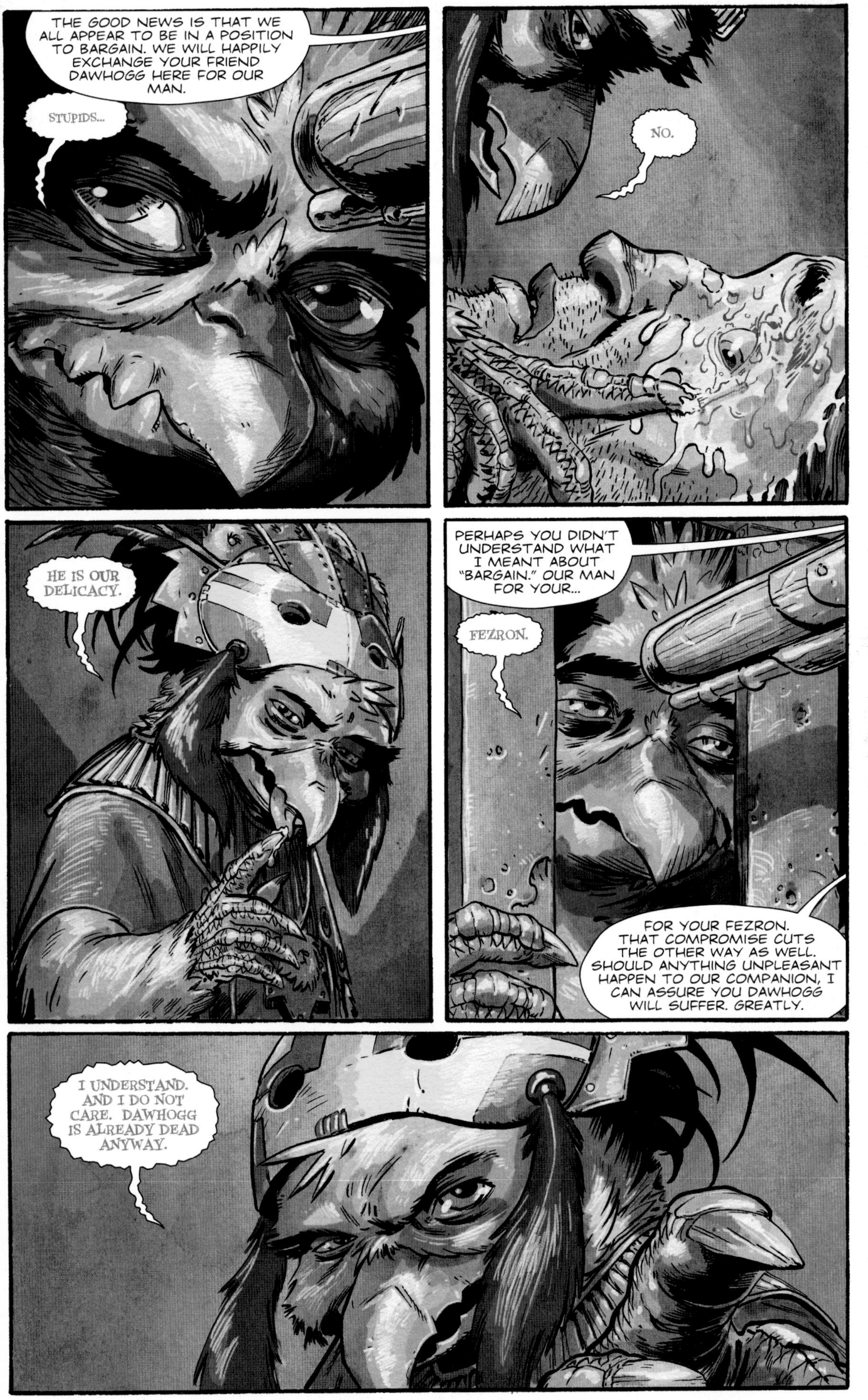
THE GOOD NEWS IS THAT WE ALL APPEAR TO BE IN A POSITION TO BARGAIN. WE WILL HAPPILY EXCHANGE YOUR FRIEND DAWHOGG HERE FOR OUR MAN.
STUPIDS...
NO.
HE IS OUR DELICACY.
PERHAPS YOU DIDN'T UNDERSTAND WHAT I MEANT ABOUT "BARGAIN." OUR MAN FOR YOUR...
FEZRON.
FOR YOUR FEZRON. THAT COMPROMISE CUTS THE OTHER WAY AS WELL. SHOULD ANYTHING UNPLEASANT HAPPEN TO OUR COMPANION, I CAN ASSURE YOU DAWHOGG WILL SUFFER. GREATLY.
I UNDERSTAND. AND I DO NOT CARE. DAWHOGG IS ALREADY DEAD ANYWAY.

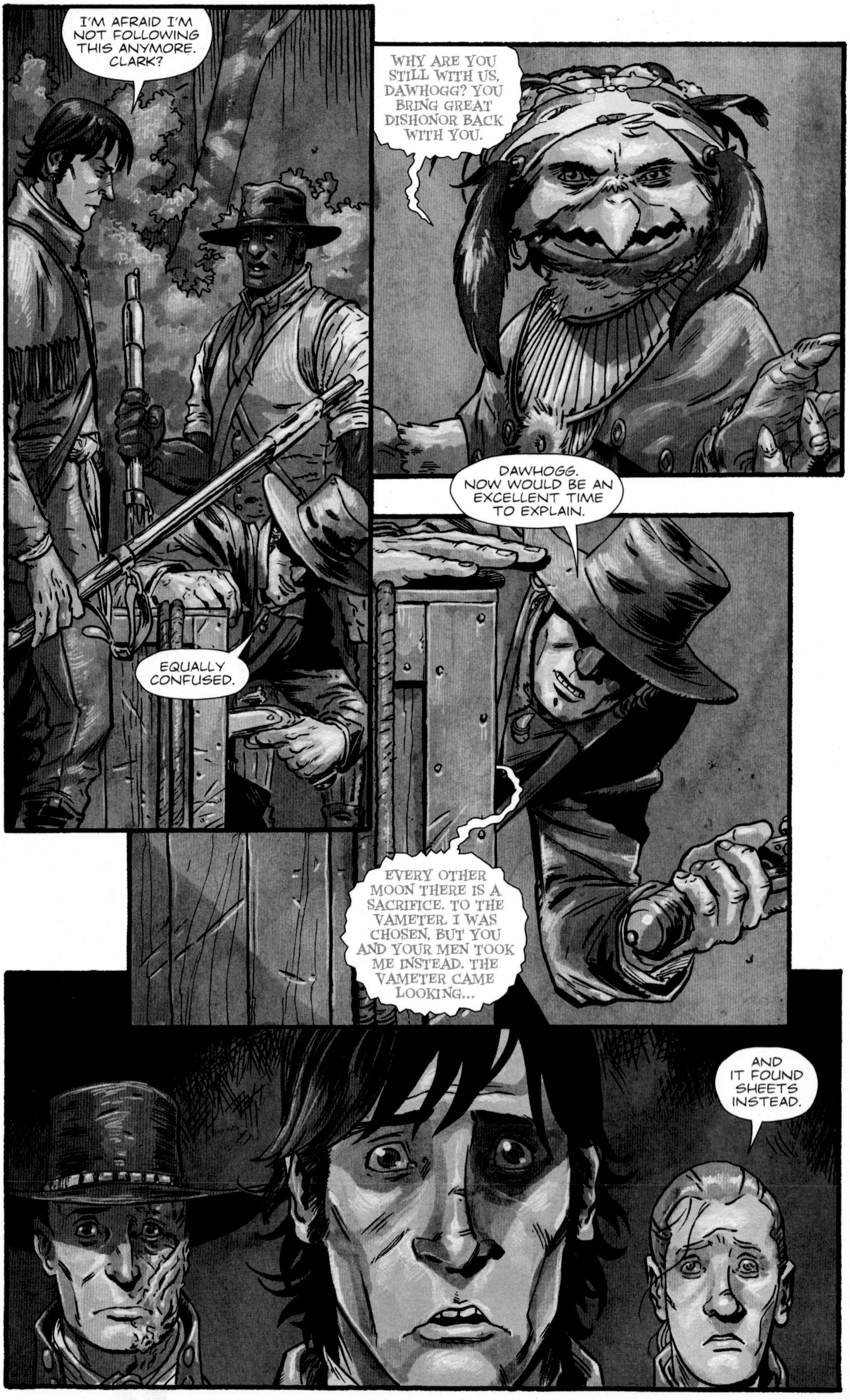
I'M AFRAID I'M NOT FOLLOWING THIS ANYMORE. CLARK?
EQUALLY CONFUSED.
WHY ARE YOU STILL WITH US, DAWHOGG? YOU BRING GREAT DISHONOR BACK WITH YOU.
DAWHOGG. NOW WOULD BE AN EXCELLENT TIME TO EXPLAIN.
EVERY OTHER MOON THERE IS A SACRIFICE. TO THE VAMETER. I WAS CHOSEN, BUT YOU AND YOUR MEN TOOK ME INSTEAD. THE VAMETER CAME LOOKING...
AND IT FOUND SHEETS INSTEAD.

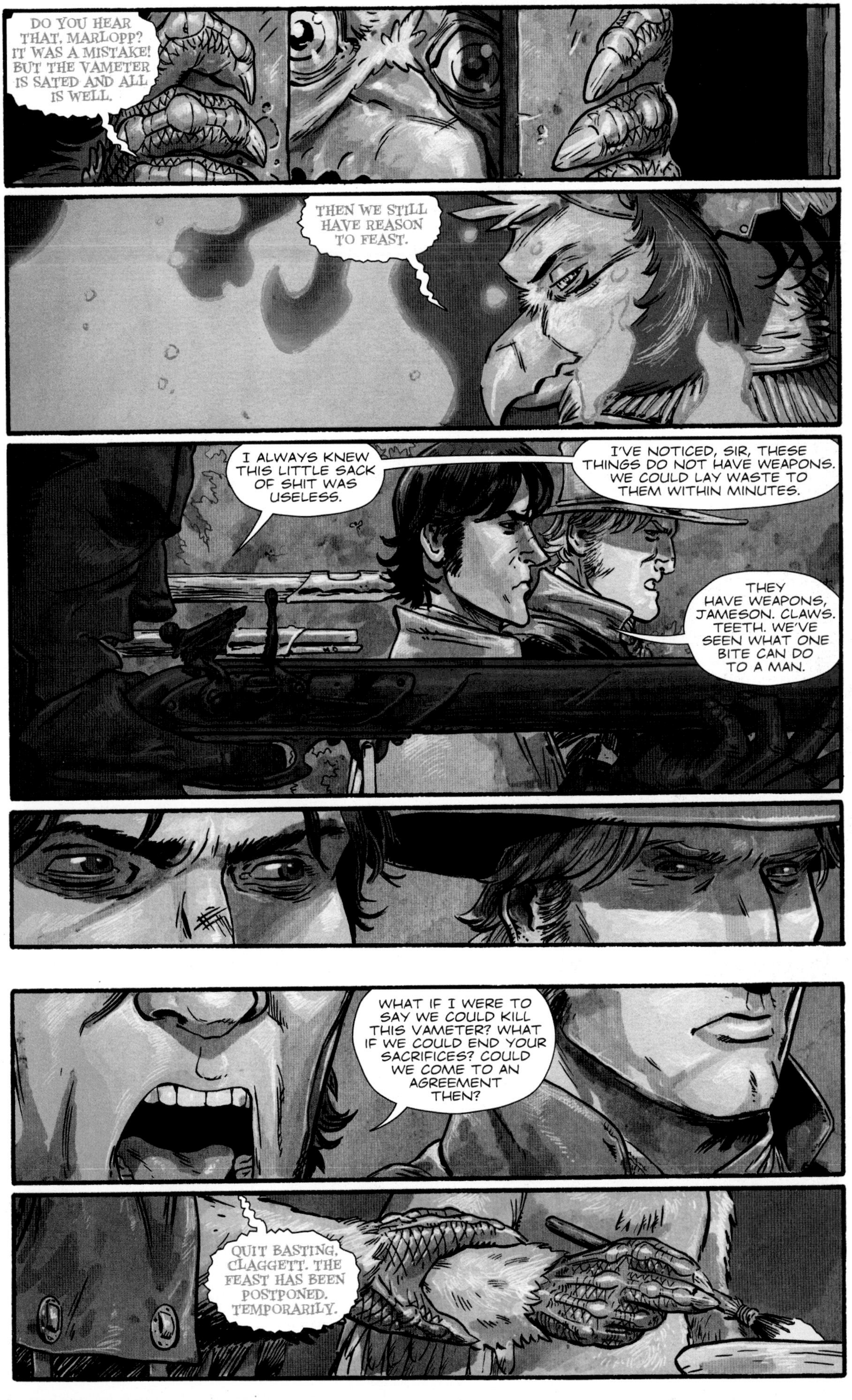
DO YOU HEAR THAT, MARLOPP? IT WAS A MISTAKE! BUT THE VAMETER IS SATED AND ALL IS WELL.
THEN WE STILL HAVE REASON TO FEAST.
I ALWAYS KNEW THIS LITTLE SACK OF SHIT WAS USELESS.
I'VE NOTICED, SIR, THESE THINGS DO NOT HAVE WEAPONS. WE COULD LAY WASTE TO THEM WITHIN MINUTES.
THEY HAVE WEAPONS, JAMESON. CLAWS. TEETH. WE'VE SEEN WHAT ONE BITE CAN DO TO A MAN.
WHAT IF I WERE TO SAY WE COULD KILL THIS VAMETER? WHAT IF WE COULD END YOUR SACRIFICES? COULD WE COME TO AN AGREEMENT THEN?
QUIT BASTING, CLAGGETT. THE FEAST HAS BEEN POSTPONED. TEMPORARILY.

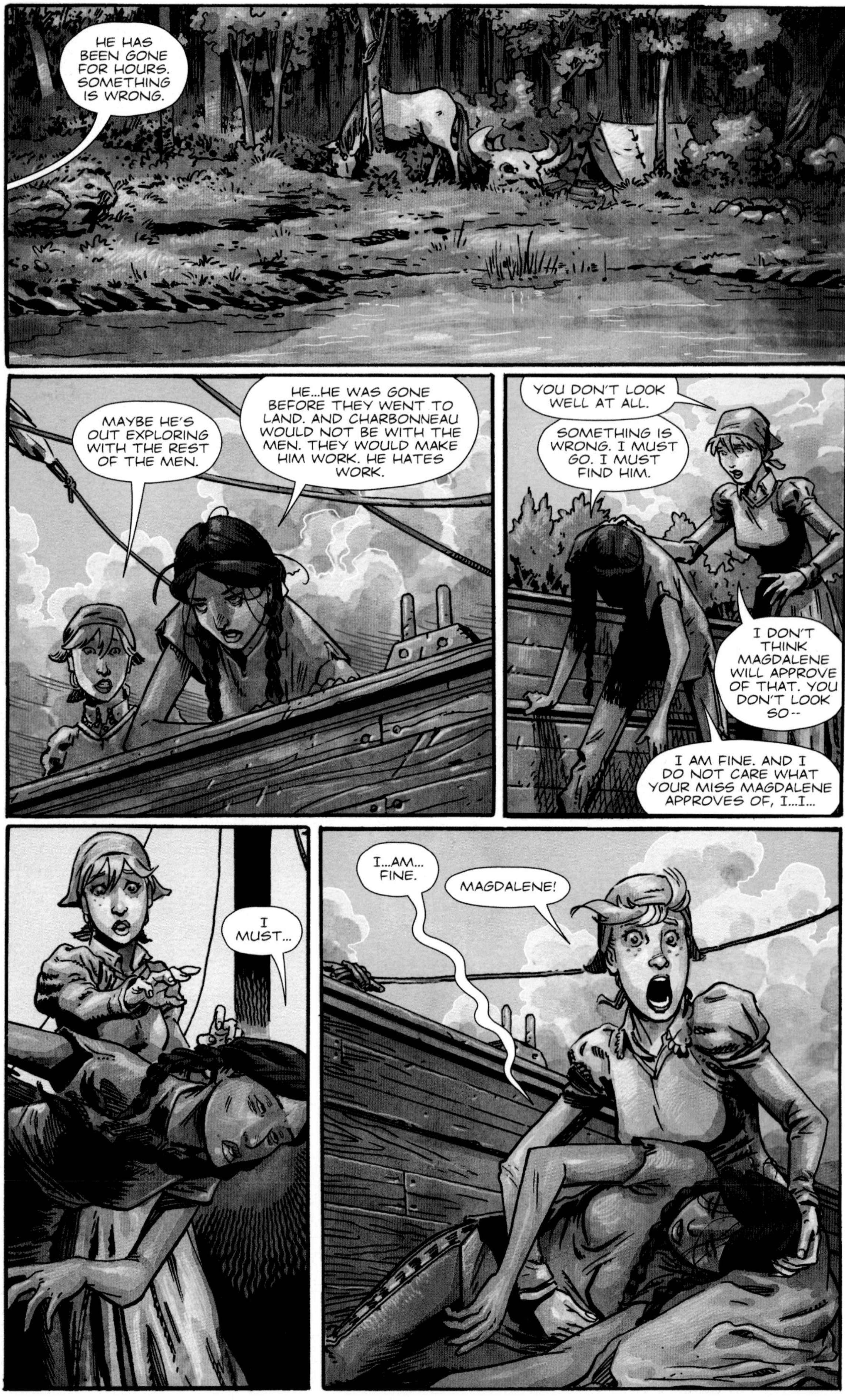
HE HAS BEEN GONE FOR HOURS. SOMETHING IS WRONG.
MAYBE HE'S OUT EXPLORING WITH THE REST OF THE MEN.
HE...HE WAS GONE BEFORE THEY WENT TO LAND. AND CHARBONNEAU WOULD NOT BE WITH THE MEN. THEY WOULD MAKE HIM WORK. HE HATES WORK.
YOU DON'T LOOK WELL AT ALL.
SOMETHING IS WRONG. I MUST GO. I MUST FIND HIM.
I DON'T THINK MAGDALENE WILL APPROVE OF THAT. YOU DON'T LOOK SO--
I AM FINE. AND I DO NOT CARE WHAT YOUR MISS MAGDALENE APPROVES OF, I...I...
I MUST...
I...AM... FINE.
MAGDALENE!

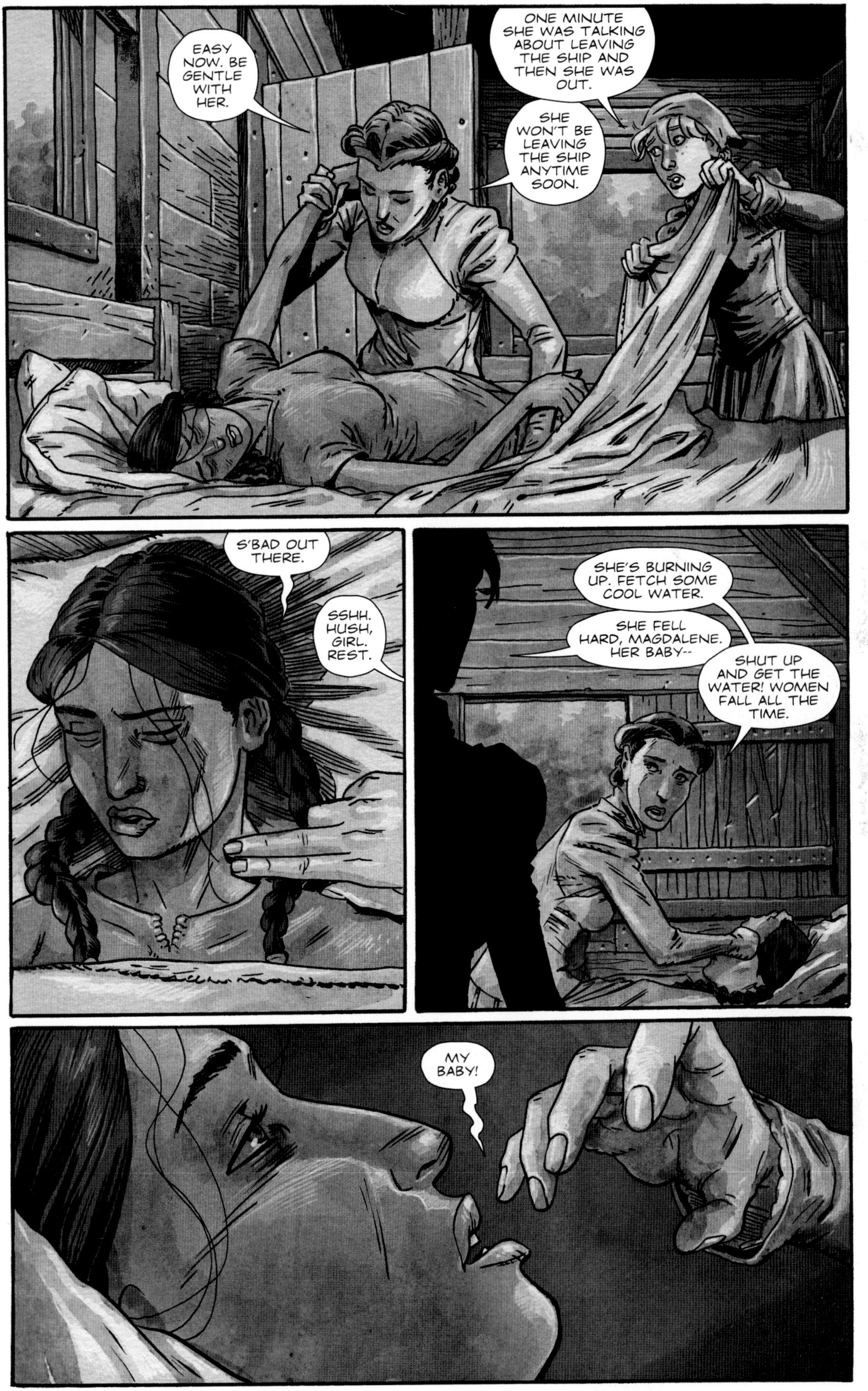
EASY NOW. BE GENTLE WITH HER.
ONE MINUTE SHE WAS TALKING ABOUT LEAVING THE SHIP AND THEN SHE WAS OUT.
SHE WON'T BE LEAVING THE SHIP ANYTIME SOON.
S'BAD OUT THERE.
SSHH. HUSH, GIRL. REST.
SHE'S BURNING UP. FETCH SOME COOL WATER.
SHE FELL HARD, MAGDALENE. HER BABY--
SHUT UP AND GET THE WATER! WOMEN FALL ALL THE TIME.
MY BABY!

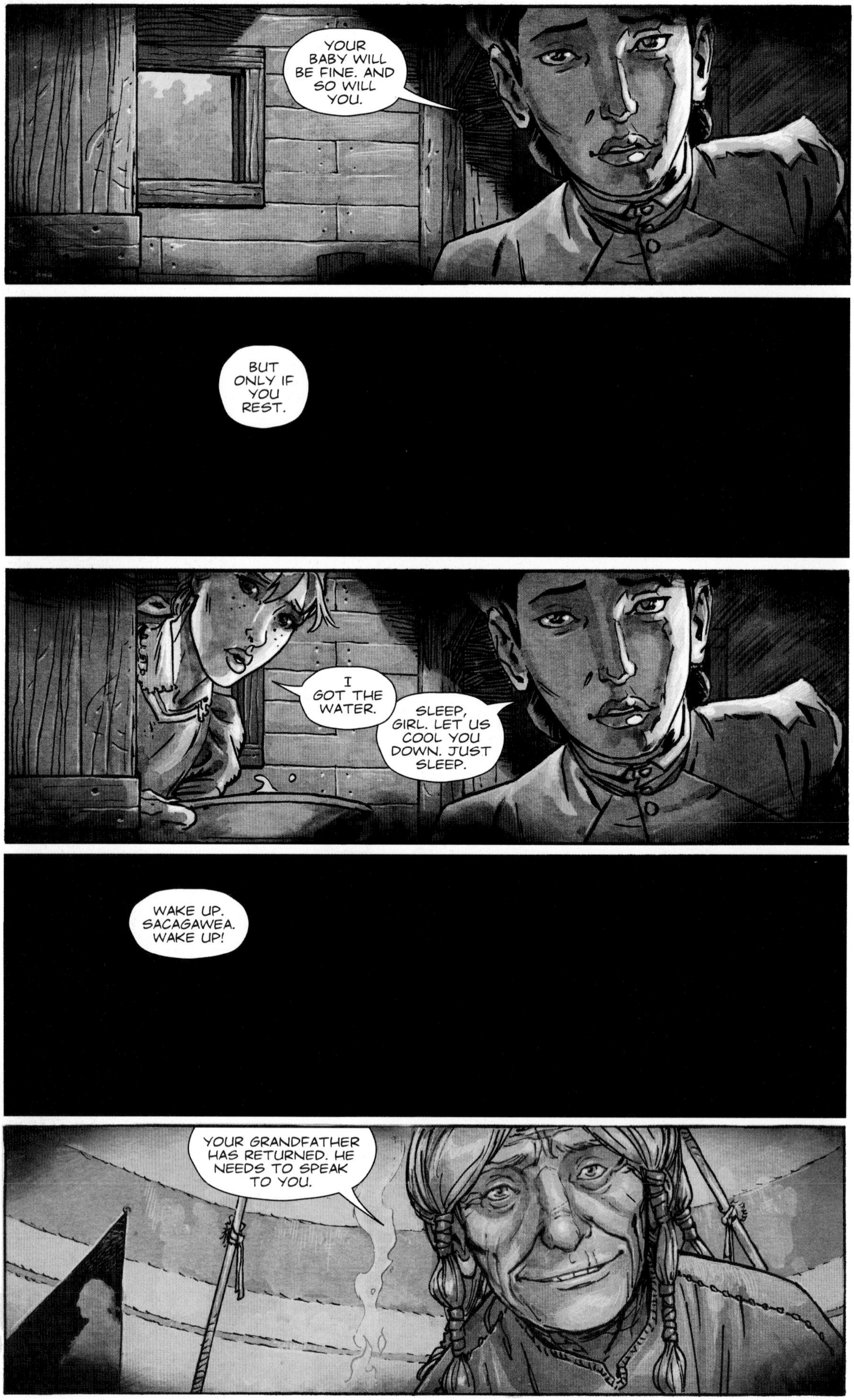
YOUR BABY WILL BE FINE. AND SO WILL YOU.
BUT ONLY IF YOU REST.
I GOT THE WATER.
SLEEP, GIRL. LET US COOL YOU DOWN. JUST SLEEP.
WAKE UP. SACAGAWEA. WAKE UP!
YOUR GRANDFATHER HAS RETURNED. HE NEEDS TO SPEAK TO YOU.

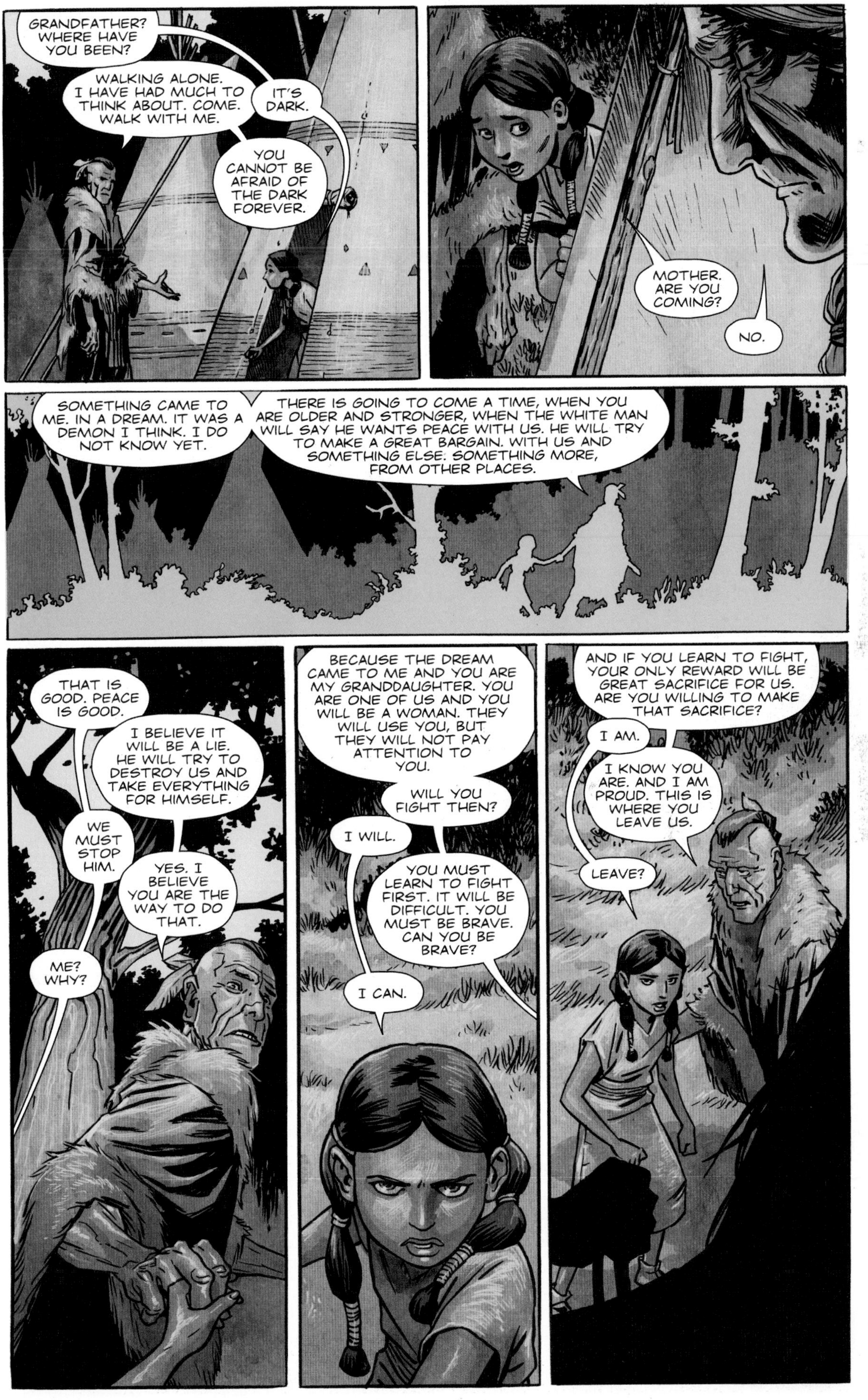
GRANDFATHER? WHERE HAVE YOU BEEN?
WALKING ALONE. I HAVE HAD MUCH TO THINK ABOUT. COME. WALK WITH ME.
IT'S DARK.
YOU CANNOT BE AFRAID OF THE DARK FOREVER.
MOTHER. ARE YOU COMING?
NO.
SOMETHING CAME TO ME. IN A DREAM. IT WAS A DEMON I THINK. I DO NOT KNOW YET.
THERE IS GOING TO COME A TIME, WHEN YOU ARE OLDER AND STRONGER, WHEN THE WHITE MAN WILL SAY HE WANTS PEACE WITH US. HE WILL TRY TO MAKE A GREAT BARGAIN. WITH US AND SOMETHING ELSE. SOMETHING MORE, FROM OTHER PLACES.
THAT IS GOOD. PEACE IS GOOD.
I BELIEVE IT WILL BE A LIE. HE WILL TRY TO DESTROY US AND TAKE EVERYTHING FOR HIMSELF.
WE MUST STOP HIM.
YES. I BELIEVE YOU ARE THE WAY TO DO THAT.
ME? WHY?
BECAUSE THE DREAM CAME TO ME AND YOU ARE MY GRANDDAUGHTER. YOU ARE ONE OF US AND YOU WILL BE A WOMAN. THEY WILL USE YOU, BUT THEY WILL NOT PAY ATTENTION TO YOU.
WILL YOU FIGHT THEN?
I WILL.
YOU MUST LEARN TO FIGHT FIRST. IT WILL BE DIFFICULT. YOU MUST BE BRAVE. CAN YOU BE BRAVE?
I CAN.
AND IF YOU LEARN TO FIGHT, YOUR ONLY REWARD WILL BE GREAT SACRIFICE FOR US. ARE YOU WILLING TO MAKE THAT SACRIFICE?
I AM.
I KNOW YOU ARE. AND I AM PROUD. THIS IS WHERE YOU LEAVE US.
LEAVE?

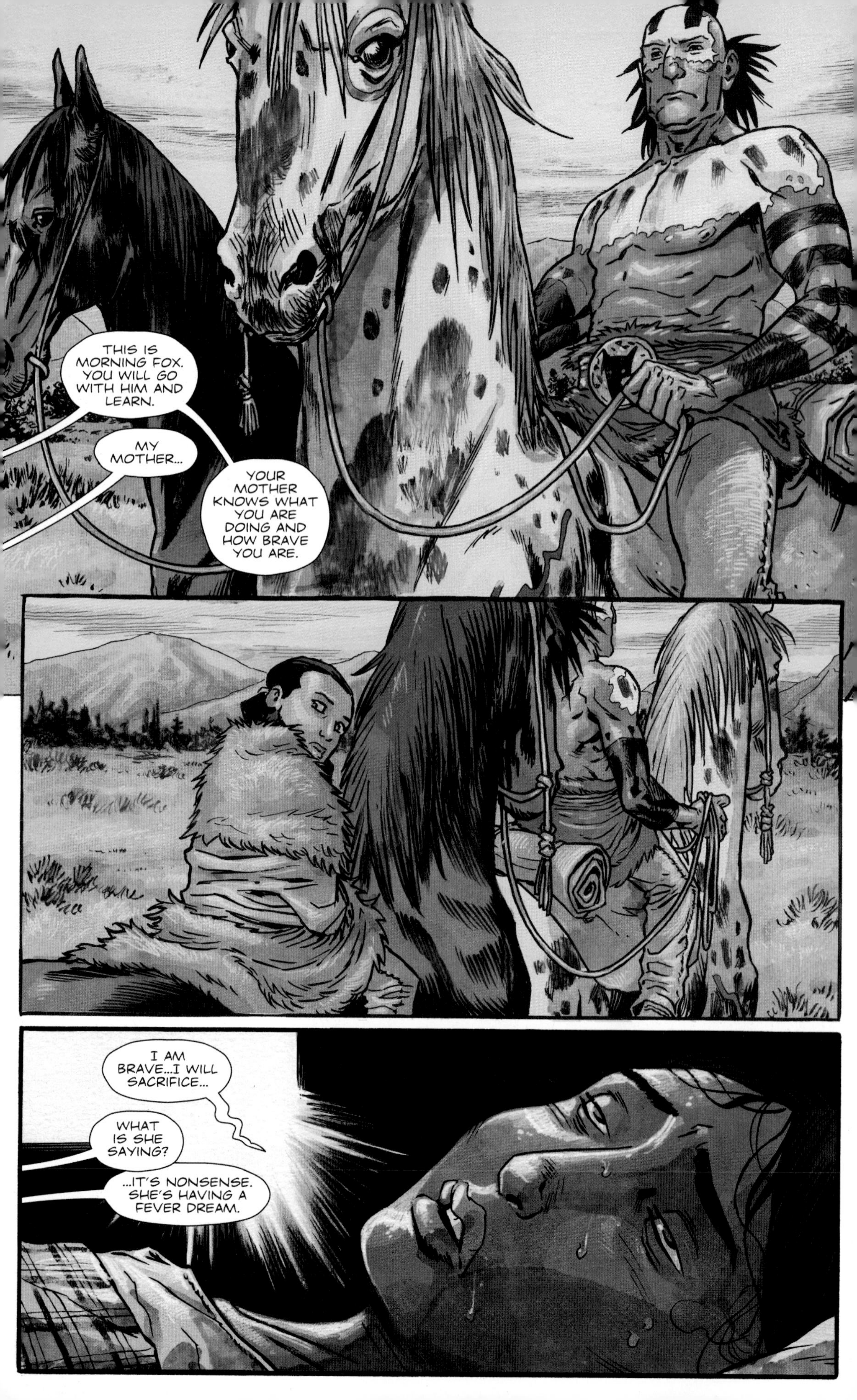
THIS IS MORNING FOX. YOU WILL GO WITH HIM AND LEARN.
MY MOTHER...
YOUR MOTHER KNOWS WHAT YOU ARE DOING AND HOW BRAVE YOU ARE.
I AM BRAVE...I WILL SACRIFICE...
WHAT IS SHE SAYING?
...IT'S NONSENSE. SHE'S HAVING A FEVER DREAM.

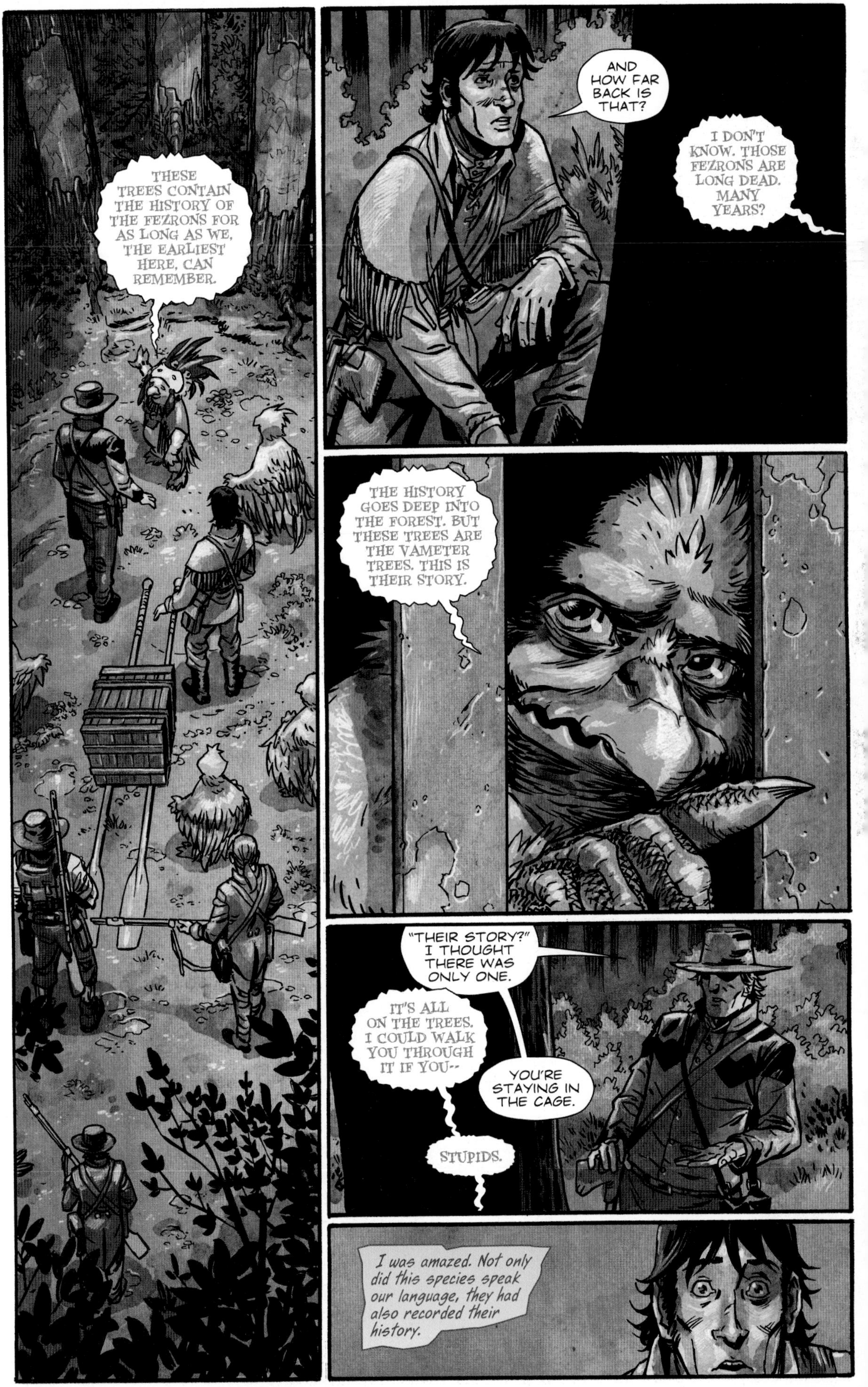
THESE TREES CONTAIN THE HISTORY OF THE FEZRONS FOR AS LONG AS WE, THE EARLIEST HERE, CAN REMEMBER.
AND HOW FAR BACK IS THAT?
I DON'T KNOW. THOSE FEZRONS ARE LONG DEAD. MANY YEARS?
THE HISTORY GOES DEEP INTO THE FOREST. BUT THESE TREES ARE THE VAMETER TREES. THIS IS THEIR STORY.
"THEIR STORY?" I THOUGHT THERE WAS ONLY ONE.
IT'S ALL ON THE TREES. I COULD WALK YOU THROUGH IT IF YOU--
YOU'RE STAYING IN THE CAGE.
STUPIDS.
I was amazed. Not only did this species speak our language, they had also recorded their history.

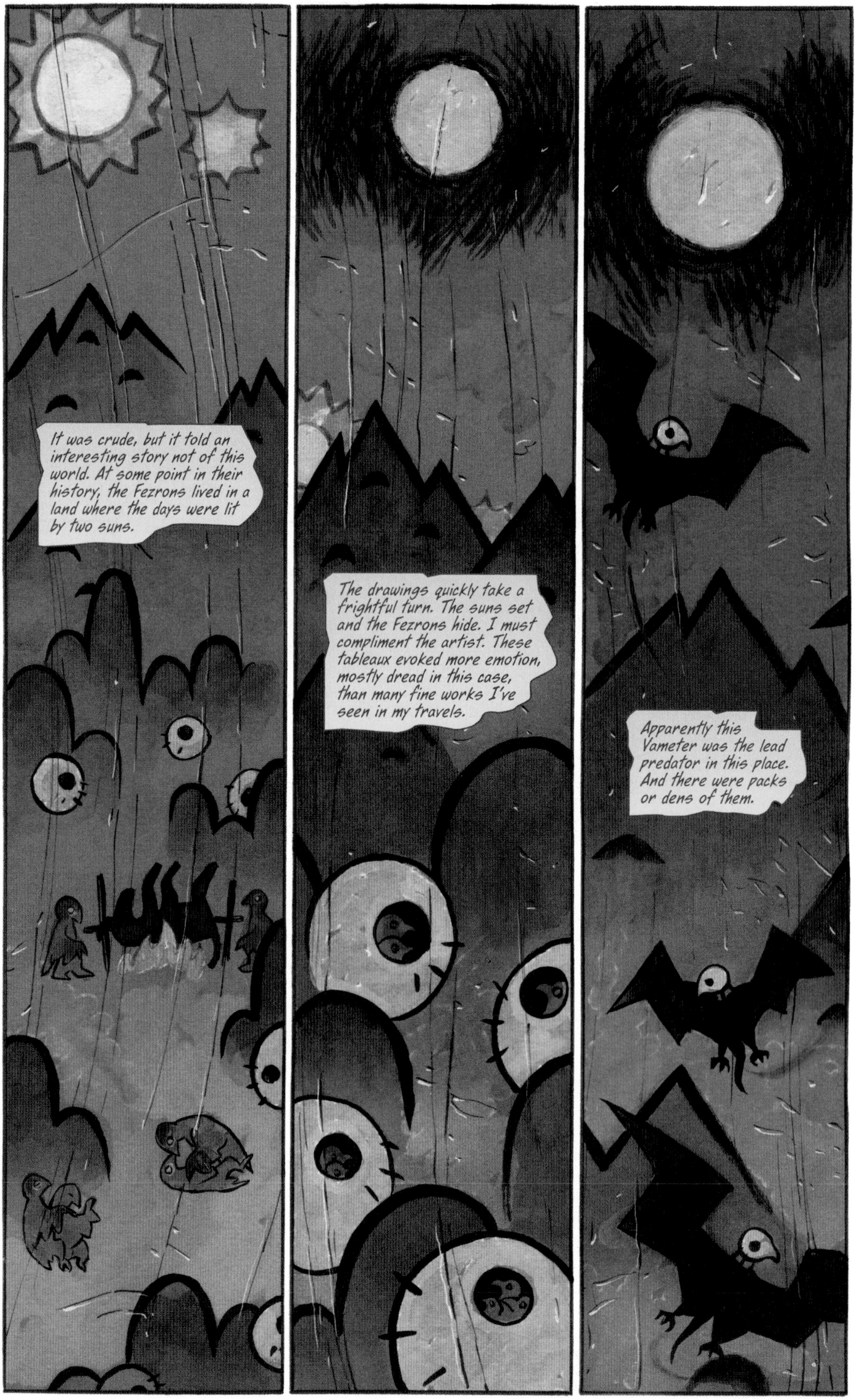
It was crude, but it told an interesting story not of this world. At some point in their history, the Fezrons lived in a land where the days were lit by two suns.
The drawings quickly take a frightful turn. The suns set and the Fezrons hide. I must compliment the artist. These tableaux evoked more emotion, mostly dread in this case, than many fine works I've seen in my travels.
Apparently this Vameter was the lead predator in this place. And there were packs or dens of them.

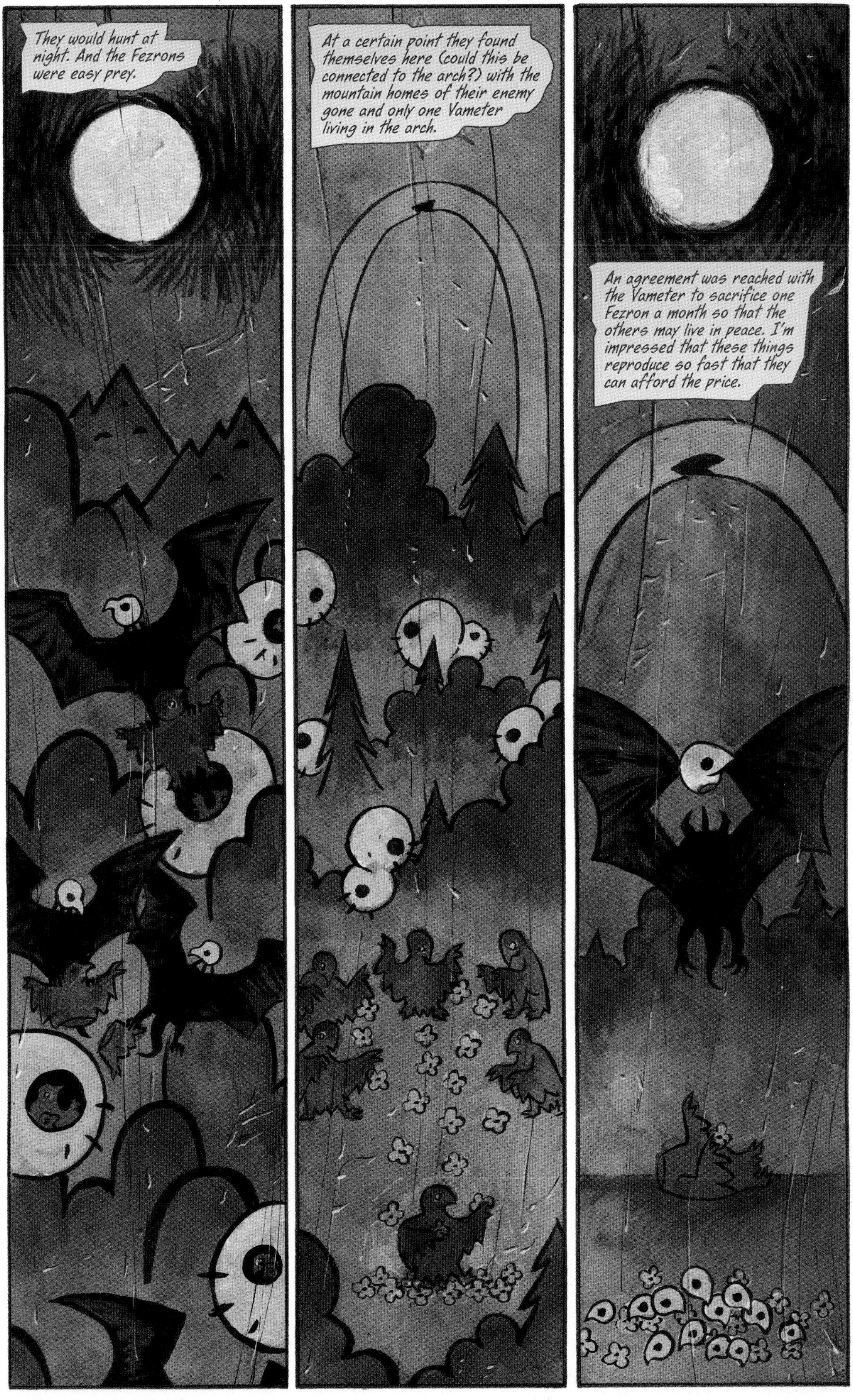
They would hunt at night. And the Fezrons were easy prey.
At a certain point they found themselves here (could this be connected to the arch?) with the mountain homes of their enemy gone and only one Vameter living in the arch.
An agreement was reached with the Vameter to sacrifice one Fezron a month so that the others may live in peace. I'm impressed that these things reproduce so fast that they can afford the price.

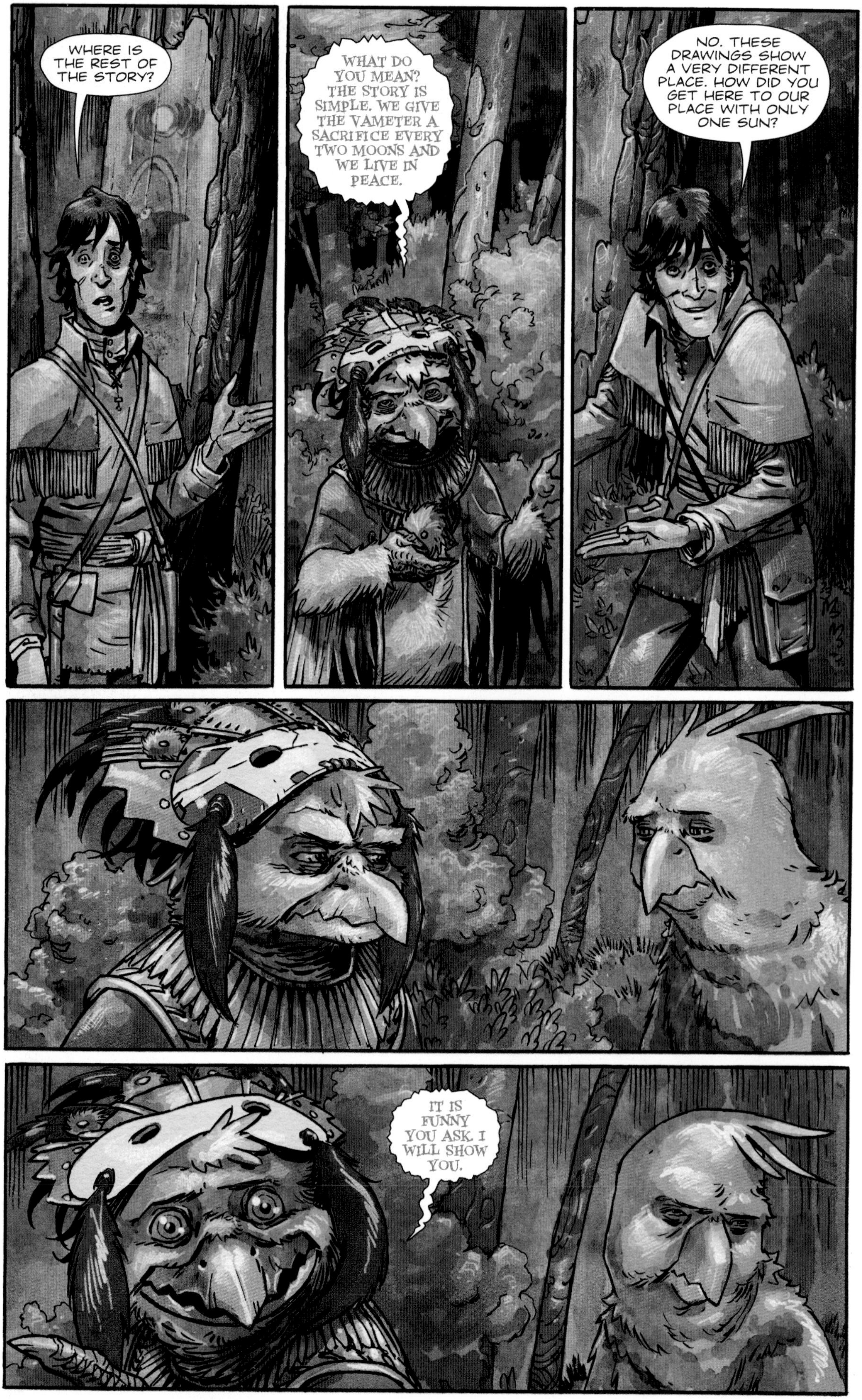
WHERE IS THE REST OF THE STORY?
WHAT DO YOU MEAN? THE STORY IS SIMPLE. WE GIVE THE VAMETER A SACRIFICE EVERY TWO MOONS AND WE LIVE IN PEACE.
NO. THESE DRAWINGS SHOW A VERY DIFFERENT PLACE. HOW DID YOU GET HERE TO OUR PLACE WITH ONLY ONE SUN?
IT IS FUNNY YOU ASK. I WILL SHOW YOU.

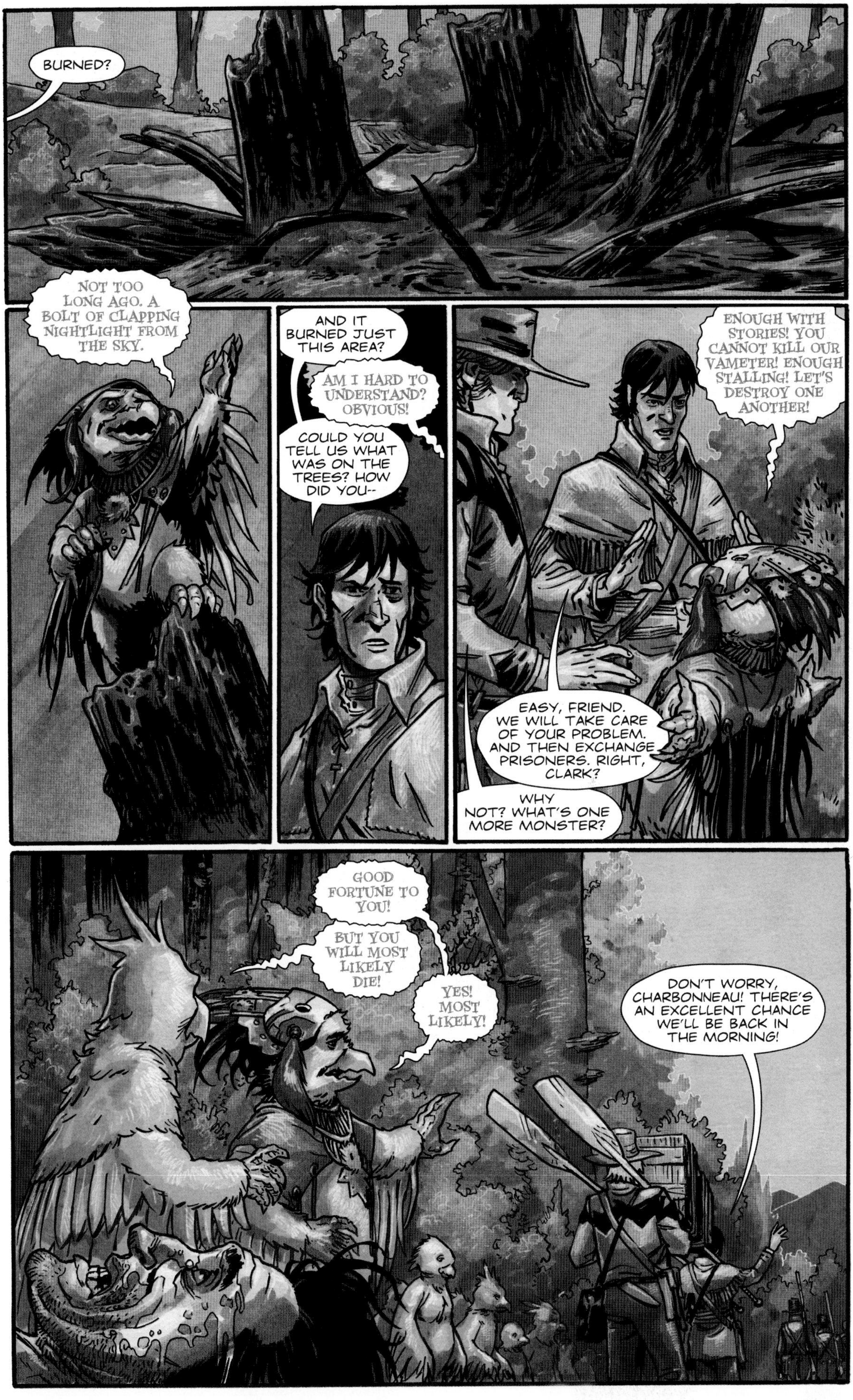
BURNED?
NOT TOO LONG AGO. A BOLT OF CLAPPING NIGHTLIGHT FROM THE SKY.
AND IT BURNED JUST THIS AREA?
AM I HARD TO UNDERSTAND? OBVIOUS!
COULD YOU TELL US WHAT WAS ON THE TREES? HOW DID YOU--
ENOUGH WITH STORIES! YOU CANNOT KILL OUR VAMETER! ENOUGH STALLING! LET'S DESTROY ONE ANOTHER!
EASY, FRIEND. WE WILL TAKE CARE OF YOUR PROBLEM. AND THEN EXCHANGE PRISONERS. RIGHT, CLARK?
WHY NOT? WHAT'S ONE MORE MONSTER?
GOOD FORTUNE TO YOU!
BUT YOU WILL MOST LIKELY DIE!
YES! MOST LIKELY!
DON'T WORRY, CHARBONNEAU! THERE'S AN EXCELLENT CHANCE WE'LL BE BACK IN THE MORNING!

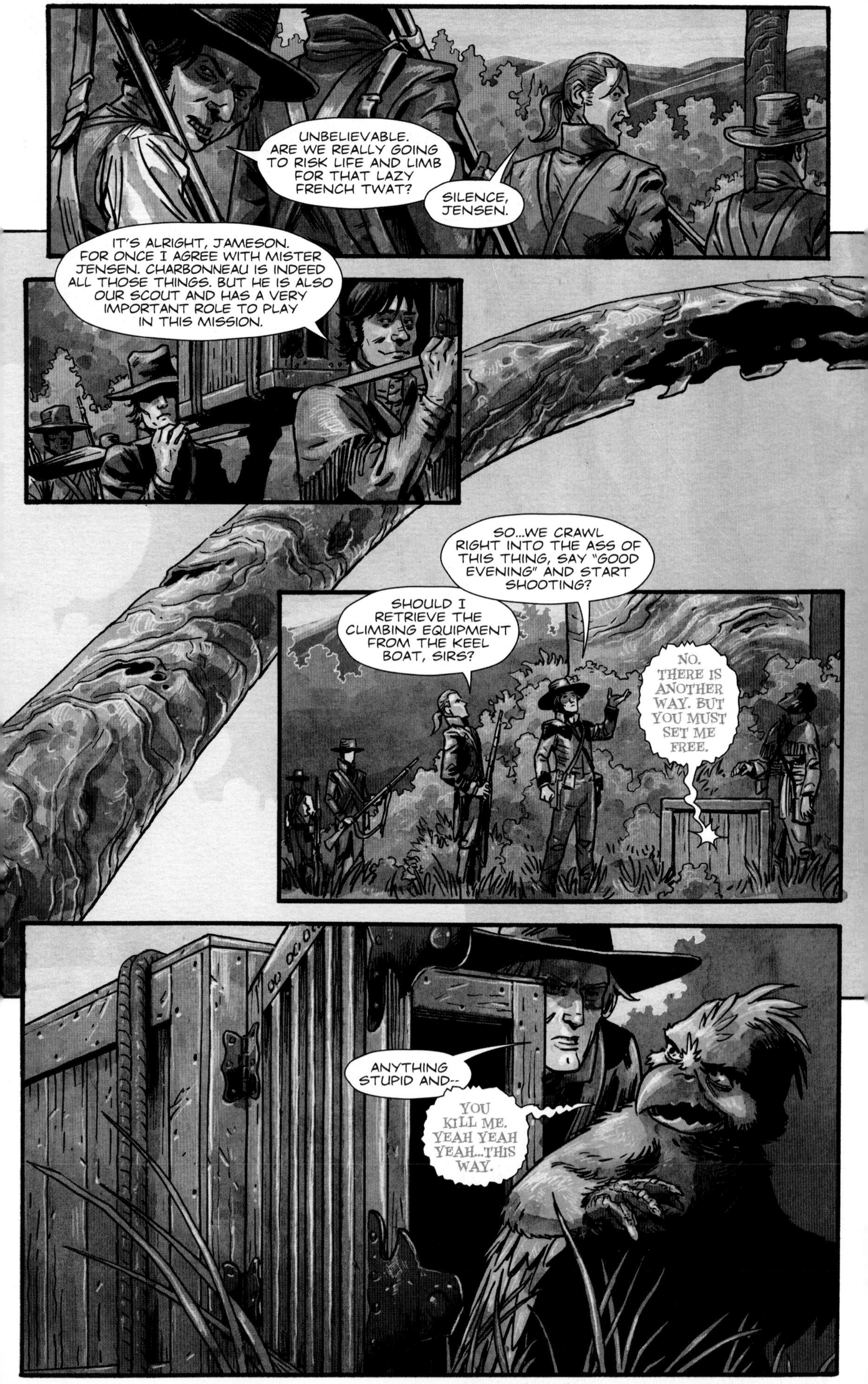
UNBELIEVABLE. ARE WE REALLY GOING TO RISK LIFE AND LIMB FOR THAT LAZY FRENCH TWAT?
SILENCE, JENSEN.
IT'S ALRIGHT, JAMESON. FOR ONCE I AGREE WITH MISTER JENSEN. CHARBONNEAU IS INDEED ALL THOSE THINGS. BUT HE IS ALSO OUR SCOUT AND HAS A VERY IMPORTANT ROLE TO PLAY IN THIS MISSION.
SO...WE CRAWL RIGHT INTO THE ASS OF THIS THING, SAY "GOOD EVENING" AND START SHOOTING?
SHOULD I RETRIEVE THE CLIMBING EQUIPMENT FROM THE KEEL BOAT, SIRS?
NO. THERE IS ANOTHER WAY. BUT YOU MUST SET ME FREE.
ANYTHING STUPID AND--
YOU KILL ME. YEAH YEAH YEAH...THIS WAY.

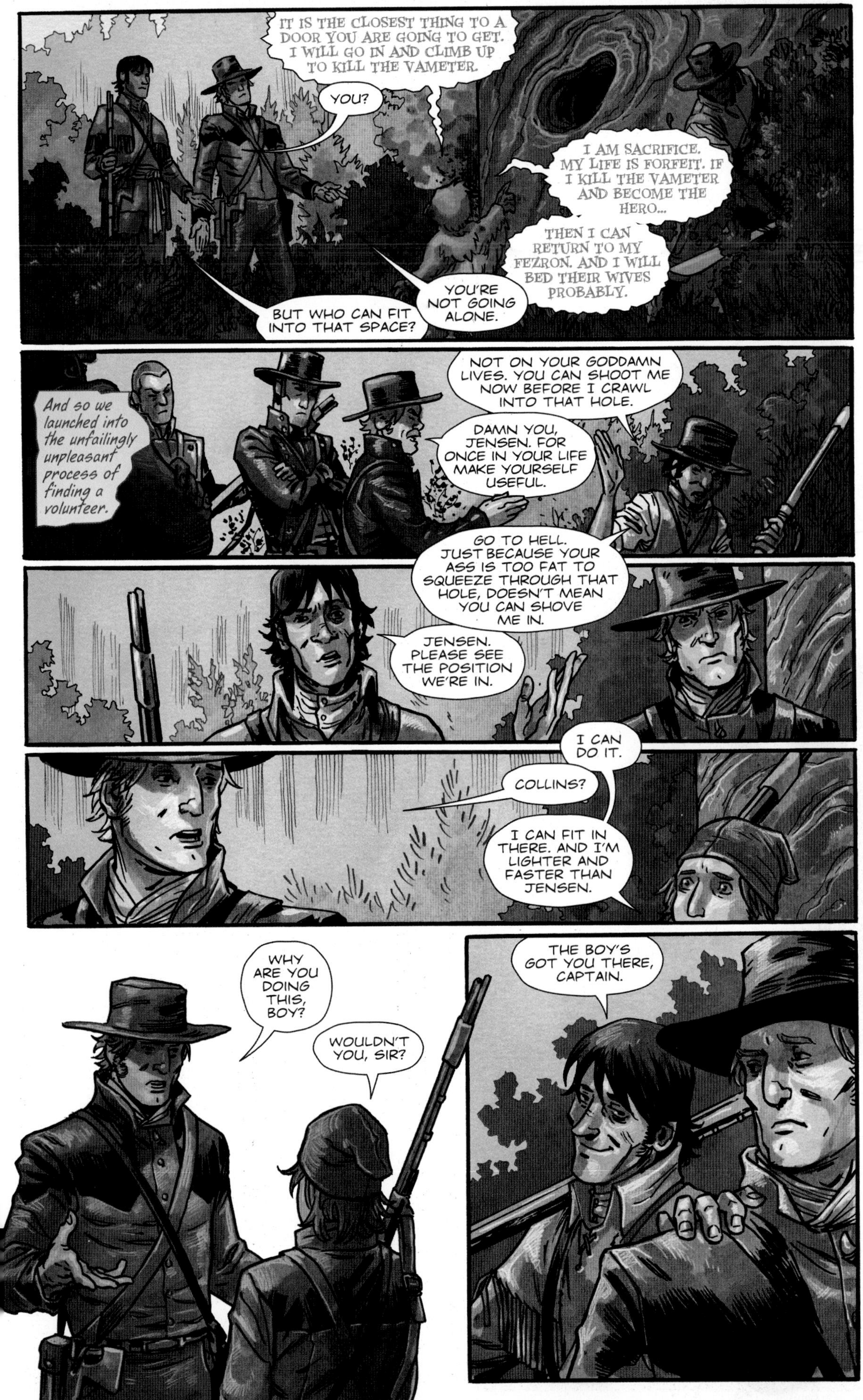
IT IS THE CLOSEST THING TO A DOOR YOU ARE GOING TO GET. I WILL GO IN AND CLIMB UP TO KILL THE VAMETER.
YOU?
I AM SACRIFICE. MY LIFE IS FORFEIT. IF I KILL THE VAMETER AND BECOME THE HERO...
THEN I CAN RETURN TO MY FEZRON. AND I WILL BED THEIR WIVES PROBABLY.
BUT WHO CAN FIT INTO THAT SPACE?
YOU'RE NOT GOING ALONE.
And so we launched into the unfailingly unpleasant process of finding a volunteer.
NOT ON YOUR GODDAMN LIVES. YOU CAN SHOOT ME NOW BEFORE I CRAWL INTO THAT HOLE.
DAMN YOU, JENSEN. FOR ONCE IN YOUR LIFE MAKE YOURSELF USEFUL.
GO TO HELL. JUST BECAUSE YOUR ASS IS TOO FAT TO SQUEEZE THROUGH THAT HOLE, DOESN'T MEAN YOU CAN SHOVE ME IN.
JENSEN. PLEASE SEE THE POSITION WE'RE IN.
I CAN DO IT.
COLLINS?
I CAN FIT IN THERE. AND I'M LIGHTER AND FASTER THAN JENSEN.
WHY ARE YOU DOING THIS, BOY?
WOULDN'T YOU, SIR?
THE BOY'S GOT YOU THERE, CAPTAIN.

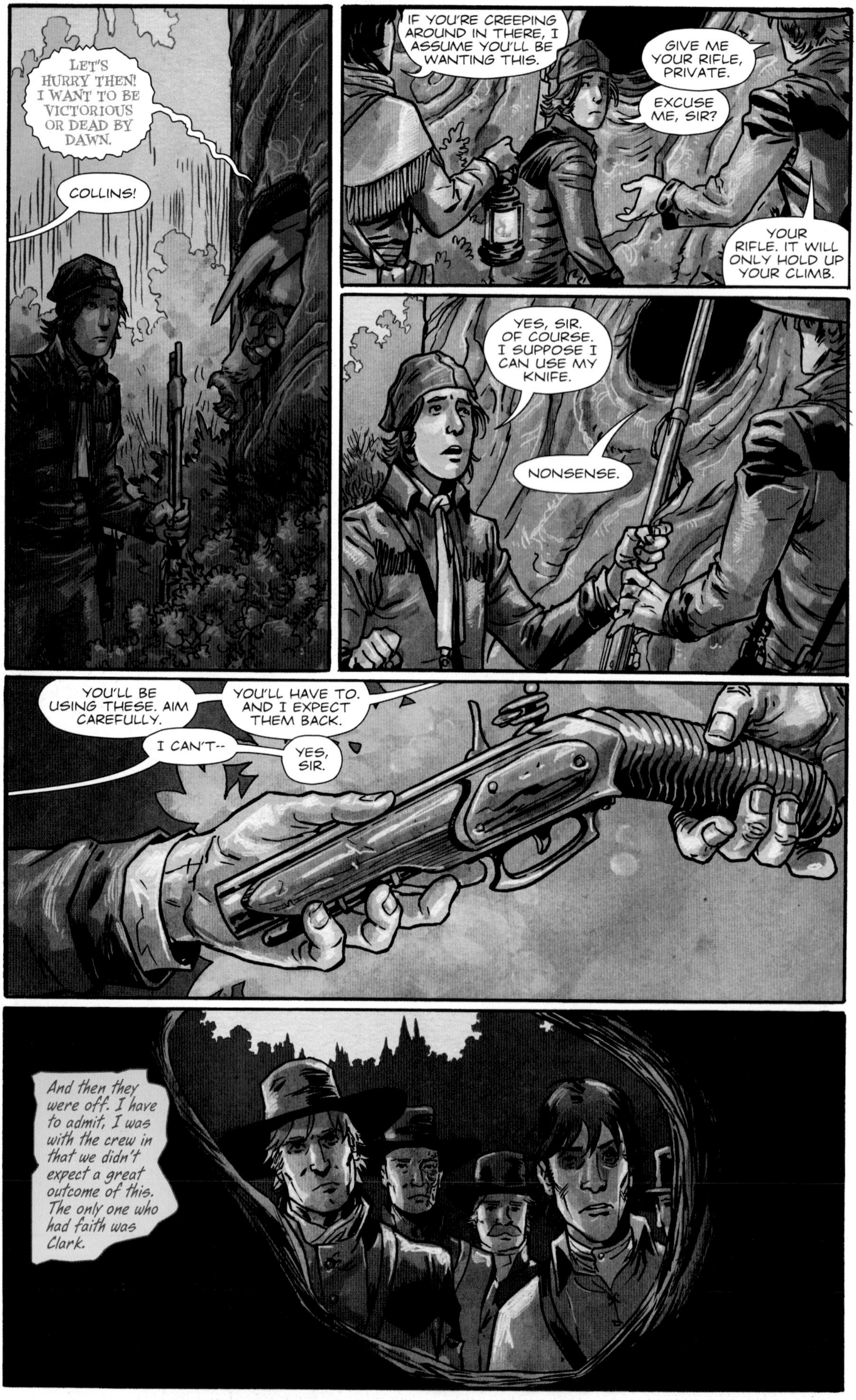
LET'S HURRY THEN! I WANT TO BE VICTORIOUS OR DEAD BY DAWN.
COLLINS!
IF YOU'RE CREEPING AROUND IN THERE, I ASSUME YOU'LL BE WANTING THIS.
GIVE ME YOUR RIFLE, PRIVATE.
EXCUSE ME, SIR?
YOUR RIFLE. IT WILL ONLY HOLD UP YOUR CLIMB.
YES, SIR. OF COURSE. I SUPPOSE I CAN USE MY KNIFE.
NONSENSE.
YOU'LL BE USING THESE. AIM CAREFULLY.
I CAN'T--
YOU'LL HAVE TO. AND I EXPECT THEM BACK.
YES, SIR.
And then they were off. I have to admit, I was with the crew in that we didn't expect a great outcome of this. The only one who had faith was Clark.

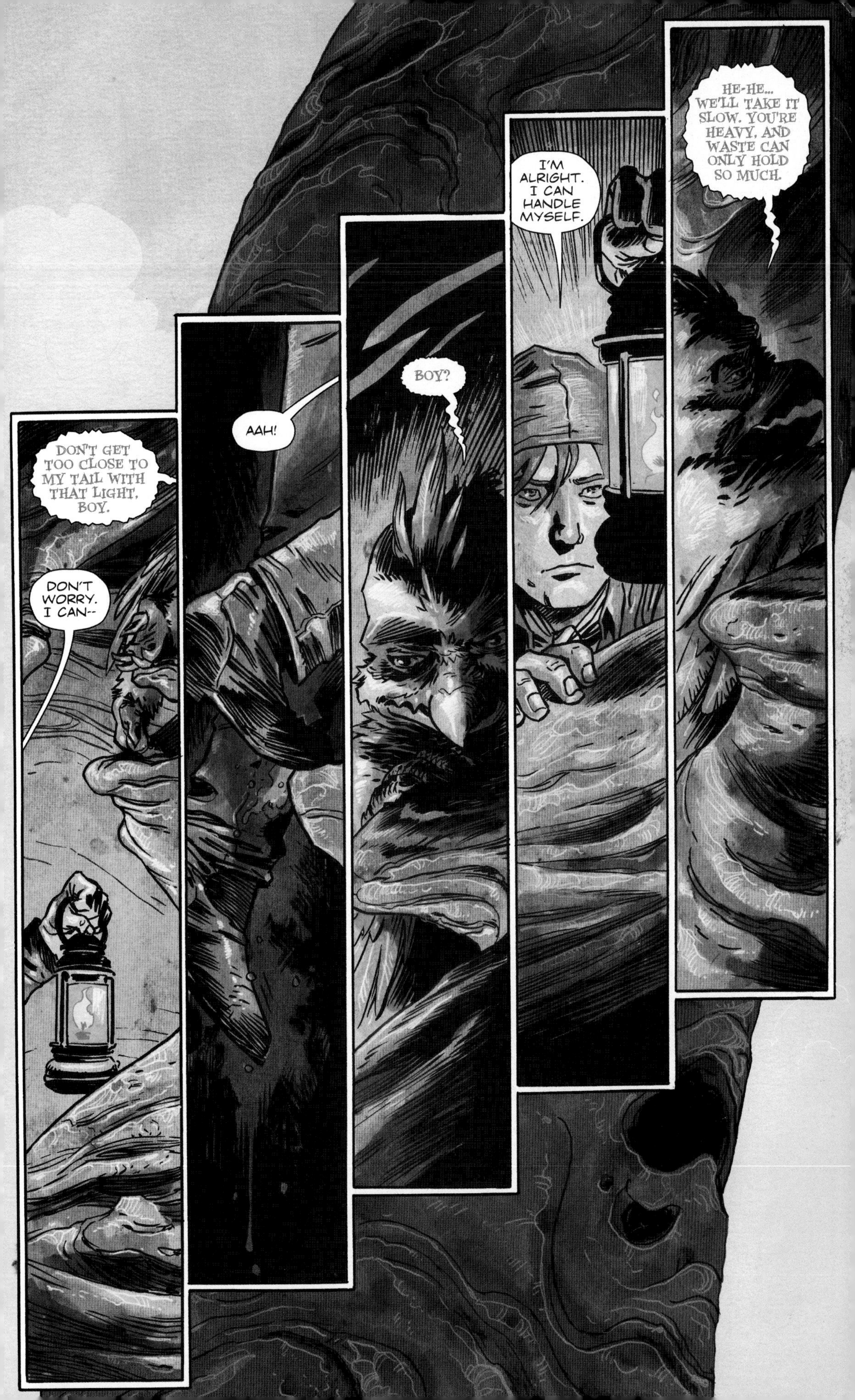
DON'T GET TOO CLOSE TO MY TAIL WITH THAT LIGHT, BOY.
DON'T WORRY. I CAN--
AAH!
BOY?
I'M ALRIGHT. I CAN HANDLE MYSELF.
HE-HE... WE'LL TAKE IT SLOW. YOU'RE HEAVY, AND WASTE CAN ONLY HOLD SO MUCH.

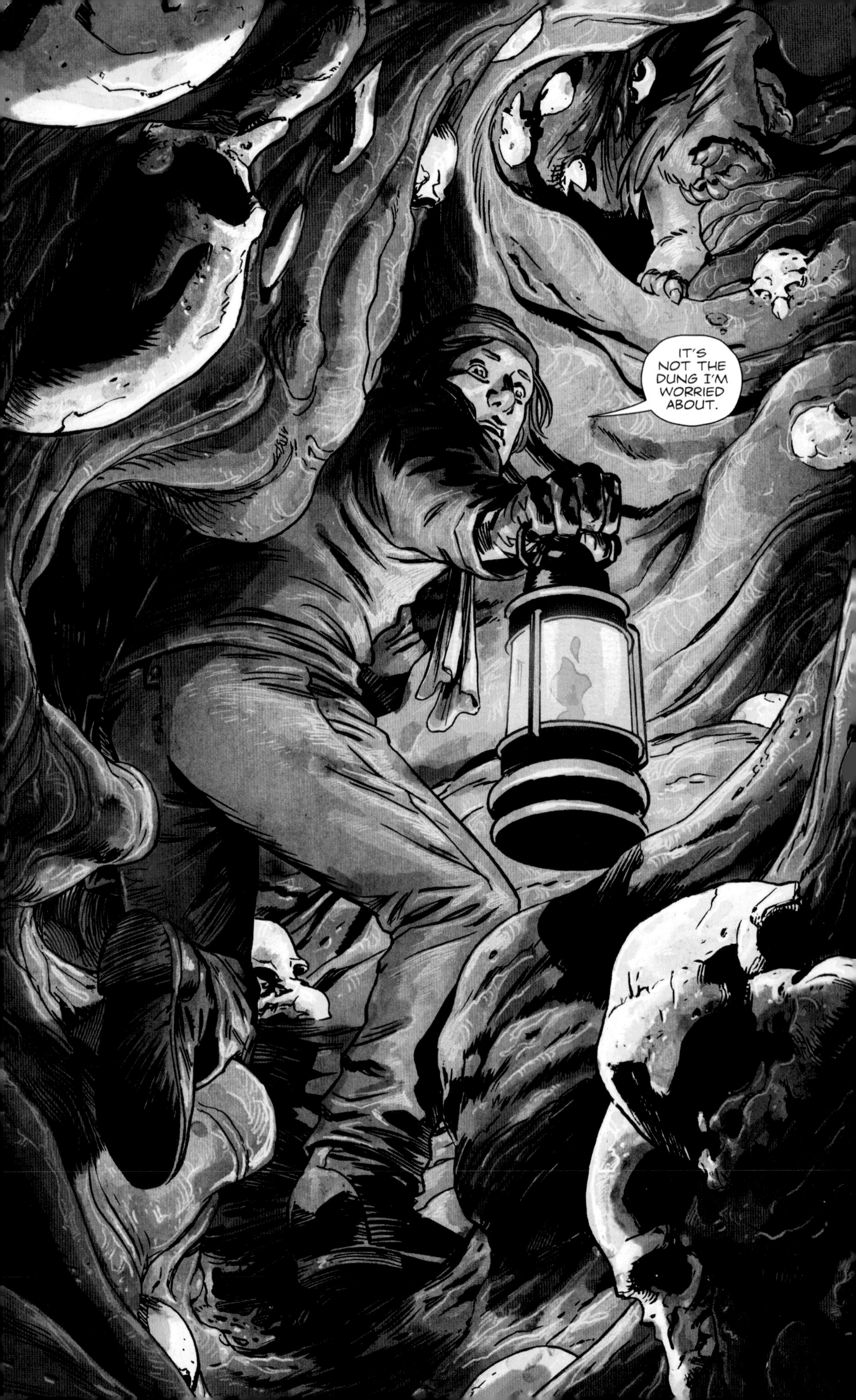
IT'S NOT THE DUNG I'M WORRIED ABOUT.

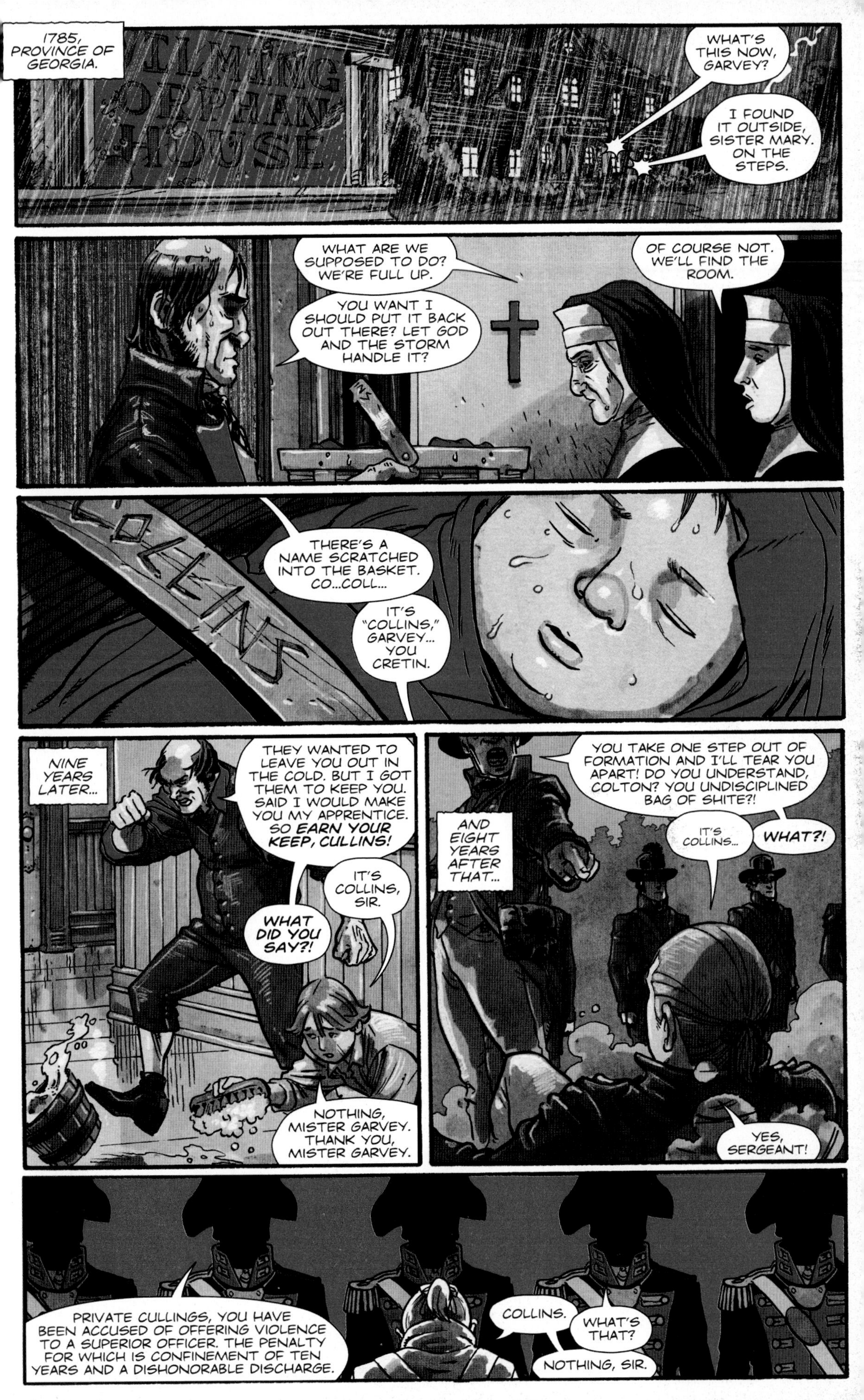

1785, PROVINCE OF GEORGIA.
ORPHAN HOUSE
WHAT'S THIS NOW, GARVEY?
I FOUND IT OUTSIDE, SISTER MARY. ON THE STEPS.
WHAT ARE WE SUPPOSED TO DO? WE'RE FULL UP.
YOU WANT I SHOULD PUT IT BACK OUT THERE? LET GOD AND THE STORM HANDLE IT?
OF COURSE NOT. WE'LL FIND THE ROOM.
COLLINS
THERE'S A NAME SCRATCHED INTO THE BASKET. CO...COLL...
IT'S "COLLINS," GARVEY... YOU CRETIN.
NINE YEARS LATER...
THEY WANTED TO LEAVE YOU OUT IN THE COLD. BUT I GOT THEM TO KEEP YOU. SAID I WOULD MAKE YOU MY APPRENTICE. SO EARN YOUR KEEP, CULLINS!
IT'S COLLINS, SIR.
WHAT DID YOU SAY?!
NOTHING, MISTER GARVEY. THANK YOU, MISTER GARVEY.
AND EIGHT YEARS AFTER THAT...
YOU TAKE ONE STEP OUT OF FORMATION AND I'LL TEAR YOU APART! DO YOU UNDERSTAND, COLTON? YOU UNDISCIPLINED BAG OF SHITE?!
IT'S COLLINS...
WHAT?!
YES, SERGEANT!
PRIVATE CULLINGS, YOU HAVE BEEN ACCUSED OF OFFERING VIOLENCE TO A SUPERIOR OFFICER. THE PENALTY FOR WHICH IS CONFINEMENT OF TEN YEARS AND A DISHONORABLE DISCHARGE.
COLLINS.
WHAT'S THAT?
NOTHING, SIR.

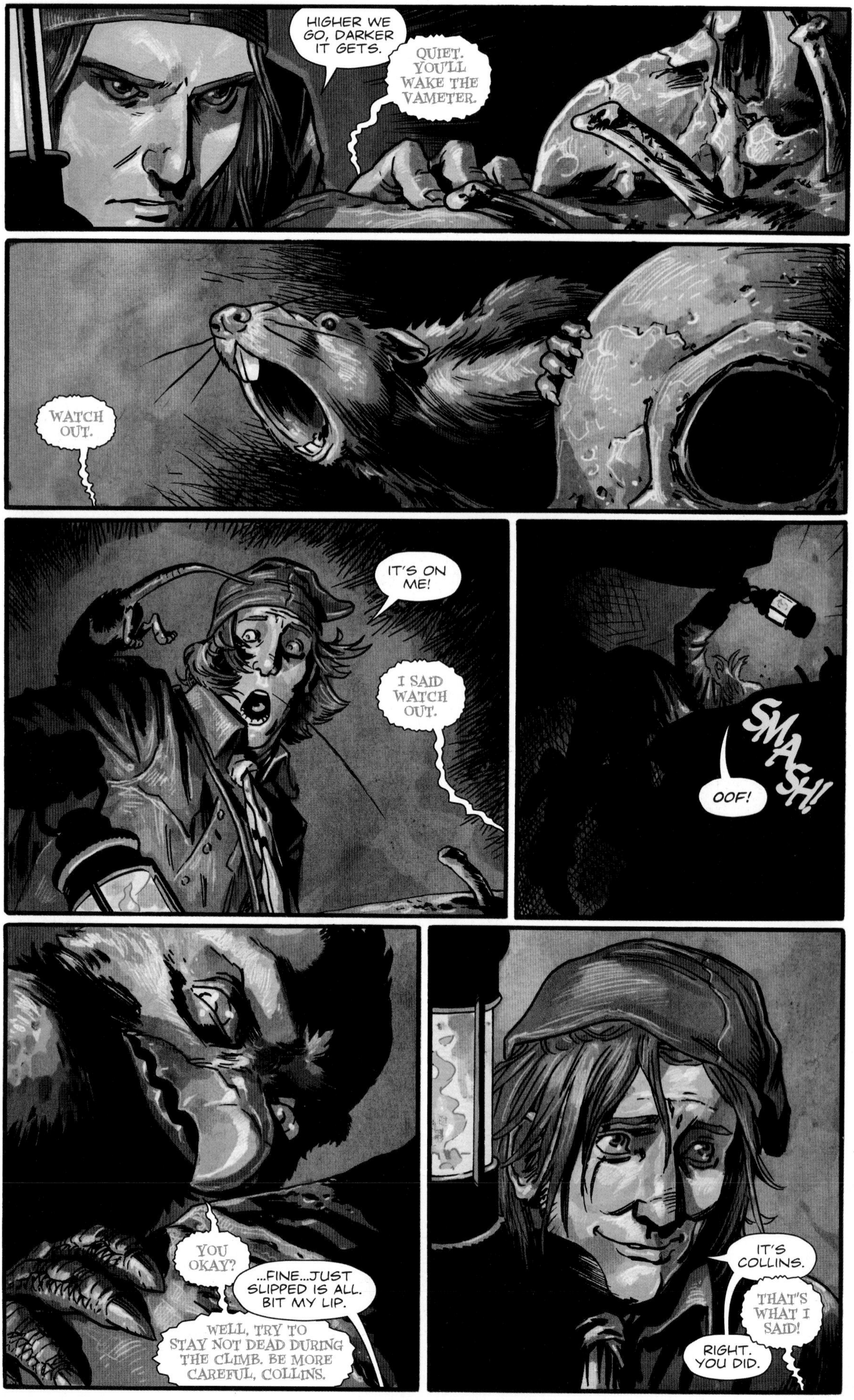
HIGHER WE GO, DARKER IT GETS.
QUIET. YOU'LL WAKE THE VAMETER.
WATCH OUT.
IT'S ON ME!
I SAID WATCH OUT.
SMASH!
OOF!
YOU OKAY?
...FINE...JUST SLIPPED IS ALL. BIT MY LIP.
WELL, TRY TO STAY NOT DEAD DURING THE CLIMB. BE MORE CAREFUL, COLLINS.
IT'S COLLINS.
THAT'S WHAT I SAID!
RIGHT. YOU DID.

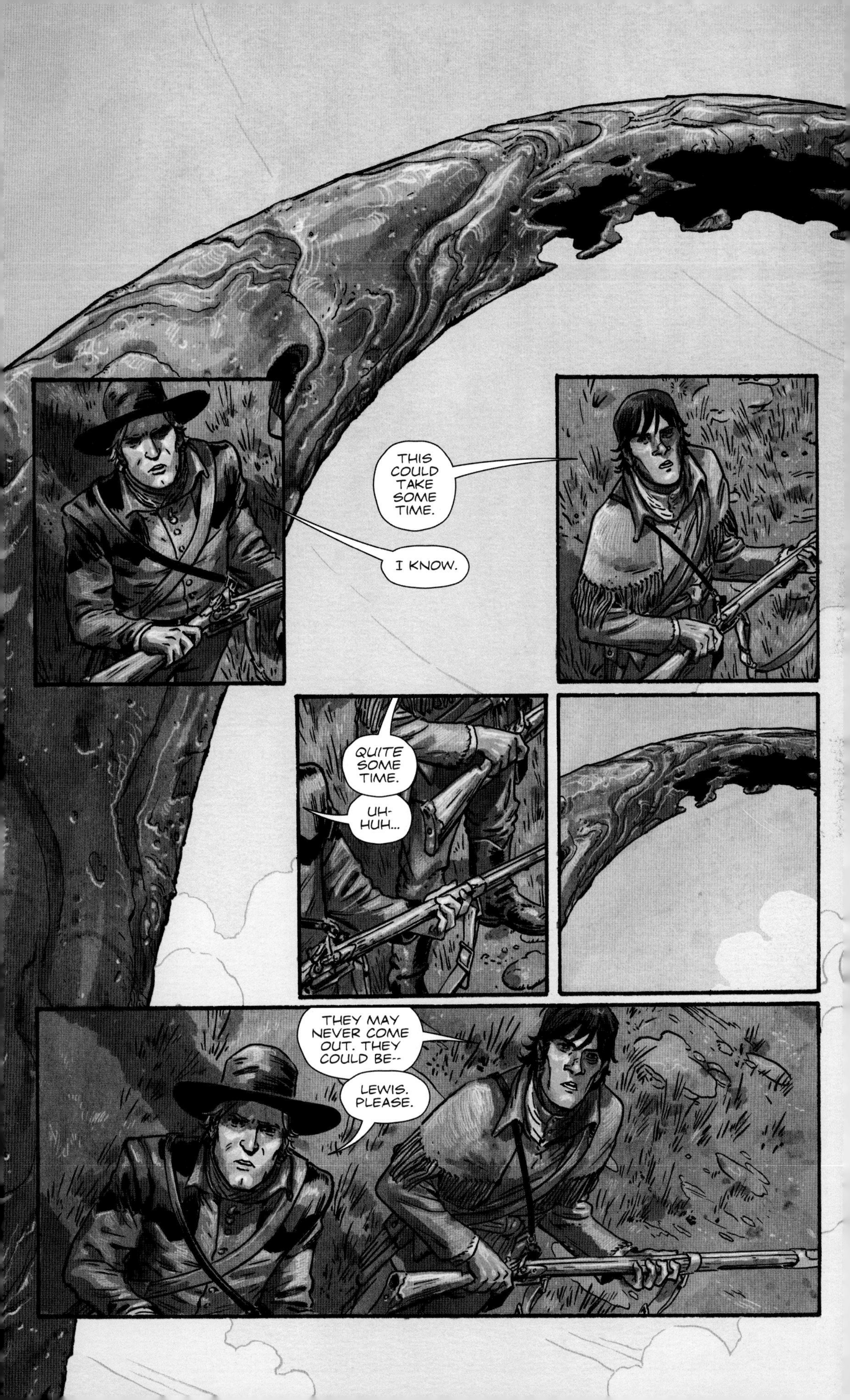
THIS COULD TAKE SOME TIME.
I KNOW.
QUITE SOME TIME.
UH-HUH...
THEY MAY NEVER COME OUT. THEY COULD BE--
LEWIS. PLEASE.

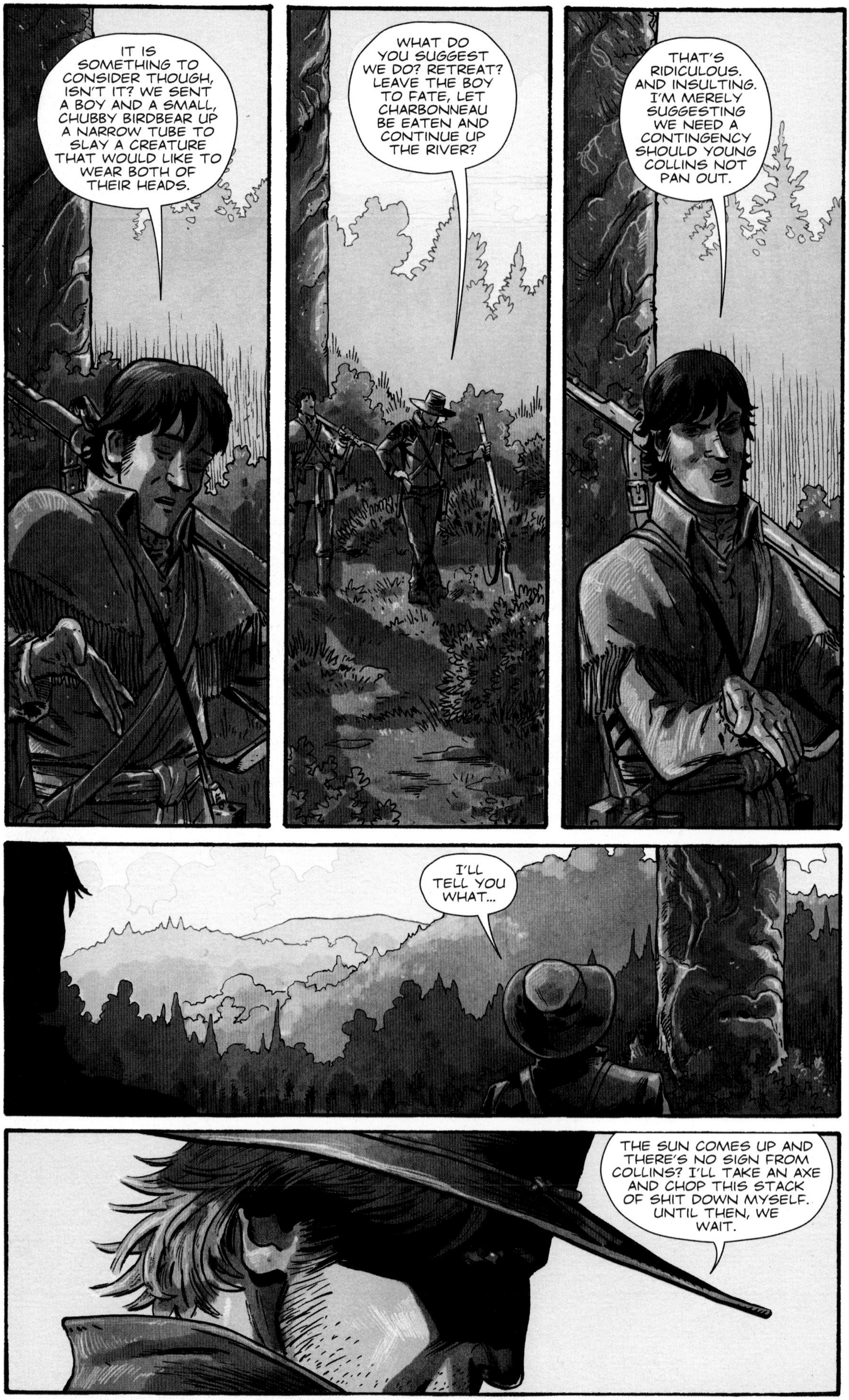
IT IS SOMETHING TO CONSIDER THOUGH, ISN'T IT? WE SENT A BOY AND A SMALL, CHUBBY BIRDBEAR UP A NARROW TUBE TO SLAY A CREATURE THAT WOULD LIKE TO WEAR BOTH OF THEIR HEADS.
WHAT DO YOU SUGGEST WE DO? RETREAT? LEAVE THE BOY TO FATE, LET CHARBONNEAU BE EATEN AND CONTINUE UP THE RIVER?
THAT'S RIDICULOUS. AND INSULTING. I'M MERELY SUGGESTING WE NEED A CONTINGENCY SHOULD YOUNG COLLINS NOT PAN OUT.
I'LL TELL YOU WHAT...
THE SUN COMES UP AND THERE'S NO SIGN FROM COLLINS? I'LL TAKE AN AXE AND CHOP THIS STACK OF SHIT DOWN MYSELF. UNTIL THEN, WE WAIT.

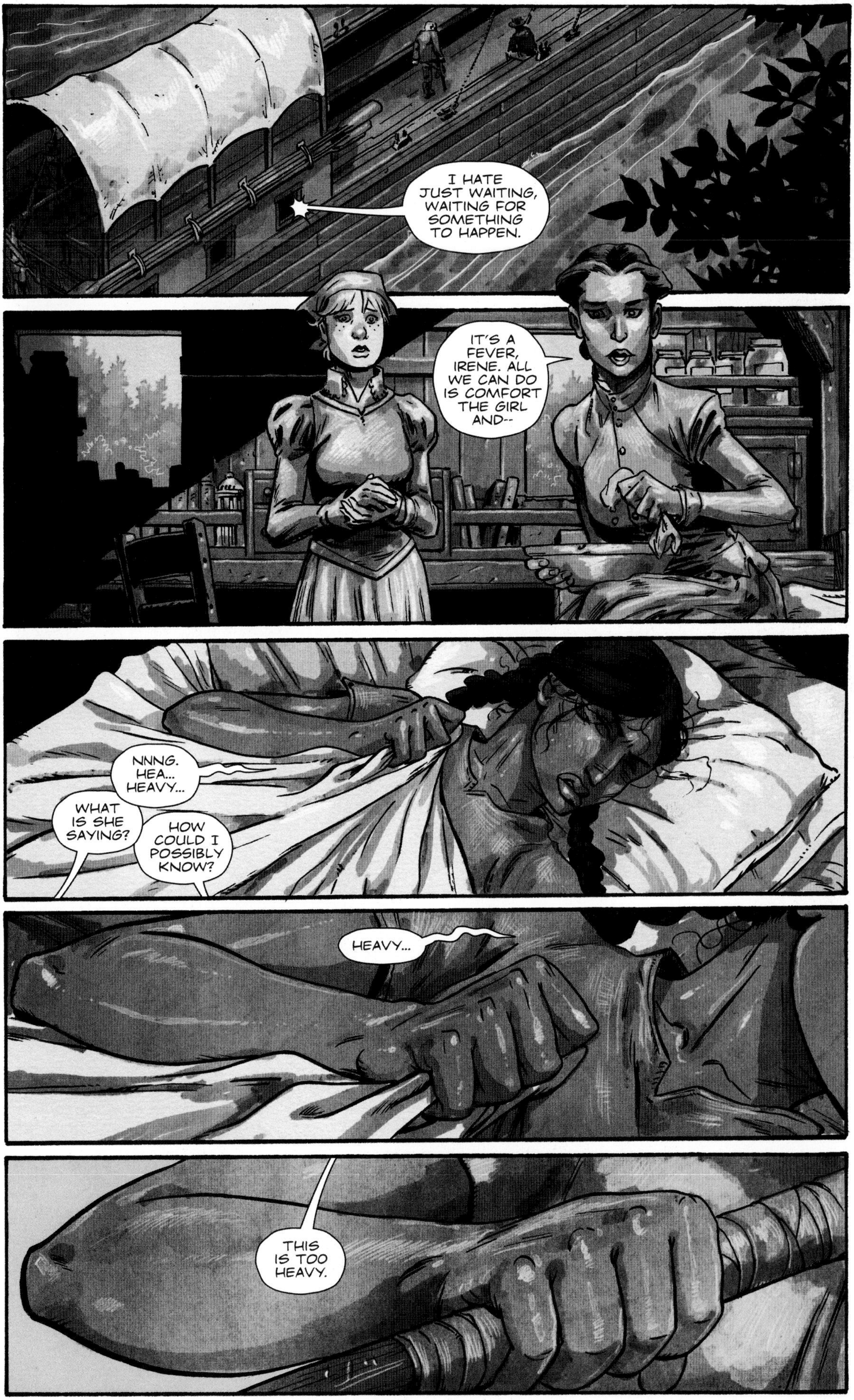
I HATE JUST WAITING, WAITING FOR SOMETHING TO HAPPEN.
IT'S A FEVER, IRENE. ALL WE CAN DO IS COMFORT THE GIRL AND--
NNNG. HEA... HEAVY...
WHAT IS SHE SAYING?
HOW COULD I POSSIBLY KNOW?
HEAVY...
THIS IS TOO HEAVY.

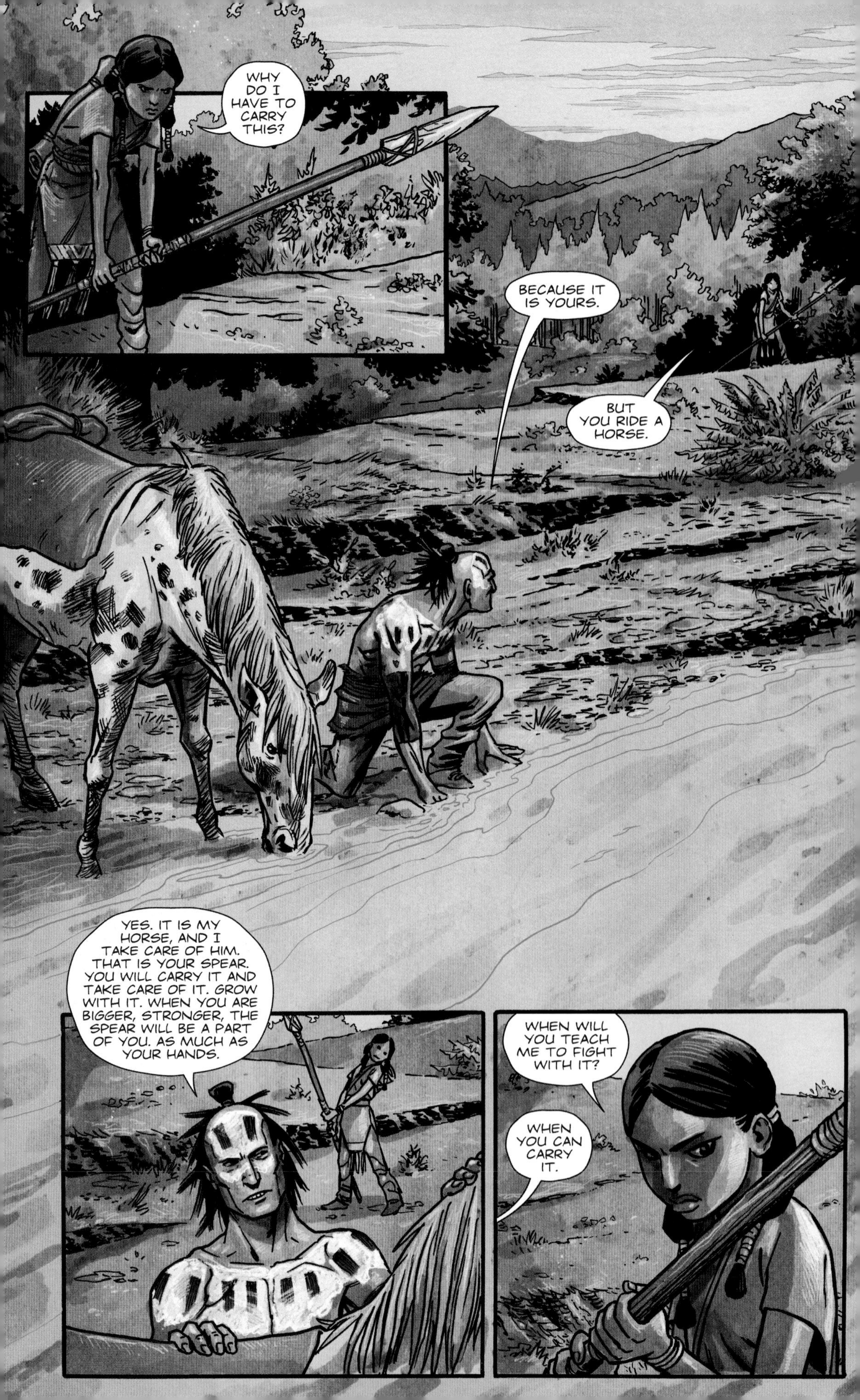
WHY DO I HAVE TO CARRY THIS?
BECAUSE IT IS YOURS.
BUT YOU RIDE A HORSE.
YES. IT IS MY HORSE, AND I TAKE CARE OF HIM. THAT IS YOUR SPEAR. YOU WILL CARRY IT AND TAKE CARE OF IT. GROW WITH IT. WHEN YOU ARE BIGGER, STRONGER, THE SPEAR WILL BE A PART OF YOU. AS MUCH AS YOUR HANDS.
WHEN WILL YOU TEACH ME TO FIGHT WITH IT?
WHEN YOU CAN CARRY IT.

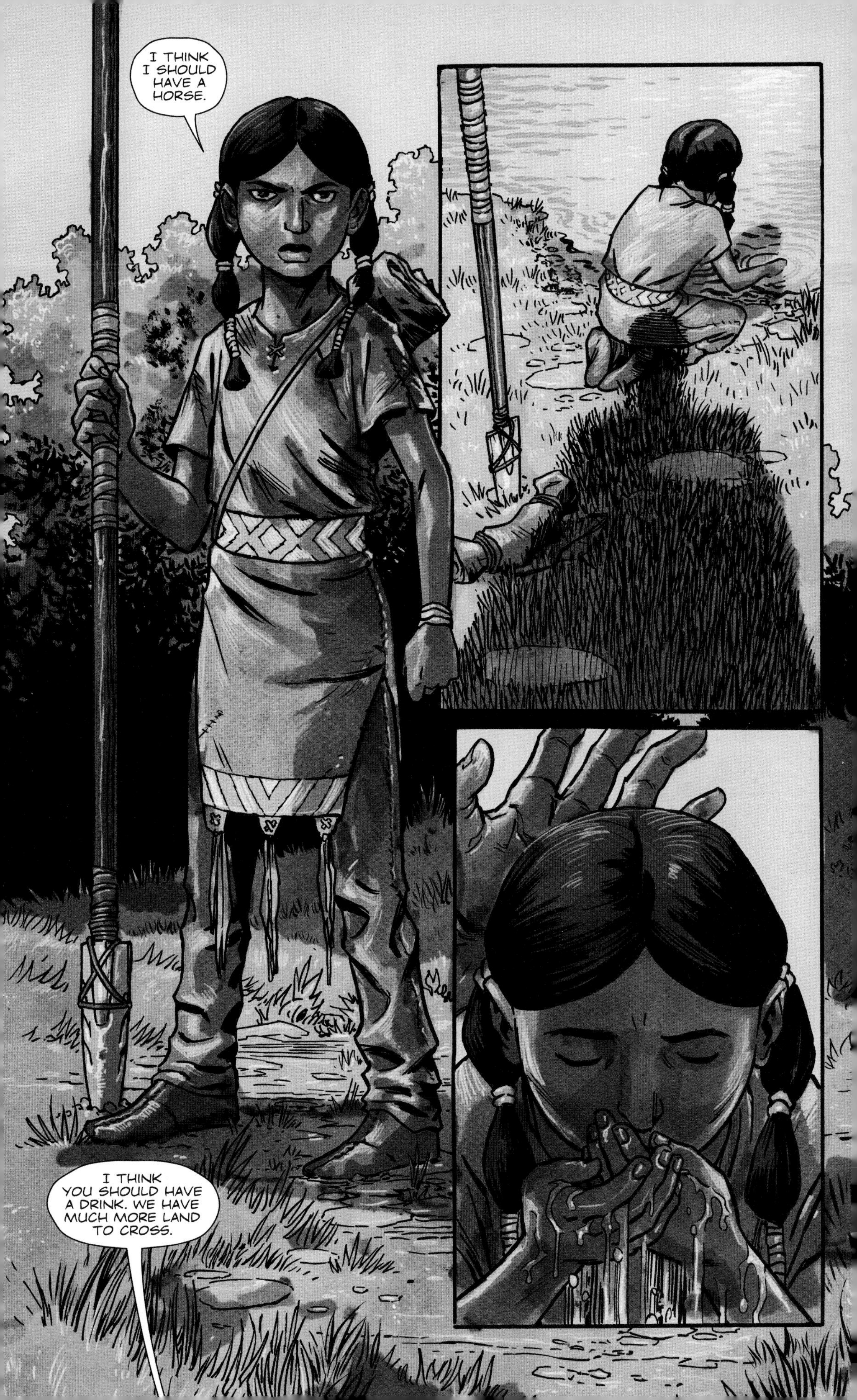
I THINK I SHOULD HAVE A HORSE.
I THINK YOU SHOULD HAVE A DRINK. WE HAVE MUCH MORE LAND TO CROSS.

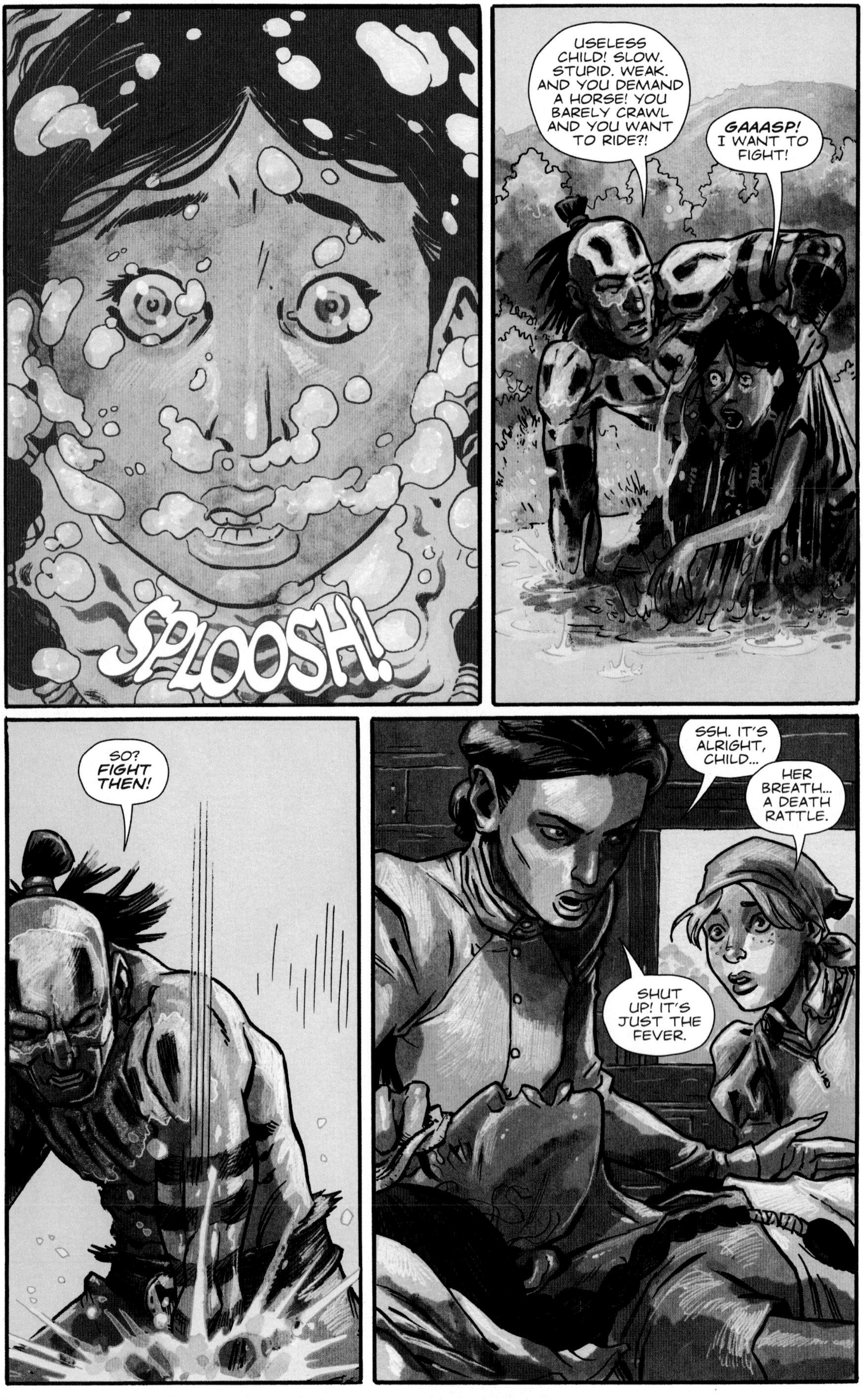
SPLOOSH!
USELESS CHILD! SLOW. STUPID. WEAK. AND YOU DEMAND A HORSE! YOU BARELY CRAWL AND YOU WANT TO RIDE?!
GAAASP! I WANT TO FIGHT!
SO? FIGHT THEN!
SSH. IT'S ALRIGHT, CHILD...
HER BREATH... A DEATH RATTLE.
SHUT UP! IT'S JUST THE FEVER.

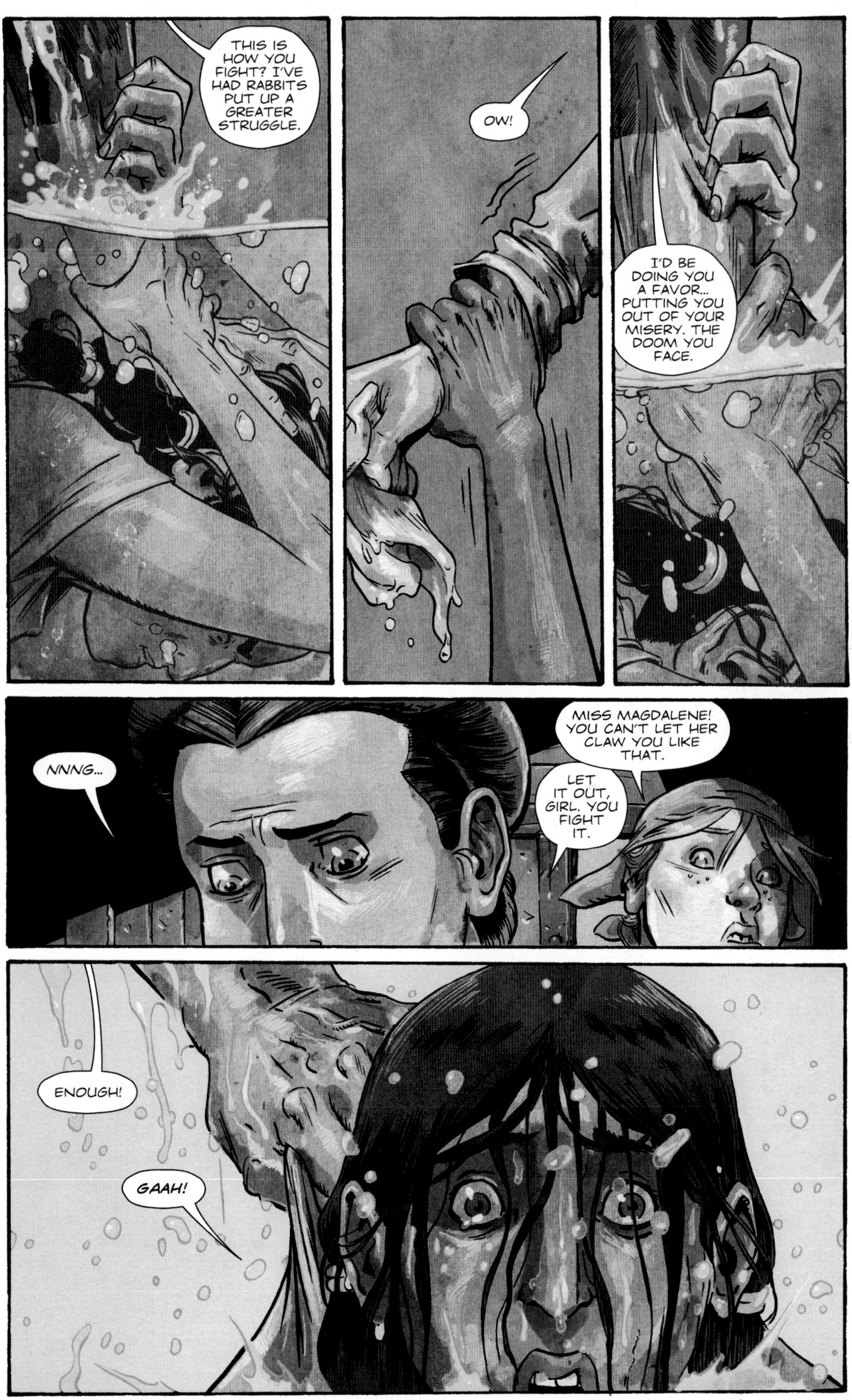
THIS IS HOW YOU FIGHT? I'VE HAD RABBITS PUT UP A GREATER STRUGGLE.
OW!
I'D BE DOING YOU A FAVOR... PUTTING YOU OUT OF YOUR MISERY. THE DOOM YOU FACE.
NNNG...
MISS MAGDALENE! YOU CAN'T LET HER CLAW YOU LIKE THAT.
LET IT OUT, GIRL. YOU FIGHT IT.
ENOUGH!
GAAH!

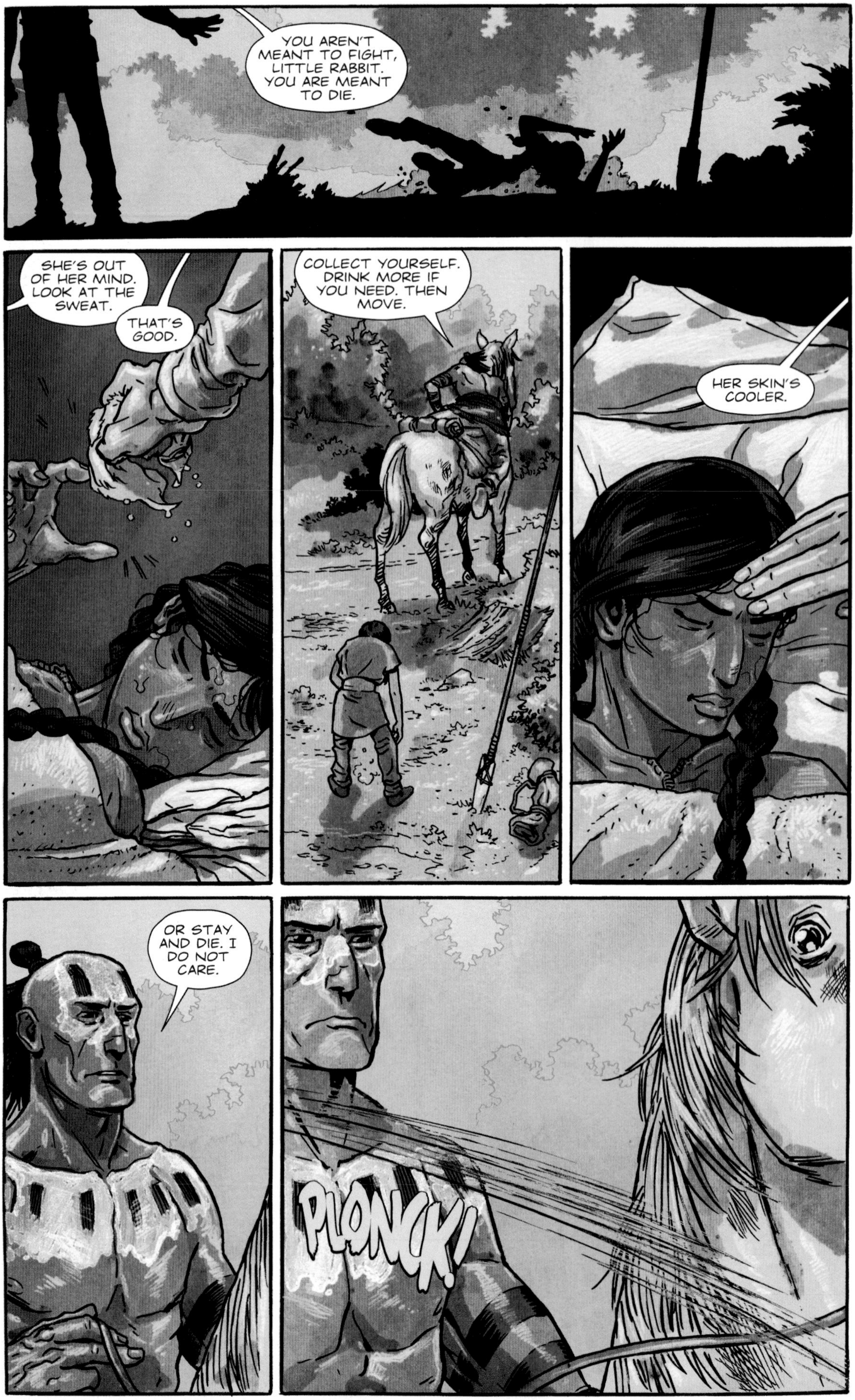
YOU AREN'T MEANT TO FIGHT, LITTLE RABBIT. YOU ARE MEANT TO DIE.
SHE'S OUT OF HER MIND. LOOK AT THE SWEAT.
THAT'S GOOD.
COLLECT YOURSELF. DRINK MORE IF YOU NEED. THEN MOVE.
HER SKIN'S COOLER.
OR STAY AND DIE. I DO NOT CARE.
PLONCK!

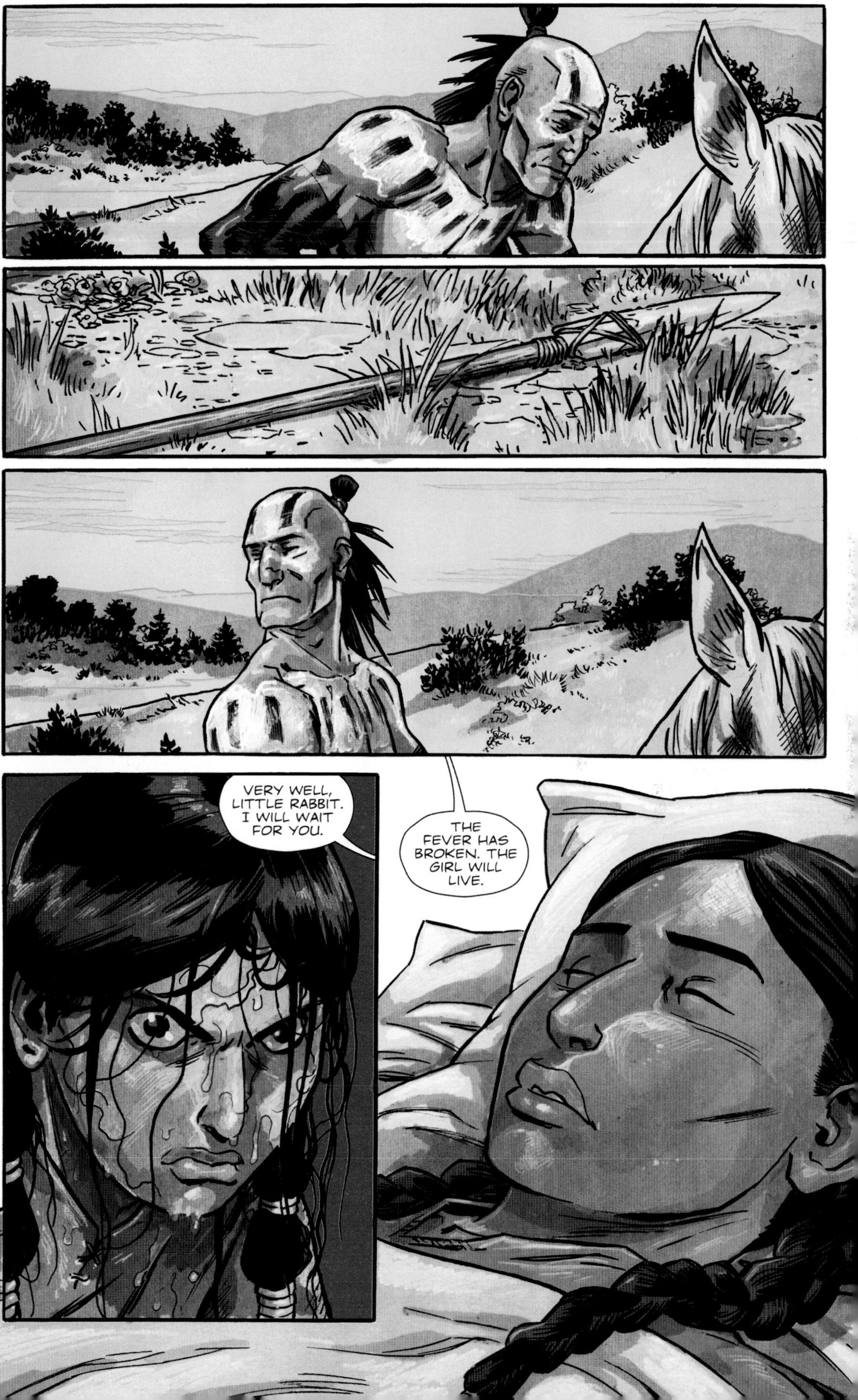
VERY WELL, LITTLE RABBIT. I WILL WAIT FOR YOU.
THE FEVER HAS BROKEN. THE GIRL WILL LIVE.

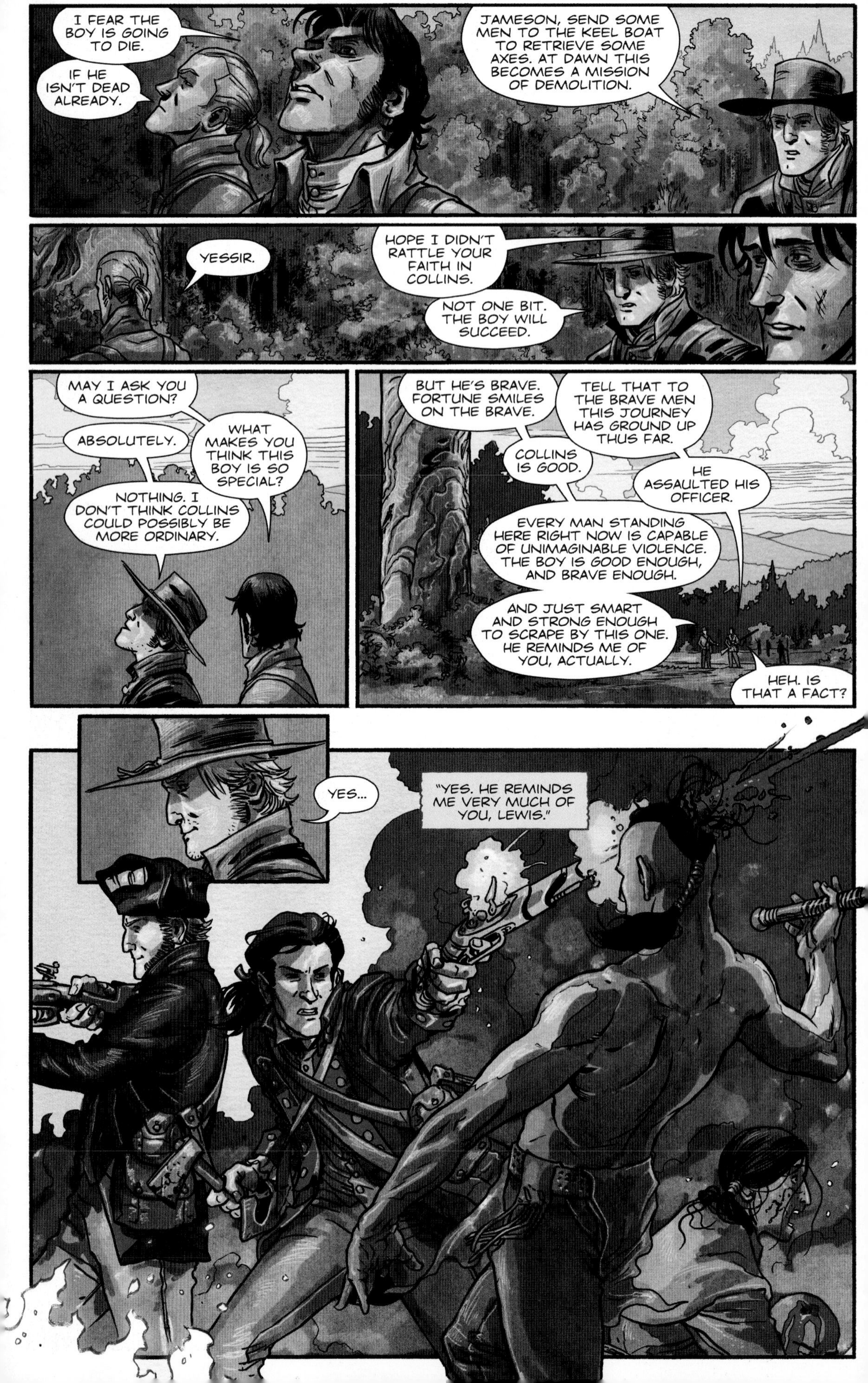
I FEAR THE BOY IS GOING TO DIE.
IF HE ISN'T DEAD ALREADY.
JAMESON, SEND SOME MEN TO THE KEEL BOAT TO RETRIEVE SOME AXES. AT DAWN THIS BECOMES A MISSION OF DEMOLITION.
YESSIR.
HOPE I DIDN'T RATTLE YOUR FAITH IN COLLINS.
NOT ONE BIT. THE BOY WILL SUCCEED.
MAY I ASK YOU A QUESTION?
ABSOLUTELY.
WHAT MAKES YOU THINK THIS BOY IS SO SPECIAL?
NOTHING. I DON'T THINK COLLINS COULD POSSIBLY BE MORE ORDINARY.
BUT HE'S BRAVE. FORTUNE SMILES ON THE BRAVE.
TELL THAT TO THE BRAVE MEN THIS JOURNEY HAS GROUND UP THUS FAR.
COLLINS IS GOOD.
HE ASSAULTED HIS OFFICER.
EVERY MAN STANDING HERE RIGHT NOW IS CAPABLE OF UNIMAGINABLE VIOLENCE. THE BOY IS GOOD ENOUGH, AND BRAVE ENOUGH.
AND JUST SMART AND STRONG ENOUGH TO SCRAPE BY THIS ONE. HE REMINDS ME OF YOU, ACTUALLY.
HEH. IS THAT A FACT?
YES...
"YES. HE REMINDS ME VERY MUCH OF YOU, LEWIS."

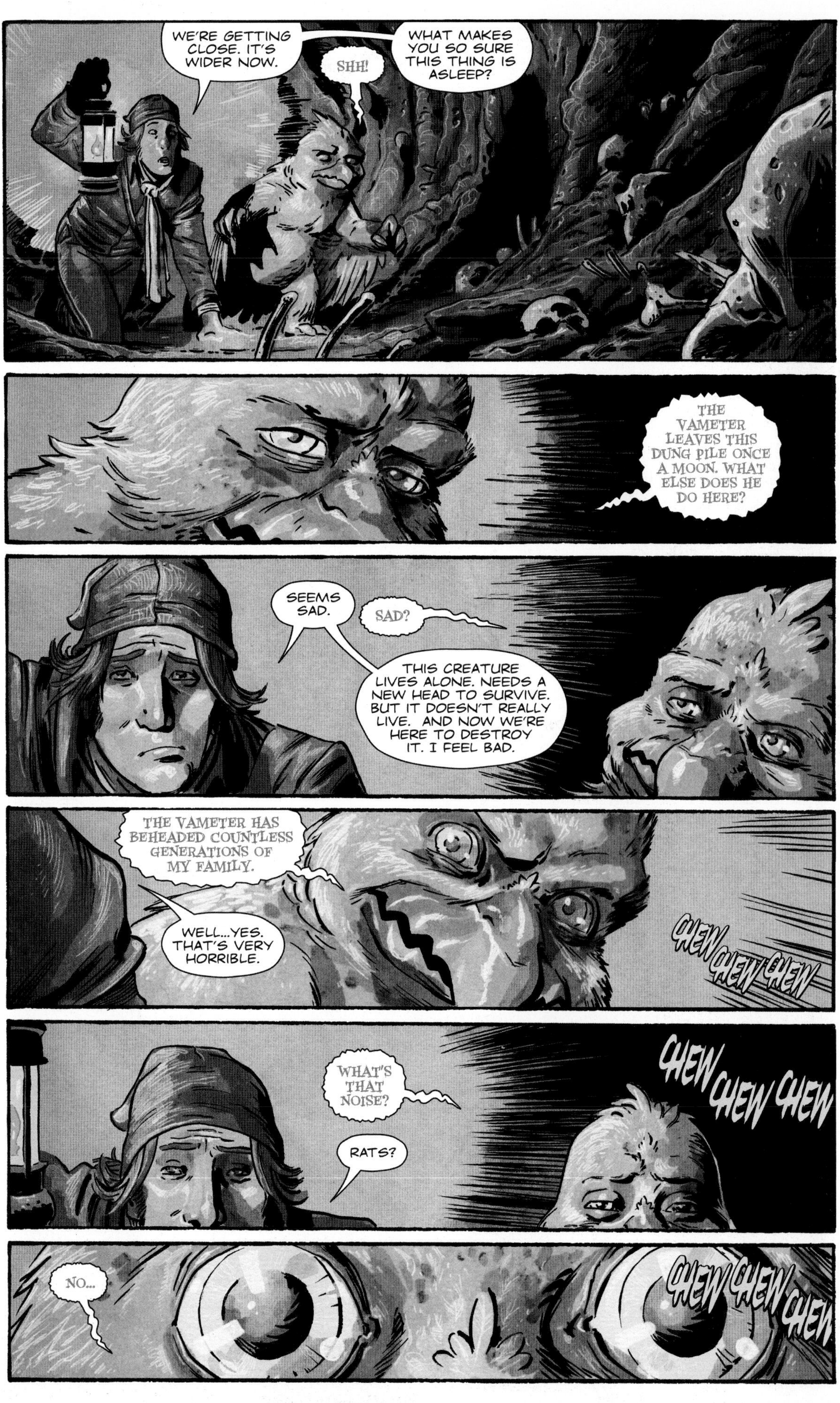
WE'RE GETTING CLOSE. IT'S WIDER NOW.
SHH!
WHAT MAKES YOU SO SURE THIS THING IS ASLEEP?
THE VAMETER LEAVES THIS DUNG PILE ONCE A MOON. WHAT ELSE DOES HE DO HERE?
SEEMS SAD.
SAD?
THIS CREATURE LIVES ALONE. NEEDS A NEW HEAD TO SURVIVE. BUT IT DOESN'T REALLY LIVE. AND NOW WE'RE HERE TO DESTROY IT. I FEEL BAD.
THE VAMETER HAS BEHEADED COUNTLESS GENERATIONS OF MY FAMILY.
WELL...YES. THAT'S VERY HORRIBLE.
CHEW CHEW CHEW
WHAT'S THAT NOISE?
RATS?
CHEW CHEW CHEW
NO...
CHEW CHEW CHEW

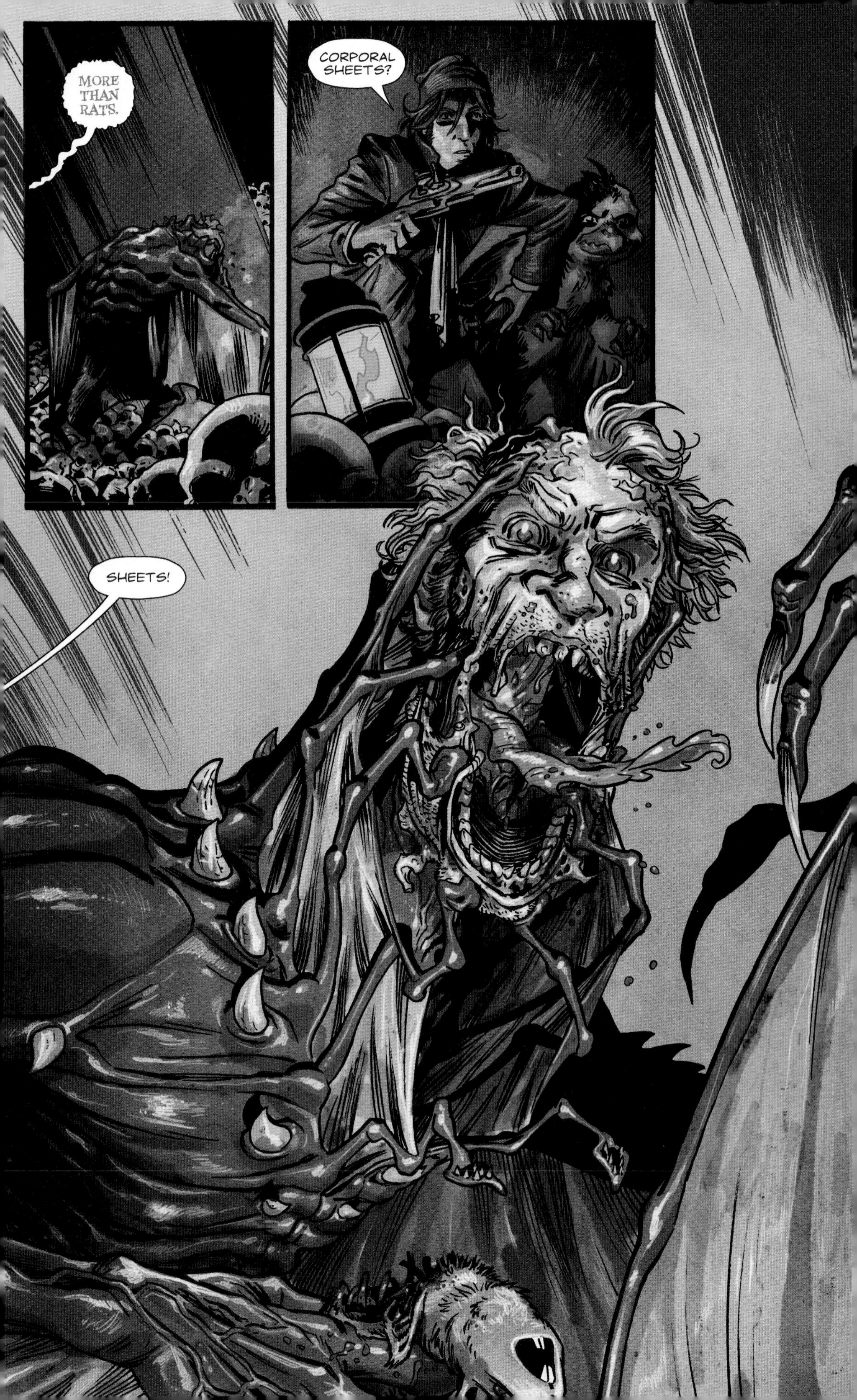
MORE THAN RATS.
CORPORAL SHEETS?
SHEETS!

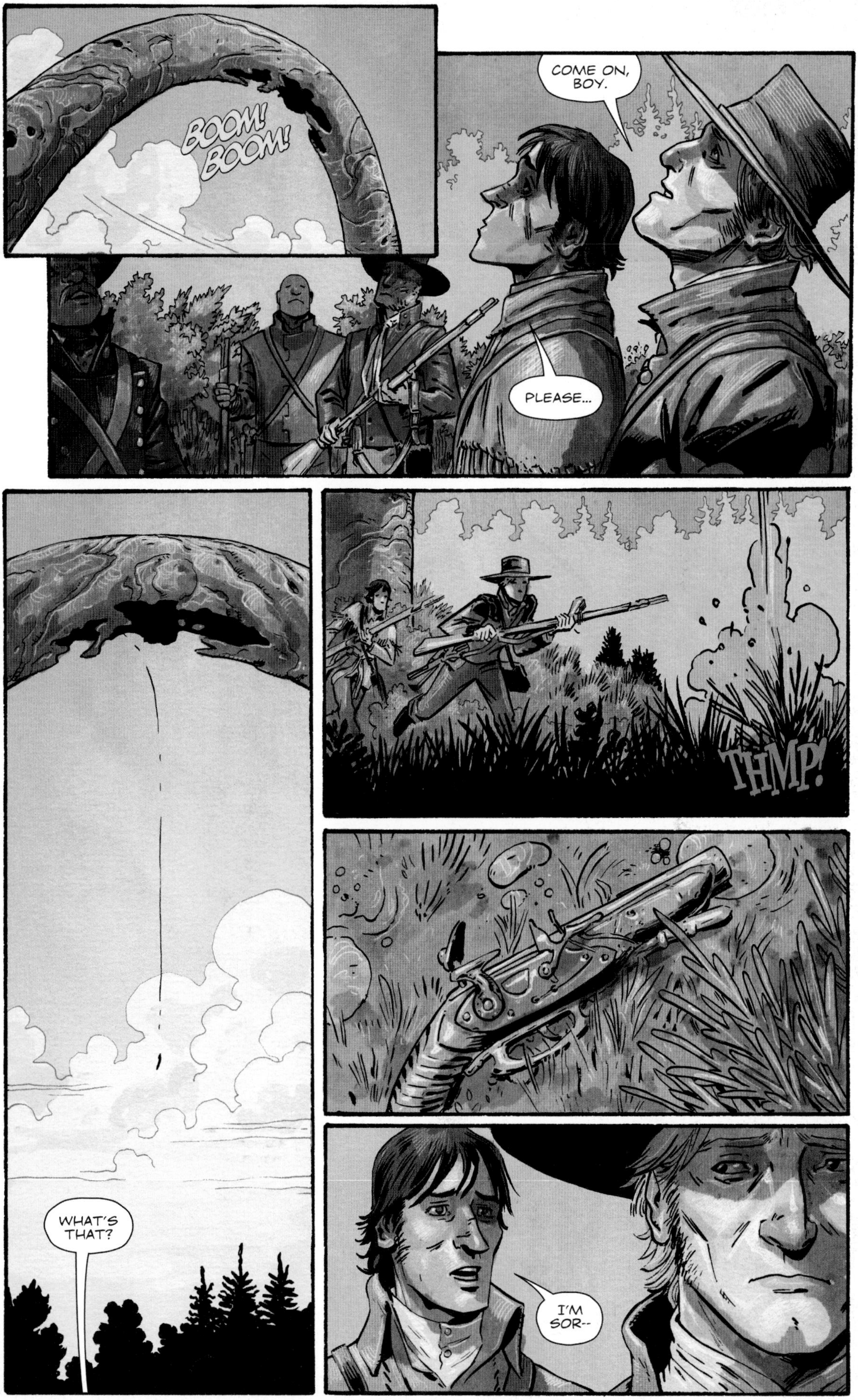
BOOM!
BOOM!
COME ON, BOY.
PLEASE...
WHAT'S THAT?
THMP!
I'M SOR--

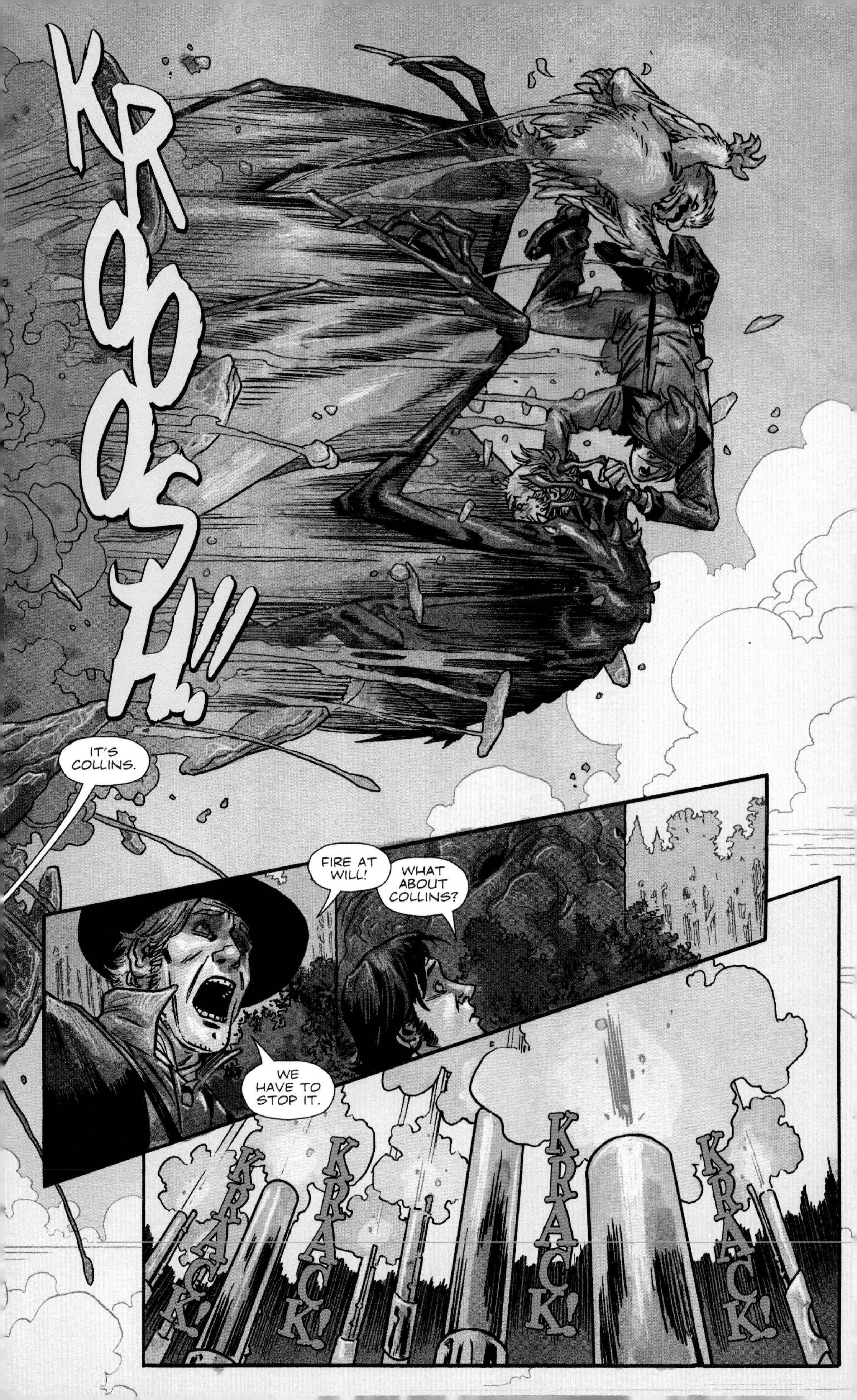
KROOSH!!
IT'S COLLINS.
FIRE AT WILL!
WHAT ABOUT COLLINS?
WE HAVE TO STOP IT.
KRACK!
KRACK!
KRACK!
KRACK!

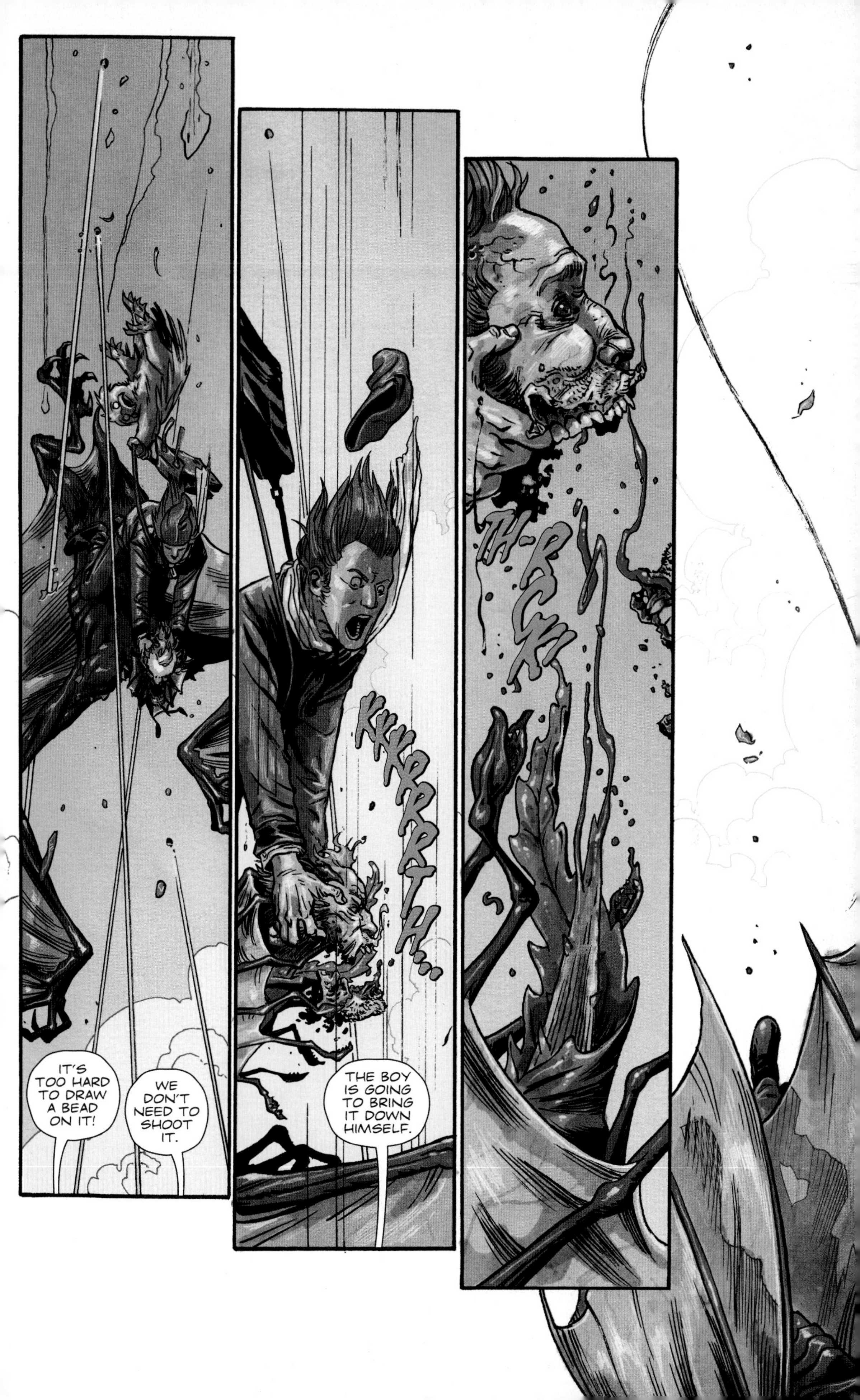
IT'S TOO HARD TO DRAW A BEAD ON IT!
WE DON'T NEED TO SHOOT IT.
KKKRRRRTH...
THE BOY IS GOING TO BRING IT DOWN HIMSELF.
TH-RCK!

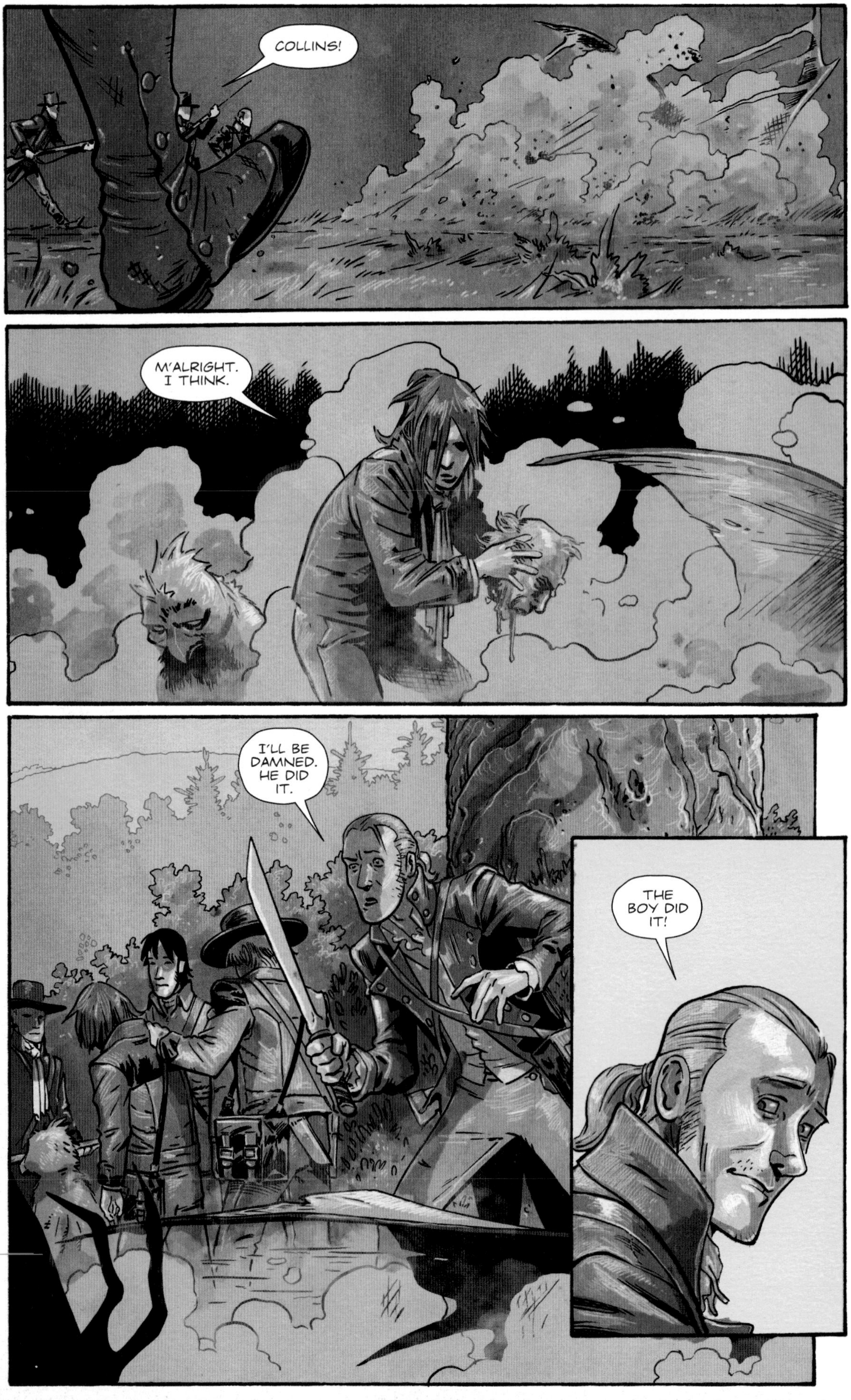
COLLINS!
M'ALRIGHT. I THINK.
I'LL BE DAMNED. HE DID IT.
THE BOY DID IT!

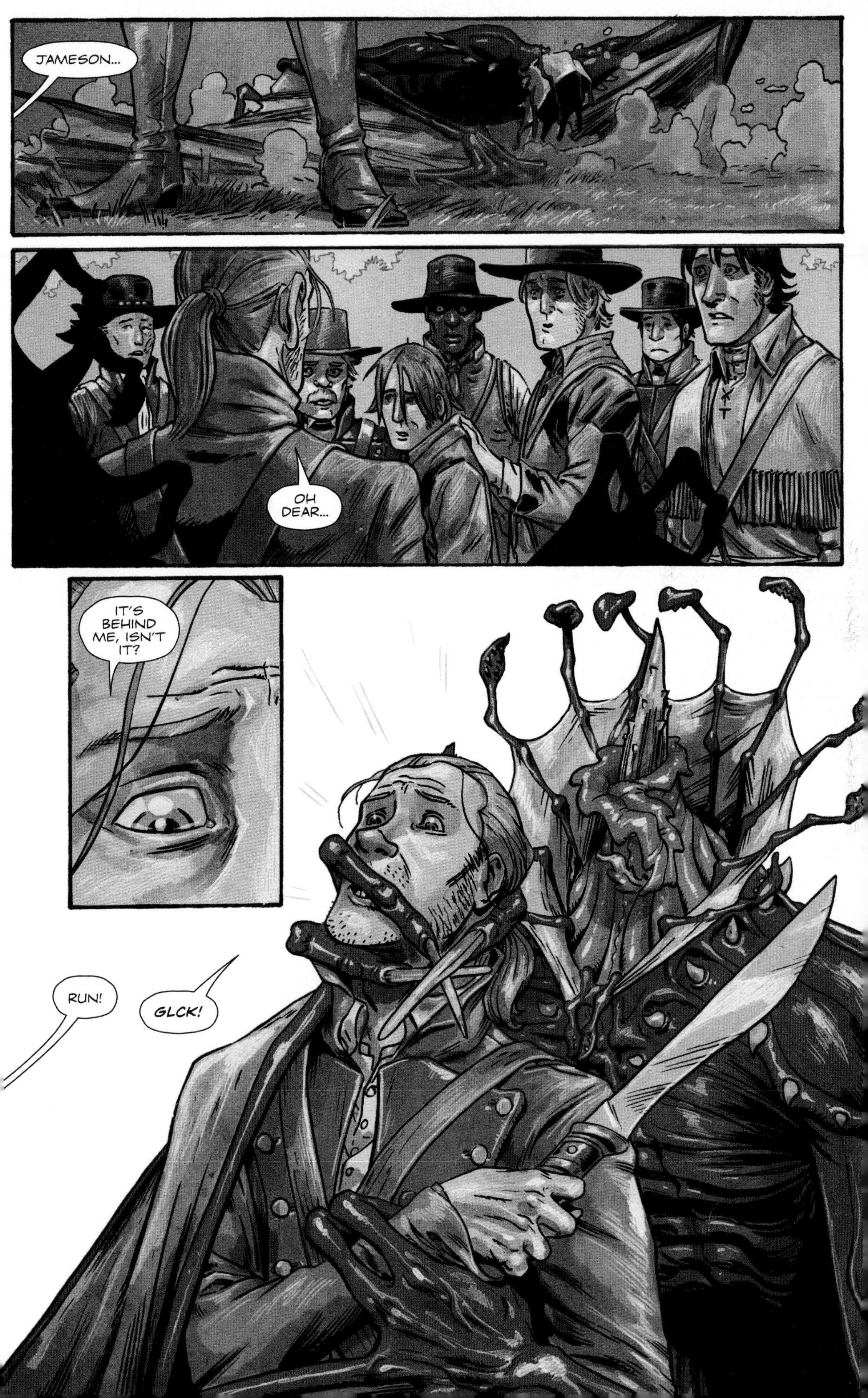
JAMESON...
OH DEAR...
IT'S BEHIND ME, ISN'T IT?
RUN!
GLCK!

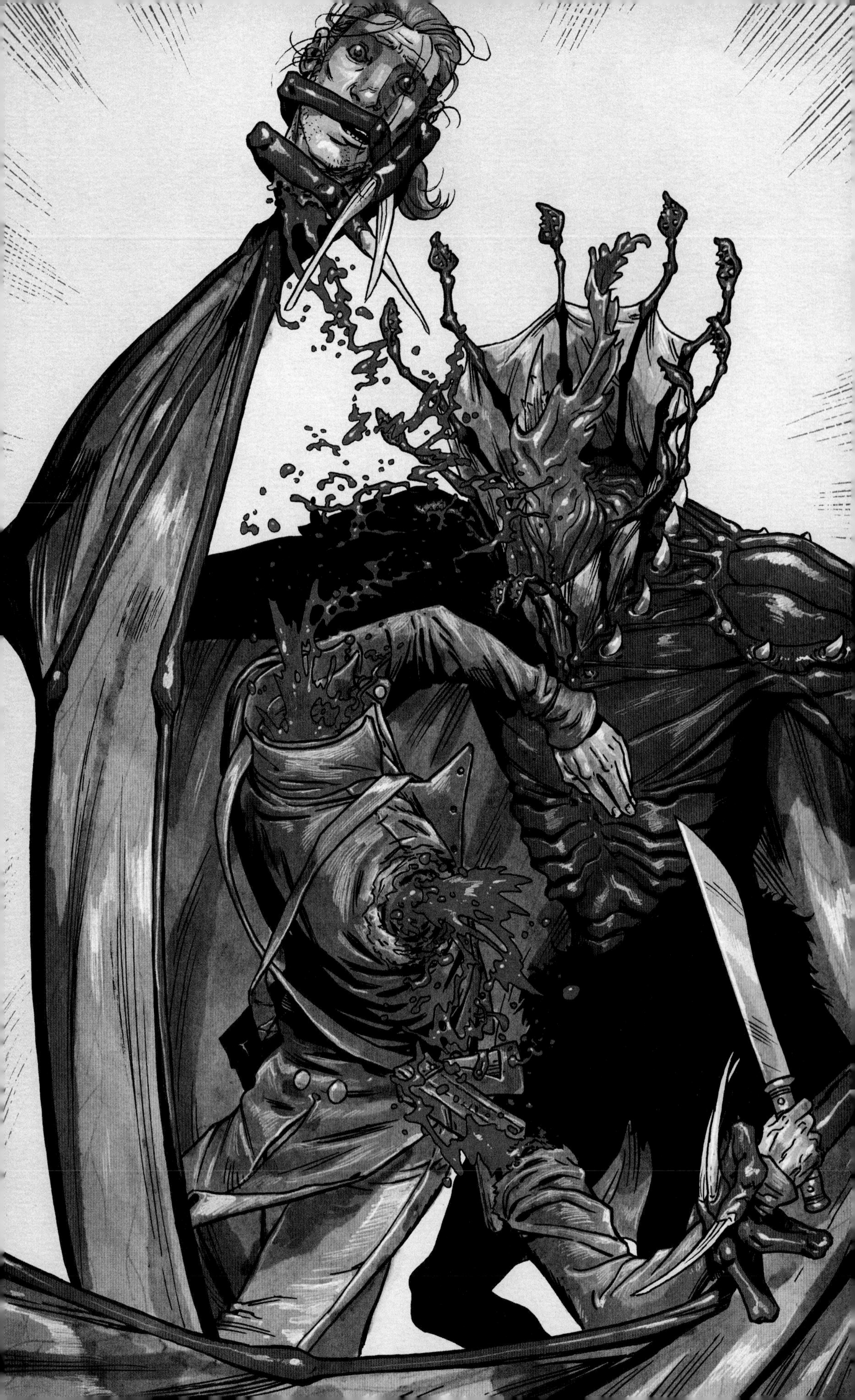

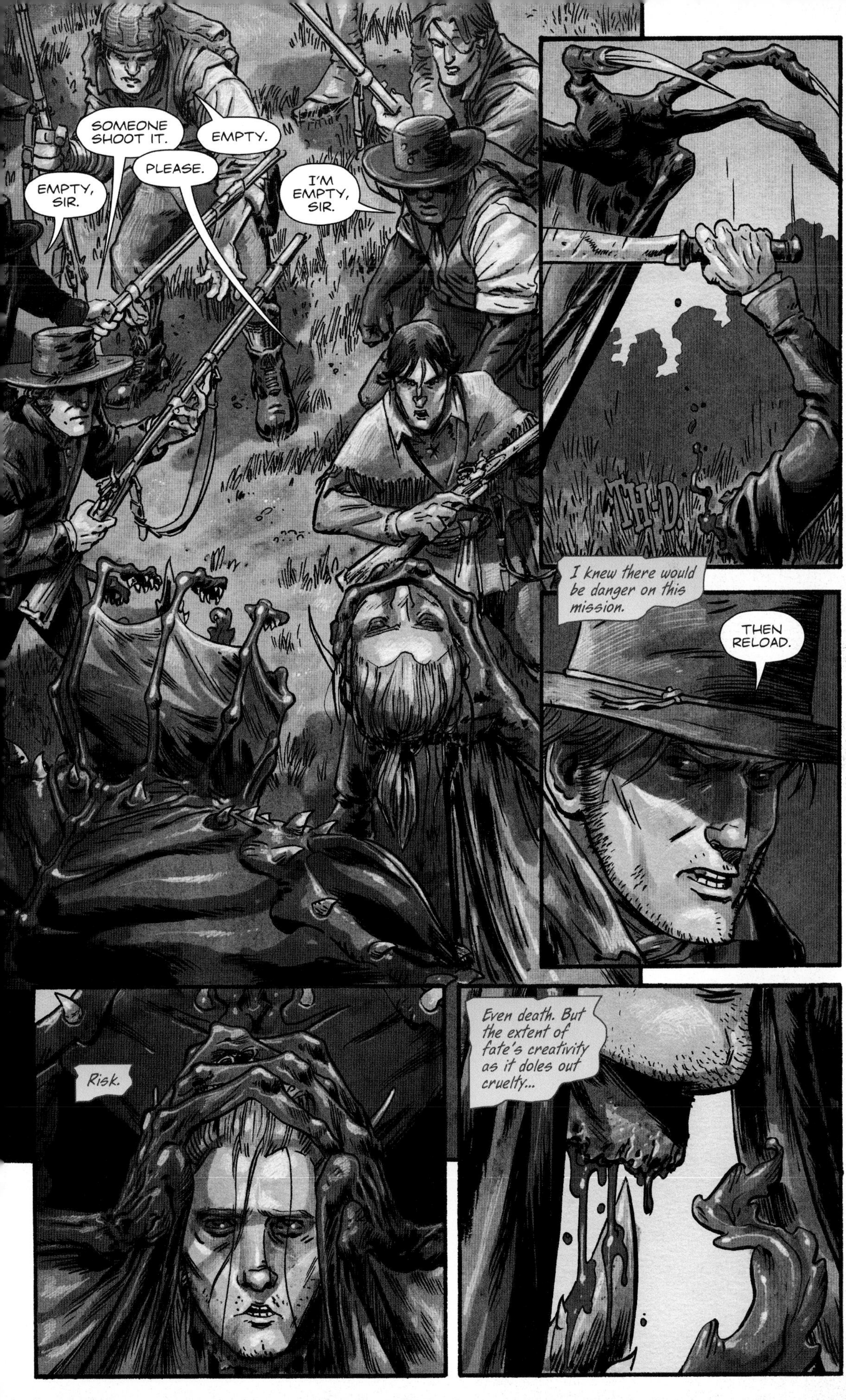
SOMEONE SHOOT IT.
EMPTY.
EMPTY, SIR.
PLEASE.
I'M EMPTY, SIR.
TH-D.
I knew there would be danger on this mission.
THEN RELOAD.
Risk.
Even death. But the extent of fate's creativity as it doles out cruelty...

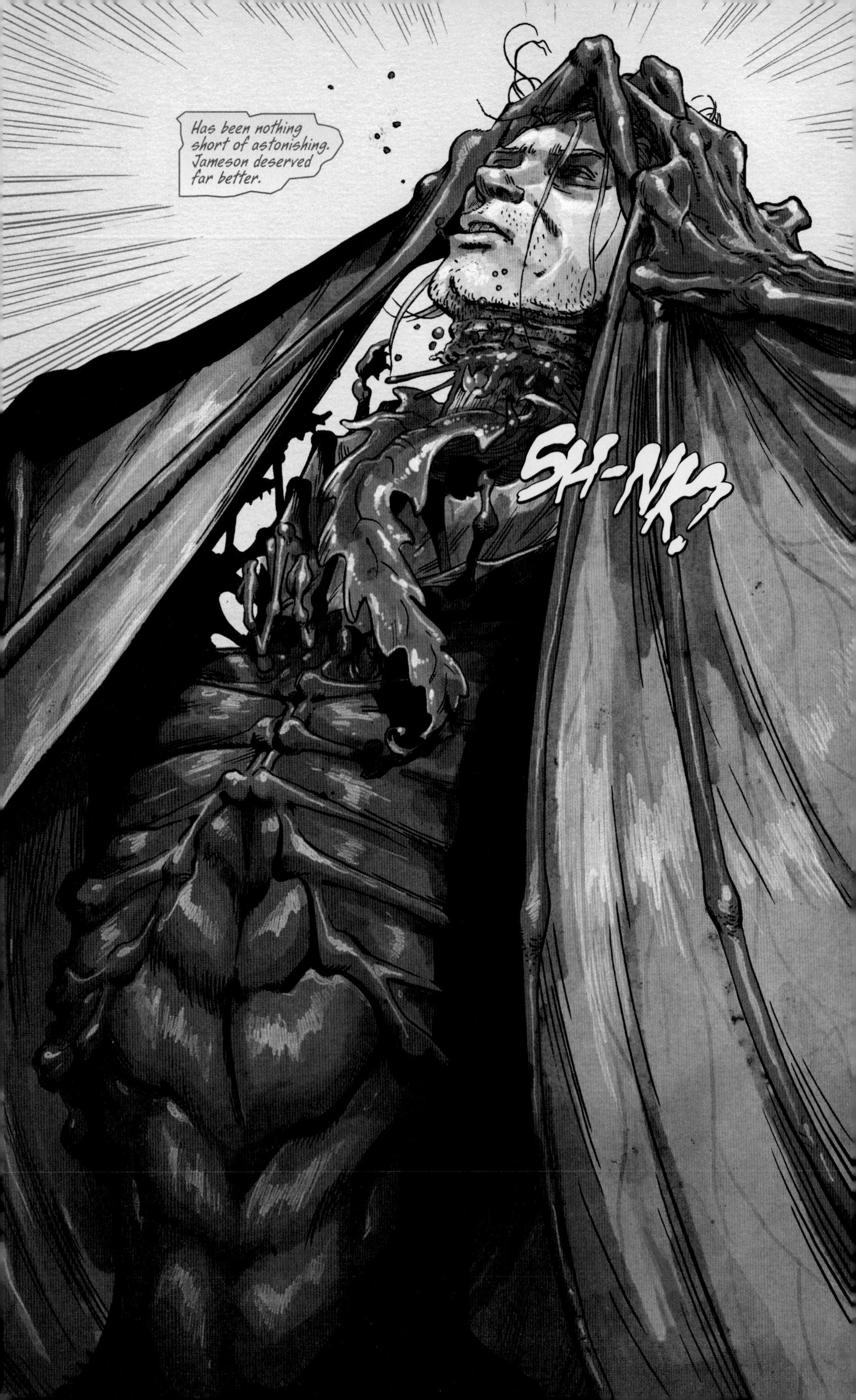
Has been nothing short of astonishing. Jameson deserved far better.
SH-NK!

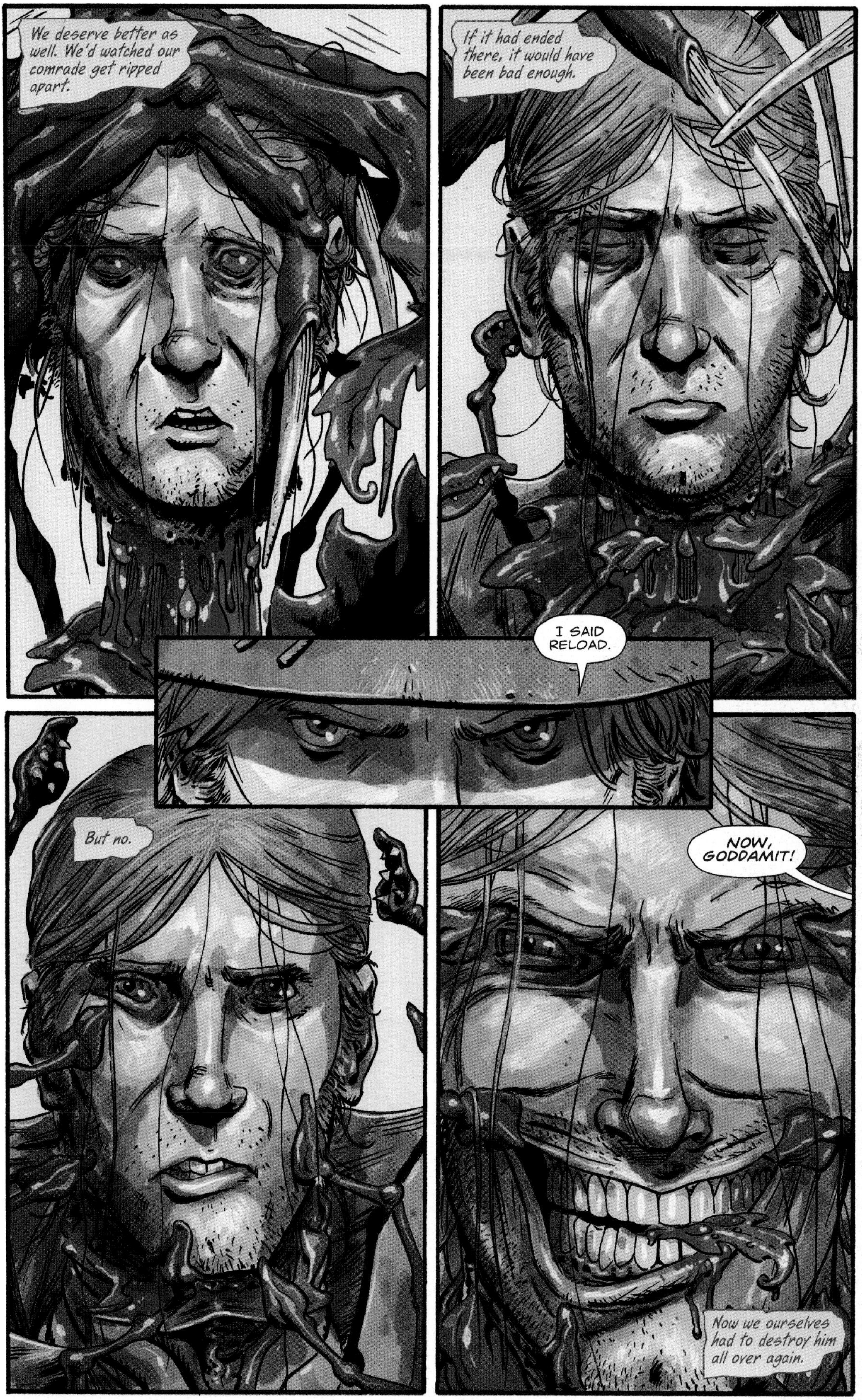
We deserve better as well. We'd watched our comrade get ripped apart.
If it had ended there, it would have been bad enough.
I SAID RELOAD.
But no.
NOW, GODDAMIT!
Now we ourselves had to destroy him all over again.

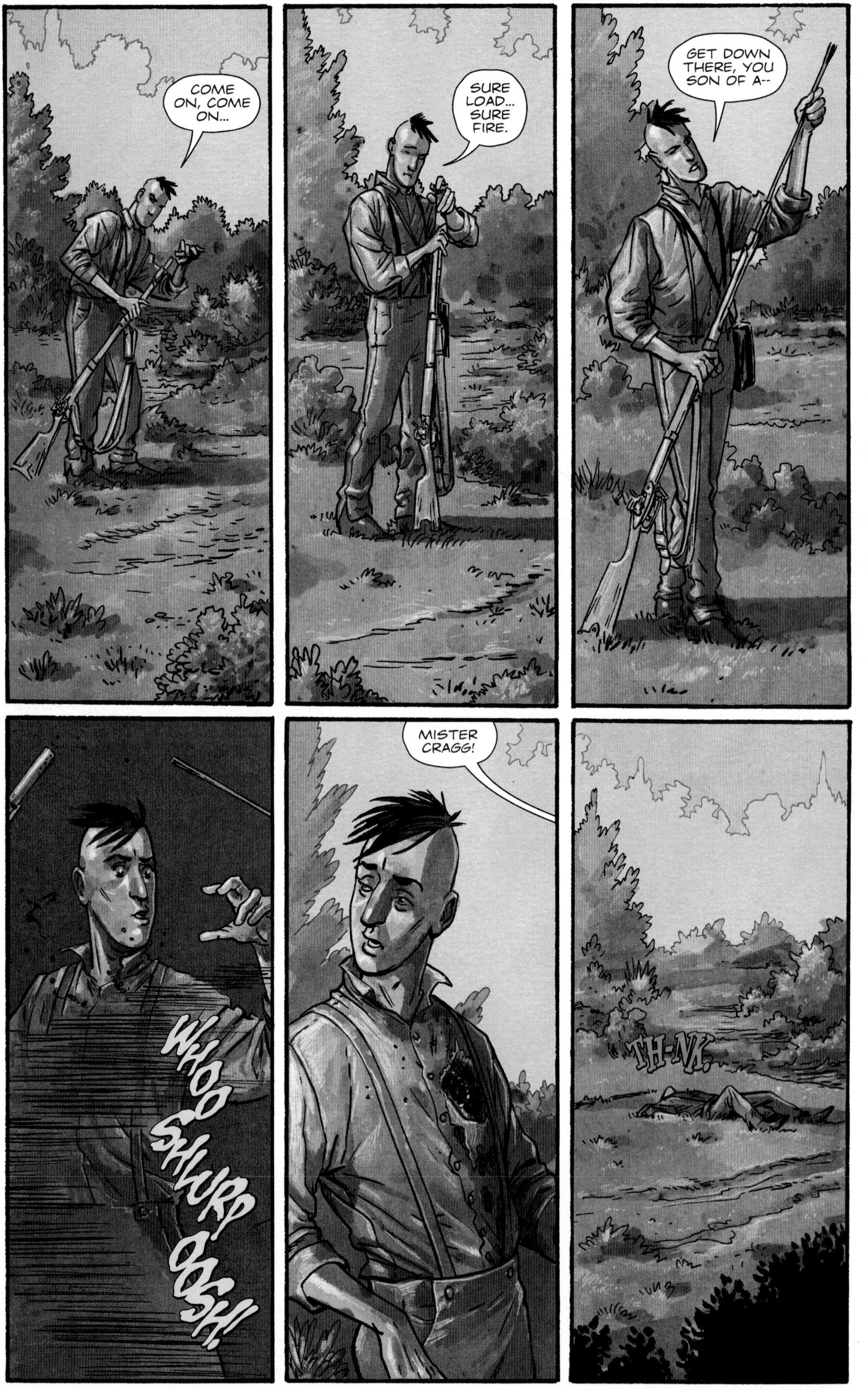
COME ON, COME ON...
SURE LOAD... SURE FIRE.
GET DOWN THERE, YOU SON OF A--
WHOOSHLURPOOSH!
MISTER CRAGG!
TH-NK.

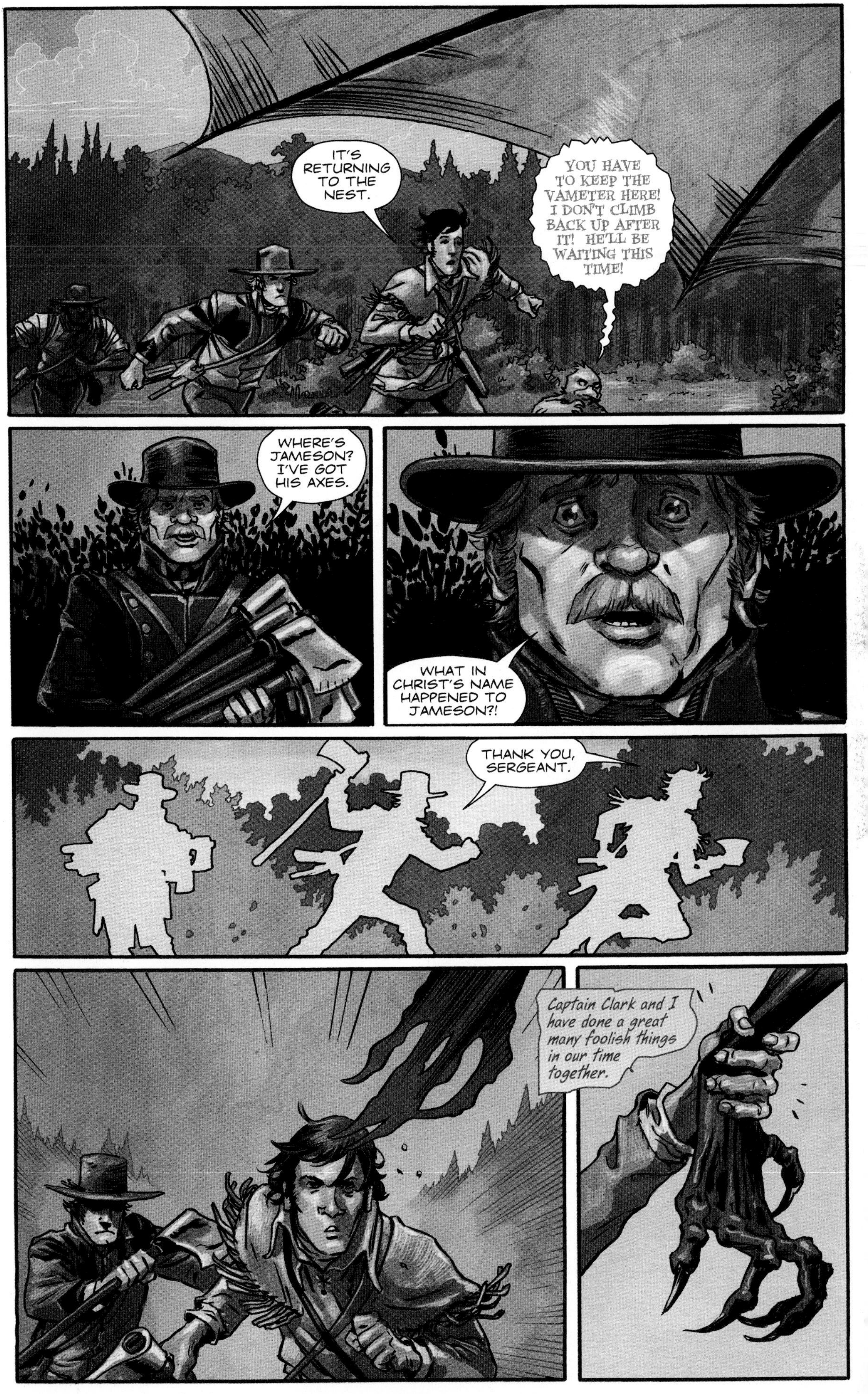
IT'S RETURNING TO THE NEST.
YOU HAVE TO KEEP THE VAMETER HERE! I DON'T CLIMB BACK UP AFTER IT! HE'LL BE WAITING THIS TIME!
WHERE'S JAMESON? I'VE GOT HIS AXES.
WHAT IN CHRIST'S NAME HAPPENED TO JAMESON?!
THANK YOU, SERGEANT.
Captain Clark and I have done a great many foolish things in our time together.

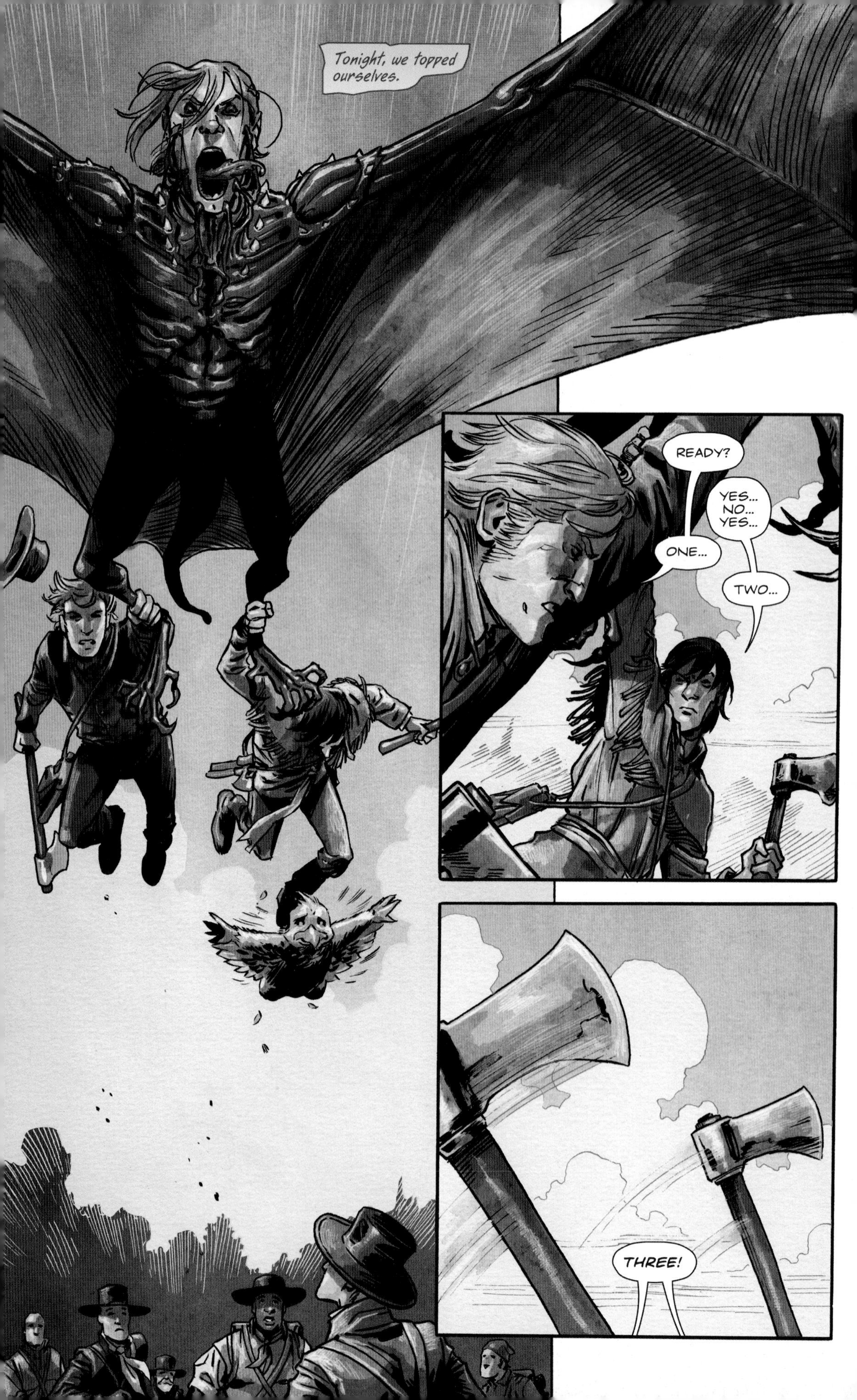
Tonight, we topped ourselves.
READY?
YES... NO... YES...
ONE...
TWO...
THREE!

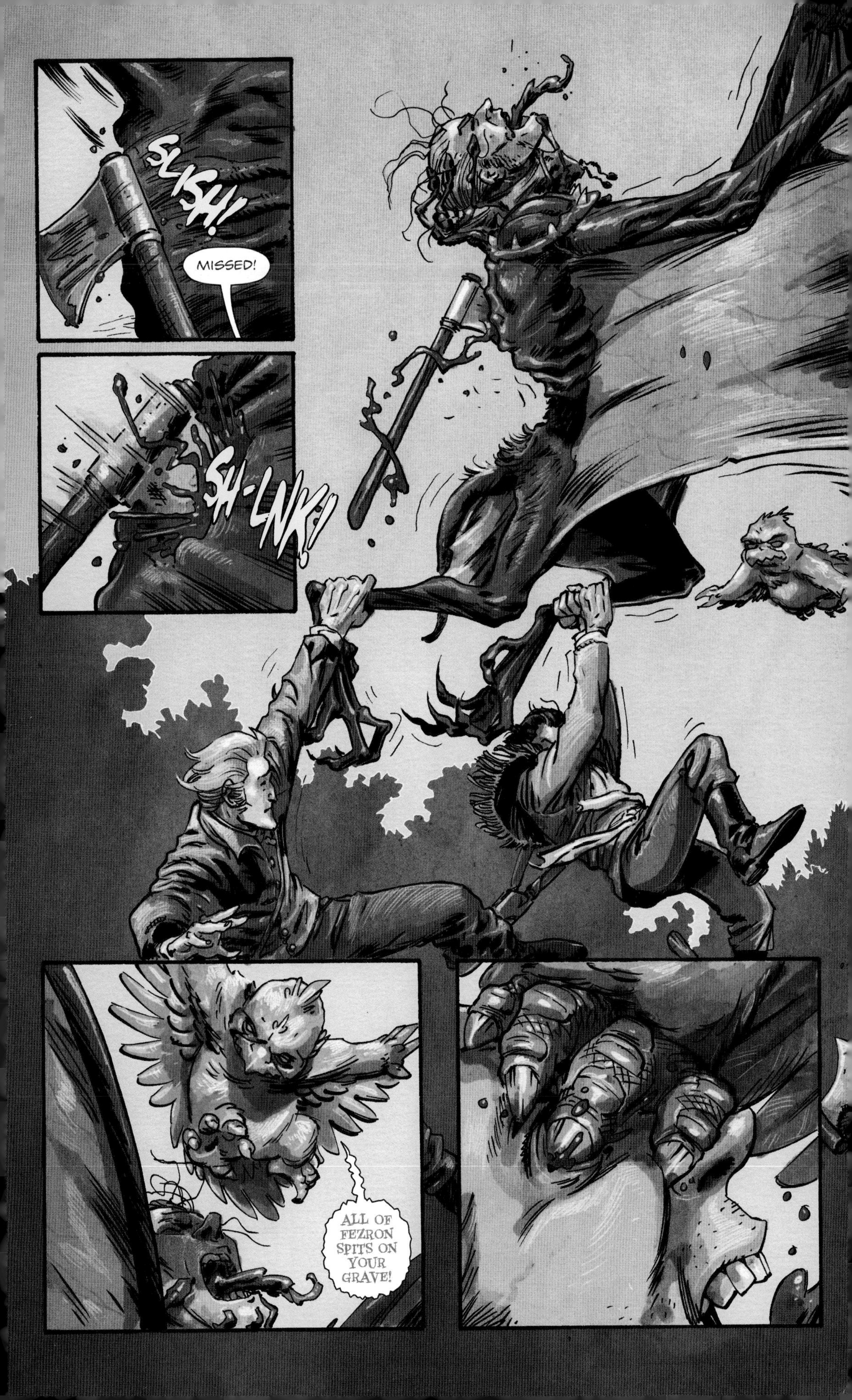
SLISH!
MISSED!
SH-LNK!!
ALL OF FEZRON SPITS ON YOUR GRAVE!

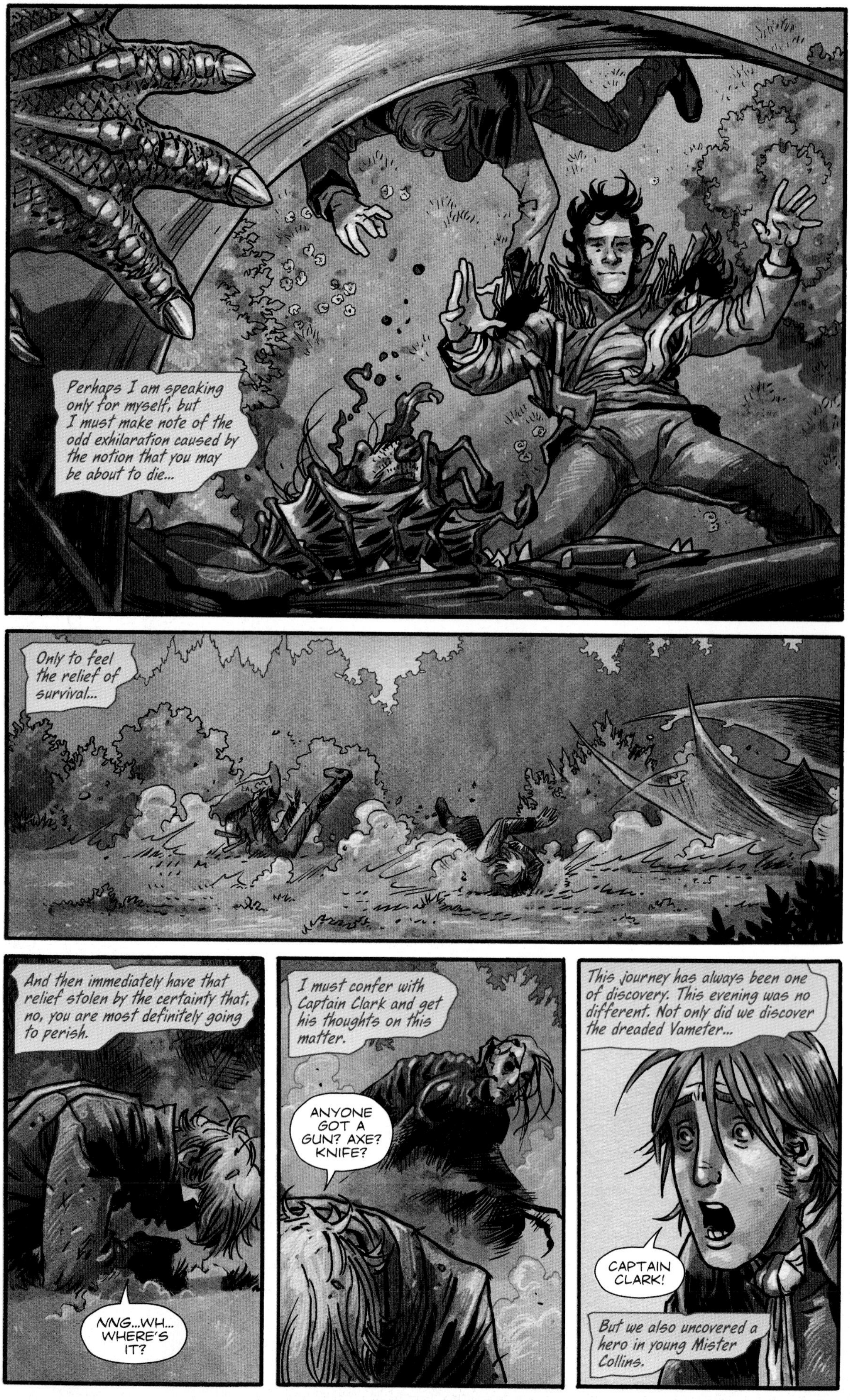

Perhaps I am speaking only for myself, but I must make note of the odd exhilaration caused by the notion that you may be about to die...
Only to feel the relief of survival...
And then immediately have that relief stolen by the certainty that, no, you are most definitely going to perish.
NNG...WH... WHERE'S IT?
I must confer with Captain Clark and get his thoughts on this matter.
ANYONE GOT A GUN? AXE? KNIFE?
This journey has always been one of discovery. This evening was no different. Not only did we discover the dreaded Vameter...
CAPTAIN CLARK!
But we also uncovered a hero in young Mister Collins.

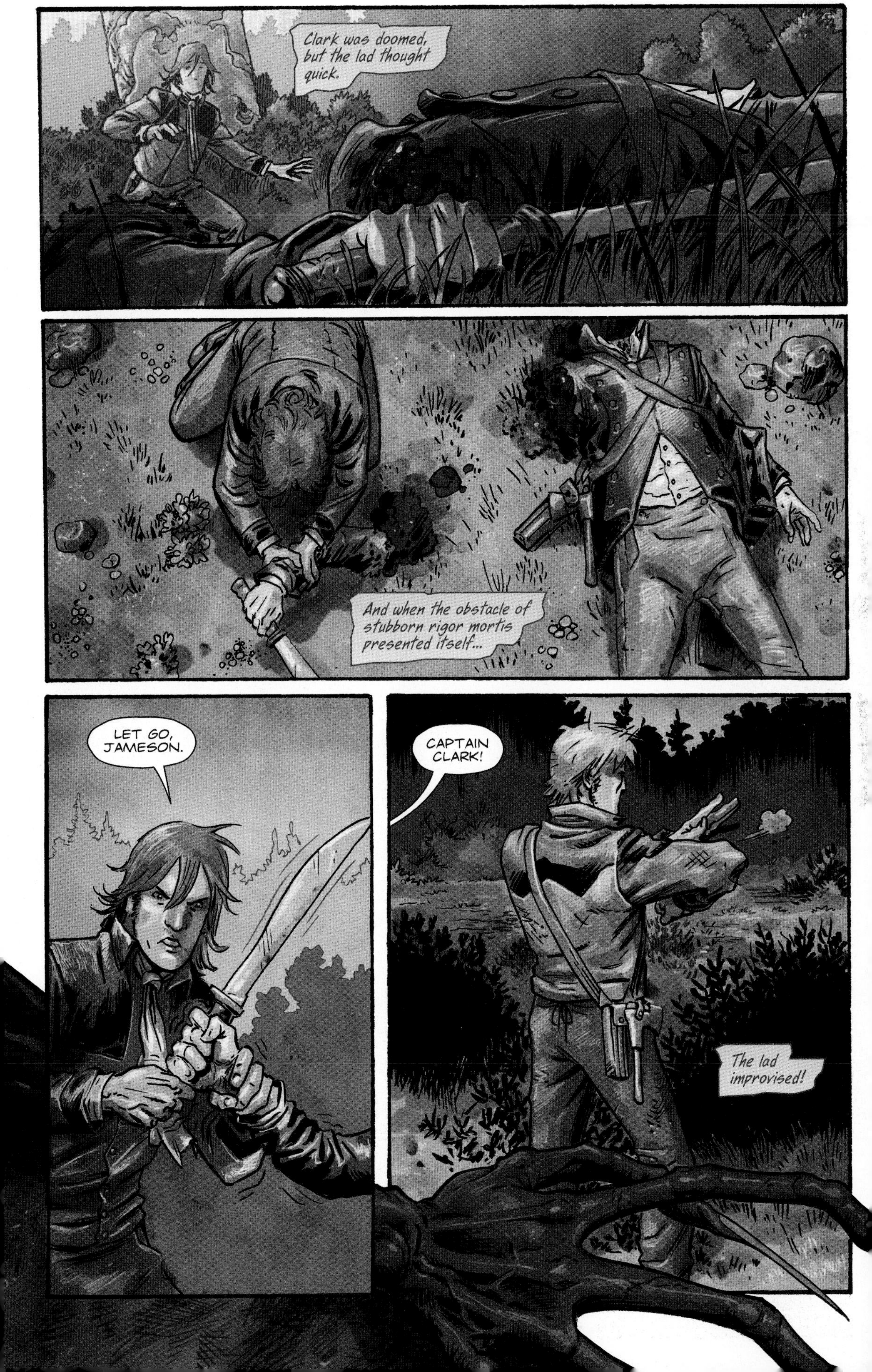
Clark was doomed, but the lad thought quick.
And when the obstacle of stubborn rigor mortis presented itself...
LET GO, JAMESON.
CAPTAIN CLARK!
The lad improvised!

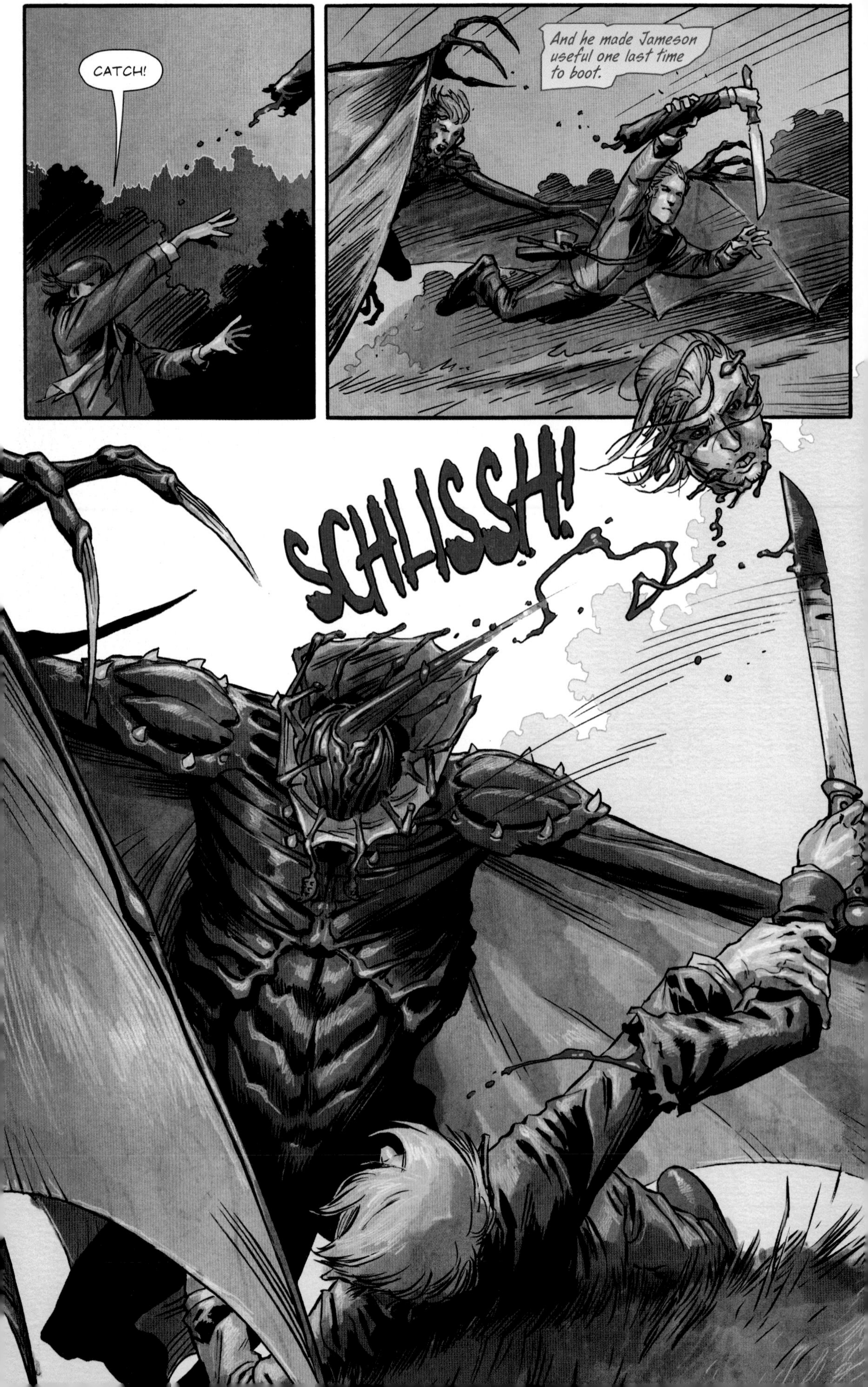
CATCH!
And he made Jameson useful one last time to boot.
SCHLISSH!

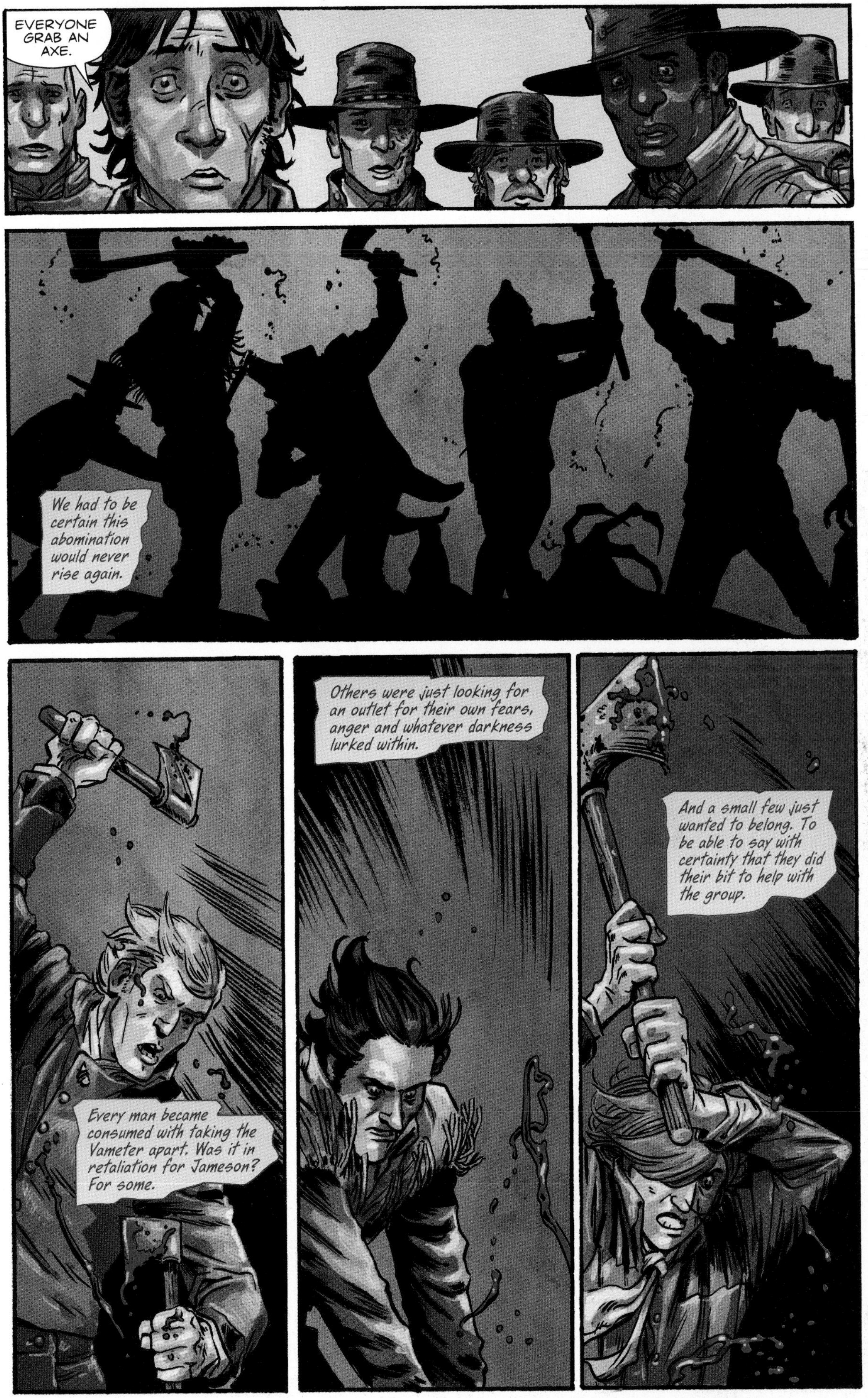
EVERYONE GRAB AN AXE.
We had to be certain this abomination would never rise again.
Every man became consumed with taking the Vameter apart. Was it in retaliation for Jameson? For some.
Others were just looking for an outlet for their own fears, anger and whatever darkness lurked within.
And a small few just wanted to belong. To be able to say with certainty that they did their bit to help with the group.

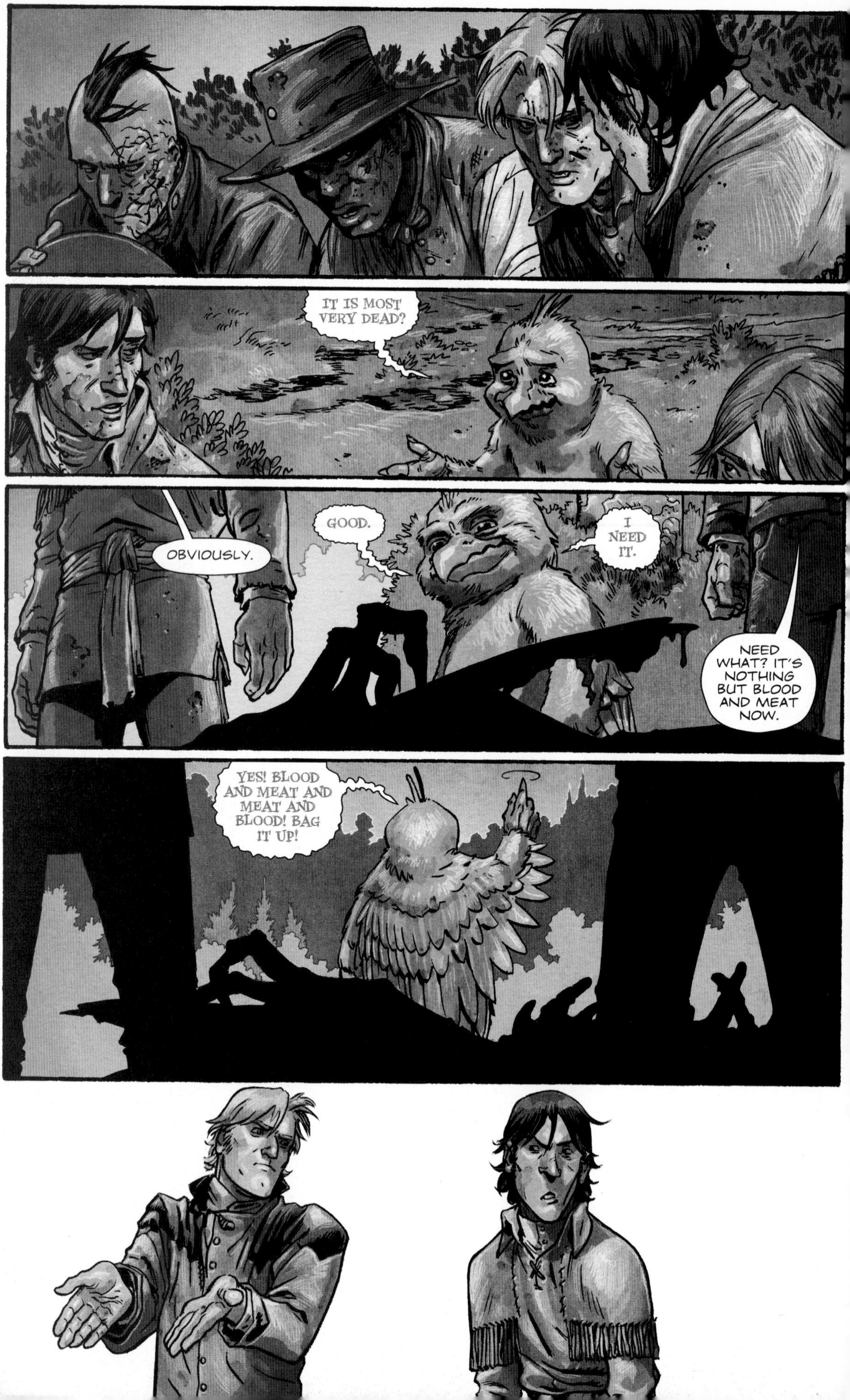

IT IS MOST VERY DEAD?
OBVIOUSLY.
GOOD.
I NEED IT.
NEED WHAT? IT'S NOTHING BUT BLOOD AND MEAT NOW.
YES! BLOOD AND MEAT AND MEAT AND BLOOD! BAG IT UP!

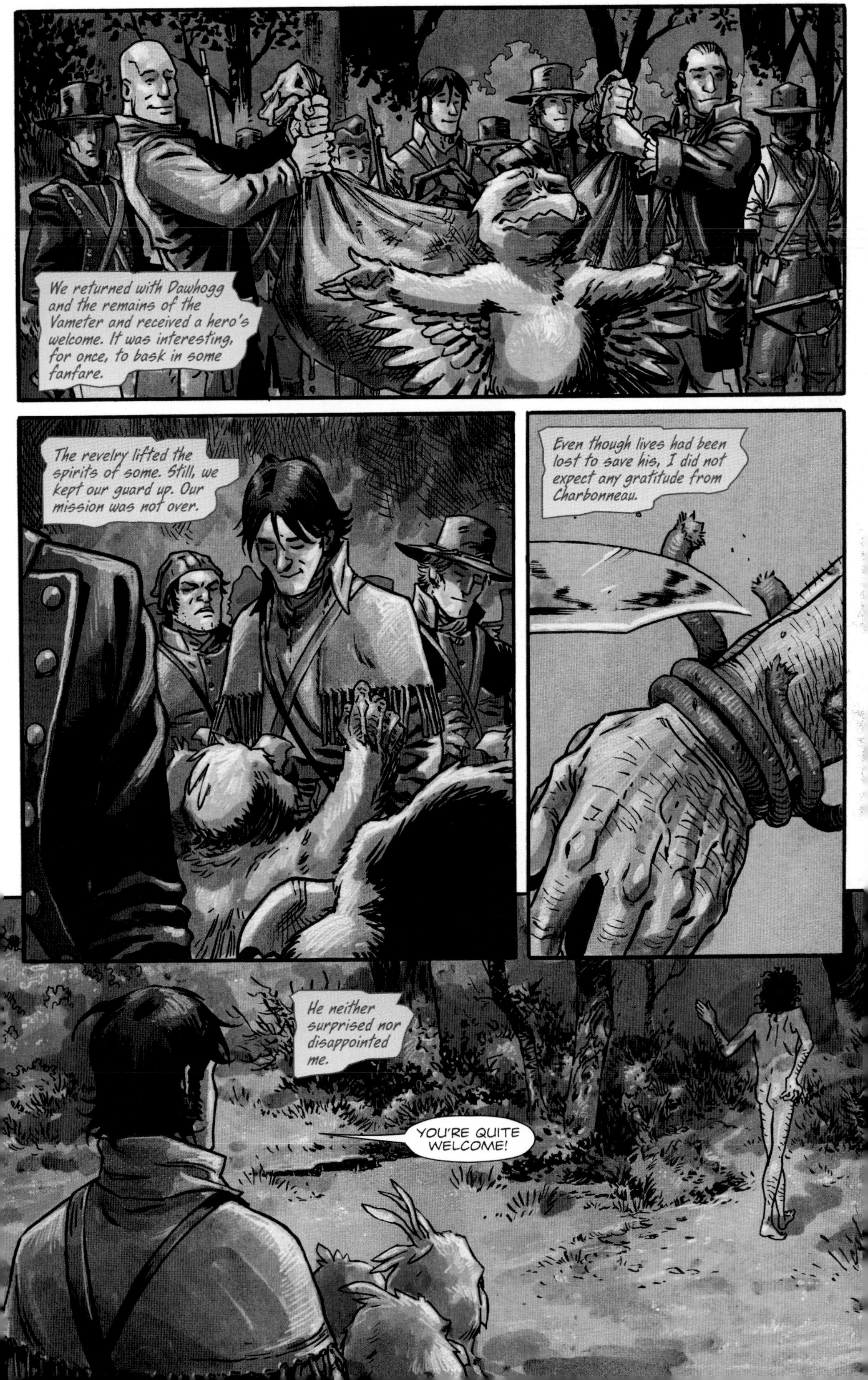

We returned with Dawhogg and the remains of the Vameter and received a hero's welcome. It was interesting, for once, to bask in some fanfare.
The revelry lifted the spirits of some. Still, we kept our guard up. Our mission was not over.
Even though lives had been lost to save his, I did not expect any gratitude from Charbonneau.
He neither surprised nor disappointed me.
YOU'RE QUITE WELCOME!

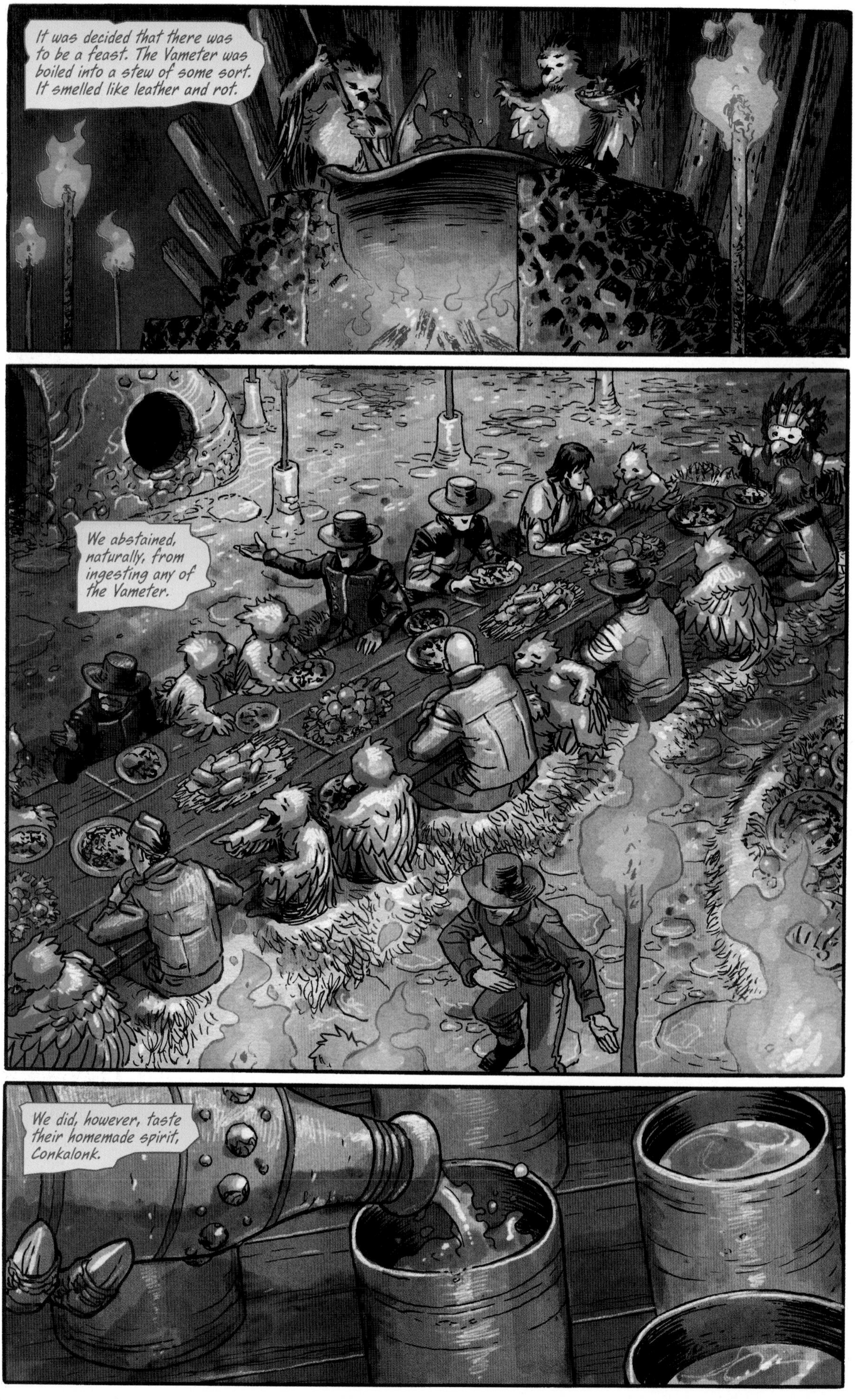
It was decided that there was to be a feast. The Vameter was boiled into a stew of some sort. It smelled like leather and rot.
We abstained, naturally, from ingesting any of the Vameter.
We did, however, taste their homemade spirit, Conkalonk.

The Conkalonk had no effect on the men. The Fezron, however, became quite intoxicated.

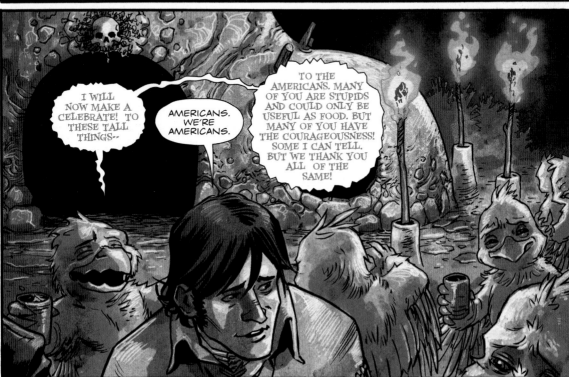

I WILL NOW MAKE A CELEBRATE! TO THESE TALL THINGS--

AMERICANS. WE'RE AMERICANS.

TO THE AMERICANS. MANY OF YOU ARE STUPIDS AND COULD ONLY BE USEFUL AS FOOD. BUT MANY OF YOU HAVE THE COURAGEOUSNESS! SOME I CAN TELL. BUT WE THANK YOU ALL OF THE SAME!

I permitted a small ration of the rum to be shared among the men. Enough to be sociable, but not to impair judgement.

Etten refused his share of rum. He claimed it was in protest. However, I believe a portion of his decision had to do with fear. I cannot blame him. He was almost done in by Dawhogg's poisonous bite.

THERE'S NO WAY IN HELL I'M CELEBRATING WITH THESE VERMIN.

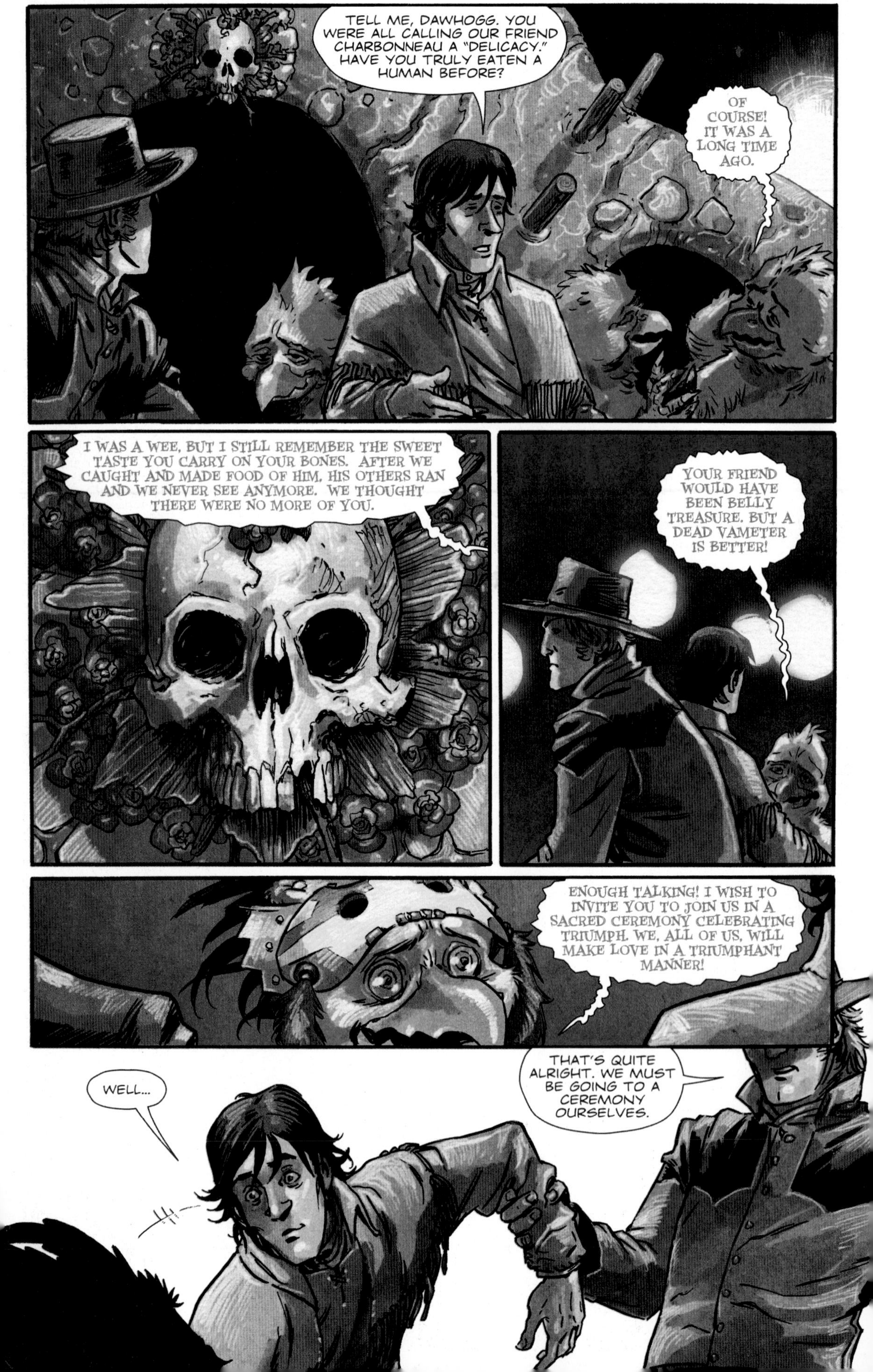
TELL ME, DAWHOGG. YOU WERE ALL CALLING OUR FRIEND CHARBONNEAU A "DELICACY." HAVE YOU TRULY EATEN A HUMAN BEFORE?
OF COURSE! IT WAS A LONG TIME AGO.
I WAS A WEE, BUT I STILL REMEMBER THE SWEET TASTE YOU CARRY ON YOUR BONES. AFTER WE CAUGHT AND MADE FOOD OF HIM, HIS OTHERS RAN AND WE NEVER SEE ANYMORE. WE THOUGHT THERE WERE NO MORE OF YOU.
YOUR FRIEND WOULD HAVE BEEN BELLY TREASURE. BUT A DEAD VAMETER IS BETTER!
ENOUGH TALKING! I WISH TO INVITE YOU TO JOIN US IN A SACRED CEREMONY CELEBRATING TRIUMPH. WE, ALL OF US, WILL MAKE LOVE IN A TRIUMPHANT MANNER!
WELL...
THAT'S QUITE ALRIGHT. WE MUST BE GOING TO A CEREMONY OURSELVES.

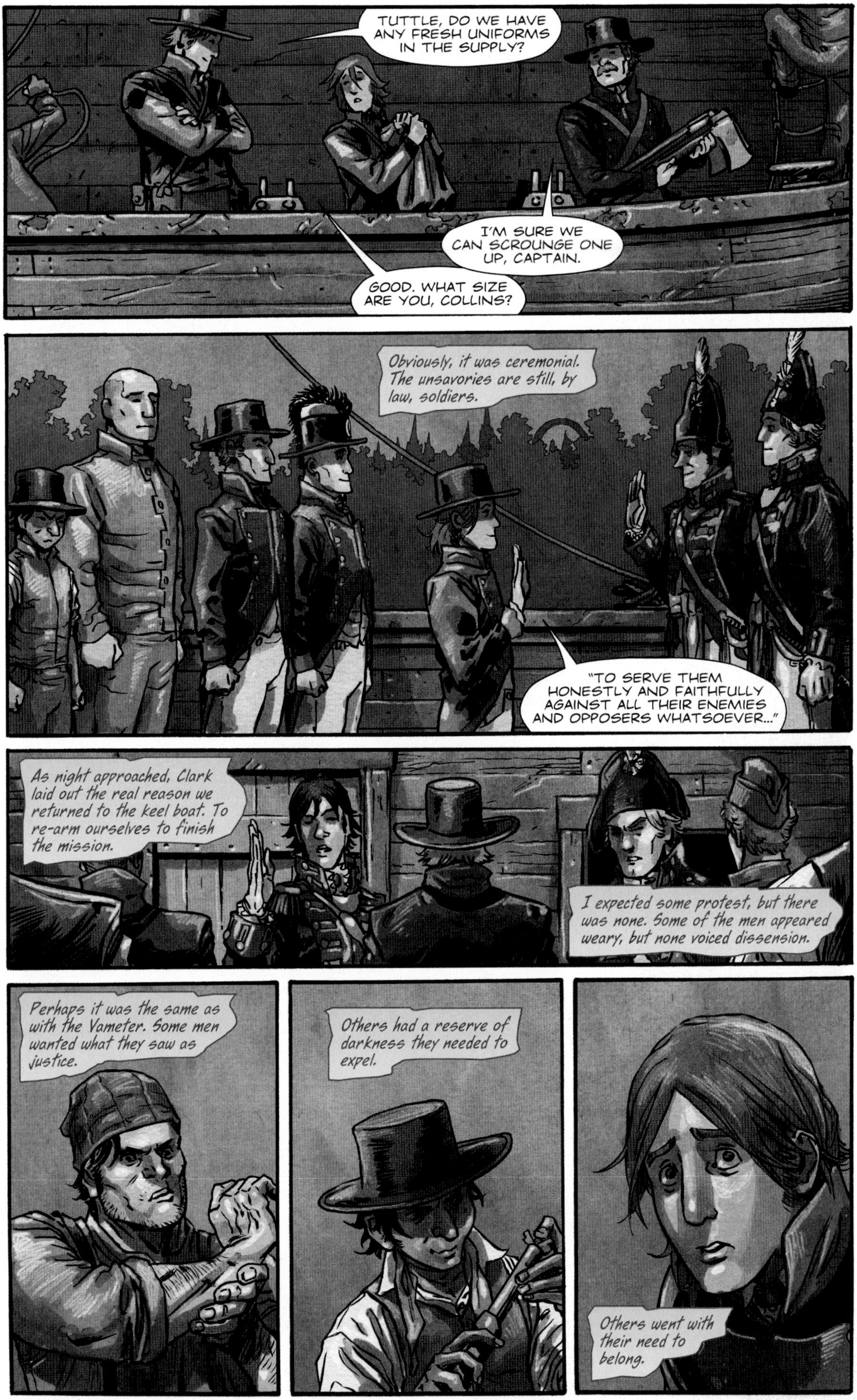
TUTTLE, DO WE HAVE ANY FRESH UNIFORMS IN THE SUPPLY?
I'M SURE WE CAN SCROUNGE ONE UP, CAPTAIN.
GOOD. WHAT SIZE ARE YOU, COLLINS?
Obviously, it was ceremonial. The unsavories are still, by law, soldiers.
"TO SERVE THEM HONESTLY AND FAITHFULLY AGAINST ALL THEIR ENEMIES AND OPPOSERS WHATSOEVER..."
As night approached, Clark laid out the real reason we returned to the keel boat. To re-arm ourselves to finish the mission.
I expected some protest, but there was none. Some of the men appeared weary, but none voiced dissension.
Perhaps it was the same as with the Vameter. Some men wanted what they saw as justice.
Others had a reserve of darkness they needed to expel.
Others went with their need to belong.

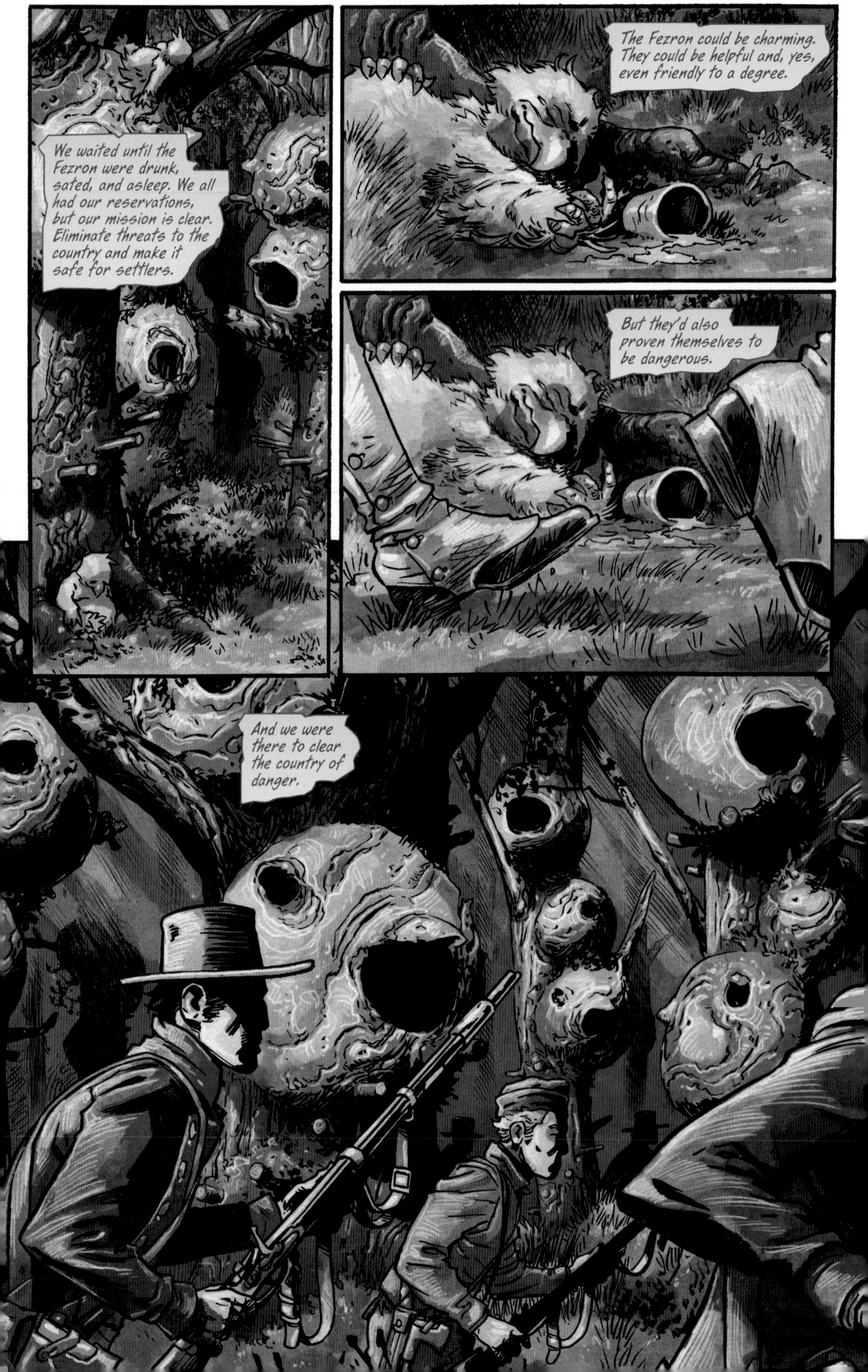
We waited until the Fezron were drunk, sated, and asleep. We all had our reservations, but our mission is clear. Eliminate threats to the country and make it safe for settlers.
The Fezron could be charming. They could be helpful and, yes, even friendly to a degree.
But they'd also proven themselves to be dangerous.
And we were there to clear the country of danger.

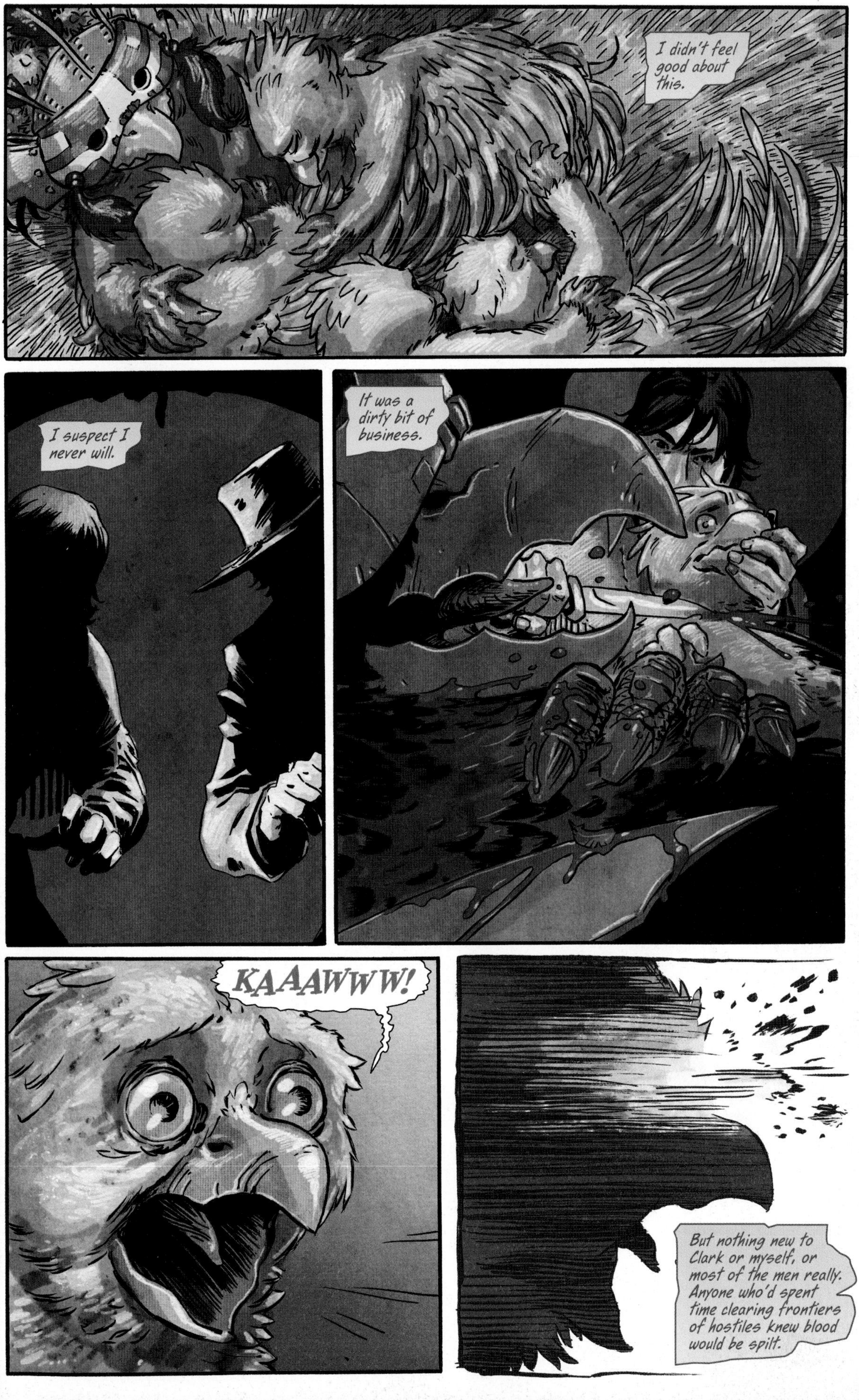
I didn't feel good about this.
I suspect I never will.
It was a dirty bit of business.
KAAAWWW!
But nothing new to Clark or myself, or most of the men really. Anyone who'd spent time clearing frontiers of hostiles knew blood would be spilt.

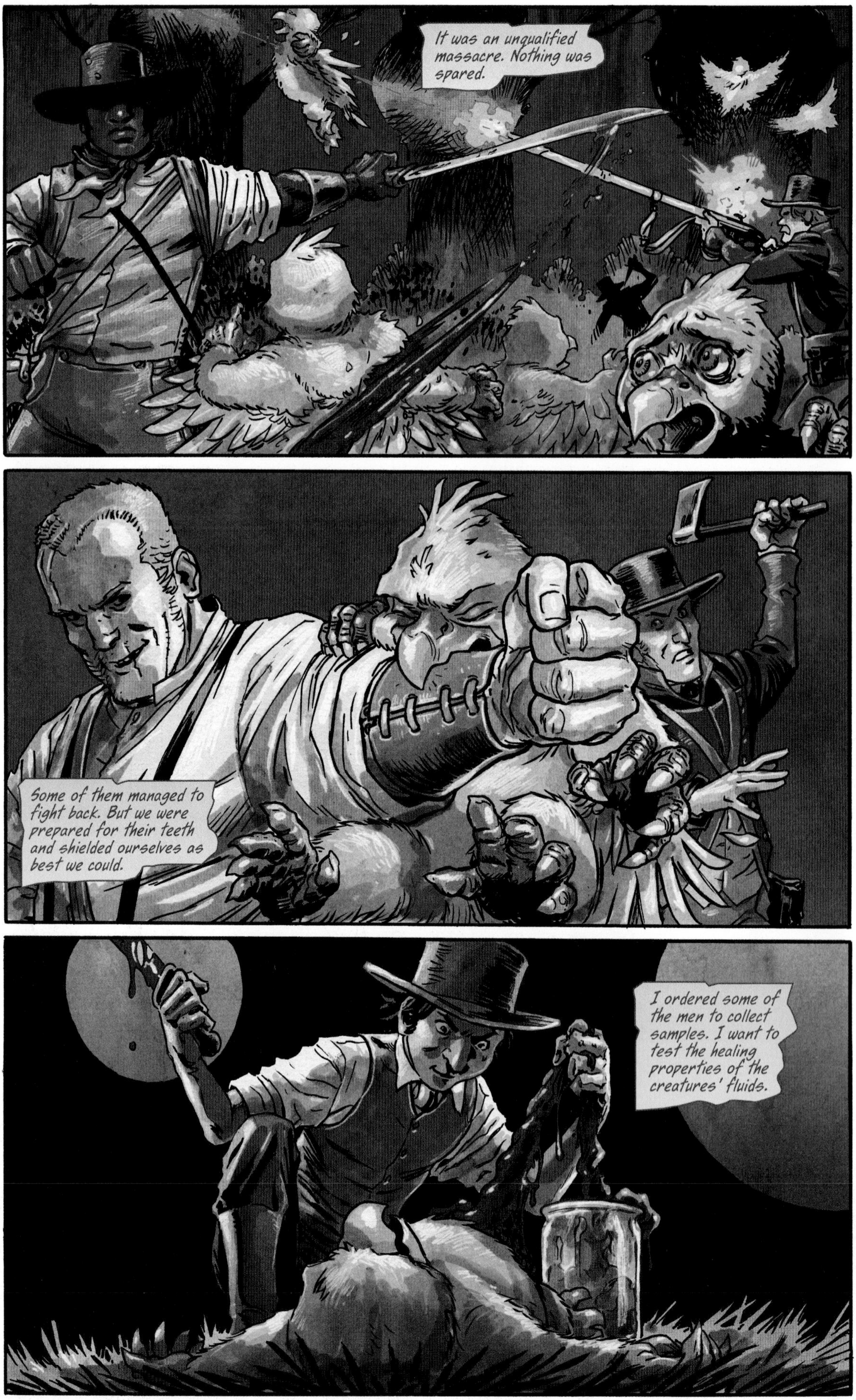
It was an unqualified massacre. Nothing was spared.
Some of them managed to fight back. But we were prepared for their teeth and shielded ourselves as best we could.
I ordered some of the men to collect samples. I want to test the healing properties of the creatures' fluids.

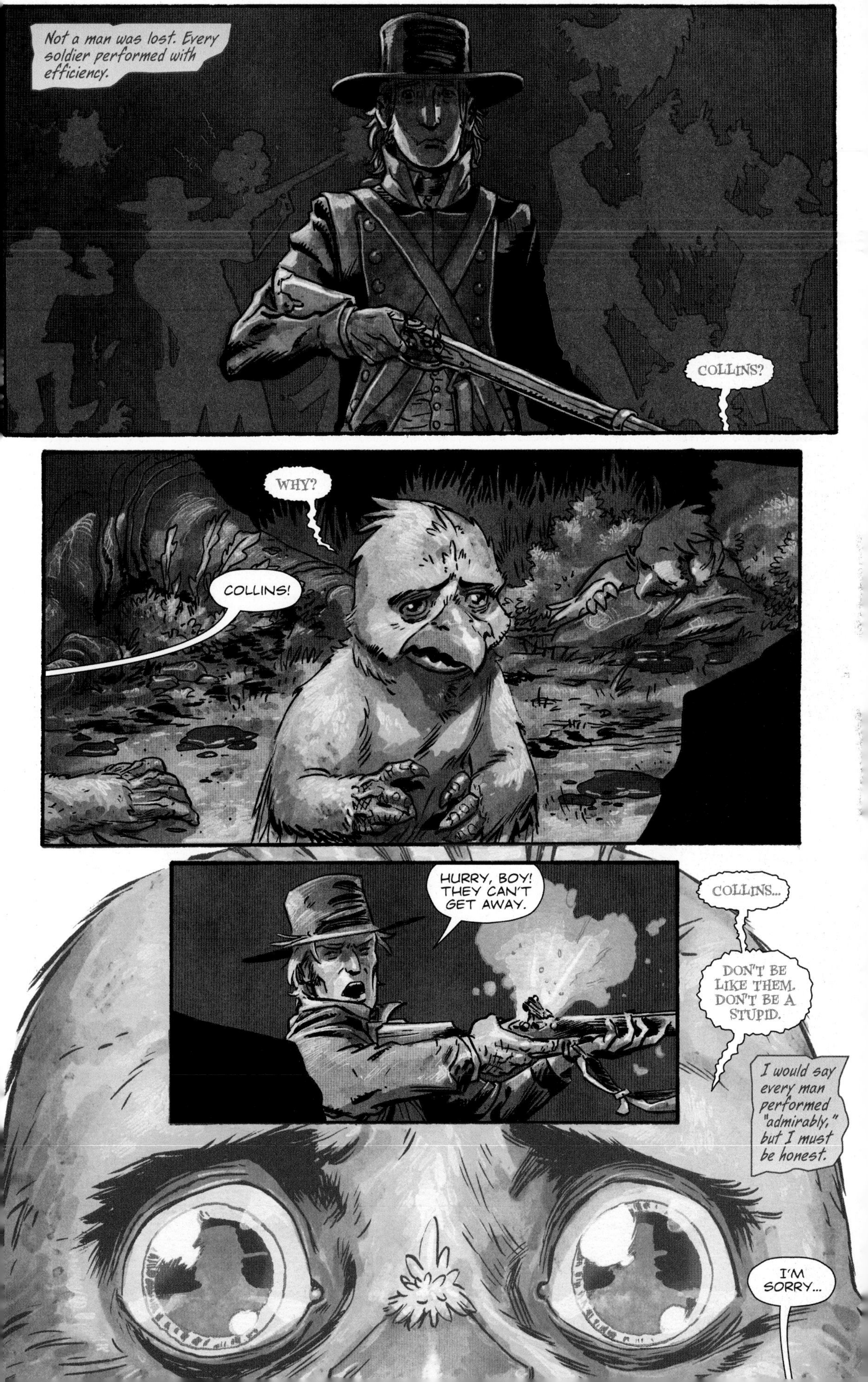
Not a man was lost. Every soldier performed with efficiency.
COLLINS?
WHY?
COLLINS!
HURRY, BOY! THEY CAN'T GET AWAY.
COLLINS...
DON'T BE LIKE THEM. DON'T BE A STUPID.
I would say every man performed "admirably," but I must be honest.
I'M SORRY...

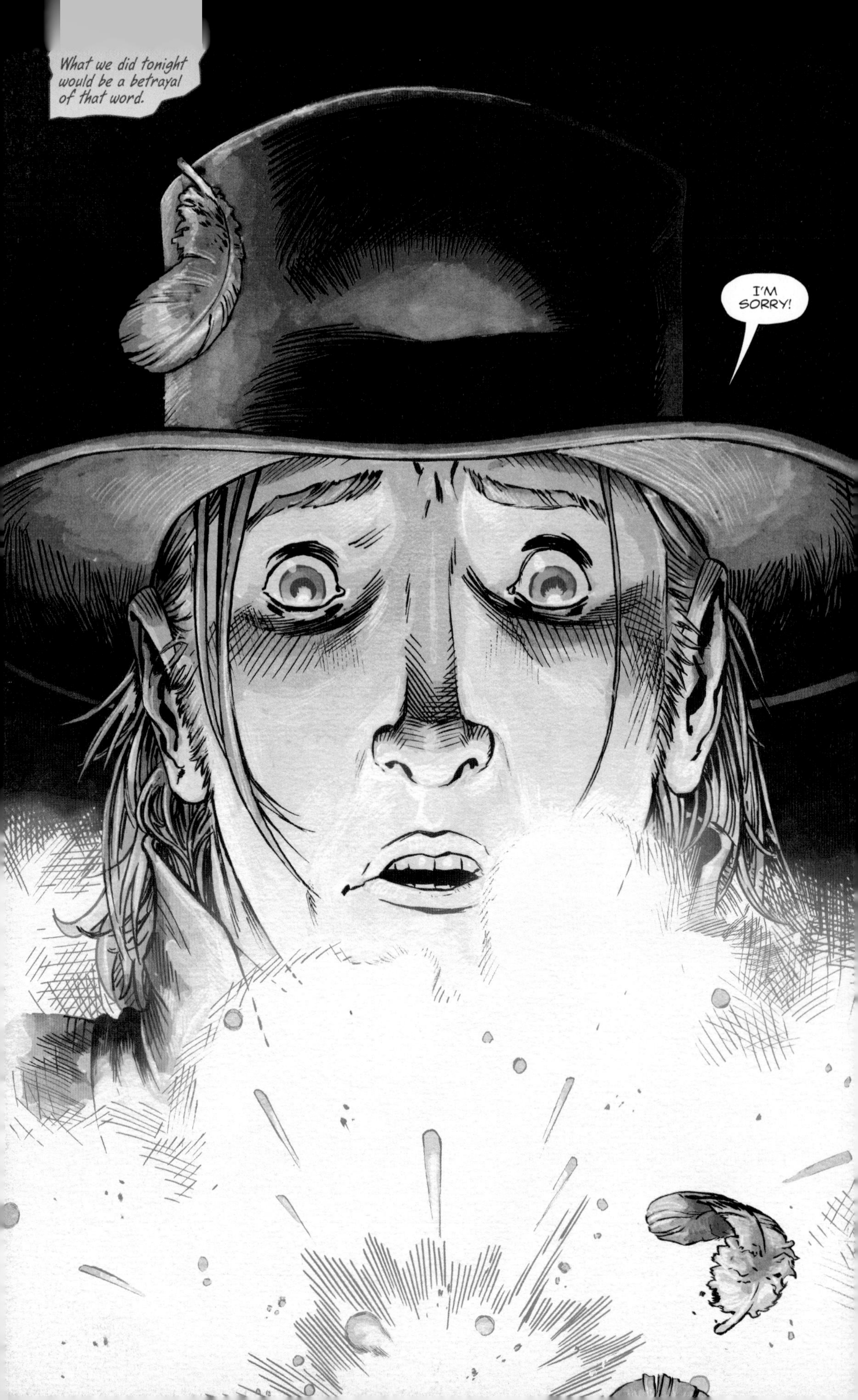
What we did tonight would be a betrayal of that word.
I'M SORRY!

To be continued...

FOR MORE TALES FROM ROBERT KIRKMAN AND SKYBOUND

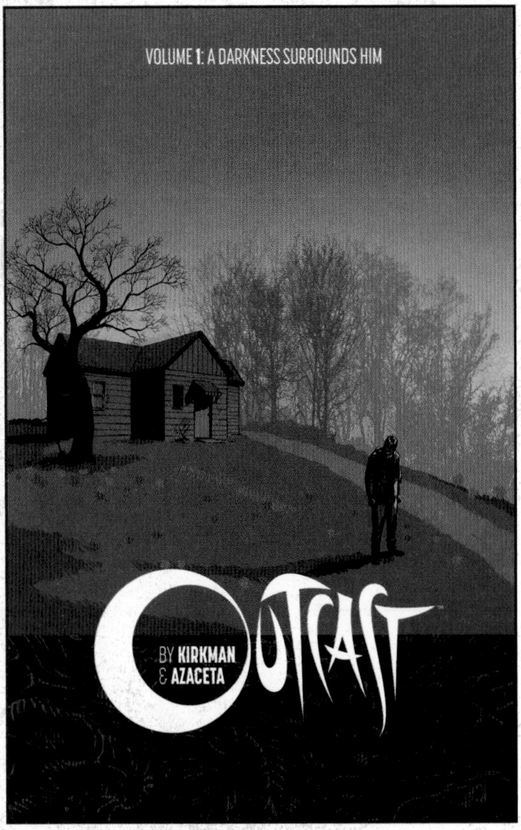
VOLUME 1: A DARKNESS SURROUNDS HIM
OUTCAST
BY KIRKMAN
& AZACETA

VOL. 1: A DARKNESS SURROUNDS HIM TP
ISBN: 978-1-63215-053-0
$9.99

VOL. 2: A VAST AND UNENDING RUIN TP
ISBN: 978-1-63215-448-4
$14.99

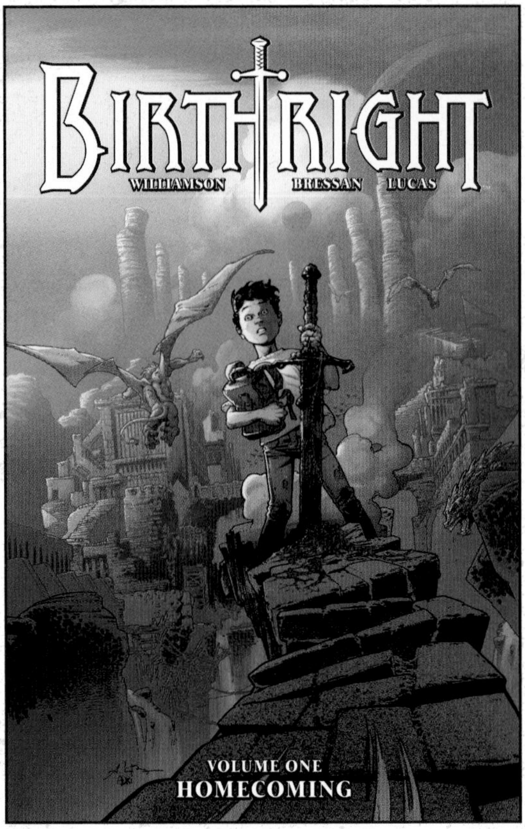
BIRTHRIGHT
WILLIAMSON
BRESSAN
LUCAS
VOLUME ONE
HOMECOMING

VOL. 1: HOMECOMING TP
ISBN: 978-1-63215-231-2
$9.99

VOL. 2: CALL TO ADVENTURE TP
ISBN: 978-1-63215-446-0
$12.99

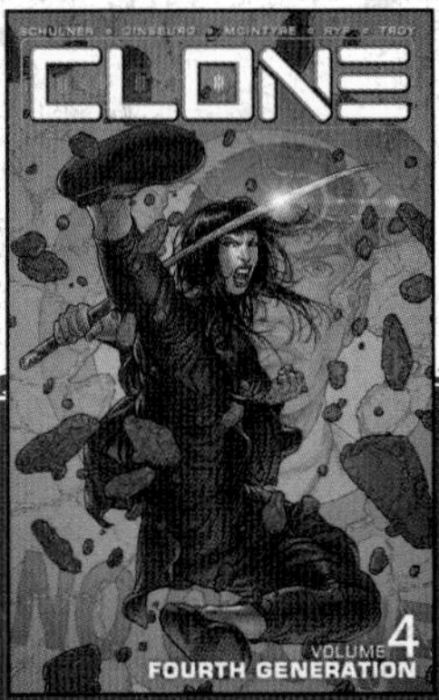
CLONE
VOLUME 4
FOURTH GENERATION

VOL. 1: FIRST GENERATION TP
ISBN: 978-1-60706-683-5
$12.99

VOL. 2: SECOND GENERATION TP
ISBN: 978-1-60706-830-3
$12.99

VOL. 3: THIRD GENERATION TP
ISBN: 978-1-60706-939-3
$12.99

VOL. 4: FOURTH GENERATION TP
ISBN: 978-1-63215-036-3
$12.99

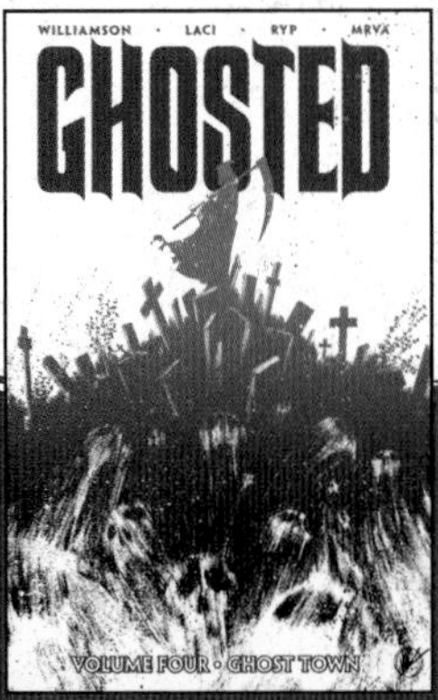
WILLIAMSON · LACI · RYP · MRVA
GHOSTED
VOLUME FOUR · GHOST TOWN

VOL. 1: HAUNTED HEIST TP
ISBN: 978-1-60706-836-5
$9.99

VOL. 2: BOOKS OF THE DEAD TP
ISBN: 978-1-63215-046-2
$12.99

VOL. 3: DEATH WISH TP
ISBN: 978-1-63215-051-6
$12.99

VOL. 4: GHOST TOWN TP
ISBN: 978-1-63215-317-3
$12.99

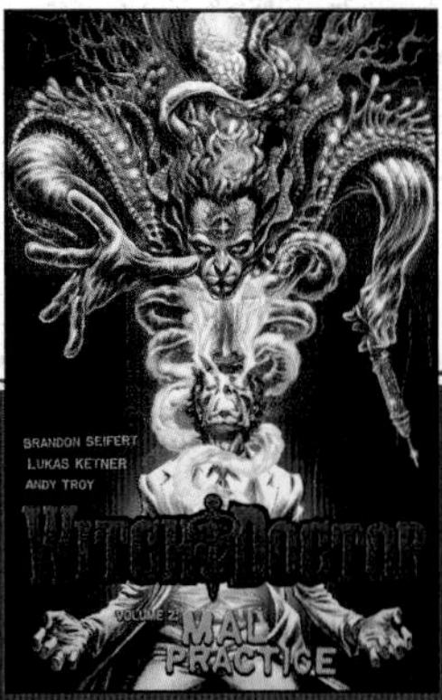
BRANDON SEIFERT
LUKAS KETNER
ANDY TROY
MAL PRACTICE

VOL. 1: UNDER THE KNIFE TP
ISBN: 978-1-60706-441-1
$12.99

VOL. 2: MAL PRACTICE TP
ISBN: 978-1-60706-693-4
$14.99

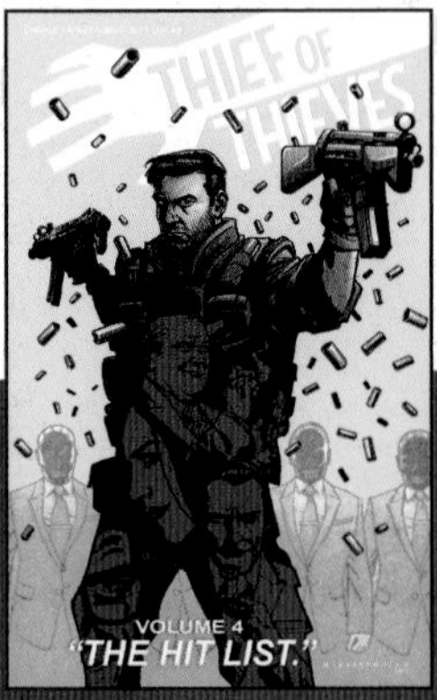
VOLUME 4
"THE HIT LIST."

VOL. 1: "I QUIT."
ISBN: 978-1-60706-592-0
$14.99

VOL. 2: "HELP ME."
ISBN: 978-1-60706-676-7
$14.99

VOL. 3: "VENICE."
ISBN: 978-1-60706-844-0
$14.99

VOL. 4: "THE HIT LIST."
ISBN: 978-1-63215-037-0
$14.99

FOR MORE OF THE WALKING DEAD

TRADEPAPERBACKS

ROBERT KIRKMAN TONY MOORE
THE WALKING DEAD
VOLUME 1
DAYS GONE BYE

VOL. 1: DAYS GONE BYE TP
ISBN: 978-1-58240-672-5
$14.99
VOL. 2: MILES BEHIND US TP
ISBN: 978-1-58240-775-3
$14.99
VOL. 3: SAFETY BEHIND BARS TP
ISBN: 978-1-58240-805-7
$14.99
VOL. 4: THE HEART'S DESIRE TP
ISBN: 978-1-58240-530-8
$14.99
VOL. 5: THE BEST DEFENSE TP
ISBN: 978-1-58240-612-1
$14.99
VOL. 6: THIS SORROWFUL LIFE TP
ISBN: 978-1-58240-684-8
$14.99
VOL. 7: THE CALM BEFORE TP
ISBN: 978-1-58240-828-6
$14.99

VOL. 8: MADE TO SUFFER TP
ISBN: 978-1-58240-883-5
$14.99
VOL. 9: HERE WE REMAIN TP
ISBN: 978-1-60706-022-2
$14.99
VOL. 10: WHAT WE BECOME TP
ISBN: 978-1-60706-075-8
$14.99
VOL. 11: FEAR THE HUNTERS TP
ISBN: 978-1-60706-181-6
$14.99
VOL. 12: LIFE AMONG THEM TP
ISBN: 978-1-60706-254-7
$14.99
VOL. 13: TOO FAR GONE TP
ISBN: 978-1-60706-329-2
$14.99
VOL. 14: NO WAY OUT TP
ISBN: 978-1-60706-392-6
$14.99

VOL. 15: WE FIND OURSELVES TP
ISBN: 978-1-60706-440-4
$14.99
VOL. 16: A LARGER WORLD TP
ISBN: 978-1-60706-559-3
$14.99
VOL. 17: SOMETHING TO FEAR TP
ISBN: 978-1-60706-615-6
$14.99
VOL. 18: WHAT COMES AFTER TP
ISBN: 978-1-60706-687-3
$14.99
VOL. 19: MARCH TO WAR TP
ISBN: 978-1-60706-818-1
$14.99
VOL. 20: ALL OUT WAR PART ONE TP
ISBN: 978-1-60706-882-2
$14.99
VOL. 21: ALL OUT WAR PART TWO TP
ISBN: 978-1-63215-030-1
$14.99

VOL. 22: A NEW BEGINNING TP
ISBN: 978-1-63215-041-7
$14.99
VOL. 23: WHISPERS INTO SCREAMS TP
ISBN: 978-1-63215-258-9
$14.99
VOL. 24: LIFE AND DEATH TP
ISBN: 978-1-63215-402-6
$14.99
VOL. 1: SPANISH EDITION TP
ISBN: 978-1-60706-797-9
$14.99
VOL. 2: SPANISH EDITION TP
ISBN: 978-1-60706-845-7
$14.99
VOL. 3: SPANISH EDITION TP
ISBN: 978-1-60706-883-9
$14.99
VOL. 4: SPANISH EDITION TP
ISBN: 978-1-63215-035-6
$14.99

HARDCOVERS

THE WALKING DEAD
BOOK ONE
a continuing story of survival horror.

BOOK ONE HC
ISBN: 978-1-58240-619-0
$34.99
BOOK TWO HC
ISBN: 978-1-58240-698-5
$34.99
BOOK THREE HC
ISBN: 978-1-58240-825-5
$34.99
BOOK FOUR HC
ISBN: 978-1-60706-000-0
$34.99
BOOK FIVE HC
ISBN: 978-1-60706-171-7
$34.99
BOOK SIX HC
ISBN: 978-1-60706-327-8
$34.99
BOOK SEVEN HC
ISBN: 978-1-60706-439-8
$34.99
BOOK EIGHT HC
ISBN: 978-1-60706-593-7
$34.99
BOOK NINE HC
ISBN: 978-1-60706-798-6
$34.99
BOOK TEN HC
ISBN: 978-1-63215-034-9
$34.99
BOOK ELEVEN HC
ISBN: 978-1-63215-271-8
$34.99

COMPENDIUMS

The ultimate edition of The New York Times bestseller!
THE WALKING DEAD
COMPENDIUM ONE
Robert Kirkman • Charlie Adlard • Tony Moore • Cliff Rathburn

COMPENDIUM TP, VOL. 1
ISBN: 978-1-60706-076-5
$59.99
COMPENDIUM TP, VOL. 2
ISBN: 978-1-60706-596-8
$59.99
COMPENDIUM TP, VOL. 3
ISBN: 978-1-63215-456-9
$59.99

SPECIALTY BOOKS

THE WALKING DEAD
THE COVERS

THE WALKING DEAD: THE COVERS, VOL. 1 HC
ISBN: 978-1-60706-002-4
$24.99
THE WALKING DEAD SURVIVORS' GUIDE
ISBN: 978-1-60706-458-9
$12.99
THE WALKING DEAD: ALL OUT WAR HC
ISBN: 978-1-63215-038-7
$34.99

OMNIBUS

THE WALKING DEAD

OMNIBUS, VOL. 1
ISBN: 978-1-60706-503-6
$100.00
OMNIBUS, VOL. 2
ISBN: 978-1-60706-515-9
$100.00
OMNIBUS, VOL. 3
ISBN: 978-1-60706-330-8
$100.00
OMNIBUS, VOL. 4
ISBN: 978-1-60706-616-3
$100.00
OMNIBUS, VOL. 5
ISBN: 978-1-63215-042-4
$100.00

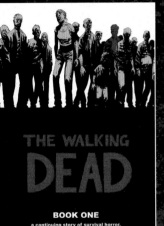

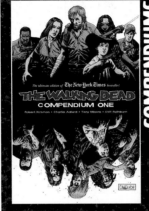

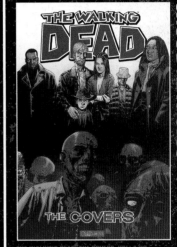

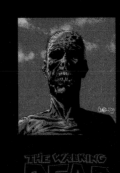

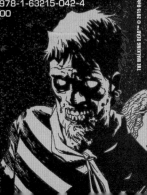

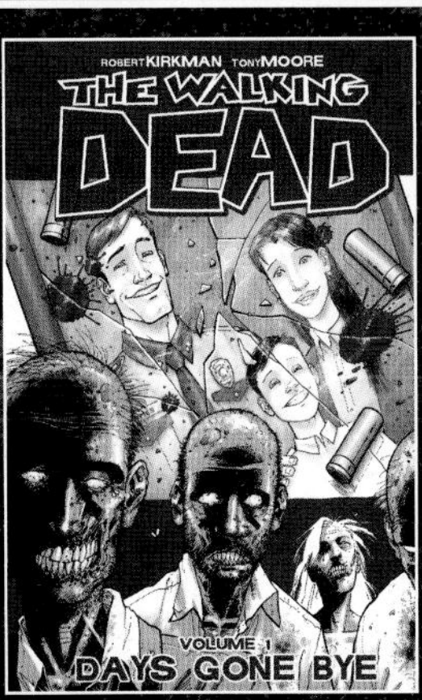

FOR MORE OF INVINCIBLE

TRADEPAPERBACKS

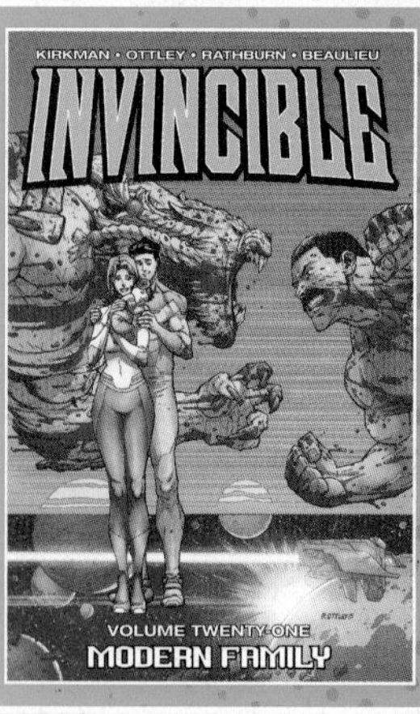
KIRKMAN • OTTLEY • RATHBURN • BEAULIEU
INVINCIBLE
VOLUME TWENTY-ONE
MODERN FAMILY

VOL. 1: FAMILY MATTERS TP
ISBN: 978-1-58240-711-1
$12.99
VOL. 2: EIGHT IS ENOUGH TP
ISBN: 978-1-58240-347-2
$12.99
VOL. 3: PERFECT STRANGERS TP
ISBN: 978-1-58240-793-7
$12.99
VOL. 4: HEAD OF THE CLASS TP
ISBN: 978-1-58240-440-2
$14.95
VOL. 5: THE FACTS OF LIFE TP
ISBN: 978-1-58240-554-4
$14.99
VOL. 6: A DIFFERENT WORLD TP
ISBN: 978-1-58240-579-7
$14.99
VOL. 7: THREE'S COMPANY TP
ISBN: 978-1-58240-656-5
$14.99
VOL. 8: MY FAVORITE MARTIAN TP
ISBN: 978-1-58240-683-1
$14.99
VOL. 9: OUT OF THIS WORLD TP
ISBN: 978-1-58240-827-9
$14.99
VOL. 10: WHO'S THE BOSS TP
ISBN: 978-1-60706-013-0
$16.99
VOL. 11: HAPPY DAYS TP
ISBN: 978-1-60706-062-8
$16.99
VOL. 12: STILL STANDING TP
ISBN: 978-1-60706-166-3
$16.99
VOL. 13: GROWING PAINS TP
ISBN: 978-1-60706-251-6
$16.99
VOL. 14: THE VILTRUMITE WAR TP
ISBN: 978-1-60706-367-4
$19.99
VOL. 15: GET SMART TP
ISBN: 978-1-60706-498-5
$16.99
VOL. 16: FAMILY TIES TP
ISBN: 978-1-60706-579-1
$16.99
VOL. 17: WHAT'S HAPPENING TP
ISBN: 978-1-60706-662-0
$16.99
VOL. 18: DEATH OF EVERYONE TP
ISBN: 978-1-60706-762-7
$16.99
VOL. 19: THE WAR AT HOME TP
ISBN: 978-1-60706-856-3
$16.99
VOL. 20: FRIENDS TP
ISBN: 978-1-63215-043-1
$16.99
VOL. 21: MODERN FAMILY TP
ISBN: 978-1-63215-318-0
$16.99
THE OFFICIAL HANDBOOK OF THE INVINCIBLE UNIVERSE TP
ISBN: 978-1-58240-831-6
$12.99
INVINCIBLE PRESENTS, VOL. 1: ATOM EVE & REX SPLODE TP
ISBN: 978-1-60706-255-4
$14.99

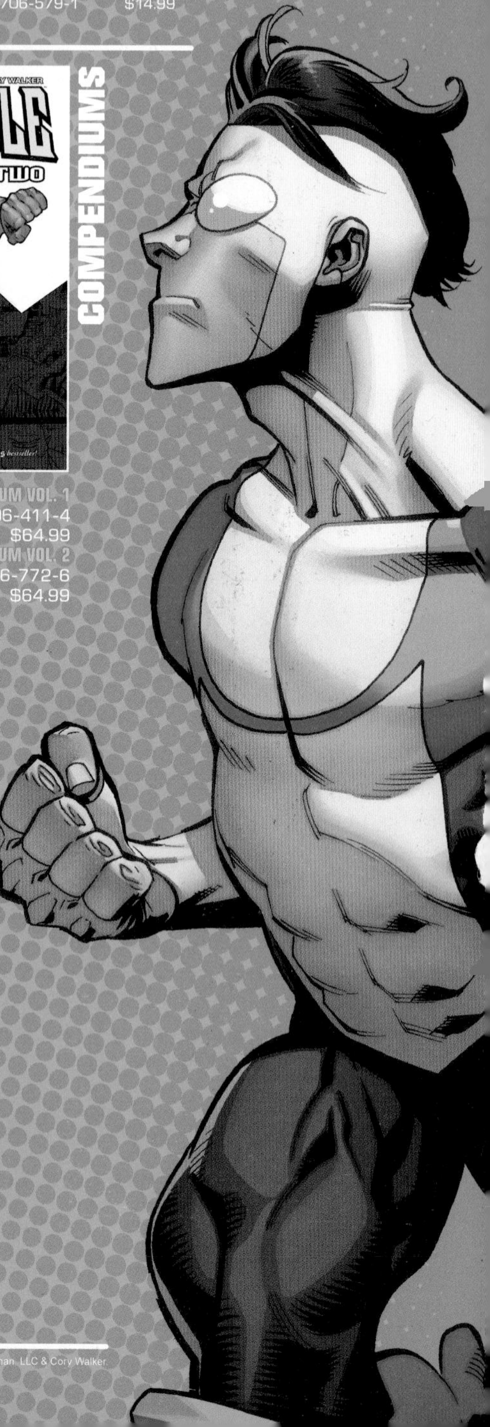

COMPLETE LIBRARY

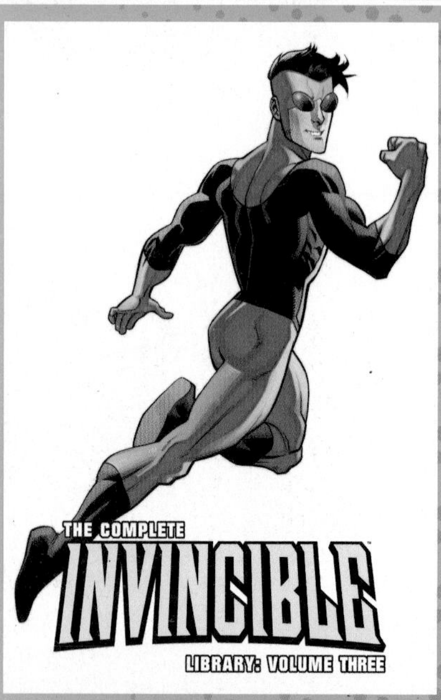
THE COMPLETE
INVINCIBLE
LIBRARY: VOLUME THREE

THE COMPLETE INVINCIBLE LIBRARY, VOL. 2 HC
ISBN: 978-1-60706-112-0
$125.00
THE COMPLETE INVINCIBLE LIBRARY, VOL. 3 HC
ISBN: 978-1-60706-421-3
$125.00

COMPENDIUMS

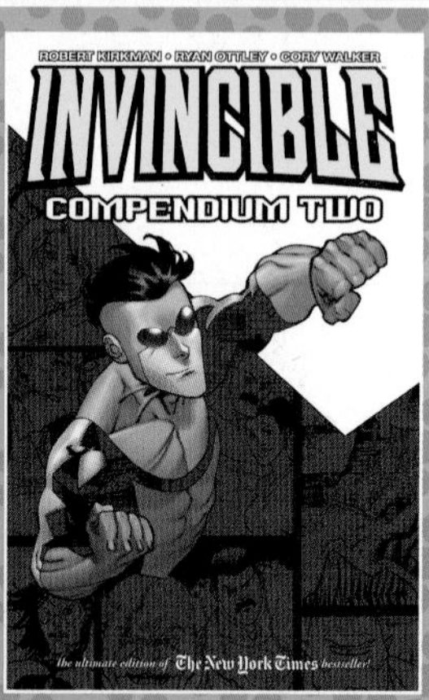
ROBERT KIRKMAN • RYAN OTTLEY • CORY WALKER
INVINCIBLE
COMPENDIUM TWO
the ultimate edition of The New York Times bestseller!

COMPENDIUM VOL. 1
ISBN: 978-1-60706-411-4
$64.99
COMPENDIUM VOL. 2
ISBN: 978-1-60706-772-6
$64.99

ULTIMATE COLLECTIONS

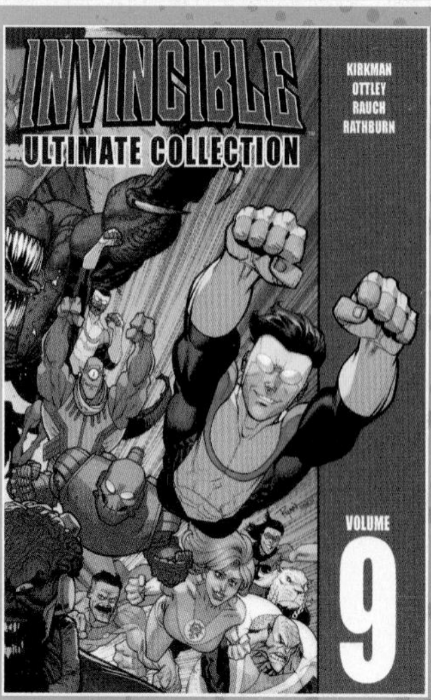
INVINCIBLE
ULTIMATE COLLECTION
KIRKMAN
OTTLEY
RAUCH
RATHBURN
VOLUME
9

ULTIMATE COLLECTION, VOL. 1 HC
ISBN 978-1-58240-500-1
$34.95
ULTIMATE COLLECTION, VOL. 2 HC
ISBN: 978-1-58240-594-0
$34.99
ULTIMATE COLLECTION, VOL. 3 HC
ISBN: 978-1-58240-763-0
$34.99
ULTIMATE COLLECTION, VOL. 4 HC
ISBN: 978-1-58240-989-4
$34.99
ULTIMATE COLLECTION, VOL. 5 HC
ISBN: 978-1-60706-116-8
$34.99
ULTIMATE COLLECTION, VOL. 6 HC
ISBN: 978-1-60706-360-5
$34.99
ULTIMATE COLLECTION, VOL. 7 HC
ISBN: 978-1-60706-509-8
$39.99
ULTIMATE COLLECTION, VOL. 8 HC
ISBN: 978-1-60706-680-4
$39.99
ULTIMATE COLLECTION, VOL. 9 HC
ISBN: 978-1-63215-032-5
$39.99